Bloody Hell

An Anthology of UK Indie Horror

Cover by Rachael Rose

Proofread by Mary Hoyle

Published by Mark of the Witch Press

All rights reserved. No part of this book may be reproduced or used in any manner without the prior written permission of the copyright owner, except for the use of brief quotations in a book review.

Copyright © 2024 Sarah Mosley All rights reserved.

This book is dedicated to readers who support self-published and independent authors.

Without you, there would be no us.

We appreciate you more than you could ever know.

EDITOR NOTE:

This book is written in British English. Therefore, dear American readers, there may be a few less z's than you're anticipating. We Brits also spell some words differently too, don't worry about it. These aren't typos, I promise.

Each of these stories is written in the author's own unique style, and therefore there may be slight formatting and stylistic differences between the stories. This is intentional, and a way to celebrate the individuality of each author.

Contents

1. HUNGRY IS TH' BODACH by Dr. Stuart Knott 1
2. DARKNESS BLOOMS by David K Slater 14
3. THE SLEEP DEMON by Jessica Huntley 27
4. THE SYN-EATER OF LANCASTER by MJ Mars 35
5. TO BE A MAN OF MAN by J C Michael 46
6. THE GOD BOTHERERS by Ashley Lister 54
7. WRONG LANE by Stephen Barnard 64
8. THE HUNT by EC Samuels 75
9. CYTHRAUL by Lee Allen 88
10. PERGYL by C S Jones 107
11. SOUNDS OF THE FOREST by Brad Thomas 115
12. THE DARK HEART by Jim Ody 123
13. MERRY BLOODY CHRISTMAS by Alexandra Nisneru 134
14. MURDER IN THE VIDEO STORE by Bethany Russo 142
15. THE MOOR-FOLK AND THE POET by Philip Alexander Baker 155
16. SAND by David Watkins 168
17. THE JOKE by Tom Carter 181
18. BROMPTON ROAD by Elizabeth J Brown 194
19. SKATE *BORED* by Tim Stephens 209
20. BONE ZIPPER by William Long 219
21. PLOUGH MONDAY by Benjamin Langley 229
22. MEMENTO MORI by Marie Sinadjan 241
23. THE MILL OF SHATTERED BONE by Mark M.J. Green 250
24. WORST HALLOWEEN EVER! by M.L. Rayner 261
25. THE HARLEQUIN by Elijah Frost 276
26. DOWN T'PIT by Sarah Jules 288
27. THEY STALK THE ROWS by Leigh Kenny 300

Acknowledgements 312
About the Authors 313
About the Editor 320
About the Illustrator 320

Stories Map

Should you fancy taking a spooky tour of the beautiful British Isles, here's where the stories are based.

Foreword

Allow me to give you a bit of background into the conception of *Bloody Hell: An Anthology of Indie Horror*. I'll be quick, I promise, and then you can get to the good stuff.

In October 2022, I published my first book, *Found You*. I'd spent the previous four years of my life working on other people's books (as a freelance writer and editor) and I came to the realisation that I should probably write a book of my own. I self-published it, with the support of my friends and family, but otherwise alone. Then, a few months later, I was invited to join a Facebook group called *British Authors of Horror, Dark Fantasy, and Bloody Thrillers* – it was in this group that I started to make connections with other authors. You see, writing books and publishing them can be a lonely game if you haven't yet found your people. And, let me tell you, I didn't just find my people, I found life-long friends. When I went on to publish my second book, *Don't Lie*, and my third book, *You Invited It In*, I came to understand the real value of community. I was amazed by how readily my fellow authors would provide help and support, feedback, and answer even the silliest of questions. To me, it felt like something just clicked. No longer was I a lone author, trying to figure things out on my own. I had a community of people cheering for me, as I did for them.

I floated the idea of creating an anthology to celebrate the incredible community in the UK indie horror space, thinking that a handful of people might want to join me in the endeavour. I never expected such a positive response, with many authors who I deeply admire wanting to take part. Somehow, I found myself leading the charge, which was both flattering and nerve-wracking. We decided in-lieu of a theme, the only requirement was that the stories be set in the UK – how better to celebrate UK indie horror authors, than by setting all of our stories in the UK? As the stories started rolling in, I knew that this anthology was going to be remarkable.

The stories are a testament to how wide the horror genre truly is – we have a quiet horror story about death personified, we have a gruesome story of murderous cattle, we have ghosts, spiders, sin-eaters, and everything in between. Each author brings to the table their own unique style of storytelling. This anthology is as much a celebration of our differences, as it is our similarities. It is a celebration of the community we have created, where we cheer for the success of others, knowing that there is space for all of us, and we can all be successful.

In this anthology, we have debut authors, we have veterans. We have authors who lean more toward thrillers, and authors who lean more toward the extreme. At the end of the book, I have included all of the authors' bios and social media links so you can check out more of their work (and you should, because they're all doing great things).

Alongside these stories are illustrations from the talented Rachael Rose (whose information you'll also find at the back of the book). Rachael Rose just so happens to be my tattoo artist. We spent a lot of time together last year while she covered up some of the not-so-great tattoos I got in my early twenties. When I mentioned the anthology I was putting together, she (serendipitously) said that she would love to do the illustrations, and… here we are! Her illustrations take this anthology to the next level, I'm sure you'll agree. I am thrilled to have her onboard.

I am extremely proud to be an indie horror author. The community is so full of talent, of respect, and of support. I am especially proud to be a *UK* indie horror author. Our little island(s) is putting out some of the best horror in the world, and holding its own against the big-guns. We may be small, but we are mighty. *Bloody Hell: An Anthology of UK Indie Horror* is, hopefully, the first in a chain of anthologies championing UK indie horror voices. Perhaps ironically, horror (whether books or films) is a safe space for many of us, and I feel fortunate that I am able to play a small part in that.

Okay, what are we waiting for? Are you ready to tour the UK (with a final pit-stop in Ireland), taking in the sights, sounds, and scares as you go? Buckle up, and let's do this!

Sarah Jules

June 2024

1. HUNGRY IS TH' BODACH

by Dr. Stuart Knott

Glen Affric, Scotland.

Freya Walsh elbowed open the cabin door and tripped her way inside, cursing under her breath and glaring reproachfully down at the raised door lip.

Ev'ry damn time!

When she was but a wee lass, Freya tripped like that every time she and her parents visited the old family cabin each summer. The lip was even splintered and worn from where her buckled shoes had caught it in her excitement, happy to be out in the wilds of nature and cosied up to her parents on the big, battered sofa before the fireplace.

Freya set her suitcase aside, sighing, and breathed in the musty cabin scent of pine, wizened wood, and, in a word, home. She wandered, thin arms hugged across her breasts, and absently blew a strand of hair from her face, barely aware of the tears trickling down her face. The cabin was nestled off a beaten path some ten miles between Fasnakyle (home of a gothic monstrosity more Lovecraft than the power plant her long-dead ded had worked at) and the popular hiking site that was the majestic Glen Affric. Todd had cursed a storm, forcing their hulking Land Rover through the overgrowth and shallow streams that had escaped from the River Glass. For Freya, it was almost worth the ass ache to see the magnificent view from the cabin's streaked windows and feel a small sense of comfort from its walls.

She could hear him grumbling outside; he was always muttering some such haver and she'd learned, long ago, to simply tune it out. A part of her - the bonnie girl who had fallen for him at university some eight years ago and gotten swept up in a romance that had cost her friends, family… and more - wanted to help unload their bags. It had been her idea to return to the dingy family cabin after all, and he'd regularly reminded her of that during the nearly twelve-hour drive from their quaint Hammersmith apartment.

"It woulda been cheaper to fly!" he'd admonish every time they came to the slightest delay, be it roadworks, a stranded vehicle, or traffic simply working against them.

It had taken them the better part of two days to make the trip. She had, at first, tried to convince Todd to take it in turns to drive and just power through the entire journey but he'd insisted on stopping on the outskirts of Beattock for a good night's rest.

Well… what *he* considered to be a good night's rest. Freya still ached from the bruises at her hips and below her ribs from his lusts, but it was all a price she'd promised herself she'd pay to get him back up this way. If it meant paying through the nose for his petrol and constant snacks and with her body to distract him from asking questions about why they were returning to where their little girl had died, then all the better.

Freya moved to the doorway and watched as Todd hauled his suitcase from the truck. Behind him, great pine trees swayed on a light breeze, their leaves almost hypnotic against the perpetually grey, cloudy sky that dominated the rugged landscape of Glen Affric. Beyond the trees, thick and twisted and aged, loomed a vast mountain range; as a child, she had stared up, awestruck, from her ded's shoulders at the ominous girth of Càrn Eige, with its snow-tinted allure, and longed to venture higher into the swirling mists that obscured its peak.

Keep the heid! he'd say, patting her knobbly knees playfully. *Yer just a wee bairn… but mebbe when you're a bit bigger.*

Freya was sure that day had come when she and Todd came here all those years ago; seven years to the day, not that it seemed he realised. He'd always been adventurous; he'd even been on the university canoe team (*Three bronze, two silver, one gold!* he'd proudly proclaim any time anyone asked about his medals) and volunteered with the Cub Scouts whenever he could. For the longest time, Freya had hated this; the other mams fawned over him and she wanted to claw their sparkling eyes out whenever they pouted over him, but she couldn't care less these days, not after what'd happened at the cabin seven years ago.

Freya composed herself and touched her husband lightly on his shoulder. "Leave the rest," she purred. "It's awfy dreich oot there here; let's git inside."

Todd slammed the truck door and looked at her with a mixture of impatience and affront. Inwardly, Freya smirked; he hated when her accent slipped through, and she'd allowed it to slowly creep in the longer their trip had progressed.

"Fine." He shouldered a large holdall. "These're the last ones, anyway."

The cabin was smaller than she remembered it being as a child; smaller, even, than she remembered it from seven years ago. The dark corners seemed thicker, the floorboards creakier, and drapes and furnishings mustier. As Todd growled and fiddled with the generator, Freya wandered through the main lounge, where a large CRT television sat in the far corner, caked in dust, before the comfy sofa. Freya ran her dainty fingertips over the cabinet in the opposite corner, regarding her tired – but determined – complexion as the lights flickered to life.

Behind the glass of the cabinet, which warped her visage, Freya gazed at the trinkets of her childhood. Plates, a teapot set, oddly shaped rocks (*Cairns*, her ded's voice echoed in her head), and framed pictures of her as a grinning child in the arms of her parents, now long gone and no doubt disappointed at the state of their family cabin and the horrendous thoughts running through their only daughter's head.

"I'm makin' tea," Todd called. "D'you want one?"

Freya saw her reflection twist into a scowl. Tea. Like tea would make anything better!

No, I don't feckin' want ta, yee eejit! she wanted to scream, clawing at his smug, self-righteous face.

Instead, she took a breath and said that would be lovely, thank you, and continued to do everything in her limited power to keep from looking at the large brick fireplace that dominated the lounge's main wall.

Her skin icy cold, her hands trembling, Freya shuffled towards the fireplace on legs that felt numb, sure – almost hopeful – that she would black out at any moment. While the cabin was sturdy and built from thick wooden logs, a shambles of a brick chimney stabbed at an angle into the lounge like a dagger into the wildlands around them. It crumbled at the touch and made a hell of a mess; she could still hear her mam complaining about the speckles of grit that fell to the hackit, patchwork rug that still covered the bare floorboards before it. The fireplace was black and dark, still filled with ash and the charred remains of logs behind the rusted, scorched iron gate that her ded had installed to keep the whole place from going up in flames… and undesirables getting out.

Keep th' fire burnin', Mam would sing every night after they locked and bolted and boarded up every door and window against the elements.

Mustn't let th' fire go out, Ded would say as the windows howled, branches cracked, and the clouds thundered overhead.

Freya dropped to one knee, wincing as her bruises cried in protest, and gently pulled open the iron gate. A waft of incinerated wood greeted her on a puff of soot and she coughed into her elbow, poking at the fragmented remains with a poker, afraid to get too close. She was so fixated that she jumped when Todd shoved a steaming cup of tea in her face.

"Ta," she mumbled. Freya took a sip and winced; always too much sugar!

"I'm gonna start unpackin'," Todd said.

Freya raised an eyebrow at him. She knew exactly what he was getting at, but she'd gotten him back to the cabin now; there wouldn't be any more sex, any more 'role play'… any more anything.

"You do that," she turned back to the fireplace, its innards as black as the Earl of Hell's waistcoat.

Todd stomped off, sulking, and Freya tossed her tea into the fireplace. *All he had t'do was keep it hot!* she thought bitterly as she slumped to the sofa, the little iron gate left open, the chimney free from obstructions.

You're a good lass, Freya, Ded would say, *but these here woods are full o' dark things. We gots t'respect their ways if they're t'leave us be.*

Little Freya had snuggled close to her ded, cosying under a large quilt before the flickering fire as Mam had pottered in the kitchen making beef stew with extra tatties and tea that had anything but sugar in it. She was comforted by his warmth, the strength of his arms, and knew that nothing could harm them if they hunkered down together and kept the fire burning. Nature would leave them well enough alone and welcome them warmly in the morning.

Y'still believe that bedtime crap? Todd had scoffed when he'd seen her arranging freshly cut logs in the fireplace. *No bogeymen're gonna come creepin' down the chimney! Grow up!*

Baby Maisie, named after her Granny, had been cooing from her travel cot, her brunette hair curled around the ears, her tentative stumps of teeth glistening behind a beaming smile. For as long as Freya could remember, she'd longed for a child but had been plagued, three times, by miscarriage after miscarriage. The first had been before she even met Todd and after a random one-night stand with a guy whose name she couldn't remember much less his face. The second had been a couple of months into her relationship with Todd and had been a very quick and clinical affair; she simply went to the twelve-week scan and was told there was nothing there. Todd, who had believed she'd made up the pregnancy in the first place, had barely batted an eyelid and it took her stomach swelling to the size of a basketball for him to even acknowledge she was pregnant with Maisie soon after… and even then he was, as her ded has always said, little more than a wallydrag.

While Freya had longed for children, Todd had never seemed all that bothered. Her getting pregnant had upended his perfectly maintained routines and forced him to marry her and struggle with things like night-time feeds and nappy changing when he'd rather be on the basketball court, cave diving, or leering over that slutty blonde that was always clinging to him when they went out for drinks.

Still, Freya never had any reason to believe he'd harm Baby Maisie; Todd was very gentle with her, almost treating her like porcelain, and the exact opposite of how he could be after a few beers or when his lusts got the better of him. She'd hoped that bringing Baby Maisie to the old cabin, reconnecting them all to nature, and rambling in the woods with the gurgling babe strapped to their backs, would help him see the benefits of having a little girl to follow in his footsteps and share his passions with. Instead, much like now, Todd had complained on the entire drive; they'd had to stop constantly to tend to Baby Maisie's needs, she'd kept him up every night with her teething screams, and he had been ratty with them both on the entire trip, refusing to let Freya drive so he could act like a pariah every time they stopped.

So, when they got to the cabin and the first thing Freya had done after setting Baby Maisie in her travel cot was get the fireplace going, Todd had been less than impressed.

Haud yer wheesht! Freya had hissed, smacking him, afraid his tirade would wake the baby.

He'd thrown his hands up in despair and stormed off to unload the truck. *You're as barmy as your mother was!*

Freya had pulled a footstool closer to Baby Maisie's cot and fawned over her. She used to sleep so peacefully when she wasn't wracked by coughs or tetchy from a wet nappy, and Freya marvelled that something so beautiful could've come from her. She'd gently stroked the baby's plump, red cheek and, barely aware of it, whispered a ditty so quietly it was more like a breath:

Aingeal, aingeal.
Bairn and wean, laddie or lass.
Keep th' fire burning,
Be not gallus; hold your sass.
Keep th' logs hot.
For hungry is th' Bodach.

Freya blinked back to reality; the lounge was cold and very empty without the crib. She could still see the marks in the dust of the floorboards where it had stood, next to the sofa, a wonderful, babbling babe sleeping soundless, naïve to the dangers lurking from the darkness of the fireplace.

All Todd wanted was to get blabbered and get her in the bedroom. Freya had tried to fight him off, but she'd been a bit younger than, a bit happier; a bit more likely to enjoy their carnal acts.

The baby's fine, he'd insisted, slobbering on her neck, his hands clutching at every part of her.

A euphoria had swept over her. *Maybe this is it*, she'd thought. The moment the spark rekindled and their life as a proper family could begin. She'd been sure that the fire had been burning; it had been at dinner, and she'd told Todd to keep it going when she'd showered, and, as he entered her, she had no reason to think otherwise.

And then the dawn had come. Freya woke to an empty bed; Todd's side was cold, indicating he'd been up for some time, which was very unusual. He had never once woken in the night to tend to Baby Maisie.

Freya had slipped on a robe and padded into the lounge, expecting to find Todd brewing tea or making toast or watching television from the sofa, and instead found him standing in the centre of the rug, a dumbfounded expression on his face.

"What's…?" her question was replaced by an inconsolable wail as Freya saw the crib was empty; streaks of soot stained the chipped wooden edging.

Footprints, small and faded, led from the crib to the fireplace, which yawned open; the black, stone-cold logs lay crumbling on the cabin floorboards. Amidst the ashes and the spikes of charred bark, Freya had spotted, through her tears, a single, tiny sock.

Dr. Jay had said it was common to ascribe impossible explanations to such horrific events, that it made perfect sense for her to retreat to her mam's warnings of a wilted, goblin-like figure that clambered down chimneys to steal unattended babies. It was, as he put it, a 'coping mechanism' to deal with an unimaginable trauma.

Todd, of course, had pleaded innocence. He'd been surprisingly distraught and proactive, calling in the local police and joining the three-day manhunt through the wilds of Glen Affric, venturing as far as the mighty Tom a' Choinich and finding nothing but rain, wildlife, mud pits, and the odd dank, yawning cave.

Freya hadn't liked what the police implied about her and found it curious that Todd was questioned for so long. Ultimately, the investigation simply petered out, with the overall suggestion being that... someone... must've entered the cabin during the night and taken the baby.

"Get tae!" Freya would scoff each time and return, again and again, to the cold, dead fireplace that, had it been lit, would've deterred the Bodach.

Six weeks with Dr. Jay had taught her to keep such rantings to herself. People looked at her like she was crazy when she insisted that Todd's stupidity had allowed the gnarled, warped creature to sidle down the chimney and take their sleeping baby. Her mam would've believed her; so, too, would her ded. They knew of the dark, hidden forces lurking in the deepest depth of the highlands and the ages-old woodland; they'd tried to warn her, keep her safe, but her caution had been seen as madness by the one man who should've trusted her instincts.

Now, seven years to the day, they were back. Seven years of trying to move on and to rebuild her reputation, which had seen even casual acquaintances give her guarded looks. No one judged or questioned him, and *he* was the one who let the fire go out! *He* discovered the empty crib and those horrible little footprints but kept that information to himself while Freya endured Dr. Jay's condescending gaze and constant scribbling in his notebook. *She* was the fruit loop, the neglectful mother, the fragile woman crippled by grief and what was he? The model husband: strong, *so* brave, supportive, for hadn't *he* paid for her therapy and recovery?

Why... yes, yes he had.

Seven years of playing the doting, affectionate, happy wife. She'd never brought up the subject of babies again and had taken down every photo of Baby Maisie; she hid them in a box under the bed and sat crying over them every day when Todd was at work. Seven years of acquiescing to his every whim, of never questioning him, all to lure him into a false sense of security. It'd taken weeks of convincing, of sexual favours that left her feeling cheap, but it had finally worked, and they were back, surrounded by the darkness and ghosts and a lifetime of forgotten and unrealised hopes and dreams.

"Comin' t'bed, babe?" Todd's head poked out from behind the bedroom door.

Freya's head snapped up sharply; in the blink of an eye, her scowling visage changed to a warm smile. "Come 'ave a coorie on the sofa wimme."

Todd ducked back into the bedroom with a roll of his eyes, no doubt to pull on some clothes to protect against the chill of the lounge. Without the fire burning, the cabin's temperature dropped considerably; Freya could see her breath in the air as she bolted the front door absent-mindedly. She stepped to the small kitchen area and felt warmed by the grey mountains beyond the trees, which loomed darkly as the sun faded.

I'll finally head up there t'morrow, she thought.

Todd came padding into the lounge wearing a dressing gown and slippers. He thumbed on the television and was greeted by a screen full of static. He settled on the sofa and jabbed at the gizmo, playing with its functions until finally tuning into a channel.

"Thought you want t'snuggle?" he said without looking around.

Freya swirled the rest of the powder into Todd's cup; a splash of milk and it looked just like any other normal cup of tea. She brought it over to him and he took it gratefully, sipping from it as she sat next to him.

"Y'not havin' one?"

"I'm all tea'd out," she gave a wry smile.

Within an hour, the concoction took its toll. Todd's eyes grew heavy, and his head lolled until he was snoring, chin pressed to his chest. Freya poked him, shook him roughly by the shoulder, but still he slept. Freya rose, shut off the television, and opened the iron gate wide, and tossed that dirty, ragged, forgotten sock to the fireplace's gaping maw. Then, she settled in the same chair her mam used to rock in with her knitting, and waited, patiently.

Darkness settled in outside; clouds rolled overhead, racing towards a storm further down the valley. The forest's thick shadows enveloped the cabin, leaving its lights like flickering stars against the night sky. Freya stared at the sock in the dead fireplace where her father had stoked the flames to keep them warm and stave off the evils that haunted the ignorant and the foolhardy. As Todd snored, oblivious, she swallowed with a boiling mixture of anticipation, horror, and gratitude as the lightest sprinkle of dirt and rocks fell from the chimney.

Freya glanced at where Baby Maisie's cot had been, now a vacant space as large and empty as the hole in her heart, then glared at the man who had let her down… or welcomed in the creature as she now did.

More debris fell in a light sprinkle onto the ashen remains of logs older than humanity, and which guarded this ancient wilderness. A small scraping echoed, like the scratching of rats in the attic, and a low, gurgling titter drifted to her ears.

Freya sat completely still, watching with expectation as strands of tangled, matted hair drooped from the chimney; as skeletal, clawed hands clutched snatched up the sock; as a leering, goblin's face with pinpricks for eyes peered from the darkness.

The thing was hunched, toad-like, and impossibly gaunt; she could see its spine protruding beneath its slick, leathery skin. The Bodach skulked across the rug, leaving sooty prints in its wake. It wore a tattered loin cloth and a shoelace necklace from which trinkets – torn mittens, tiny teeth, even a chubby digit or two – dangled. It padded across the floor like a lizard, barely making a sound, and glared at Freya, who sat transfixed.

The Bodach's face was a twisted, wrinkled mess; its brow was furrowed with constant disgust and its tiny, glittering black eyes gleamed maliciously beneath its bushy eyebrows. A nose – long, sharp, and crooked–cast a shadow over its chapped, thick lips. It smiled at her with longing, revealing rotten, crooked teeth; a forked tongue licked unspeakable drool from its chops, some of which was stuck in its wispy beard.

"Yer lookin' a bit peely wally, yah hairy coo," it chuckled spitefully.

Freya swallowed, held her nerve, and kept her eyes locked with the creature's black pits. She tried to speak but managed only a strangled croak as it swallowed Baby Maisie's sock whole. As tears fell down her cheeks, Freya simply nodded towards Todd's sleeping form.

The Bodach regarded Todd and sniffed; its features screwed up in a look of loathing. It ran its long, chipped fingernails over Todd's sleeping form and pinched at his flesh. Clatty gloop fell from its eye when it raised a bushy eyebrow at her.

"Whit's fur ye'll no go by ye," it slurred.

"Haud yer weesht!" Freya tried to sound defiant but failed miserably.

The Bodach cackled and clapped its wet claws together, amused, then craned its head back. Its jaw opened wide, its mouth splitting into a rictus grin, exposing jagged fangs and a sore-encrusted palate. Freya forced herself to watch, with only the slightest wince, as the Bodach tore into Todd's jugular.

The arterial spray – worsened by Todd's sudden death spasms – splashed Freya's face. She barely noticed. She simply rocked in her chair, weeping, kneading her hands together, and watched as the Bodach ripped tendons and muscles with its few (but powerful) teeth.

"Don't it gee-in yee the boak?" the Bodach chuckled, viscera dribbling from its lips.

Mechanically, like a mannequin, Freya shook her head. She thought of Baby Maisie, so small and innocent and with no choice but to trust her parents to care for her. Freya felt nothing but hatred and revulsion not just for the wretched goblin before her, but the fandan it was feasting on.

Satisfied with its taster, the Bodach gripped Todd's lifeless body – still spurting blood, still jerking involuntarily – by the ankle and dragged it back towards the fireplace. The Bodach manhandled the bleeding corpse with the strength and skill of a hunter with a fresh kill and clamped its claw-like hands to the chimney, ready to haul its latest feast up and away into the thick woods.

Before it vanished from sight, scurrying up the chimney like a spider with a helpless fly held in its webbing, it tipped Freya a spiteful wink.

"Lang may yer lum reek!"

Freya sat alone in the gloom of her childhood cabin, the stench of soot and blood in the air, her husband's blood still drying on her cheeks.

"Haste ye back," she whimpered quietly into the darkness.

2. DARKNESS BLOOMS

by David K Slater

The Tees Valley, England.

It had just begun to rain when Marcus Bradbury arrived home. He parked his black BMW in the driveway and hurried inside. His lavish five-bedroom house was filled with signs of a life he had not lived. Walls and shelves were decorated with tokens and trinkets from countries he had visited but never truly seen.

There were hundreds of books filling the shelves in Marcus' study, covering a variety of topics. He scanned through the art section feverishly, pulling out volumes, dropping them to the floor if they didn't contain what he was looking for. He searched quickly through the indexes, finally coming to a halt when he saw the name Leonard Biagi.

He had shown the semi-detached fixer-upper earlier in the day as part of an estate, to a run-of-the-mill old hag named Agnes Griss. Of course, the office sent him to cart her to and from the property. As soon as they had passed the threshold of the place, she started rooting through her dead sister Marcia's photo albums and opening music boxes. A bingo card of cookie-cutter Hallmark moments. One particularly filthy part of her inheritance was Luca, a tuxedo cat the size of a turkey, who was constantly underfoot. At one point, Marcus found himself in a darkened bedroom with Agnes, and when he pulled at a light string overhead, an attic stair trap almost brained him for his trouble.

The painting the old woman found in the attic had been covered in a tarp and secured with twine. When she pulled back the tarp, both of their eyes lit up. It was a gothic landscape, showing a black lake overlooked by a row of dilapidated, terraced houses on a cobbled street. Against his policy of downplaying the value of plunder in front of clients, Marcus had snatched it up, cutting his thumb and splattering the cracks of the frame with blood. When he looked down to wipe it off, the old wood had already absorbed it. In the pictured lake, there was the floating, bloated body of a man, face down. Writing daubed in the bottom corner said, 'Darkness Blooms - Leonard Biagi'. He knew when she snatched it back that Agnes would never give it up, no matter what the price.

Marcus hurried to his study desk, flicking through the pages until the yawning cut on his thumb dripped blood onto the page which bore Leonard's name. He sucked at the open wound and looked with wide eyes at the page. Images of paintings similar to the ones he saw in the attic at Marcia's house were there, strange renderings of dark landscapes and what looked like mossy stone and wooden men standing in ritual, but alas, not the one he so desired.

Biagi's work was limited and much sought after by collectors, so the absence of this painting from the book made Marcus feel it was all the more valuable. The old devil had even been rumoured to have carved up servants for leather when new canvas was scarce. Everything Marcus came across was sorted in his mental file by price, not value. When he looked into that painting, however, something reared up inside him, a dark, sweating thing.

He looked up from the roll-top into an ornate mirror. Marcus spent his career disguising a cold distance from others with a winning smile made up of pearly white teeth. They were too big, too straight and too many in number. When he smiled, the muscles in his face contorted and signified happiness and friendliness, but his eyes didn't change. They were locked into a stare, and saw no joy in the world; only potential for personal gain. Sticking his scavenger's fingers in the ruins of other people's lives had given him a very comfortable living, but this was different.

Marcus Bradbury slammed the book closed and looked around, then inspected the wound on his thumb, still open, still oozing blood.

"It's mine," he said to his wolf-toothed reflection.

* * *

Agnes sat in the armchair, Marcia's favourite, and bit into a sugar-coated doughnut. As was always the case, jam trickled down the side of her hand. Almost as soon as the cold, handsome young man had dropped her at her door, she had felt the cold touch of unfinished business. Agnes had showered and packed a small overnight bag, then took a cab back to Marcia's again, to stay.

She had found a box of photo albums under a coffee table in the living room and decided to take a trip down Memory Lane. The plastic covers on the pages had crackled and peeled apart as she turned them, giving off a musky smell she associated with memories from long ago. Agnes had closed the book when the images of younger, happier days became too real to handle.

Letting out a scornful sigh, she angled her hand in a way that would restrict the flow of the jam towards her arm, but was unsuccessful. It made its way to the sleeve of her cardigan, immediately soaking in. She licked most of it off her hand, setting down the photo album she was perusing, then stood up from her armchair with a dramatic, groaning sigh.

As she went into the kitchen to soak the sticky cuff of her sleeve, Luca followed her in, circling around her legs.

"Oh, Luca-di-pooka, I'm sorry, where are my manners?"

She picked up a bowl from the drainer, filling it with water and placed it on the floor. Luca lapped at it contentedly.

"Who's a good boy?" she said, patting him on the side, then heading upstairs for bed.

* * *

Marcus woke in a cold sweat; his sheets, drenched and tangled around him like a net. He couldn't even remember going to bed. Shadows of the branches from trees outside cast over him, waving like long, wiry arms with uneven bony fingers, scratching at the surface of some parallel world, trying in vain to break through.

He found himself back inside his beloved BMW, wide awake, as though the blackest Vietnamese coffee ran through his veins; but still, somehow, asleep at the wheel. He was completely lost in a fog of thought, following the lines in the middle of the road through the darkness. One after another, they slowly turned red, until they became splashes of blood. He rubbed his eyes with the palm of his hand, wiping beads of sweat from his brow, and the road came back into focus.

Before he knew it, Marcus was standing by Marcia Griss' front door. With barely a moment's thought, he robotically punched his hand through the window to open it, despite having the key box code. He stepped in, quickly closing the door behind him. Moving around the house like a bloodhound, he searched quickly and quietly for his prize, but each room came up empty.

A whispering sound startled him, and he almost hit his face on a door frame. Luca appeared from the kitchen, growling at his hated enemy. Why was he here?

"Jesus... Go away, you fat little bastard," Marcus said as the cat's growl became a howl. Luca hissed loudly before Marcus rushed over, grabbing him tightly around the neck with both hands. Luca's growl became muted, his back feet kicking wildly against Marcus' arms. They cut him deeply, ripping long strips of skin from his forearms, leaving them resembling one of those oranges that you can't quite peel. Luca's feline neck swivelled like a turret, burying his fangs in the web of Marcus' right hand up to the gum, he then dropped to the floor and disappeared. Marcus struggled as he silently screamed and clutched at his horribly punctured hand.

Agnes was sound asleep, wrapped in the glow of her television set. A Sunday afternoon-grade murder mystery played loudly. She had always preferred to sleep with some background noise, ever since her husband died. It made her feel less alone, but tonight... she was not alone.

Marcus gently opened the bedroom door and spotted the painting leaning against the wall. As he crept inside, within arm's length of it, he tread on a creaking floorboard.

He glanced up to see a figure suddenly sat up in bed, propped at an uneasy-looking angle. Eyes bloodshot and bulging, tongue lolling from her mouth, grey, clammy skin covered in dark blue veins. Like a corpse, he thought.

The invader shook his head, and when his eyes cleared, it was the old woman again. Her eyes weren't even fully open when she looked up at him.

"Marcus? What are you..."

He grabbed a cushion from the chair beside her bed, thrusting it down over her face. She gasped and struggled, her pale weak limbs flailing around wildly. Suddenly, her resolve increased, and she reached upwards, scratching and jamming her thumb into his eye. Marcus screamed and turned his face away. 'You fucking…'

Releasing his grip on the pillow, Marcus grabbed her by the throat, he felt her larynx start to crumble in his fist. He rained down punches into her face, and it wasn't long before all of her fight was gone. Grabbing the lamp from beside her bed, he smashed it onto her battered and bloodied head. Marcus kept swinging, over and over, until the bulb shattered and the ceramic base collapsed. Eventually, he was left only clutching the wires and broken remnants of the lamp.

He turned away from what was left of Agnes, and stared through bloodshot eyes at the painting, as the colours swirled and the water rippled. Brushing the hair from his blood-splattered face, Marcus let out a sigh of relief. What had started as theft had turned into a spiteful bludgeoning. He hadn't thought any of this through.

"Another spot of tea, Vicar?" said a voice from the TV. "Lovely, I could murder one of those scones…"

Marcus stood up and turned it off, plunging the room into shadows. For a moment, he stood motionless like a waxwork in a chamber of horrors. From outside, his silhouette was visible through the window, silently gasping for breath.

* * *

The world became snatches of spinning, lunatic reality. Marcus remembered flashing lights streaking across his vision, then the smoking, twisted wreckage of a car. Seconds later, it seemed, he found himself in a darkened woodland, feeling as though he had been running all night. High above, through the tops of the trees, he could just make out the colours of fading daylight.

His eyes darted from side to side, looking for something he couldn't see, but somehow knew to be there. The old wooden men, covered in earth and moss, staggered in the shadows all around him. They were too slow to chase him, but there was no rush, he had nowhere to go. He was a fly dissolving in the jaws of a Venus flytrap.

Suddenly, it was as though the trees had stepped aside and created a clearing ahead of him. Marcus ran on ragged legs, with sore, rasping lungs, to the safety of the open space. As he stumbled into the dying light, he saw a lake and a row of houses outstretched along a cobbled street on the opposite side. There was a sharp, aching throb of feedback in his ears, like cold metal spikes, and he dropped to his knees at the water's edge. It began to ripple and splash, and Marcus attempted to stand, but he felt cold, dead hands grab him by both arms. He couldn't turn his head from the black water. Then, he was rattled to his core when he saw the faintest reflection of light against amber eyes staring up at him from the water's depths. Far away, he heard the sounds of screaming, and slowly came to realise that the screams were his own.

* * *

Marcus leapt out of bed, wrenched from unconsciousness by his own shrieking. He scanned the room, half expecting to find that the visions from his nightmare had followed him into the waking world. He went to the bathroom to splash cold water on his face, and winced at the scratches he was covered with, both feline and human. His left eye had begun to sink in, collapsing on itself like a grape left in the sun. His eyelid hung in shreds. An infection was already setting in; he shivered and stared at himself before vomiting into the sink.

The telephone seemed like it had been ringing for hours.

BEEP "Hi, Marcus? It's John. Are you there? Look, it's been a few days now... We're starting to get a bit worried... Let me know if you're getting our messages. Call me back."

Marcus sat at his kitchen table eating a bowl of cereal like a zombie. He remained transfixed on the painting, like a magic eye picture, his focus locked on something deep inside it; looking for a sign, waiting for a message. His eyes opened wide, and dropped the bowl on the table, spilling the last of its contents. Marcus took out his mobile phone and dialled, suddenly manic with life again.

"Hey John, sorry I missed your call! I can't talk now, but I've had to go out of town for a few days. I'll be in touch." He rang off, then threw his phone at the wall, shattering it into a hundred worthless pieces.

Outside the world was flat and grey, already dusk. The rest of the houses on the street were little more than 2-D facades. Marcus looked to the horizon; a blood orange sun cowered low in the sky.

The engine growled to life as Marcus fled, gripping the steering wheel tightly. He drove as if some dark mother was beckoning him to their breast, and passed a crooked street sign. 'You are now entering Calmouth. Please drive safely' it read, as he ploughed onwards into the night.

Up ahead, the road flickered like an old projector screen, and Marcus looked in the rearview mirror. His eye was swollen and bruised, if he didn't seek medical attention, he would surely suffer permanent damage. Who was he kidding? That ship had already sailed. The best a doctor could do was rip the damn thing out. He spun around maniacally to check the back seat, hoping to catch a glimpse of the figures he'd spotted behind him just a moment ago. Nobody there. They never had been there, only the painting.

He knew from now on, there would always be something frightening, lingering just beyond his peripheral vision.

The road narrowed, towering trees and dense foliage blacked out the moon and stars. Shadows danced on either side of the car, and it was impossible for Marcus to tell how long he had been on this ghost train. Maybe he'd always been there. Suddenly, the road through the woods opened up to daylight. The dense forest had disguised the warm, safe feeling that is afforded by the morning sun. Marcus knew the safety it brought was only an illusion.

At the edge of the blackened wood, jagged branches stuck outward from the trees, like frozen and rotting moss-covered hands. They tried desperately to stop anyone from leaving, but Marcus flew by them in the safety of his car. As he pulled around the side of the lake, he saw the row of dilapidated terraced houses along a small cobbled road. They looked like concrete alien vessels, dropped from space and ruined by time, now unable to return home. They were of no value or use to anyone, but Marcus was overjoyed and filled with dread at the same time when he saw them. A rattling sound emitted from the hood of his car as he drew closer, and the moment the wheels touched the cobbles of Lakeside Terrace, his car died and rolled to a stop.

Marcus opened the glovebox and fished around beneath a stack of papers. He stuffed a long object into his breast pocket, then stepped out of the car, quickly moving to the trunk to open it. Inside was Agnes' body, wrapped in blood-stained bed sheets. Marcus stood for a long moment, then pulled her out of the trunk and waded out into the water, dunking her in. He looked into the water, deeper than he thought possible. There, he saw something that he couldn't comprehend.

A once white temple, faded and coated in centuries of algae and decay. Leading to the temple was a humped bridge, sandwiched on either side by scores of flailing arms of the damned. Marcus knew in an instant that these were the lost souls of those who had tried to buy their way into paradise and found a home in the coldest darkness imaginable. He looked longer, deeper into the black water, and somehow he felt something he could not see, a voice, whispering to him. Marcus shook himself free of the trance and made a run for his car. The sun was going down so quickly that it was almost as if it were falling from the sky.

He jumped into the car, but the engine sputtered and died. After grabbing the painting from the back seat, Marcus ran towards the houses, in the hope they might offer some protection from the things that lurked in the night. The door was locked, no way inside. He rushed down the steps and headed to the next house. The steps cracked beneath his feet as he bounded, and, with all his remaining strength, he threw himself against the weather-beaten door. It burst open in a cloud of dust and splinters, and once inside, he froze as if someone had walked over his grave. There were gaping holes in the floorboards and the stone fireplace was cracked and cobwebbed, the yellowed wallpaper peeling off in great strips. The house was almost certainly haunted, and by something much worse than ghosts.

Marcus settled for the box bedroom upstairs, towards the back of the house. It felt like the kind of space you would give to a child, or an unwelcome guest. He propped the painting against the back wall, and braced himself against the door, glancing around frantically.

Through the cracks in the walls, Marcus watched the daylight recede. Then, slowly and deliberately, the footsteps came, dragging as they moved around the house searching for him. A dull, metallic drone made his ears ache, and he could see lights flashing outside. Then, a heavy pounding at the door began. Marcus stifled a scream as the door started to crack and splinter behind him.

Green, inhuman arms burst through the old wooden door, and Marcus screamed until his lungs burned. He became dizzy, reaching an almost euphoric state as they dragged him out of the house, heels bumping down the stone steps. They pulled him across the slippery black cobbled street, and his vision was a kaleidoscope of colours and swirling lights. Marcus lacked the motor function to turn his head, even to see the creatures that held him so tightly. Even if he could have, he would not have dared. The breeze was cool against his sweat-drenched skin, and the slippery, cobbled street squeaked under the soles of his shoes, still wet from the lake.

His delirium faded momentarily, and in the sky above, he saw stars bursting into existence and billowing clouds rolling by. Marcus was turned around and saw the black water at his feet, alive with ripples. Something enormous and ancient was being summoned, arising from the depths. The creatures of wood and stone pulled him further into the lake until he was submerged to the waist, soaking wet and freezing. Even through the shadowy depths, Marcus's one good eye spotted the shape moving ever closer, like a weather balloon floating up from the bottom of the lake. The splashing of the water became evermore frantic, then, the creature showed itself.

First, the eyes rose above the water, those awful amber eyes with a stare that looked upon Marcus with equal measures of coldness and disdain. The skin of its bloated body was similar to a crocodile, but with a living ecosystem of smaller creatures plastered across it. The parasites squealed, writhed and glistened on the moonlight. Bubbles foamed at their disgusting mouths as they tasted the air for the first time in a century. The creature appeared to be some prehistoric amphibian. Like a giant toad which only rose to the surface when the sacrifice was brought to its shore. When fate drew its prey into a metaphysical web and rang the dinner bell.

The body of the creature raised from below water level and began to reach for Marcus, with arms, and arms, and arms! Marcus shook all over as if electrocuted, but the servants of the beast marched him deeper into the freezing black water. Flowers of the darkest violet and magenta began to bloom on the creature's shoulders. Opening wide, drinking in the moonlight.

Marcus suddenly remembered who he was, and what he had done. Nothing on Earth or from the depths would stop him now. Marcus freed an arm from one of the wooden men and reached into his jacket pocket. The hunting knife from the glovebox glinted in the exploding cosmos overhead, and he began to swipe wildly at the beast.

The monster plunged one of its many hands, like a trident, with its sharp, jagged fingers, deep into his chest. Marcus screamed, bearing his blood-stained teeth. He was far too stubborn to be taken quietly into its arms. Violently, he stabbed the appendage protruding from his chest, the creature recoiled in pain, letting out a scream from its fat, swollen mouth which gasped like a fish out of water; its eyes widened in horror. The flowers on its shoulders immediately putrified and wilted, letting out a dying gasp of spores. Quickly it began to retreat and descend into the lake once more. The surface became a swirling, roiling blackness, and the houses around him filled with beckoning shadows, full of misery and dread.

Marcus saw a new light in the forest, and its beacon made him feel as though it had all been predetermined somehow. Even in his depravity, he'd served a purpose, even as a pawn. He watched as his lifeblood poured from the hole in his chest, becoming a dark stain even over the black water.

The men of wood and stone simply released Marcus, then turned and slowly walked away, swallowed up quickly by the darkness of the woods. He fell face down in the water with his eyes open, and looked once again into the deep, letting shock take him. The silhouette of the beast made its retreat to the depths, but there, beyond it, Marcus could again see the spires of the submerged temple. He longed to call it home, but he knew that it never would be.

An axis of the Universe shifted, and in his ears, the sounds of metallic distortion subsided, replaced with that of something scratching against canvas. He felt the damp, bristled points poking into his back, stroking him calmingly as the black water filled his lungs, opening capillaries wide, pushing out every last bubble of air.

Everything became still, frozen in time.

* * *

After making his last purpose-filled stroke, Leonard Biagi dropped his brush into the water-filled jar beside him, the black paint diffused and dissolved, spiralling upwards, contaminating the water with its darkness. He had almost called for Miss Griss to replace the water, but laughed instead, realising she was no longer in his employ. Then, showing a row of yellowing teeth, he reached around to caress the canvas with his filthy, gnarled fingers. She was still here, after all, he thought.

His tired eyes, with deep black rings around them, were locked into a crazy stare; he hadn't slept in days. His grin was maniacal; he had created something magnificent today. Outside, through his bedroom window, the sounds of splashing water could be heard from the lake.

3. THE SLEEP DEMON

by Jessica Huntley

There are some unfortunate people who experience a frightening phenomenon, something that would terrify even the bravest of souls. This phenomenon includes temporary paralysis when falling asleep or waking up and some can even experience different sensations such as a tight chest, hallucinations, and a perceived presence of something else *in the room. These hallucinations are different from nightmares because the person involved is not asleep and is semi-aware during the episode. PTSD can be attributed to this condition. It is commonly known as* The Sleep Demon.

The Lake District, England.

Amber's small, adolescent body trembled under her duvet. Her skin was slick with sweat, yet goosebumps prickled her from head to toe. Cherry Hollow, the small town in the Lake District she called home, was experiencing a heat wave unlike any other she'd experienced in her thirteen years, yet she couldn't stop shaking from the chills surrounding her, even in slumber.

It had taken longer than usual to drift off to sleep. Usually, she'd be asleep within minutes of her head hitting the soft pillow, but ever since the events of the 20th of July, sleep had become an elusive and slippery creature to catch and control. And it was getting worse each night.

Two weeks had passed since that fateful day at Beaker Ravine, and she hadn't spoken to her three remaining best friends since. The memories plagued her during every waking moment and, when she finally did fall into dreamland, they haunted her dreams too. She wished she'd never gone to Beaker Ravine that day. It was cordoned off for a reason.

Amber thrashed her head from side to side. Her arms went rigid at her sides, her fingers grasping the bed sheets so hard she untucked them and balled them up with her fists.

'No!' she cried out. 'Please … stop …'

It was the summer holidays. She and her friends were supposed to be enjoying the sunshine and getting up to no good. It's what they'd planned to do all year. This summer they'd all turn into teenagers, but now one of them would never grow older, not even by a single day. He would forever remain a twelve-year-old boy … until the end of time.

Amber sucked in a breath as if it were her last. She needed to wake up.

It had almost caught her …

She'd barely left her house in two weeks and lay awake long into the night staring at the ceiling, too afraid to fall asleep in case it came back. Last night the elusive creature known as *sleep* had finally taken her to the dark place, to the depths of her subconscious. That was the most dangerous place of all; a place she feared to go.

Amber's eyes flew open, and she exhaled a long sigh, glad to be free from that terrible nightmare. But she couldn't move ...

Not again ...

Her bladder released itself and she could do nothing to stop the trickle of urine. A warm, wet sensation spread around her bottom as she blinked, and tears spilled from her eyes. A cold chill crept up her spine, one vertebra at a time and her feet tingled.

It was coming ...

She didn't have a name for it yet, but it was some sort of sleep demon. Part human and part creature, it morphed from nothing but black smoke and transformed into a hideous monster with a skeletal body and long arms, ending in sharp claws. It visited her in her dreams, but that wasn't the worst part. The worst part was that when she woke up the terror didn't stop. It often followed her into the real world.

Amber willed her body to move, but her muscles refused to cooperate. They were locked tight as her mind raced and her eyes darted from side to side, but her body lay perfectly still, trapped within itself.

Is it finally going to get me?
Am I going to die?

She didn't know what was happening. She became paralysed every time she woke up. The only movement was her body shivering from fear and cold as it rattled her insides.

The Sleep Demon was close, yet it remained in the strange phase between the dream world and reality. She could feel its warm breath on her face, its weight pressing down on her flat chest, but she couldn't see it. She couldn't close her eyes either.

But she could *feel* it.

Please, stop.

But it wouldn't stop. She knew it wouldn't because The Sleep Demon had only started visiting her since *that* day. It was her doing. It was all in her head.

It wasn't real, yet she knew her *fear* was real.

How long was this torment going to last?

She didn't know how much longer she could bear it. She hadn't told her parents yet, not about the thing that haunted her. But they knew something wasn't quite right due to her constant nightmares and wetting the bed.

How could she tell them? She'd promised her friends; made a blood oath. There was no way she could tell the truth about what happened to Kieran that day. She'd have to live with the knowledge and guilt forever. Maybe this strange entity would eventually go away on its own.

Gradually, Amber's muscles relaxed, and the weight lifted from her chest. Sometimes the sensation lasted only a few seconds and other times it lasted much longer. She wondered if one day the pressure would never be released, and she'd be trapped inside her own body forever.

She sucked in a breath and attempted to count the plastic glow-in-the-dark stars on her ceiling, remnants of her younger years. There were twenty-five …

Once she'd counted them several times, her body was her own again. She shuffled her bottom up the bed out of the wet area and drew her knees to her chest, wrapping her arms around them. She sobbed quiet tears as the room turned colder.

It wasn't over yet.

It never was.

Just when she thought it had freed her from its icy grasp, The Sleep Demon returned.

Amber looked around her room, dimly lit by the moonlight outside her window. Everything was as it should be: her wardrobe door was closed, the desk and chair sat in one corner. Her toy box, filled with her old juvenile toys she told her parents she was too old to play with yet couldn't bear to throw away, sat in the opposite corner.

Everything was as it should be: except it wasn't, and it never would be again.

Amber's eyes flicked to her window, which was closed. The branches of the tree outside brushed lightly on the pane. Her father had been meaning to get a ladder, climb the tree and cut down the long branches, but hadn't got around to doing it yet.

Through the thin curtains and with the moonlight backlighting them, the tree branches reminded Amber of the long, spindly arms of The Sleep Demon. The pale lilac curtains blew gently at the corners, but the window remained closed.

Amber breathed out. The air around her turned icy and she shivered. She needed to get out of her wet pyjamas and change her bedding. Ordinarily, she'd go and wake her mother who'd then help her with it, but she didn't want to wake her; not again.

Without turning on the light, she changed out of her pyjamas and took the wet sheets off the bed, placing them in the wash basket on the landing, before wrapping herself in her pink, fluffy dressing gown and going downstairs. She settled herself on the sofa and pulled a blanket over herself and up to her chin.

A long creak echoed behind her, but Amber remained facing forward. Even when a dark shadow passed over her face and a cold, skeletal hand stroked her hair, she stayed perfectly still.

'I'm sorry,' she whispered to the empty room.

The next morning, Amber woke to the smell of her mother's cooking. She didn't remember drifting off to sleep, but she must have done at some point. Now, in the bright morning sunlight, her surroundings looked much less foreboding and sinister. There was no large, scary demon standing behind her.

But it was still there.

That feeling inside.

Which was the same thing.

'Amber, baby, did you have another bad night?' asked her mother from the kitchen doorway. Amber nodded, her cheeks burning. 'Don't worry. I'll get your sheets washed.'

Amber watched her mother put her sheets into the washing machine. The idea of telling her parents about her nighttime visitor filled her with so much fear it made her chest tight. She couldn't tell a soul. She'd made the ultimate promise.

'I heard from Kieran's mother last night,' said Amber's mother as she turned back to the stove.

Amber stood up and walked into the kitchen area. She almost lost her balance as she slid her bottom onto the chair at the kitchen table. Hearing *his* name was like a punch in the gut. She felt out of breath, as if she was trying to paddle up for air, but her face never broke the surface.

'I'm afraid there's still been no sign of Kieran,' she added. 'They're calling off the search for now.'

Amber nodded, keeping her head down as she listened. She didn't want to listen. She didn't want to hear any of it. She never wanted to hear his name ever again. He was gone. That was the end of it. The local community had sent wave after wave of search parties out to look for him, but only she knew they'd never find him. Not unless they knew where to look.

'Have you spoken to any of your friends lately?' her mother asked.

Amber heard the question but didn't reply. She was too distracted by the pounding in her head and the shortness of her breath.

'Amber … are you okay?'

'Mum … I …' Her pupils dilated and her mouth dropped open as a huge creature transformed from nothing but black smoke. It towered over her mother, casting a dark shadow. Her mother didn't notice as it took a long, slender claw and sliced it slowly across her throat.

Amber screamed as blood spurted from her mother's neck, soaking her white blouse in crimson.

But her mother didn't choke or drop to the floor in agony as the life drained from her body. She continued to stare at Amber with a frown on her face, asking her over and over if she was okay and what was wrong.

The darkness swallowed Amber and she fell to the floor.

A bright light brought her round from her dreamless sleep. Her mother's voice drifted in the distance. As her eyes fluttered open, she saw her mother's face smiling down at her. Her throat was no longer slashed and there was no strange creature lurking in the corner.

'What happened, Mum?' asked Amber.

'You fainted, baby. I called the doctor and he's checking to make sure you're okay.'

Amber sat up straighter. She was in her bed, safe and warm. A middle-aged man in a white coat stood at the bottom of her bed. He had kind eyes and dark hair flecked with grey.

'Hello, Amber. Glad to see you're awake. You took a pretty nasty fall when you fainted. Can I get you to look into the light for me?' Amber went through the motions of following the doctor's orders for a few minutes. 'I'm glad to say there's no concussion,' he said once he'd completed his checks.

'Why did she faint?' asked her mother.

'It's difficult to say. She's perfectly healthy, although, by the looks of those dark bags under your eyes, I suggest a decent night's sleep.'

Amber leaned back against her pillow. 'I can't sleep.'

'Why's that, Amber?' asked the doctor.

Her mother took a small step forward. 'She's been struggling to sleep ever since... her friend disappeared a few weeks ago.'

'Ah, yes, Kieran Jones. I'm so sorry. It must be a very traumatic and confusing time for you.'

Amber nodded, blinking away the tears.

The doctor continued, 'It must be hard not knowing what happened to him. Would you like to talk to someone about it? A professional, perhaps?' He turned to her mother. 'If that's something you'd like to pursue, I can provide the details of a child therapist.'

Amber's mother shook her head lightly. 'Thank you, but we'll have to talk about it as a family first.'

'Of course.' He turned to Amber. 'Plenty of fluids and rest for you, young lady. You'll be just fine.' He patted her leg through the sheet. 'I'll see myself out, Mrs Walker.'

'Thank you, Doctor.'

'Any time.'

With one last smile, he walked from the room, leaving Amber lying on the bed in silence as she stared out of the window at the branches of the tree. In the daylight, they didn't appear so scary and menacing. But she knew, come the darkness, they would spring to life again, twisting and clawing at her windowpane.

'I'll come and check on you in a few minutes. I need to do a few chores, okay?'

Amber nodded and then took a deep breath. 'Mum,' she said quietly.

'Yes, baby?'

'I love you.'

'I love you too.'

Amber heard her mother pull the door not quite closed and walk down the stairs. She continued to stare at the tree branches, as the wind knocked them against the glass.

Her eyes threatened to close, but she fought as hard as she could. She didn't want to sleep ever again. She couldn't. Because in her dreams, she'd see it. She'd always see it. And when she was awake, it was there too.

Forever.

It wasn't merely a sleep demon. It was more than that.

It was The Creature.

And it was never going to leave her alone until she told the truth.

Amber's story continues in The Darkness Within Ourselves, *available wherever you buy books.*

4. THE SYN-EATER OF LANCASTER

by MJ Mars

Lancaster, England.

On the morning of the last hanging, Barnabas Swain peered into the looking glass and frowned at the gnarled reflection staring back at him. Twelve years of sin eating had taken their toll on his face, and, at 31-years of age, he saw similarities in the lines and sagging jowls of his own father, who had passed ten years prior at the age of 45.

Barnabas carefully buttoned his black woollen shirt and straightened the fall of the material over his shoulders. He felt it was his duty to present himself as neatly as possible. Although he was certain the dead could not bear witness to the act of his profession, he believed it was only right to treat the bodies with the respect he might offer the living. He smoothed the front of the shirt with his hands, marvelling at the quality of the material. When he had first begun sin eating, he barely had enough money for a paltry meal each day. It was known as a profession of the impoverished – because so few would desire to do it, only the desperate might apply.

The first few years he had roamed from town-to-town, as and when a person nearing death requested his attendance. The days were long and the travel treacherous, but he found solace in the fact that he was offering comfort to the families of those at the point of death.

He would turn up to the house of the afflicted, solemn, and quiet as he was shown to the room of the invalid or the recently deceased. The practice was designed to absolve those who were not baptised, or those whose sins may have overridden their initial invitation through St Peter's gates. Once his client had breathed their last, Barnabas took pride in the lifting of the bread, holding it over the recently stilled chest of those who had passed over. The incantation was one that had been taught to him by a retired sin eater in the vestibule of a hushed church after-hours, and he knew it by heart. His words took the sinful acts that clouded the soul of the recently deceased and transferred them into the bread. Carefully, he would eat every morsel of the bread, washed down with a small chalice of wine. The chalice had been tarnished a little over the years, only shining where his fingers clutched the sides each time it was lifted to his mouth above a slightly stinking corpse.

But the tough days of travelling to necessity ended for him seven years previously, when he was called to attend to the priest at Lancaster Castle. A man condemned to hang had requested absolution upon death and had paid the priest handsomely from his family's inheritance to have his sins cleared. Barnabas had arrived when requested, shown into the lower room of the grand castle, where the hanged man lay still on a wooden table. The skin of his throat bore a purple line that made the young sin eater flinch for a moment. But within a moment he had gathered his wits and set about following the steps to cleanse the prisoner's soul.

The priest, one Reverend Carmichael, had been waiting for him outside the chamber, and had asked that Barnabas follow him to the priory nearby. There, he would offer the sin eater a rite of protection since he had been charged with taking on the sin of a condemned murderer.

Barnabas had followed eagerly. It was true that from the moment he had swallowed the bread and wine containing the soul of the villain, it had sat heavier than the usual clientele; women who had been forced to give up a child to the workhouse, or the petty thieves who had not been baptised and feared for their souls in the afterlife. He had sat and drank another wine with Carmichael as the priest spoke gentle words pertaining to spiritual protection, until Barnabas had felt the contents of his stomach lurch.

Anticipating the oncoming surge, the priest had swiftly held forth a brass bowl into which Barnabas vomited the bread, wine, and presumably, any unforgiven sin from the hanged felon.

"Do forgive me!" he had blurted, shamefully wiping his mouth with his sleeve, and attempting to scurry away with the bowl of mess.

"Nonsense," the priest chastised. "You are in a house of the Lord, and this was in response to you being cleansed of sin. I do not doubt you needed it."

Barnabas watched as the priest covered the slopping bowl with his own folded stole, slipping it into the room next door so as not to continue embarrassing the young man. When he returned, gently smiling, Barnabas asked, "Have I condemned that poor man's soul by failing to digest the sin?"

Carmichael shook his head. "You have done your duty, my good man. In fact, are you due to stay a while in Lancaster? I have another prisoner who has requested absolution of this kind. He is due to swing by a week on Wednesday."

"That is… most unusual, Vicar. Usually, my services are not requested in the same town for months on end."

The priest sat back in the seat opposite the sin eater. "That may be so. But word spreads fast in a prison such as the castle of Lancaster. When one man hears of a chance to cleanse his soul, others tend to follow suit. He has agreed to pay me handsomely for the request. Which gives me heed to repay you for today's services…"

At the thought of spending another week in the city, Barnabas's mind had flitted instantly to the pricey charge of the room he had been granted at the local inn, and the even pricier ale at the public house along the road. But upon sight of the money in the priest's hand reaching across the short gap between their chairs, any consideration of his former poverty dissipated. "This must be for some other work undertaken today, Sir. I have never been paid so handsomely for my services in the past."

"You forget perhaps that the cleansing requested of you today was for one who had done despicable deeds in the eyes of the law and of the Lord. Such pains in taking on the stain of these extreme actions should be suitably rewarded."

Wide-eyed, Barnabas had taken the money from the priest's warm palm, awe-struck.

"And, if you will return next week in service of my next execution, you will be just as handsomely in pocket."

So, Barnabas had remained in Lancaster. And a regular stream of requests came to him from Lancaster's gaol within the castle walls. After each instance of sin eating, the priest would take him for his own spiritual cleansing. It happened so often that Barnabas had learned to lose his shame over the purging of his stomach contents. And he was reassured each time that the Lord had accepted that the cleansing of the felon's soul had been completed. He took the money, and on he stayed. Living a wealthier and more comfortable lifestyle than any sin eater before him.

***

The prisoner lay out on a wooden table, a burlap cloth covering his modesty. His chest was bare, revealing the muck, scars, and bruises Barnabas so often witnessed on the bodies of those who had been incarcerated for the most heinous of crimes.

Despite the circumstances, the room had a reverence to it in its simplicity. The grey stone of the castle floor and walls brought a sense of light through the shadowy corners, and the sweet scent of the hay that scattered the floor masked any smell of decay that might have already begun to permeate from the corpse.

Barnabas put his work bag on a stool that had been positioned near the head of the dead man and opened the latch. He did such movements slowly and with care, as he found that any noise made in the presence of the recently deceased brought with it a feeling of blasphemy. He lifted the brass chalice, placing it beside the bag on the stool top. Carefully, he filled the cup with claret and took the recently baked bread roll from its cloth wrapping. When he first began as a sin eater, he could only afford to bring with him the stalest of cob ends, cringing when the crumbs scattered over the bed linen of those he tended to. But that morning he had passed by the finest baker's stall, taking the still-warm and fine-scented roll from the first batch of the day. Fortune had certainly decided to favour him in his endeavours.

Unlike the poor wretch that lay before him.

The man was wiry but finely muscled, the type of frame he might see on a chap who was used to fleeing and climbing, ducking into small spaces, and creeping away from police or rivals. His knuckles were swollen and purpled with bruises from fistfights, and the sin eater could only assume that those scraps had occurred within the castle walls. But from fights with fellow incarcerates or guards, he wouldn't dare to hazard a guess.

Dark stubble scattered the rogue's pocked chin and cheeks, and his dark-shadowed and sunken eyes were half-open. The eyeballs turned down to the side, as if he were trying to get a glimpse of Barnabas's shoes. Around his neck, the burning bruise left by the rope blazed reddish purple.

Averting his gaze, Barnabas set to the task at hand. No matter what the man had done in this life, he had a right to absolution in the next. He held the bread over his sunken chest and began the incantation.

After the first line, he broke a thumb-sized piece of the bread and placed it in his mouth. He began to chew.

The fine crust around the bun shattered to pieces on his tongue, tasting a slightly burned tang from the fires mixing with the gentle malt of the dough. He swallowed, chasing the first sin with a gulp of the wine.

That, too, tasted slightly burnt.

The concoction felt instantly heavy in his stomach, and, as though his body had now been trained to repel the mixture, he covered his mouth when a belch rose from deep inside. He flushed in shame, sending his apologies to the man lying before him.

Before he could dwell any more on the discomfort of his task, he set about reciting the next line. Every bite of sin-absorbed bread felt somehow more laborious. His tongue felt dry, no matter how often he swilled the crumbs with the claret. His stomach twisted and turned, and more than once he feared the poor man's sins might be regurgitated all over his body before the cleansing was complete.

Finally, Barnabas managed to grit out the last line of the ancient text and stuff the final crust of bread into his mouth. Sickness pulsed through him in a wave now, the cooked dough feeling like hot coals in his belly. He gulped the wine and began to pack up his bag, keen to hurry across to the priory where Carmichael could give him his own blessing before the mess rushed from his body.

The door to the room squeaked open, and the young assistant to the hangman peered at Barnabas, wide-eyed.

Swallowing, Barnabas forced a smile. "I'm working with Vicar Carmichael," he reassured the squire.

The boy pulled a face. "I shouldn't think you'd have any business in 'ere with 'im if that's true."

Patience thinning as his stomach gave a loud warning growl, Barnabas tried to keep the smile plastered to his face. "I perform a rite after death that allows the soul to find peace. It was requested by the prisoner."

A bark of laughter from the young man caught Barnabas short. "From 'im? I do doubt it, Sir. That's Derek Warner. The Devil's Cordwain."

The nickname sounded familiar, but the confusion must have been clear from Barnabas's sick expression.

The squire jabbed at the table with the toe of his own boot, sending it rocking. The corpse's eyes fell even deeper down in the sockets, until only a small crescent of darkness appeared over the lid in each eye. "He's the cobbler what took all those kiddies and put them in the fire for the demons to eat. There ain't a scrap of repentance in this one, friend. The whole city would gladly watch him hang thrice-more. He cursed us all on the gallows, and all."

"How so?"

"Said he would take the whole town to hell with 'im. Mark his words." The boy had the decency to look a little uneasy at that point, and the hair on his arms stuck up as a chill scurried over his skin. "Well, it's all mouth up there, ain't it. A bit of chat for the *Gazette*. But I tell you one thing I know; that man was not looking for no repentance in the afterlife. Warner wanted to head straight down to carry on making boots in hell."

Saliva bloomed at the back of the sin eater's throat, alarm growing inside him. "I...I have to be going, now."

"Yeah. You tell the vicar he sent you to the wrong man." The boy laughed again, the sound stark in the stone chamber. "If The Devil's Cordwain woke up in Heaven, he'd be furious! Wouldn't you, you evil so-and-so."

The squire nudged the table again, and Warner's forearm on the left-hand side jerked upwards, as if it wanted to throw a punch.

Both the boy and Barnabas jumped in shock, but the squire gave a nervous giggle this time and shook his head. "Don't worry, they often do that. The hangman says it's each little part of the body shutting down on itself one by one. I think something different, mind."

Despite being so eager to leave, Barnabas found himself asking, "What is it that you believe?"

"Me? I think the innocent ones are trying to cling on. Grab at life, you know?"

Barnabas looked to the murderer's face and found that it wasn't only the arm that had moved. The eyes had lifted in the sockets. They appeared to be staring right at him. "And the guilty?" he pressed, his voice a shaking whisper.

"Oh, they're reaching out to grab us, alright. He said 'imself: He wants to take us all down with 'im."

***

Barnabas hurried across the pathway to the looming priory building. He pushed through the doors and stumbled to the vicar's room.

Reverend Carmichael sat in his chair, ready and waiting for the ritual. Upon seeing the sin eater's appearance, he clambered to his feet. "Barnabas? Whatever is the matter?"

"Derek Warner. You told me he hired me with willing for a cleansed soul."

The priest's expression faltered slightly. "Indeed."

"I am told this cannot be the truth. That the man whose sins I just consumed was more than in cahoots with the Devil himself." At mentioning the consumption of sin, the bread flamed inside him. He hunched over, saliva streaming from his lips.

Carmichael reached for the bowl, eager to catch the mess, but Barnabas flailed an arm in anger. The dish clattered to the floor and rolled away, clattering noisily as it came to rest at the door of the chamber.

"You've taken leave of your senses!" the holy man exclaimed.

Barnabas spat, crumbs of bread dappling the foaming wad that hit the church floor. "I have not! I have merely been enlightened to the fact that my actions have been folly. How many more sinners have I taken on without necessity?"

The priest's expression softened, and he moved to Barnabas's side as he hunched over his knees, gasping for air. Carmichael rubbed his back in comforting strokes. "Do believe me, young man, it was a necessity."

At the softness of his voice and the soothing comfort of his hand, Barnabas felt a moment of regret at his rash actions. Perhaps the priest had reason to try and gain repentance for these damned souls. Perhaps Carmichael felt it was his mission to at least try and absolve them of sin at their final hour. He spied the bowl laying across the room and winced with guilt as he recalled thrashing it from the holy man's arms. He would feel even more regret if he made a mess in the room. He gagged and covered his mouth with his hand. "Ugh, Reverend… do forgive me. I fear I'm going to…"

In a swift motion, the vicar clasped the back of Barnabas's neck and shoved him toward a chest that stood up against the wall. Barnabas landed heavily on his knees in front of it. A sour, pus-like scent drifted up from the air around the chest. He heaved, feeling the cursed liquid rushing up his windpipe.

The vicar still clawed at the sin eater's neck with one hand and, with the other, prised open the clasp of the chest. He flung wide the lid and forced Barnabas's head inside just as the bile began to pour from his mouth.

At first, Barnabas could not breathe in to smell the stench from within the chest. But, as the ruby-red vomit coursed from his stomach, he was aware that it was splashing against liquid that was already inside the chest. Red liquid congealed with sodden gobbets of pale matter. Bread.

Then, between agonised retches, he huffed in a deep breath and the stench assailed him.

This was seven years of his own sin-laden vomit.

Once Barnabas was completely purged of the Devil's Cordwain's futile cleanse, Carmichael let go of his neck and stood over the box, chanting the words that he used to say with a hand over Barnabas's head, the charade of protection in the air. The vicar lifted his eyes to the sky with a grin. If the stench bothered him in the least, he did not show it. In fact, he appeared to revel in it.

He turned to Barnabas, glee in his eyes. "Oh, my dear sin eater. I had hoped for at least three more good souls to be brought forth to the box. But, since you will no longer be in my services, this will have to do. And do nicely it will."

Still gulping for air, drool spilling down his chin, Barnabas blinked through tears as the priest rubbed his hands together over the box of bile as though it were a fine recipe.

"And now, the final ritual can begin. You've done well, my soul eater."

"Sin eater," Barnabas managed to gasp.

Carmichael snorted at the correction. "Perhaps once. But under my care you have been collecting the most heinous souls that have ever graced the hangman's noose of Lancaster. And here they are."

The sin eater watched Carmichael spread his arms over the box. He looked down with pride, as though it were his own babe or a creation of some majesty for all to admire. In a low voice, the vicar began to chant.

There came a squelching sound from within the chest.

The gastric mess slopped and splashed as something began to move within it. A grotesque red form, dripping chewed bread and stale claret, began to rise from the centre of the box as though it were fresh bread baking within.

A hand clasped the rim of the box. It slopped vomit on the floor, its fingers long and congealed with red and white gunk.

Barnabas screamed and, before he could stop himself, raced to stop the vicar's chant. He pushed the holy man, never dreaming in all his born days that he would have cause to take such an action.

They both tumbled to the ground.

Unused to fistfights, Barnabas was dazed for a moment, until a flash of gold rushed towards the side of his temple and the brass plate that had been used to catch his vomit on multiple occasions smashed into his skull, knocking him away from the vicar.

Unconscious for a moment, he woke blearily to the nightmare of more creatures rising out of the box. Dozens.

"Arise my children!" the vicar cried. He opened the back door, then turned tail and ran in the opposite direction, through the grand priory hall.

Barnabas staggered from the room and raced in the vicar's footsteps. Dizzily, he clung to the backs of the pulpits as he passed by the rows. A steady trickle of blood pulsed down the side of his head. He made it outside as screams began to erupt from the nearby castle.

A figure burst from the castle's hanging entrance and pelted up the pathway towards him. The young squire. When the hysterical boy's gaze fell on Barnabas, he gripped his shoulders and sobbed. "The Devil's Cordwain… he said he'd take us all down to Hell with him. They're here. The demons are here!"

The boy's eyes widened, peering at something behind Barnabas. The sin eater turned and saw a creature born of his own foul stomach contents leering out of the doorway. Its limbs were long and dripped bile. Its mouth widened in a sodden grin. When it leapt onto Barnabas, he smelled the slight waft of claret and bread over the rankness of the mouldering vomitus.

The finest bread that Lancaster had to offer.

5. TO BE A MAN OF MAN

by J C Michael

Isle of Man, England.

Whatever it was that they had given me in the bitter tea had taken hold to the point where I could barely stand. My eyes were half closed, partially from the stinging wind and fine drizzle which whipped across my face, and partly from the drug-laced beverage I'd consumed earlier in the evening, which made my eyelids feel unusually heavy, particularly the right-hand side where my face felt numb. I'd stood there, shivering, Meg by my side, as the sound of drums and chanting in a language I had no hope of understanding competed with the gale. As the chant intensified, and the speed of the beat increased, Meg took my hand and led me away, the ritual left to continue without me, yet only temporarily, for I knew my role, and the thought of what was to come filled my confused mind with a fear that would have been terror had it not been for whatever they had used to dull my senses, and ensure my participation.

As we had walked down the hill I had seen the mist rising on the sea and could only wonder if what I had been told over the past day could really be true. That the ancient protector of the island, Manannan, the Son of the Sea, would rise from the depths to accept my sacrifice. The ritual was nothing short of barbaric, and, had it been explained to me prior to being plied with alcohol, and then the tea which had initially paralysed me, I would have run. Run all the way back to the ferry in Douglas and, had there been no vessel in the dock, swam back to England and escaped this madness. Yet I couldn't run then, let alone swim, nor can I run now. I could barely walk, and was glad when we reached the small hut where I was told to wait, and where I now sit.

I suppose, as I wait for the inevitable, that I should start from the beginning, although telling any tale when my mind is as mangled as it presently is will no doubt prove difficult. I shall also choose to ignore the *fact* that I am recounting my story in the presence of an albino hedgehog, who may not really be there at all, but is happily snuffling around the hut, yet occasionally pausing to fix me with a quizzical look from its piercing red eyes. Meg? Oh, she's returned to the ritual. At least it's warm in here, with a fire burning in the middle of the room and the smoke escaping from a small hole in the roof. There's also a low table filled with food. Bread. Cheese. Scallops. Fruit. Eating is the last thing on my mind, but it's nice to be catered for. Now where was I? In a hut. Sat on a bench decked in furs. Story? Oh yes, forgive me, did I say I was somewhat befuddled?

We had met through online dating, and before you start I know you should be careful about who you meet on the internet, and I was. We spoke at length on the phone a number of times before our first date, and when an introvert like me can spend four hours on a call then surely there's a connection. Still, I did my due diligence. She was a writer, like me, not my genre, admittedly, but it explained why she'd 'matched' with me when the other 'likes' and 'swipes' I'd made had failed to reach anyone who deemed me worthy of such a reciprocal gesture. I'm a thriller guy, and she writes some strange niche alternative history romance that sounds like werewolf porn, but her work checked out, and 'knotting' is now a thing I know more about than I care to. More importantly, I found her on LinkedIn, and yes, she'd held some decent jobs, had owned her own business, and but for one white lie, her school dates giving away she was slightly older than her dating profile declared, verified via her Companies House entry may I add, all appeared legit. So, we met for a meal. It went well. We went to the cinema, which went even better, and we went to a pub quiz, which went better still. We even won, the two of us, leaving a team of six disgruntled locals in our wake. Seven years single and I was finding happiness. We booked a weekend away in a glamping pod by the East Yorkshire coast. We walked. We talked. We slept together. The sex was amazing. The next day we visited Rudston monolith, the tallest standing stone in the UK, and it was there, as she lent her long, lithe body against the ancient stone, that she told me she wanted to take me home. At first, I thought she meant the small village she lived in near Doncaster, but she laughed, a soft, sweet laugh that I was falling in love with, and said no. Her real home. The Isle of Man.

Now my knowledge of the Isle of Man was limited at that point to a vague awareness of tailless cats and motorbike races but she explained how her family had lived there for generations and that her father, Magnus, was ill and she should really visit. Having lost my own father recently I empathised, and for all it wouldn't be the nicest reason to take a trip away, the thought of more time with her filled me with joy. How I feel like a gullible bugger now, eh? Besides, she offered to pay for the crossing, and said we could stay on the family farm, so two weeks later we were on our way. Admittedly I was a little wary of how fast things were moving, but she told me to put my 'manxiety' on hold, and I was smitten. Totally drawn in by professional, sensible, caring Megan, who I felt able to be open with about anything, and who was never judgemental about my past and previous issues. Not to mention besotted by Meg, her wild and hedonistic side, a side I'd only glimpsed but who I wanted more than anything. Megan for the boardroom, Meg for the bedroom. Combined, they had stolen my heart.

Looking back, maybe there were warning signs, pesky red flags I'd chosen to ignore. Her interest in paganism for one, but that's not too unusual, or how quick she was to lure me away with a siren's song of a sick father and how she was scared to fall in love, but couldn't help herself. The fact her favourite film was Midsommar, Christ, I should've picked up on that one. Or her two brothers, Alex and Orry, who collected us from the ferry and drove us over the island to the farm near Peel, two hulking brutes with shaved heads and very little to say. But yet again, I'd done my research. Her father had sat on the island's parliament, the Tynwald, and was a member of the 'House of Keys'. He was well respected, as was the family, and his own brother, who welcomed us on arrival at the farm and hugged me like an old friend, was a senior police officer. I should've known that 'the establishment' and 'people you should trust' are not necessarily one and the same, but I'm not a conspiracy nut, just a regular guy. There's nothing regular about my current situation though is there? I'm tripping my tits off on God knows what, wittering on to an imaginary hedgehog, who thankfully doesn't talk back, and barely able to move, let alone escape. If I was a man prone to profanity, I would say I was fucked.

My eyes are stinging now from the smoke and the wind is building outside, rattling the timbers of the hut which, while cosy, is still but a wooden shed on an exposed hillside. I can't tell how long I've been here, nor do I know how long the preparations for the ritual take, but the feeling of dread upon me provides an intuition that it won't be long. Meg and I had taken a drink with Magnus, a man whose jaundiced skin and hacking cough betrayed the severity of whatever ailed him. We partook in a strong spirit I was told was distilled there on the farm, and akin to the whiskies of the Scots and Irish who held a degree of kinship with the Manx people native to the island. Following that, and a meal of lamb and potatoes, I had been offered what I was told was a traditional herbal tea. It was bitter, yet I was polite. I drank it, and if my fate hadn't been sealed the moment I returned Megan's 'like' and offer of a 'last first date', it was sealed with that first sip. Not long after I'd drained my cup, and wondered at the roots mingled with the leaves in the bottom, did I begin to feel woozy. There was a conversation going on around me in what I could only assume was Manx, an offshoot of Gaelic and too alien from English for me to fathom. Meg, her brothers, her father, and her uncle, all busily chatting, then hastily making calls. Then, Meg took my hand. She explained, as my terror mounted, the role of the second-born child. A role to be performed by them, be they male, or their lover, their substitute, be they female. A role in a ceremony which was performed once a generation to ensure the protection of Manannan, and the prosperity of the island. In the days of the pagans and the Norse, the whole island would gather, but since the days of the English only the few had kept the old ways alive, ensuring the harvest, and in more recent years the good fortune brought by tech companies, online gambling, and tax haven status. I would've laughed, if my facial muscles had been capable of movement. I would've run, had I not been rooted to my chair, I would've yelled to be let go, but my vocal chords refused.

"From the hill of Barrule, on the ancient stone of sacrifice, a man shall be offered, and in return prosperity shalt be granted. For Manannan, Son of the Sea, Protector of the Isle, whose mists kept the Romans from our shores, whose trickery drove the Norse back into the sea until betrayed, who has watched over us under the rule of the Scots and the English, we give thanks, and give our offering. On a clear day seven kingdoms can be seen, England, Scotland, Ireland, and Wales, as ruled by men, and the kingdoms of the Sea, of the Otherworld, and of Man, who shall be ruled by Manannan, and Manannan alone. 'Tis the place of the second born of the first family to guarantee and make such sacrifice, a sacrifice to be cast from on high to the depths of the sea below. Their wings unfurl from their back as they take flight before they dive gull-like to the waves below. Their sacrifice willingly accepted, and our protection renewed for another generation". That's how she explained it to me, in the soft, melodic voice that had entranced me since I'd heard it for the very first time. It was almost poetic, "It isn't as bad as it sounds," she had said, "the back is sliced open, but there's little pain. The nightshade and mushrooms see to that. The skin is unfurled, and the ribs hooked from the spine to be folded outwards, but there's no suffering at that point, for death comes quickly." I'd tried to scream.

The hut door is open, the wind whistling in and driving the stinging smoke into my eyes. I try to blink away tears as Meg approaches me, her long green robes wet from the rain and sticking to her body. I know that she is naked underneath, as she had dressed in front of me, seductive and playful, and her body presses against me as she lifts me, but I'm in no fit state to be aroused. My own robes are white, and soon to be splattered with blood. Her blonde hair is shot through with grey a shade lighter than the grey of her eyes. Her lips are thin, and curled in a smile. I don't feel like smiling, and I stumble on jelly legs. Strong arms catch me, one of her brothers, but I don't know which, as he's wearing a mask with shaggy black hair spilling over his face, and bulls horns. "He is Buggane," she whispers, but the word means nothing to me.

Taking an arm apiece they lead me outside and back up the hill, towards the stone. I know that it is close to the edge of the cliff, and that soon a body shall plummet down to the sea below, where Manannan will claim his due. The chanting has ceased, as have the drums. There are a dozen or so robed figures, all in hooded green robes, and holding torches which burn despite the wind and the rain. There's also another masked figure, this one a boar with long tusks, and by its stocky build I have my suspicions that it's none other than Uncle Edmund, who tomorrow morning will presumably file a report detailing a missing person, or tragic accident. Tonight will be swept under the carpet, and life will move on, for most. By the stone stands Magnus, bare chested, exposing a tattoo of a leg, bent at the knee, rising from his crotch. I almost laugh, as I realise that the design makes a triskelion with his own two legs, but the large black spaniel by his side growls through bared teeth as if in warning. "Heed the Moddey Dhoo," whispers Meg into my ear as she and her brother all but drag me onwards. As I approach, a figure steps forward and removes his robe, the youngest of the three children of Magnus, Orry. In his hand is a knife, long and wicked, and as he holds it above his head the remaining robed figures begin to chant again, "Fragarach. Fragarach. Fragarach."

Orry and I exchange a look, he knows what is coming, and that he has had little choice but to wait for this day since the day of his birth. I pity him as he passes me the knife, and it feels heavy, yet comfortable, in my hand. I know what I must do. Everything had been explained as Meg had made love to me earlier that evening, the paralysis from the tea loosening its grip as she sat on what she called "the beast between my legs". I was left under no illusion that should I fail to do as expected, I would be killed in Orry's place, and how can it be murder, when the victim goes so willingly? Alex, the Bugane, is by my side, and holding something that looks like a claw hammer. I have no doubt such an implement will break ribs as if they were matchsticks, that particular activity being his role to play in this madness. His breathing is heavy with anticipation, whereas I feel like being sick. Magnus is watching on, and I wonder if he will have the strength to throw his son's corpse into the sea, or if Uncle Edmund will assist. Orry just smiles, before silently turning his back to me. The chanting stops. Meg kisses my neck and holds my hand "It's time to become a man of Man," she says as I begin to slice open her brother from the nape of his neck to the small of his back. It's easier than I thought it would be, and his screams fill the night air.

6. THE GOD BOTHERERS

by Ashley Lister

North of England.

"There are three types of people who answer the door," Brother Black explained. "And the commonest type are the abusive ones."

Brother Green swallowed nervously. "Abusive? Will they try and hit us?"

Brother Black smiled warmly. "Usually they prefer verbal abuse," he explained. "They'll tell us to go away. They'll probably swear and act like godless heathens as they chase us from their doorstep and tell us to 'eff-the-eff off', but they seldom resort to physical violence."

Brother Green sighed with relief. He was prepared to do a lot for his Lord and saviour. He was prepared to devote his days off to the great man in the sky. He was willing to give over 25% of his income to the church's coffers. He was happy to sing the praises of his beloved God to anyone who would care to listen. But he wasn't sure he could tolerate the threat of physical abuse.

It was a miserable winter Wednesday and the sky was the colour of a brimming ashtray. Like a million other urban sprawls in the UK, the backstreet terraces of this town were tightly packed together. The buildings were striving to look inconspicuous whilst the brothers from the Church of the Holy Grail walked past their curtained windows in search of souls that could be saved.

"You said there were three types of people we'd encounter," Brother Green reminded his superior. This was his first recruiting trip, and he was anxious to learn as much as possible from a church elder with the experience of Brother Black, a man who had been with the Church of the Holy Grail for more than a decade. "What are the other two types of people?"

Brother Black's smile widened. He was a handsome man, somewhere in his mid-thirties, Brother Green guessed, but with glints of steel darkening the jet-black hair at his temples so that he looked a little like a maturing George Clooney. Dressed all in black, save for the Roman collar around his throat, he looked imposing, but approachable. The uniform jackets that they both wore were large enough to conceal a Bible in the left inside pocket and a hefty crucifix in the right.

"The second type we'll encounter," Brother Black said, "are the ones who welcome us with open arms. They're the ones who give us a proper cup of tea and they often put out the good biscuits."

Brother Green licked his lips, knowing that 'the good biscuits' were the ones that had chocolate coating but no thumbprints.

"The welcoming ones are the ones who want to learn the word of our Lord and saviour," Brother Black explained. "They're the ones who are eager to become members of the Church of the Holy Grail."

Brother Green was warmed by the idea of meeting such spiritually open people and he found himself returning Brother Black's smile. "I suspect the welcoming ones are the smallest group, aren't they?"

Brother Black shook his head and said, "The smallest group, thankfully, are the dæmons. But they're the reason why I do this each week."

"Dæmons?" Brother Green repeated. He studied Brother Black to see if the man was having a joke with him but there was no suggestion of amusement in his expression. "Do you mean metaphorical dæmons?" he asked warily, not sure what a metaphorical dæmon might be. "Or do you mean something more literal?"

"Dæmons," Brother Black said again. "Godless heathen dæmons who suck the soul from a victim's body, strip the skin from their flesh whilst they're alive and squirming, and then slaughter their victims as part of a fiendish Satanic ritual." He noticed the expression of concern on Brother Green's face and added, "But, as I said before, even though that's my main reason for going door-to-door, dæmons are the smallest group we encounter."

They walked in silence for a moment before Brother Green found the courage to ask a question. "What do these dæmons do?" Trying to bring a moment's levity to the conversation, desperate to believe that Brother Black had been attempting to make a joke, he said, "I take it these dæmons don't bring out the tea and biscuits like the welcoming ones."

Brother Black stopped and considered him for a moment. There was no hint of amusement in his features. He looked as solemn as a cancer diagnosis. "As a matter of fact," he began.

"Dæmons are very likely to bring out the tea and biscuits. Dæmons will always try to engage the likes of you and me."

Brother Green raised an eyebrow, wondering if the man genuinely believed in dæmons. More likely, Brother Green told himself, he was being subjected to some sort of prank. Admittedly, none of the elders in the Church of the Holy Grail were known for their sense of humour but Brother Green figured all places had their own hazing rituals. He figured that he was enduring the equivalent teasing that happened to a building site apprentice being asked to collect an order of tartan paint, a glass hammer or a ladder bag.

"Why do these dæmons bring out the tea and biscuits?" he asked.

"They try to lull us into a false sense of security," Brother Black explained. "You take a nice biscuit, or you sip at a cup of tea, and then you find you've been drugged."

"Drugged!"

"Once you're sat there, paralysed with the narcotics they've put into your tea and biscuits, the dæmon will suck out your soul and devour it. Then, whilst you're still alive, the dæmon will start to peel the skin from your body. I saw one work on your predecessor, and she was merciless. She removed the skin from his hand, as though she was taking off a glove. He was left with the bare flesh of his fingers, hand and forearm, exposed to the elements. The hypnotic drug she'd given him meant he couldn't move. But you could see in his face that he could still experience pain. At least, you could see that in his face, until she removed the skin from there as well."

Brother Green wondered if he was about to vomit. He placed a protective hand over his mouth and stopped himself from dry-heaving.

Brother Black shook his head as though coming out of a trance and said, "All of which is why you will need to have the godly weapons of your book and your cross with you at all times." He paused and patted his pockets, seeming to smile when he touched the reassuring presence of his Bible and crucifix. Brother Green followed his example and felt the bulky weight of the godly weapons in his own pockets.

"Keep those with you," Brother Black insisted. "And be on the lookout for the signs."

"Signs?"

"Typically, they're just signs of occult worship, idolatry and vice," Brother Black explained. "But I'll show you when we see them." They had arrived at the first door on the street and he tapped loudly and confidently, knock-knockity-knock-knock, on the glass pane in the centre.

Brother Green's heart was hammering inside his chest, and he realised he was silently praying that no one would answer the door. He didn't want to suffer the verbal abuse that Brother Black had said would come from the majority of houses and he certainly didn't want to encounter a soul-sucking dæmon who was going to strip the skin from his bones and then kill him.

Brother Black knocked again. Knock-knockity-knock-knock.

"Who is it?" called a female voice. The door opened partially, and a tired face stared out at them both from the shadows within. There was suspicion in her sunken eyes and a vape pen dangling from the corner of her mouth. "Who are you?"

"I'm Brother Black. This is Brother Green. We're here from the Church of the Holy Grail."

"Fuck off!"

The door slammed in their faces.

Brother Black shrugged philosophically and moved onto the next door. Brother Green marvelled that the man had accepted such bald rudeness without any sign of upset. He watched his colleague approach the next house with his smile unperturbed and he delivered the same cheery knock-knockity-knock-knock he had rapped out before.

This time he was told to get fucked.

They had gone down the street, being enjoined to, "piss off", "go bother someone else", and "get a proper job instead of fiddling with kids." They were almost at the end of the road before an elderly woman opened the door and invited them both inside.

She looked like the epitome of a sweet grandmother. Her hair was a cap of tight, white curls. Her eyes were wrinkled with laughter lines and her smile was made up of porcelain white dentures. The air that wafted from inside her house smelled of synthetic lavender and freshly baked cookies.

"I've heard about your church," she said cheerfully. "And I've been curious to learn more. Would you care to come inside for some tea and biscuits?"

Brother Black thanked her and said they would appreciate that opportunity. They were escorted into a room that was prim, tidy and had clearly been decorated by someone whose taste belonged to an era that was now in the history books. The walls were decorated with a floral print paper, occasionally broken by pictures of giddily smiling grandchildren and pastel-coloured watercolours. The floor was carpeted with a busy Axminster and the furniture looked like the dictionary definition of chintz.

"Make yourselves comfortable, gentlemen," she said. "I'll be back with the tea and biscuits in just a moment."

And then Brother Green and Brother Black were alone.

"Is this one of the welcoming ones?" Brother Green asked in a confidential whisper. He figured it was the sort of ridiculous question that would make Brother Black smile. After walking down a street of repeated verbal abuse, he didn't think it would be possible to imagine a warmer welcome than the one they had received from this sweet little old lady. "She is a welcoming one, isn't she?"

Brother Black shrugged and glanced around the room. His lips were set in a scowl of disapproval. "Some of the signs we look out for in a dæmon house are visible here."

"What sort of signs?" Brother Green asked, scouring the room with a curious gaze that saw nothing. He was wondering if there should be an inverted crucifix on one wall, or a chalice filled with the blood of a virgin on the mantelpiece, or a sacrificed goat in front of the fireplace.

"Books that discuss witchcraft," Brother Black said, pointing at a paperback on the coffee table. "Pictures of the false Madonna," he added with another gesture. "And signs of a penchant for vice."

Brother Green frowned as he considered the evidence. "Is that really a book on witchcraft? It looks like one of the Harry Potter books. Maybe *Chamber of Secrets*?"

"Those books promote witchcraft," Brother Black assured him. His tone was suddenly resolute, and Brother Green knew the topic of books on witchcraft was not up for discussion. It would only take a moment and he would be quoting Exodus 22:18 "Thou shalt not suffer a witch to live."

"But the false Madonna," Brother Green noted. "Isn't that just a vinyl sleeve for the *Like a Virgin* album?"

Brother Black considered him with eyes that were wide with the threat of repercussions. "Jonah, 2:8," he said piously. "Those who cling to worthless idols turn away from God's love for them." He pointed at the album sleeve and asked, "Do you believe that woman to be the real Madonna?"

Rather than get into an argument about the identity of Madonna, Brother Green asked, "Why do you say she's got a penchant for vice?"

Brother Black nodded at the keyring on the table and Brother Green saw it was from the Mecca Bingo. He didn't need that one explaining. Gambling was a vice, he conceded, and bingo was one of the oldest forms of gambling, so he supposed that was a reasonable accusation. But, whilst he didn't want to undermine the authority of Brother Black, he truly believed the evidence against this elderly woman was so flimsy it couldn't even be described as circumstantial.

"I've put milk and sugar on the tray," the little old lady said, returning to the room and carrying a large tray burdened with teapot, cups, saucers and trimmings. "But we'll need to leave the tea to steep for a moment if you want the full flavour of this Twinning's breakfast tea."

She placed the drinks on a table in the centre of the room and waited for Brother Black and Brother Green to sit on the chintzy settee. Once they were settled, she placed herself in the room's only armchair and stared at them. Brother Green reached for a biscuit, but Brother Black slapped his hand away.

"For those who are led by the Spirit of God are the children of God," said Brother Black solemnly. He was staring at the elderly lady as he spoke. Brother Green recognised the words from *Romans 8:14*. He made another attempt to take a biscuit but, again, Brother Black slapped his hand away. Once again, Brother Black said, "For those who are led by the Spirit of God are the children of God."

"What does that mean?" the little old lady asked. She had a puzzled expression on her face, her dentures appearing as she gave Brother Black a polite smile. However, Brother Green figured that his colleague had seen something more than her likeable grin. From the way he acted, it was almost as though he had seen her eyes turn crimson whilst horns grew out of her head.

Brother Black leapt up from his seat on the settee and pointed an accusatory finger at her. "You are a dæmon!" he declared. He took the huge crucifix from inside his jacket pocket and smashed it against the elderly woman's head.

Brother Green watched in stunned horror.

The crucifix was large and heavy, fashioned from silver, and weighing a couple of pounds. When it hit the woman's head there was a cracking sound, like an egg being broken.

"Dæmon!" Brother Black bellowed, hitting her again. "Leave this woman's body and return to the Hell from whence you came!" Again and again, he used the outsize cross as a weapon, slapping her across the face with it so that her head twisted in one direction and then the other.

A spray of blood swept over the tea tray and Brother Green could feel his interest in the biscuits dwindling.

The woman was elderly, and her skin lacked the elasticity to cope with this level of abuse. A strip of flesh across her forehead tore away and then, with each swipe of the cross, her injuries seemed to worsen. As Brother Green watched, he saw one of her eyes being taken out by the vicious assault. Her cheekbones were pulverised by the silver bars of the crucifix and one vicious blow took her false teeth out and sent them spinning to a corner of the room.

It took a good twenty minutes before Brother Black was finally finished.

Brother Green sat on the settee, watching the display and wondering if he had really seen the outrageous display of violence. Looking at the remains of the elderly woman, her face stripped to a blood-red skull with empty eye sockets and cracks in her cranium, he supposed he couldn't argue with the evidence of his own eyes.

"Our work here is done," Brother Black said, putting the crucifix back into his inside pocket. "We've vanquished the dæmon that possessed this unfortunate soul. We must move on."

Brother Green wanted to ask if that was what they had really done, but he didn't dare question the man standing beside him. He nodded agreement, followed Brother Black's example in wiping fingerprints from every surface they had touched, and then followed him out of the house.

"Is that the first time you've seen a dæmon being vanquished?" Brother Black asked as they returned to the street and closed the elderly lady's door behind them.

"It is," Brother Green replied. He didn't dare say more for fear that the words might be accompanied by him hurling vomit to the floor.

"It's very satisfying work," Brother Black admitted. "I'll let you vanquish the next one, if you like."

Brother Green wanted to demur, but he could sense he was under his colleague's scrutiny. If he said anything at this moment that suggested he didn't agree with Brother Black's beliefs and attitudes, he knew he would suffer the same fate that had just been administered to the elderly woman.

"That would be very kind of you," Brother Green said easily.

Brother Black nodded, turned to the next house and rapped briskly on the door. Knock-knockity-knock-knock. As they waited for a response, Brother Green found himself silently praying that the person inside the home would just open the door and tell them to fuck off.

7. WRONG LANE

by Stephen Barnard

Bolton, England.

Aaron Langer indicated to come off the southbound carriageway of the M61 – at Junction 6 – just as he did every day. A creature of habit, he flicked the left-hand stem on the battered Land Rover's steering column as soon as he passed the three-striped marker for the exit slip road. Once moving up the ramp he stayed right, to facilitate his clockwise journey around the exit roundabout; he would enter at 6 o'clock and leave at 3 o'clock, taking the Westhoughton and Chorley exit, having driven through 270 degrees.

There was a queue, but there always was; out of the three lanes to choose from at the top of the ramp the right-hand one was always the busiest, mainly because it was the one that had to contend most carefully with the oncoming traffic from the right-hand side. The other two lanes went left, towards Horwich and Bolton, and could exit the roundabout much more quickly and safely.

That was how it was supposed to be, anyway.

The arrows – freshly re-painted on the tarmac – even indicated it: two arrows going left, only one going right. Except, there were those people that didn't like to queue in the right-hand lane with everyone else, but zipped up the middle one instead. Once at the top, the curvature of the roundabout gave them half a car length's lead on the idling car to the right. They would take advantage of this, and once it was safe to go, they would accelerate away, not to go left towards Horwich and the Middlebrook retail park, but to cut across the front of the car that had been patiently waiting for its moment in the correct lane.

Aaron was often one of the cars patiently waiting in the correct lane. And he hated those drivers that cut across him, stealing his spot.

He didn't tolerate it anymore, and relished the chance to take these idiots on.

When his moment came to be at the top of the right-hand lane, eyes firmly fixed on the body of traffic coming across him from the right, he could sense a car pulling up to his left. Of course, it could make a swift exit towards Horwich as it was supposed to, but he doubted it – he expected it to try and take his spot.

Aaron afforded a quick glance: a Honda Civic. *Let's see if it wants to take on a Land Rover.*

There was a suitable gap in the traffic flow and Aaron took his chance. He floored it and held his driving line, as he always did.

Blinkers on like a racehorse, he didn't worry about what was on his left. If the Civic was going to try and take his lane that was up to the driver. It all depended on how much it wanted to risk bouncing off the sturdy body of Aaron's jeep.

There was a flash of the red Civic ahead and to the left: it was trying to take his lane. Aaron pushed on, hands gripping the wheel tightly at ten to two.

A car horn sounded, and the Civic swerved away, having to drive on the narrow strip of chevrons that marked the roundabout's edge. The Civic then slipped in behind Aaron to avoid careening into a waiting car at the next entry point. The driver – a red-faced middle-aged man – appeared large in Aaron's rearview mirror, somehow managing to continually beep his horn, offer Aaron aggressive hand gestures, and steer the car.

Inside Aaron laughed, but didn't allow himself to outwardly chuckle.

On the bridge section of the roundabout, the M61 running underneath him, he was reminded why he did this. Tied to the rails – as there always was and had been every day for five years – were ribbons, teddies and flowers. All that time ago, some young punk in a TR7 had done to a young mother and her two kids what the Civic had just tried to do to him. The inquest reported that the rear end of the TR7 clipped the front of her Punto and she panicked and struggled to hold it. Caught in a spin, she had crashed through the rail and onto the motorway below. There they had perished. The authorities never caught up with the driver of the TR7.

Aaron went past the remembrance marker. *If I do this enough, maybe they'll stop abusing the lane.*

He exited the roundabout onto a two-lane carriageway that ran for around 200 yards called De Havilland Way. He wanted the right-hand lane again, Chorley-bound. The Civic re-appeared in the left-hand lane, heading for Westhoughton. It could have gone ahead of Aaron this time, the road in front being clear, but instead it held its position next to him. The driver's window came down, his face still puce with fury. He was screaming at Aaron. The Land Rover was old: he had to reach across to wind down the window a crack.

'-could have fucking killed me!'

Aaron checked his driving before responding. 'You were in the wrong lane!'

'No I fucking wasn't!'

'Yes you were. The arrows clearly indicate that you should have turned left to Horwich!'

They were running out of road. 'Fuckin' beardy twat!' the middle-aged man roared, and then they were at another, smaller roundabout. This time the Civic took the expected left turn and disappeared towards Westhoughton. When the route was clear, Aaron calmly headed towards Chorley on the A6.

Beardy twat – was that the best he could do? He supposed it was Aaron's most obvious feature; a little wild and unkempt, it dominated his face. It made him look a lot older than his thirty years, and that's why he liked it. A bit dishevelled, like the old Land Rover.

He thought about what to do next. He had nowhere special to go. It didn't take much deliberating to make the decision to drive all the way to Chorley, get back on the motorway at the next available point and then head south again to tackle the Junction 6 exit once more, hopefully encountering another idiot.

This time he did allow himself a chuckle.

**

It was some days later – Aaron didn't really count them – when he found himself in an abnormally long queue in the right-hand lane of the exit slip road. It was getting dark and this was rush hour traffic. He'd been in it for a good five minutes and had seen a number of cars zoom past him to his immediate left, most of them undoubtedly intending to abuse the middle lane. There were even those that had been waiting with him, only to then pull out of the proper lane to join the growing number of idiots looking to take the illegal shortcut. He knew that when he got to the top of the ramp he would have challengers on his left – maybe even two at once.

He was not disappointed. He was at the head of the queue for perhaps a second when he heard a car approach next to him – something with a souped-up engine and an unnecessarily loud exhaust. He afforded a quick glimpse and noted the low ride and black body. Then his eyes were back on the flow of traffic to the right, waiting for a gap.

When it came he swiftly adjusted pedals and surged the Land Rover forward, eyes focused dead ahead and the correct line held, as always.

The car to his left did the same, noisier than before, half a length further forward. It was a sports car shape, but an old model. It wanted Aaron's lane. He pushed the Land Rover harder so that it squealed.

The other car didn't get far enough ahead but now needed the lane. Aaron expected it to take to the chevrons, for its wheels to spit up gravel and detritus, for its driver to curse and scream. It didn't. Instead it moved right, into the front of the Land Rover. The back end pushed against his front left wheel guard and bumper. Sparks flew up.

Aaron expected the smaller car to almost bounce off, but instead it pushed against him harder and he felt it impacting on his steering. He had to grip tight to hold his line, but somehow found himself being nudged into the other lane. Behind him, someone flashed their lights.

There's going to be an accident, he thought, horrified. He would have to slow up and let the sports car have the lane.

Not just a sports car.

That was the split second he realised what it was, just as he relented and let it move in. It was a TR7.

They were on the bridge section and he glanced quickly at the floral tribute on the rails, then back at the black TR7 in front of him. Had the vehicle from five years ago been black? He couldn't remember.

Then they were off the roundabout and onto De Havilland Way. Two open lanes now, and room to manoeuvre, to pass and overtake if necessary. The TR7 was ahead of him and so Aaron, defeated, considered it done. But of course it wasn't. He noticed the silver scratches and dents on the rear of the vehicle in front and realised there had to be a conversation about the collision, insurance details shared, numbers exchanged. Would he apologise? He didn't know yet. He would follow the TR7 and wait for it to pull over.

Except that's not what it did. Before the next roundabout, it switched lanes, dropped its speed so that it seemed to reverse past him, and then slotted in behind. Aaron looked in his mirror. He couldn't see the driver. The windscreen of the TR7 was blacked out with a dark tint. *Is that even legal?* The roundabout came and Aaron took the right lane to Chorley.

The TR7 followed.

Aaron looked for a suitable place to pull over, but the A6 was pretty narrow for a stretch. Perhaps if he turned off-

The engine roared behind him and the black sports car shunted into the back of his Land Rover. Again, the impact and pressure was more than he expected from such a smaller vehicle. *This guy's crazy!* Aaron sped up; the TR7 matched him. Again, a shunt, as Aaron had to slow because of the car in front. Again, he looked in his mirror and could make out nothing.

Again, again.

Aaron was panicking now, and wondered what was best to do. There were traffic lights approaching and he feared what might happen if they turned red. There was also a fork in the road: the left-hand one took him on the more sedate route through a village called Blackrod; the right-hand one to Chorley – which was essentially straight ahead – had a wider carriageway, a 50mph speed limit, and room to overtake. That was the route: it was now all about the lights.

The car ahead went through on green, just. The lights changed to amber. Aaron pushed the Land Rover and crossed the line just as it turned to red. He crossed the yellow hatching on the road surface without interfering with other traffic. He quickly checked his mirror. The TR7 still followed, drawing a honk from the first car now crossing from the other direction.

Aaron accelerated, and straddled the central white line in order to overtake the car ahead. Beyond it, there was open road to move into – up a slope but the Land Rover could handle it.

So could the TR7, easily. It was at his rear again, and shunted him. This time, because he was doing sixty, the impact wobbled the jeep in a more exaggerated fashion and he had to grip the wheel tight to maintain his position.

He pushed on and crested the slope. He knew what to expect on the downward approach: he had driven this road thousands of times. Another set of lights, 300 yards away, this time with three options: left, right, or straight ahead. If Aaron was to shake off the lunatic behind him, he thought there was only one option he could take.

Ahead of him, cars took all three directions, the green light allowing. However, he knew it would change before he got there. He supposed he was counting on it. Ideally he'd be the first car confronted with a red light, then he could make a decision either way.

He wasn't. There were two cars ahead of him that obeyed the colour-led change of instruction. Aaron could either be stationary or reckless.

He chose the latter. He swerved into the right-hand carriageway reserved for oncoming traffic. It was only just green for them up ahead, and gears and pedals were just being engaged. He floored it, cutting across tarmac intended for vehicles from two different directions, neither of them his. Car lights approached him at speed and horns blurted. He'd committed now, and slowing would cause more damage. He veered right, looking for the turn that would take him past the Ridgeway Arms on the corner and the neighbouring train stop. Cars screamed their fury at him, and he felt a nudge on his left panel, thought he heard the tinkle of a broken light. Then he definitely did hear the impact of metal on metal, but not his. He took the turn, slipped past the pub, and left the blaring horns behind him. He felt guilty about causing an accident, but what else could he have done?

Aaron looked in his mirror. Stationary cars blocked the junction, outlined in smoke. There was no sign of the TR7. He drove on, hoping that no-one had got his licence plate.

He thought it would be a good idea to get off the main roads for a minute, just in case a witness was able to pursue. Also, he realised, he needed to catch his breath and drop his adrenalin levels. There was a housing estate up ahead on the left that – once you got past the first five houses – went round in one big loop. He would park up at the top of the loop for a few minutes, and then follow it round and out again, with a view to heading home.

He turned left into the estate.

Just ahead, at the end of the row of five houses, parked on a slant across the entrance and exit to the housing estate loop, was the black TR7.

That's impossible.

Not knowing what else to do, Aaron pulled over. As nothing else happened in the next few seconds, he formulated a plan. He would wait for the driver to get out and walk close up to the Land Rover. Then Aaron would reverse onto the shared driveway of the five houses adjacent and then speed away. Surely he could throw the guy off then?

But how did he get ahead of me to be waiting here?

Aaron didn't want to think about that. Instead he stared at the TR7.

Bizarrely, there were no markings on the front of the car. He could make out the silver scratches on the rear from their confrontation on the roundabout, but there was not a single dent or blemish at the other end, despite all the ramming and shunting.

That was when he fully took in the licence plate and momentarily lost the ability to take in new breath.

The man got out of the black sports car. He had an athletic frame covered in dark sportswear. He had brown hair, was clean-shaven, and wore sunglasses despite the absence of natural light in the early evening.

Aaron wasn't going to wait for him to get closer; he was leaving now.

Only, the Land Rover's engine had died, and no amount of aggressive key turns and pedal pumps was going to do anything. Suddenly Aaron knew, as sure as he knew anything.

The man had stepped closer, now under the glow of a street lamp. Aaron recognised the face as the shades were removed.

He realised he had no choice but to confront this... moment?

As he got out of the Land Rover he looked at the TR7's licence plate once more: L44 AAR.

He remembered it well. Just as he suddenly remembered *all* of it well.

Today's wasn't the first car accident he'd fled from.

He looked again at the scratches on the back of the TR7. He remembered deciding that there was no way he could take it to the repair garage to get them mended, not when everyone was looking for the vehicle that had caused the death of the young mother and her two infant children.

It couldn't be the same TR7, could it? He'd dumped that one in a nearby reservoir, nearly five years ago.

Wondering if he should ask the question, he looked into the eyes of the driver. His eyes. His face, minus the beard. *No, no need for conversation after all.*

But then what was this? Aaron didn't know. His younger self took a step towards him, which made Aaron back up, away from the Land Rover and towards the pavement behind.

He was standing in the middle of the entrance to the shared driveway for the adjacent houses, when he realised why he knew this estate so well. The front door to the middle house opened, and the silhouette of a man appeared against the yellow glow of the hallway light. 'Can I help you?' enquired a deep, male voice.

He still lives here, thought Aaron. *After all these years, the husband still lives here.* Aaron remembered countless times in the past, parking up in roughly the same spot the Land Rover was in now, just to wait a few minutes and then drive round the loop and off again, his inner thoughts remaining unspoken, his inner demons remaining shackled and caged.

'*Can* we help him?' asked the TR7 driver. Aaron looked up at himself. A malevolent grin was spreading across the younger face. His double came closer, an air of menace about him.

The husband at number 3 stepped out onto his path. 'Are you okay?'

'*Are* we okay?' asked... himself? He wasn't sure if words were spoken or whether this response was purely in his head. The advancing figure seemed real though, and now the unsettling grin was distorting, widening, baring teeth befitting something that belonged in Hell.

It felt appropriate.

The man from the house stepped onto the drive. 'You probably shouldn't be here.'

His now evil-looking self – as was the verbal pattern – echoed the uttered sentiment. Its eyes suddenly smashed in like broken headlights and exhaust fumes billowed out from every hole in its face. Behind, dirty water poured out of the TR7, spreading across the road with all the menace of lava, speedy, slick fingers reaching for him.

Aaron screamed, turned and ran.

He ran away from the Land Rover and TR7, away from the water, his monstrous self and the approaching widower, away from the housing estate and into the main road.

The police car was doing 40mph, lights flashing but no siren, the constable driving not yet being aware if the traffic collision he'd been called to warranted it. He didn't see the man run into the road until it was too late. The front of the car struck him at knee height and carried on, sending the man onto the bonnet and firmly into the windshield – just long enough to spread spider-web cracks all across it – then over the top of the car and into the night air.

The constable didn't see the victim land; he was too busy slamming on the brakes. The man from number 3 did though. He saw the dishevelled-looking fella who had been loitering in front of his drive, land hard on the surface of the road, head-first. He fancied he also heard the skull cave and the neck crack. He instinctively turned away, and found himself looking at the back of a Land Rover.

There was not a scratch on it.

The same couldn't be said for its owner.

8. THE HUNT

by EC Samuels

North West England.

Jenny began her nightly ritual as the clock inched towards midnight.

She was late; usually she did it at ten sharp, but she had fallen asleep on the couch and her mind was fuzzy, her movements slower than usual. She checked the living room window first, even though she knew she hadn't opened it since the weekend. Locked, just as expected. The kitchen was next. Jenny checked the windows, the door. She turned on the outside light, flooding her back garden with bright light. It looked exactly as it had looked the night before, and the night before that: knee-high grass, overgrown borders. Jenny checked the door again. *It's locked*, her subconscious said. *You've literally just checked it. The door won't have unlocked itself in ten seconds.*

I know. Jenny's fingers lingered on the handle. *But you can't be too careful, particularly now.* Her eyes went to her copy of the *Marston Bay Herald*, the local newspaper. The front page was dominated by a story about Maddie Burgess. Jenny and Maddie had never met, although Jenny was sure that she remembered the name from school. Maddie was older than Jenny by one year and lived alone in a small terraced house, three streets from Jenny's place. *Had lived*, Jenny corrected herself. Now Maddie lay in Marston Bay's morgue with three other women, all of them cold and dead, the stab wounds that had killed them stitched together by hundreds of tiny stitches. And who was to blame? The police had no idea, but four women had been murdered in Marston Bay in less than twelve months, and the others lived in fear.

Jenny tried the handle again, then headed towards the hallway, performing the same ritual with the front door. Locked, just as it had been when she checked it after her shower. She went upstairs, her slippers quiet against the carpet. Her legs felt heavy, every step an effort. Only two more sleeps until the weekend. She made a pact with herself that this weekend, she was going to have a bit of downtime. Maybe go to the gym, go for a walk, check out that new café that had opened next to the butcher's... The grass could wait another week; it wasn't like there was anyone nagging her to cut it.

The spare bedroom window was open. It was tiny, and the fresh air stopped the room from smelling too musty, but Jenny closed it anyway. *You can always open it again tomorrow.* Satisfied that the house was secure, Jenny went into the bathroom and readied herself for bed. By the time she went into her bedroom, her eyes were drooping closed and she couldn't stop yawning.

The last part of her ritual was to look out of her bedroom window. The world beyond was utterly still, each window dark, the residents asleep until tomorrow morning. *Soon I'll be one of them*, Jenny thought. Still, her eyes scanned the road, searching for anything that might be amiss. The full moon was out, showing her cars, bikes, more than one cat, but her road looked completely normal. Finally satisfied, Jenny got into bed, turned out the light, and closed her eyes.

*

In a mundane black car parked at the end of Jenny's street, Audrey shifted in the driver's seat and for what felt like the hundredth time that night, scratched the back of her neck. The first night of the full moon always did this to her. The darkness offered by the trees hid her from the worst of the glow, but a sliver of moonlight bounced off the steering wheel, and Audrey's fingers crept towards it. *Just one little taste, that's all I want ...*

The skin on Audrey's hand rippled, tearing and re-healing to accommodate her breaking and expanding bones, the nails that shot out of cuticles, becoming long and curved, thicker and sharper than any human's, digging into the steering wheel with leather-shredding force... The transformation rippled up Audrey's arm, reaching for her spine, her brain... If she gave into it then her night – not to mention the life of the girl living at number twenty-five – was over before it had begun.

Grinding her teeth, Audrey gripped the small pouch of wolfsbane inside her pocket, summoned every ounce of self-control that she possessed and yanked her hand back into the darkness of the car. The transformation stopped, but it took almost a minute for her hand to resume its human shape and even then, her middle finger refused to cooperate. Audrey massaged the finger, trying to coax the claw back into a nail. *Don't worry. We'll have our time soon enough.*

She returned her attention to number twenty-five Well Lane. The girl was getting ready for bed; Audrey tracked her movements through her house by the lights going on and off. She checked her watch. The autopsy reports said that each girl had been killed between midnight and 2 a.m. It was a little after midnight now, meaning that this guy's night was just beginning. Audrey closed her eyes and remembered the photographs, her skin tightening in a way that had nothing to do with the full moon. *He had his fun with you*, Audrey thought grimly. *Well tonight, someone's going to have a bit of fun with you, you bastard.*

Wilbur had given her the police files. Audrey had not asked how he got them but that was her brother for you: friends in lots of places, fingers in lots of pies – sometimes all the way to the shoulder. The files appeared on her coffee table a few days after the fourth girl was murdered. Audrey had picked them up, and that had been that.

His name was Kevin Bridle, or at least, that was the name he gave the police. He'd been flagged as a person of interest, but so far, no evidence had been found linking him to any of the four girls that had been murdered inside their homes on various streets within two square miles of each other. Well Lane was almost exactly equidistant between girls three and four, placing it squarely within the catchment area. Each girl lived alone, and was attacked in her home by a man who broke in via the back door. By the time the girls realised what was happening, it was too late.

Audrey had followed Bridle for weeks, learning his habits, his routines. Two weeks after the fourth girl was found, Kevin Bridle's habits and routines changed. It hadn't taken long for Audrey to realise that the girl living at number twenty-five – whoever she was – was the reason. A part of Audrey wanted to warn her, to tell the girl to move house, move town, go and live with her parents, but that wasn't how it worked. It wasn't just about getting justice when the police couldn't - wouldn't – it was about the ritual of *the hunt*. About the hunter becoming the hunted. About the scent of fear, the way it sweetened the blood, especially when the night was so very dark and the moon was so full and so very bright-

That ripple again, stronger this time, instincts passed down through generations tearing along Audrey's spine once more. Audrey put her fist in her mouth and bit down, stopping only when she tasted blood. *Soon, I promise.*

Across the street, Kevin Bridle crept between wheelie bins, pressing himself flat against the wall of number twenty-nine. Dressed all in black, he was easy to miss in the dark, especially if you were tired and all you wanted was your bed. Audrey was neither of those things. She waited until he reached the path that ran along the bottom of the gardens before getting out of the car, pausing only to remove her leather jacket. It was her favourite, and she'd lost too many clothes during the hunt as it was. Then she crossed the road in long, silent strides, following Bridle's smell: sweat, stale deodorant and beneath it all, a heady musk.

She turned onto the road just as Bridle climbed over the fence at number twenty-five. His shadowy form dropped quietly into the garden beyond. Audrey's heart began to pound.

*

Jenny woke to the sound of breaking glass.

Still cocooned in sleep, her first thought was that she was dreaming. She mumbled and turned over, burrowing deeper into her duvet. Her mind drifted aimlessly in that fuzzy space between asleep and awake, sleep slowly pulling her under...

Glass broke again, louder this time. Closer. Inside the house. Jenny's eyes flew open. *I'm not dreaming.*

She lay in bed, eyes wide, breathing heavily. Over her racing heart, she tried to focus. *Call the police.* She reached for her phone, usually on the bedside table but not tonight. *Where did it go?* After five agonisingly slow seconds, her hand finally settled on the smooth, cold surface of the phone screen, the soft, rubber case. Fingers tightened, trying to find the edges, something to grip-

She knocked the phone into the dark crevice between the bed and the bedside table.

"Shit." Jenny's whisper sounded terribly loud.

She groped for the phone, her eyes on the closed bedroom door, ears straining for any sound. Was that creak just the house, or a boot on the stairs? Images came to her then, things she'd seen in the news, pictures of happy, smiling girls butchered by an unknown man, houses within walking distance of this bedroom guarded by police, roped off by crime scene tape. Another creak, louder this time. Then a purposeful, deliberate silence. *There's someone in the house.* The thought made her whimper. She groped harder for the phone. *It's him, I know it. He's going to do to me what he did to those other girls-*

You have to fight. That thought pressed through her tears, her panic. *Fight, or you will end up like those girls.* Her whole body trembled. She bit her lip, tried to force it away, then took a deep breath and got out of bed. The carpet was cold beneath her bare feet, goosebumps prickling her arms. *Barricade the room. Find a weapon. Fight!* She ran to the bedside table and pushed it against the door. The ottoman at the end of the bed was next. Both of them felt significantly lighter than when she had lugged them upstairs and struggled to get them into place. They wouldn't stop whoever was in the house, but they might buy her a few seconds.

Beyond the door, the stairs creaked once more, then the familiar swish of shoes on carpet. Jenny froze. *He's here.* Hot piss streaked down her leg. *I don't want to die.* Her whimpering was almost impossible to stop now. *Please, God, I don't want to die.* She reached for the bedside lamp, hands suddenly slick with sweat against the cool ceramic. The footsteps got closer to the bedroom. Breathing so hard that she was almost hyperventilating, Jenny pressed herself against the wall, next to the door, and gripped the lamp. *Please don't let me die, please, please-*

To her left, the door handle was pushed down from the other side. *Oh God, this is really happening.* Only then, watching her bedroom door be opened by someone who wasn't supposed to be there, did the reality of the situation truly sink in.

The door swung towards Jenny, momentarily concealing her. A man came into her bedroom. Dressed all in black and wearing a balaclava, he seemed to fill the room, making her feel, in her piss-stained pyjamas, no bigger than a child. Less than two steps separated them; if Jenny was going to act, it had to be now.

Pushing the door with her left hand, Jenny stepped forwards and with an almighty scream, brought the lamp down as hard as she could. It landed somewhere on the man's back and immediately smashed. Ceramic shards dug into Jenny's feet but she ignored them, already out the door, racing as fast as she could towards the stairs. Her feet had barely graced two stairs when she heard a grunt behind her, then heavy, powerful footfalls heading her way. *Don't stop*, that voice inside her head said, the same one that had commanded her to fight. *If you stop, you'll freeze and you'll be dead.*

She was at the bottom of the stairs now, the front door straight ahead. It was still intact; somewhere in the recesses of her mind, she knew that meant he had come in through the back door. She pivoted almost three-hundred and sixty degrees at the bottom of the stairs, a hairpin turn that almost took her legs from under her, barrelling down the narrow hallway, passing the stairs on her right just as he came down them. A leather-encased hand made a grab for her hair; she dodged it and carried on.

The door to the kitchen was open. Ahead, the glass from the back door glittered on the tiled floor like stars. The door was open, less than twelve paces between her and the safety of the garden, the witnesses of the surrounding houses. She sprinted through the kitchen, ignoring the shards of glass that dug into her feet. *Just keep going*, her brain screamed. *Cry later, when you're safe.*

Twelve paces became ten, then eight. The garden inched deliciously closer. *I might even make it out of here after all-*

A leather fist wrapped around her hair and pulled. Pain exploded at the back of Jenny's head, bright spots flashing in her eyes. She jerked backwards, screaming, hands clawing at her scalp, feeling hot wetness. The air became alive with the smell of blood. She landed hard on the kitchen tiles, pain lancing up her side. With slow, deliberate movements, the man started dragging her back towards the stairs.

"Help!" She shrieked, wide eyes on the back door, which was now getting steadily further away. "Please! Someone help me!"

A woman stepped out of the dark living room. "I wouldn't do that if I were you, Kevin."

The man – Kevin – stopped walking. Jenny's head jerked to the left, trying desperately to find the owner of the voice. *What the hell?* Her hands, which seconds ago had been desperately trying to break the hold her attacker had on her hair, slackened off.

"Who the fuck are you?" Kevin said.

"Someone who knows who you are and what you've done. What you're trying to do to this girl." The woman stepped closer. She was tall with broad shoulders and closely cropped blonde hair. "Let her go."

Kevin paused, breathing heavily; Jenny could feel the damp heat pulsing off his body. His hand still gripped her hair, but loosened, almost infinitesimally.

"There's no good ending here for you, Kevin." The woman stepped closer; only then did Jenny notice that she was barefoot, in nothing but a vest and jogging bottoms. "All I can promise is that if you let her go and come with me, I'll make it hurt slightly less than if you fight." Her amber eyes glinted. "But please, for the girls' sake ... *fight*."

Jenny's heart lurched into her mouth. Her breath hitched, so much that she was sure she had stopped breathing. *What's going on?*

Kevin's breath quickened. His hand slackened off again, the pressure in Jenny's scalp easing just enough for her to scrabble away, bumping into the woman's legs. She looked up at Kevin, whose eyes were now darting all over the hall, returning every few seconds to the woman, who watched him, arms folded, head cocked to one side.

Muttering something that sounded like, "Bollocks," Kevin sprinted for the back door.

The woman dropped to her knees, hands pushing against the floor. Clothes tore, revealing an expanse of skin that rippled under the moonlight. Bones broke and reformed. Straw-coloured fur pushed through skin, growing and thickening. Fingers and toes grew to three, four times their natural length, nails lengthening and curving, becoming… Jenny's eyes widened. *Are those claws?* She looked at the woman's face, but it was gone, replaced by an elongated snout and wide, and a snapping mouth with teeth as long as Jenny's fingers. Only those amber eyes remained, any hint of the woman that had, until seconds ago, stood in her house.

Screaming, Jenny scrambled backwards, heading for the stairs, but the wolf's attention was wholly fixed on Kevin, who had now cleared the house and was sprinting down the garden. Growling, the wolf sprang towards the retreating man, crossing the distance that separated them in seconds. She launched herself at Kevin, landing hard on his back, both of them tumbling to the floor. Kevin tried to get up, but the wolf lunged for his neck, burying her snout in his face. Kevin screamed, but they soon became wet gurgles that turned Jenny's throat. He thrashed and struggled, but his movements became increasingly weak, erratic. After one last gurgle, he lay still.

The wolf waited, as if checking that Kevin was really dead. Then she jumped off his warm corpse. In less time than it took to blink, the wolf was gone, replaced by the woman who had, only seconds ago, stood in Jenny's hallway. Grabbing Kevin by the collar, she dragged him, one-handed, and completely naked, back towards Jenny's house, pausing only to close the ruined back door behind her.

"I need some plastic sheets," she said, dumping Kevin's body on the kitchen floor. "Do you have any?"

Jenny stared at her, eyes wide as saucers. All the blood seemed to be rushing out of her head and towards her stomach, which churned uncontrollably. Her gaze ricocheted between Kevin and the woman. The woman wiped her mouth, leaving a long, bloody trail across her face. Her bare breasts and stomach were speckled with blood. She snapped her fingers in Jenny's face.

"I need you to listen." Another snap. "Hey! Don't zone out, this is important. I need to get this piece of shit out of your house. Plastic sheets – where are they?"

Jenny heaved and covered her mouth, but it was no use. She heaved again, and vomit surged up her throat. Gagging, she leaned over and threw up. Most of it splashed up the stairs but a sizeable portion sprayed up the woman's bare legs.

"Great." The woman sighed. "Puke. My favourite."

*

Audrey dumped Kevin's body in the boot of her car. She'd pulled it round to Jenny's house, and the five seconds it took to walk from the girl's front door to her car felt like some of the longest of her life. The girl in question lingered in the doorway, chewing her nail, eyes torn between the man who had almost murdered her in her home and the neighbour's dark windows. Her eyes bore a vacant, half-crazed expression; Audrey wasn't sure if she was going to collapse or scream when she finally drove away.

"You need to get the back door sorted." Audrey reached into her glovebox and rooted around for her phone. "My uncle's a glazier; if you call him now and tell him I sent you, he'll come here and fix it before dawn." She scribbled the number down on the back of a nearby envelope and wrote 'Simon' next to it. "No charge."

Jenny's eyes remained fixed on the boot. "Wh-what are you going to do with him?"

"That's between me and him." Jenny had given Audrey some old jogging bottoms and a t-shirt that were several sizes too big; she felt strangely naked in them. Gripping Jenny's arm, she dug her fingers into the other girl's biceps until Jenny looked at her. "You can't call the cops about this."

"I-"

"I mean it, Jenny." Audrey's voice was like steel. "Trust me, the cops will be glad someone put a stop to him, but you can't call them. They can't be trusted, and cops mean questions, and me and my family hate questions." She paused. "Say it, Jenny." She dug harder, until Jenny cried out. "Say it."

"Ow! Alright, no cops!"

Audrey sighed. *I hate this part. It's like after a one-night stand where all you want to do is leave but you've both got to make polite chit-chat before you run out the door.*

"Alright." She raised her eyebrows and plastered a smile on her face. "I'll be off then. D'you need a hand cleaning up?"

Jenny stood in the kitchen doorway, her eyes on the long, bloodied smear leading from the garden to the kitchen, the hundreds of glass shards twinkling against the moonlight.

"I'll be fine," she mumbled.

Audrey nodded. "Bleach helps. And don't forget to call Simon."

She walked out of the house and closed the front door behind her. Seconds later, the key turned in the lock. Audrey smiled. *Smart girl.*

She got in her car, which was starting to smell pungent and metallic. She examined her nails under the moonlight, waiting for the ripple that always came with a full moon, but the world was quiet now. Sated. Kevin's blood gathered under her cuticles. She'd have a hell of a time getting that out.

The dashboard clock read a little after two am. She wondered if her cousin Noah was awake. *Only one way to find out.* Putting the car into gear, Audrey pulled away from the kerb.

*

Noah was not awake, and not happy about being woken up. After five minutes of consistent knocking and ten missed calls from Audrey, he opened the door in an old dressing gown and worn slippers.

"What do you want?" He whispered, squinting under the orange streetlight. "I swear, Audrey, if you wake up the baby, Caroline will take my head off my shoulders and mount it on the wall above the fireplace."

"Got something for you." Audrey gestured to her car, which she had parked outside her cousin's flat.

"Can't it wait until tomorrow?"

"No."

Sighing deeply, Noah hung his head, hands on his hips. Muttering under his breath, he threw up his hands. "Alright. Show me."

Noah followed Audrey to her car, waiting while she opened the boot. When Bridle's foot flopped out, he sprang back, clutching his chest.

"You want to tell me what that is?"

Audrey gave him a 'come on' look. "Someone who deserved it."

"According to you, they always do."

"This one really did."

Noah blew out a long breath. "Why can't you - any of you – just leave the catching of criminals to the *actual* police?"

"Because they won't and you know it."

Noah sighed, his eyes on the foot. "Hasn't it ever occurred to you that when you and your fucking family go off on this vigilante shit, you might snack on the wrong people?"

"No. And they're your family just as much as mine." Audrey eyed her cousin. "Can you help me?"

Noah's shoulders slumped, his eyes moving towards the large window emblazoned with, 'Thompson and Sons. Family butcher proudly serving Marston Bay since 1850!' He shook his head.

"Arthur would be turning in his grave if he knew. Chopping people up and serving them up alongside chicken thighs and sausages." He wiped a hand over his face. "Jesus, Audrey."

"Arthur would be pleased you're doing your civic duty." Audrey grabbed Kevin Brindle's right foot. "Think of it that way."

"Not by turning them into cannibals!"

"So save him for the out-of-towners. Or for the dogs."

"Save it for the dogs?" Noah spluttered. "You think I'd feed this piece of shit to my dog?"

Audrey grinned. "That's the spirit. Now come on, sun's coming up. Start of a new day."

9. CYTHRAUL

by Lee Allen

Anglesey, Wales.

Act I

I taste salt. Struggling for breath. I feel my skin tear. Rock rough under my grasp.

I hear screams in the wind. Her screams; cries of fury, moans of pleasure, combined in a conflicting assault on my senses. Forever ensnared by this contradiction of emotions: she is desperate desire and revolting repulsion; I despise and adore her; she is anathema and elixir. In truth, she is addiction – the euphoric, ugly sting of the needle holds nothing to her.

I cry out to God to rescue me from her constricting embrace of my mind. Yet He does not answer. Has He forsaken me? For once ensnared by her, one basks in the arms of the Devil.

The wind buffets me, slinging pellets of ice in my face, driving me against rock. On I push. This must end. And end it will, in her death. Perhaps, even then, I shall never be free of her. Our fates are entwined now, since I first beheld those eyes. But I no longer fear my penance. I shall not fear my sacrifice.

Where did it all begin? It is branded on my mind, seared into scar tissue. Worst of all is that, still, I cannot feel anything but pleasure at the recollection; I desire more. The hardest cross to bear? This began by choice. My choice to dabble in sin.

I'd often suffered periods of loneliness. I'd courted several young ladies, yet none of those dalliances progressed as I wished them and I remained a bachelor. Worse still, my siblings and cousins had each married in turn, now all raising families. Real or imagined, I felt radiating disappointment from my family at each gathering. So it must have been with some desperation I began perusing horoscopes and small advertisements relegated to the back pages of the three-sheet supplement of my daily newspaper.

I was already scoffing at myself as I shook the paper straight to read the small print, a performance at not taking any of this seriously for no one but myself. Yet as soon as I read it, it gave me pause, as if it had been written for me. Under my sign: 'in Love, someone is coming into your life who will feel like your missing piece. Very quickly it will feel as if they have always been there – your twin flame'.

All very generic, I'm sure. Only, at the bottom of the next page, in a small box amongst several, two words caught my eye. 'TWIN FLAME'. I glanced between the pages, pondering the other star signs, but found no mention of twin flames there. This could have simply been a clever marketing ploy. I returned to the small advert. 'TWIN FLAME: Agency assisting the lonely and broken-hearted to find their missing piece. Discretion guaranteed.' A "to be called for" PO address ended the advertisement.

For several days, I dismissed the notion of enquiring at this agency. It felt like desperation. Not only that: an admission of failure at the usual avenues of courtship that proved perfectly adequate for everyone else. Only the inept and undignified would resort to such measures. I certainly wasn't ready to confess to being amongst them.

But, after a rather excruciating firm dinner where it felt every other gentleman brought his bride or betrothed, I found myself drafting a letter to the agency, requesting details of their services and fees. Within only three days, I received a response detailing their courtship services, with an enclosed questionnaire, a request to include a photograph, and payee details for the cheque. Now I had come thus far, I returned the completed questionnaire, along with a photograph and a cheque for one month's services. Truthfully, I expected to hear no more once the cheque was cashed.

However, a week later I received a letter. Recognising the expensive stationery, I left the envelope unopened atop my folded newspaper. Breaking the seal may shatter the illusion the contents may be life-changing. I realised, then, I believed this may be my final chance at finding love.

Finally, curiosity got the better of me and I slid my letter-knife beneath the seam, tearing the paper. Enclosed was a brief letter explaining I'd been paired with an eligible young lady, detailing a time and venue for us to meet should we both be agreeable. Arrangements were to be made by the agency, associated costs already covered by their considerable fee.

Also enclosed was a photograph. The only information I was provided was a Christian name: Katharine. I sighed deeply as I gazed at Katharine's image, and laid it beside my letter. She was a vision of loveliness. Yet she had been deemed a suitable partner for me!

I made haste to draft my response, anxious not to lose this opportunity to another suitor or to have wasted time festering disinterest on her part. Having suffered both in the past, logic was not my advisor in such matters.

The date of our proposed meeting was two weeks hence; I led an anxious few days before I received a response. Our introduction meeting was finalised, along with confirmed details of passage.

The day arrived. I travelled to Bangor to board the ferry that would carry me across the Menai Strait to the Isle of Anglesey. It was a cool, overcast day, the wind whipping a chill around me as I stood on the deck as we made the crossing. I cast my gaze in search of Katharine amongst my fellow passengers, but could not spot her. Perhaps separate journeys had been arranged to avoid our meeting prior to the appointed time.

I traversed the island by carriage. The sky grew darker, the driver warning me a storm was coming. Remembering the treacherous current vaulting the ferry during the crossing, I didn't much look forward to the return journey late this evening.

Though it wasn't quite time for my meeting with Katharine, I bade the driver take me directly to our meeting place, always wishing to be punctual. As we climbed a narrow track, I watched the choppy ocean to my left.

The white tower of the lighthouse suddenly rose into view from behind the cliffs, stark against the slate grey of sky and ocean. It struck a lonely figure, atop its own separate isle. Narrow stone steps snaked down the cliff towards the roaring waves.

I realised the driver was speaking. We had arrived. I alighted from the carriage and looked at the small building, partially sequestered by rocks, steep stone steps etched up to its door. As the wind howled from below, carrying the cries of gulls and the deep-throated roar of Poseidon, I gazed around me at the desolate countryside. I shivered; little a result of the cold. The Smuggler's Inn, perched on the edge of the cliff, beyond it the towering lighthouse and the chilling depths of the Irish Sea, felt like a relic from a long-forgotten mariner's tale, one no one had desire to recall.

As I watched the carriage disappear around the turn in the cliff, I had the inexplicable urge to give chase and call it back. But the moment had passed, and I chided myself for even thinking it. It would be unseemly and ungentlemanly to abandon my appointment.

I averted my gaze from the lighthouse as I ascended the steps. If I could not see it, then it could not see me. Yet in the same way it remained in my peripheral, so I remained in its. I paused at the old oak door, then pushed against it.

Heat enveloped me immediately, my eyes drawn to the fire in the hearth. Uncarpeted, unfinished floorboards ran the length of the seated area, all wooden tables and wooden upholstered chairs. Heavy oak shutters stood open, letting in the dying sunlight, the chill of ocean breeze, the view of the lighthouse. I looked around me, perhaps too eagerly. There were only four occupants – two middle-aged gentlemen in the corner beneath one of the windows; an elderly lady close to the bar; the landlord behind it, perusing a newspaper. He glanced at me as I approached.

"You're expected." He motioned behind me with an indication of his head and returned to his newspaper.

I chose the table closest to the fire, heat permeating my damp clothes and chilled flesh. A waitress appeared beside me, depositing a carafe of wine, asking if I wished for a whisky or brandy while I waited. I declined, instead gingerly sipping the glass of red she'd poured. I noticed a tremor in my hand, the smooth surface of the wine tilting as if that of the roaring sea beyond the window. I scolded myself, such anxiety not befitting a man.

I glanced at my watch. Not yet the appointed time. I sipped the wine, listening to the rain as it began its patter, a steady build to a downpour. The sea raged.

I resisted the urge to check my watch a fourth time, conscious of being observed. I gazed into the flickering flames, my mind drifting.

I became aware of a presence beside me. I turned. She was there, the light of the flames dancing in the dark folds of her dress. I was unable to stifle the gasp, noticing incongruously she had not a drop of rainwater on her, wondering if she had come through the door marked 'ROOMS' beyond the bar.

She was more lovely than her photograph. An elegance to her poise no picture could capture, the reality of her features too vivid for any image; the gentle point of her nose and high cheekbones, the slope of her jaw. Her lips full and blossom pink, a hint of colour in her dark hair that glowed like burgundy dusk in the fireglow. Most startling were her eyes, glittering like sapphires, at once reading me and entrancing me. In the dancing light, she looked the angel.

I hastily (and clumsily) got to my feet.

"Katharine?" It was the first time I'd heard her name on my lips. It tasted sweet. She smiled, a shy smile, her eyes meeting mine, then averting quickly. It lit up her whole face, making her eyes shine. I felt something in my chest I'd never truly felt – a fluttering warmth.

I rounded the table to pull out her chair, debating ludicrously if I should shake her hand. She decided the greeting for me, telling me it was a pleasure to meet me and depositing a light kiss on my cheek before she sat. As I pushed her chair in for her, I felt the flush in my cheeks.

Taking my seat opposite, I was barely aware of the waitress bringing menus and pouring another glass of wine.

My lasting memory of that first meeting isn't so much the words we spoke, but how I felt. She was like the moon breaking through clouds, a rainbow on a dismal day. I'd never believed in love at first sight – entirely illogical and fantastical – but beside a crackling fire, to the increasing ferocity of rain, wind and sea, I found my faith. The talk of our journeys, work and family lives was immaterial compared to the ease we so rapidly slipped into, how we talked of plans and hopes for the future that so naturally may include the other, how my heart was bursting and featherlight every moment I gazed at her. I remember the meal tasting delicious, but there was no greater delight than Katharine's company.

As we enjoyed a sweet dessert, I felt the sting of ice clawing at my back, the fire guttering. The headache I'd been ignoring for some time knitted itself into my skull and stretched down my neck. A howl erupted through the inn.

The outer door slammed behind me; I realised it must have blown open in the wind.

"No one will be leaving here in this storm," the landlord declared. Anxiety stiffened my posture, sending a rivulet of pain up my neck and into my head.

"Edward?" Katharine placed her hand over my own, her touch the only warmth and comfort at that moment.

"The Cythraul is in the wind tonight!" The elderly lady bayed from the bar. "She sits upon the cliff calling to the lost!"

Katharine's alarm appeared to deepen by the moment. I tried to shake off my pain to fashion a look of reassurance on my face.

"Rooms are of course available," the landlord announced, ignoring the lady's doomsaying.

"Are you okay, Edward?" Katharine asked.

I nodded. "Just a headache. Probably the storm."

"You should rest. We're staying anyway." She smiled. "I'm not going anywhere. I'll see you at breakfast."

After making the necessary arrangements, I was shown to my room and brought a bowl of hot water, soap, and fresh towels. I closed my eyes against the pain, massaging my neck. I wondered if this was an omen. Yet I felt nothing but a warm glow after my evening with Katharine.

I washed before the water went cold, listening to the wind and rain, the crash of the waves far below. Through thunderous lashing, whistling wind found its way inside, carrying something mournful. I paused, listening. One could even interpret the melee as desperate calls.

Attempting to shake off my discomfort, I lay upon the bed and closed my sore eyes.

I must have slept soundly, for I recall being roused, slowly and gently, as someone cradled me. I startled, but was immediately soothed by whispers. Katharine's voice. My head rested between her neck and shoulder. In the dim light of a candle's flame, her hair took on a deep plum hue.

Her voice soothed my tired brain. Softly, she sang, notes drifting on the air to land on my skin, absorbed into my bloodstream. I closed my eyes. Her sound was divine beauty itself, so gentle. So sweet.

She sang to me of other lives, how our meeting was written in the stars. How our love burned eternal, beyond the agony of mere flesh and bone existence, the flames of our souls as fated to belong as Gemini's twins. Throughout human history, where one of us lived, the other crossed their path.

Her fingers stroked my face. My lips were moving, the confession of my heart taking me by surprise.

"Shhh."

I felt her lips against my own. I feared opening my eyes, feared her no more than a delusion.

"Drink."

I opened my eyes, watching her fingers move a phial, phosphorescent liquid frothing within.

"What is it?"

"It will help with the pain."

The glass touched my lips. I opened my mouth to receive it. The liquid was cold against the back of my throat, yet warmed me from inside out. The pain began to recede, exhaustion flooding me. Katharine held me. Through the fog of my mind, I realised she wore no more than her slip. Flesh burst from the cups at her chest, threatening to spill over. Shapely bare thighs, skin as smooth as the white silk of her meagre garment.

"Sleep now." Words slipping in a sigh into my ear.

Sleep I did. How long, I know not. But when I woke she was gone. I wondered if it had been real, if she was no more than a fever dream.

The storm had subsided to a dull roar, rain still falling steadily. Waves crashed far below, unrelenting. I drew open the shutters. I hadn't realised my room faced the lighthouse. I stared down the steep and jagged incline to the water, glimpsing the wood and rope of the bridge that joined the lighthouse's island with this one. It rocked as if many feet were crossing.

A light flashed, moving in a circular motion. Strange, I had thought the lighthouse no longer operational. Yet there it was again. The light flashed from atop the tower.

Dazzled, I turned away. The light caught a hairline crack in the wallpaper. I ran my fingers down the wall, following its descent from chest height to the ground. Stooping, I traced my fingers over the skirting board to find the crack continued through it. Rising, I found another crack continued horizontally to meet the shutters. Pushing one closed, I felt beside it, finding it hid a small nook in the crevice between wall and shutter. I pressed a finger into it, rummaging. I was rather taken by surprise to hear a small click, releasing a latch that pushed the wall out towards me. The hairline crack had been all the evidence of a hidden door.

I pulled it open, the hidden hinge inside making no sound. I grasped my candle from the bedside, holding it inside the opening, revealing a narrow space, approximately a foot in depth, a space between the walls.

I poked my head inside, brushing cobwebs from my hair. The space stretched the length of the wall. Perhaps this was how Katharine had gained entry to my room.

Emboldened by the notion of her using this passage to reach me, I crawled into the cramped space, turning sideways to fit, holding my candle aloft before me. I edged along the wall, shaking my head to loosen the sensation of cobwebs crawling over my face and head.

Reaching what must be the wall of the landing outside my room, the passage turned at a right angle to the right, continuing in the same narrow fashion. The storm sounded muted within the confines of the inn's inner structure. I turned another right angle, to the left, now surely having crossed into the second wing of rooms accessed via another staircase.

I stopped. A faint, breathy moan reached my ears.

Knowing I could trace my way in the dark, I extinguished the candle. Immediately, up ahead, I saw a glimmer of flickering light. I treaded carefully forward. A small crack at head height broke through into the room beyond. I hesitated, then bent closer to line my eye with the crack.

In semi-darkness, Katharine lay atop the bed in the centre of the room. The candle at her bedside danced light and shadow across her naked flesh. She was masturbating. In her soft moans I heard my name. I could no longer bear this strain. As I watched, her eyes closed, her legs trembling, spasms washing through her body, I pleasured myself too.

A mist of shadow blocked my view. I squinted; had the candle blown out?

An eye blinked open, staring directly into mine, fury and malice pouring from its gaze.

I recoiled, stumbling as my back hit batten and plasterboard. Katharine's light blocked, I could see nothing, but still felt that eye's scrutiny.

I was assaulted by dual urges to flee in terror and crash through the wall in a wild attempt to play the hero. Hindsight has told me neither response would have been the right course, but it was only this conflict at the time which gave me pause.

Katharine let out a cry. As the crack of light returned, I lined my eye with the slit in the timber and wallpaper. She lay, apparently in a state of comfort and peace, her eyes fluttering at the ceiling, smiling. I watched her lips mouth my name.

It was clear the room was otherwise empty. My heart was gripped by a new horror. Shame flooded my mind. That demonic presence meant Katharine no harm. Instead, it looked into my soul.

Wearily, I returned to my room. I slumped on the bed. She'd come to me and eased my pain. In return, I had betrayed her; watched her in private, intimate moments. I could take no pleasure in the knowledge it was me whom she thought of.

Beneath the snarl of thunder and rainfall, I heard footsteps outside my door, pacing all night. I heard scuttling between the walls, scratching against the other side of the secret door.

The night I fell. Intoxicated by flesh and pain. I had allowed sin into my heart; now the evils of the world dogged my every breath.

*

I hadn't anticipated sleep, yet awoke to calm having descended upon the inn. The fury had dissipated, birds calling in the morning peace. My thoughts drifted to Katharine, allowed a fleeting moment of a smile before dread took me in its grip. I didn't deserve her. Already I felt sure she was lost to me.

I considered skipping breakfast and making haste my departure. But that would be quite ungentlemanly. All thoughts of fleeing were cast aside when I opened my shutters and saw several people gathered on the cliff edge, gazing into the sea below. I left my room and joined them.

No one paid any attention to my approach. Another group was on the rocks below, surveying detritus floating in the surf – items of clothing, some travelling cases, fragments of a vessel. Splintered wood batted against rocks.

"No survivors."

The elderly woman from the bar stood to my left.

"Surely it's too early to say?"

"There never are." She turned to the lighthouse, stoic and watchful. "Woe betide any that cross her path on a night of fury."

I was confused. "The lighthouse?"

"The Cythraul. She has haunted this lighthouse for as long as it has stood. Perhaps longer. The fallen one. An angel cast out of

Heaven, or spirit of something beyond mortal man, who knows? But many have fallen prey to her. When the night is calm, you can hear the children of the shipwrecks running across the bridge. Perhaps they play, perhaps they are in search of safety.

"The boots of many a sailor march the inner sanctum of the lighthouse, in search of the hand that steered them into their doom. Those who drowned beneath decks clamber up the rocks, forever falling and climbing once more. Sometimes, when the moon is full, they can all be seen.

"But never her. Any who see her perish. She can be heard though. In the wind, she sings and she rages. Some tales tell of her twisted with hatred and thirsting for vengeance. Others as lonely. No reason she cannot be both."

"How could anyone be so cruel?"

Katharine's voice startled me. I turned to her behind us. A tear ran down her cheek.

"A damaged person causes damage to others," the lady replied, not taking her eyes from the lighthouse. "A wounded animal will fight another to the death. Why shouldn't that be evident in all God's creatures?"

Act II

Wind circles, grabbing, pulling, threatening to rip me from my feet. Rain and saltwater lash, slicing my skin, sending pellets of ice deep into my flesh. I can barely see, barely breathe. So cold. So lost.

Light flashes high above. Blinking. Beckoning. Sinking back into dark. The lighthouse, my destiny. Calling like a siren's song. I hear it now. Yet it has lost all its music. It is the screech of a banshee.

I could have avoided my fate. The night I saw a demonic eye open on my soul was a warning. There was still time to turn away.

I had sought to leave my visit to Anglesey in the past. Far easier to simply return to the humdrum of routine, the machinations of life; pretend my heart had not been touched. Far easier to be a coward and succumb to doubts and fears. While I cannot deny I was plagued with thoughts of Katharine daily, a lack of action on my part would still result in the undesired, yet safer, outcome.

Katharine, however, was plainly not content to await the letter that would never come. She wrote to me, expressing joy at our meeting, reminiscing over our dinner conversation about literature, lamenting on the horror of the shipwreck. My heart gave such a leap when I tore open the envelope, I took up my pen to respond immediately. So began our frequent correspondence.

If how I felt on the night we met was the love of which the poets speak, then the ensuing months showed the love the philosophers speak of – the meeting of hearts and minds, in intellect and understanding. My feelings grew deeper with each of her words.

Inevitably, our musings turned to how we should meet again, fantasies of walks on golden sands and along glittering canals succeeded by serious consideration of a rendezvous. Truly there was only one place to play host to our first reunion – The Smuggler's Inn.

The approaching days went in a blur, I in a bubble of contentment and eager anticipation. The day arrived to embark on my journey. Only the mildest anxiety – that frequent voice silenced by the depth of my feelings for Katharine. This time, the journey felt like stepping back in time, treading old ground to make my way back to her.

As I climbed the hill towards the inn, the lighthouse rising beyond the cliff edge, the fear she may not be here pushed its way through, having been trying to surface for the entire journey.

But she was there for me. As the path rounded the jutting rocks, I saw her at the foot of the steps. She saw me approach and her face broke into a smile. Forgetting decorum, we ran to each other and embraced. I hadn't realised until this moment quite how much I'd missed and longed for her.

So began a magical evening. Had anyone questioned me critically, I could have hardly explained it with any rational analysis. Through our letters, we had developed such a bond, as close and intimate as a couple who had known each other for years.

After dinner, we took a walk along the coastal path that ran the cliff edge. Beyond the tip of the lighthouse tower, the moon shone full and dazzling, a mass of black clouds gathering on the horizon.

Katharine shivered and I pulled her close.

"I'm so happy I met you," she murmured into my shoulder.

"And I you."

We watched the ocean reflecting the moon, the shadow of the lighthouse shimmering in the surface.

"I know you were there. The night we met."

I stilled. Unable to summon words.

"I'm glad you saw," she whispered, so faint I feared I imagined it on the wind. "I wanted you to see my pleasure from thoughts of you."

She stirred; I found myself gazing into her exquisite eyes.

"Did you…were you aware of anything else?"

She frowned, then laughed. Shook her head.

I blinked away memories of the demonic eye. The Cythraul's eye, as I had come to believe it.

"Did you feel you were being watched?"

"Only by you." Her eyes roamed my face, resting on my mouth, then met my eyes. "Will you kiss me?"

I obliged. Her mouth soft and delicate. The entire world ceased; the cold and wind and drizzle that had begun to fall receding. Time paused at her touch.

I felt her smile; pulled back and looked into her eyes.

"It's getting late." That musical lilt in her tone dizzying to my senses. We turned towards the inn. I failed to suppress a shudder as the lighthouse thudded back into my vision. All along the path, I felt its scrutiny. Once again, the eye of the Cythraul judged me.

For the sake of Katharine's reputation and polite decorum, we bid each other a chaste goodnight in the bar, taking our separate staircases away from each other.

No sooner had I closed the door to my room when Katharine was entering via the hidden door. Our mouths found each other, awakening deep, sensual longing.

Eager fingers fumbled with clothes, unbuttoning and unfastening, unravelling each other's garments. My fingers wrapped around her neck as my lips traced her jawline. She ran her hands inside my undershirt, tracing my collarbones, fingernails scraping down my chest. We discarded our clothes to the floor, dropping to the bed behind us. We may have lain there for hours simply kissing and caressing every inch of skin, for I had no concept of time outside of us holding each other.

"Can I tell you something?" She ran a hand through my hair.

"Anything." I cupped her face with my hands, softly kissing those lips.

"We were meant to find each other." She stroked my face. "No matter if it all crumbles, our love is real." She had tears in her eyes.

"I'm not going anywhere," I reassured her, kissing her mouth. "I'll never leave you."

"Promise?"

"I promise." I whispered these words into her mouth.

We made love. Afterwards, I realised her cheeks were wet with tears. Holding tight, I told her I loved her. But I was afraid. Such fear that I found my own face was wet. Though we were both silent, our crying did not cease until we slept.

When I awoke, she was gone.

I lay paralysed. If I were to move, then it became real. I feared her lost to me.

I shot upright as the storm erupted. Somewhere close, a shutter or door was caught in the fury, clattering open and closed against stone.

I knew then. Felt it deep in my bones as certainty. The Cythraul had taken her.

Frantically, I dressed, attempting to form a plan. Failing. I heard something more: beneath the storm, or part of it. At first, it sounded like screaming. The screams of many, in harmony. But as I listened, it became singing. Mournful, maybe wordless, but singing nonetheless. The song – the scream – of the Cythraul.

I flung open the shutters, searching the ocean and cliff. The lighthouse stretched into the sky. Light flashed from the tower. I looked up. Both relief and terror gripped me in unison. Katharine hung over the rail at the top, a nightdress clinging to her skin, hair plastered to her face.

As if sensing me, she turned her gaze in my direction. Even at this distance, I met her eyes. No breath entered my lungs, my heart felt it had stopped. I could have screamed and cried as if my soul wrenched from my body; instead, I remained paralysed.

They were not Katharine's eyes. Instead, I met the gaze that had looked deep into my soul.

The eyes of the Cythraul.

Act III

My balance unsteady; ground shifting beneath my feet.

Rain lashes. Waves roar below, thunder overhead. My feet slip, rope burns my hands. The light far above no longer shines, trickery for any approaching seafarers. As I was tricked.

I almost slip from the bridge again. Hands grip my arms, my legs, support my back. The children of the bridge are with me. Grouping around, guiding me across to steps ascending the rockface.

I stagger forward, climbing stone on hands and knees. More lost souls climb beside me, making the ascent they attempted so long ago from the ocean below to guide my way.

I can barely open my eyes, moving by touch alone. As I crest the final step, I collapse, heaving, desperate to catch my breath. Turning on my back, staring into the rain, the tower disappearing into black. She is up there.

My initial horror is diminishing. I should hate her, but cannot. Though I cannot equate this monster, perpetrator of such cruelty and torment, to the woman I love, I know them to be one and the same. My eyes did not lie to me, as much as I still reject the truth.

I am a fool, an addict. My rage has already burnt out; now I feel only exhaustion. Desperation. For she is still my Katharine. She must be.

I crawl to the lighthouse door. Unlocked. She expects me. I drag myself to my feet. Above, footsteps, circling the spiral staircase that climbs the interior of the tower. I follow in the dark. Behind, I hear another set of footsteps. The sailors are with me. Chaperoning me on the final part of my journey.

On and on, I circle and climb, always accompanied by footsteps, never seeing a flicker of another soul in the darkness. Finally, I reach an upper platform, an open door to the raging elements. Solitude now. They all did their part to guide me, but I must face her alone.

I step outside, the gale tearing at me, almost hurling me from the narrow balcony that circles the tip of the lighthouse. I grasp the slippery railing, peering through rain. The ocean roils far below, an angry nest of serpents.

I pull myself around. Ahead, a white shape. The creature, its back to me. Its head turns; I shudder at those eyes, raking through me in search of my soul.

But then those eyes are Katharine's. So sad. The thin nightdress clings to her body beneath, every inch of her perfection revealed to me.

"Why?" I implore.

"I've been in agony so long. Pain is all I know." She turns from me, as if she need hide tears in this storm. "I'm sure that isn't the answer you're looking for."

"What about us? Was I just another victim of your agony?"

"No." She steps towards me. "Every word I ever said to you was true. You were my salvation. You made me feel human. I only ever felt beautiful and special with you. I never want to lose that."

I close the gap between us, gazing into her lovely eyes, her perfect face.

"You never will." I kiss her lips, wet from the rain. "I'll never let you go." I wrap my arms around her. She is still my Katharine. She will always be my Katharine.

I kiss her forehead. She nestles against me. How I love her. Such a perfect, beautiful soul, mangled by pain.

I tip forward towards the railing. We slip over the side and plummet, the wind battering us, roaring. We cling to each other. For a moment, the fall feels like freedom. Falling together into eternity. Conjoined souls in flight.

We hit a wall of water, waves reaching to swallow us whole. Wrenching our arms and legs, our torsos, clamouring at our heads. Still, we hold on, pulled roughly down. We sink, still locked together.

Water fills my mouth and nose, my lungs screaming. I hold on.

Vision blurred, but we are too deep for sight to be any use. It burns, this ferocious need to breathe.

Sensation ceases. No more pain. Still, I hold on.

How I love her. My fallen one. My Cythraul.

*

Mme. Rougierre choked, heaving desperately, spluttering. She coughed saltwater over the papers on the table before her. Taking shuddering breaths, she turned in her chair away from prying eyes, as her two aides rushed to her.

The hall was silent. Never before had her audience seen her in such a frenzied grip. The same spirit coming through in all three acts, intent on telling his tale in the hoarse male voice that escaped her mouth and the spidery hand which she scrawled upon sheets that now lay scattered around her.

She looked to each of the circle, seeking the one whom this meant something to, that this man's spirit had been drawn to. Had his message been delivered?

The door at the rear of the room shut with a gentle click. A flash of plum hair passed the glazed window in the lit corridor beyond. *Mme*. Rougierre was hit with a sudden, sinking dread. Pain shot through her arthritic fingers. She struggled to unclench her fist. A piece of paper fell. Stooping, she smoothed it on her knee. On it, barely legible, she had scrawled: *A damaged soul cannot rest until consumed by its twin flame.*

Message delivered. A young woman headed into another stormy night on a quest. A hunt? For prey, or for love?

Either way, may God be with them. Evil may never truly die.

Though nor does love.

10. PERGYL

by C S Jones

Snowdonia, Wales.

How they'd reached the cabin was anyone's guess. The storm was tyrannical; biblical.

They had looked forward to taking in the majesty of the Welsh mountains while they traversed the winding roads, but visibility had been near-zero.

Now parked outside, David strained to gaze through the relentless downpour, barely making out the faint outline of the flimsy structure they would call home for the next five days. "On three, we'll make a run for it. Maggie, you look after Kira, I'll grab everything else. Dad, you've got the key, you run on ahead and get it open."

Without fuss, they darted from the car, a bolt of lightning illuminating their path. David's wife, Maggie, hunched over with baby Kira held to her chest, the raincoat wrapped around them instantly slick and heavy with rain.

David lagged behind, the rainfall quickly finding its way down his collar. Wincing at the icy trickles down his spine, he cursed under his breath and pushed on. From the boot, he carried two big cases while strapped to his back were a travel cot and backpack.

Henry, his father, was already at the door, clumsily thumbing through the slippery set of keys for the one that would grant them shelter.

In the distance, dozens of eyes watched on through the hazy dark.

They burst in, disturbing the peace and kicking up dust, announcing their arrival with booming footsteps and rumbling grumbles. Henry flicked a switch; the lights faltered, then settled to a dull hue that barely illuminated the dour room.

The grim scent of grime and earthy notes of disturbed mould laced the air, causing Maggie to wrinkle her nose. "I told you we should have turned back. Those road signs, I know they were in Welsh, but I'm telling you every one was a warning. I kept seeing the word *perygl* in a red triangle," she said and cast off her coat to bring her daughter back into the fold.

"Well, I'm sorry, Maggie, but I was a little more focused on the road. You know, so we didn't die?" said David and dropped the luggage in a violent heap, throwing up more dust.

Kira started coughing, causing David's expression to ease, "Hey, hey, I'm sorry." He said and stroked her cheek, then handed over her teddy. "Look, Mag, turning around on those roads would've been way too dangerous. Anyway, we're here now. We can actually have a holiday. Our first as a proper family." He spotted thick cobwebs covering every window, but decided not to draw attention to them. It wasn't worth setting Maggie off.

Fortunately, Maggie was too busy checking her phone when he funnelled her away, "Nothing's coming up for *perygl*. Or anything for that matter. The signal's been shocking since we passed the mines."

"Well, don't fret. We're here, safe and sound in Dad's nice, cosy cabin." David spotted a leak in the roof where murky water trickled down. "Alright, maybe it could do with a little TLC, but let's just throw the bags in the cupboard and deal with it in the morning. Once the cot is set up, we can all get some sleep."

Maggie forced a smile and put her phone away, "I can't argue with that, I'm exhausted. Pass me the backpack, all the bedtime stuff's in there. It's too late to be messing about with anything else."

Henry was already crouched, nosing through his case. He removed a number of jars and petri dishes, "Ah, good. They're not broken."

"Seriously, Dad. You can do all that in the morning. Besides, you said you were bringing us up here for a holiday. A new chapter and all that. Why'd you bring all your bug crap?"

Henry's eyes narrowed, "How many times—" he pinched the bridge of his nose. "Arachnids are not bugs, David."

David winked at Maggie, "Every time." He spotted a flash of concern cross her face, "Something wrong?"

"Wasn't your mother meant to be here already?"

David paused to consider this. "Hey, yeah, that's right. Dad, where's mum?"

Henry studied a notebook, "Oh, who knows with that woman. She's always come and gone as she pleased."

Maggie blinked, "Aren't you even bothered? What if she's outside in this? It's like a monsoon out there."

"She'll be fine, she's a strong swimmer."

Henry had always given Maggie the creeps, but this callousness was something else entirely. She was about to step towards him, but David squeezed her shoulder, shaking his head. They may not have spoken for a few years, but he knew better than to push the subject when his dad was in this mood. He grabbed the luggage bags and threw them in the under-stair cupboard. A mighty crash erupted, the bags smashing through the rotten floorboards, leaving them half-submerged. Beneath, David could swear he heard a noise. Something groaned beyond the stringent moan of the distressed wood. Tired and irritated, he ignored it and slammed the door. "Christ sake."

"What was that?" Maggie called over.

"Damn floor gave way. This place is falling apart. Seriously Dad, when were you two last here?"

Henry still thumbed his textbook, "Never have been. We only bought it last month. Once we were sure."

Ignoring Maggie's concern for his father's cryptic ramblings, David rolled his eyes and tickled his daughter's chin, "Great. Christ knows what we've let ourselves in for; this place is a shed. Still, beats a tent, I suppose. We'll sort the bags out in the morning, I'm not messing about with them now."

***

Through the thumping rain that crossed rather than crissed along the window pane, Maggie awoke in the early hours to a piercing squeal.

"Kira!" she cried and shot across the room, mother's instinct catapulting her to her daughter's cot.

Kira wailed in the darkness, the cries reaching banshee-level decibels. Bleary-eyed, David appeared over Maggie's shoulder, "What? What's going on?"

The night took shape to reveal Kira already in Maggie's arms, her tiny body writhing with a strength thought unnatural for a baby. "I... I don't-" Then a spider the size of her hand crawled from Kira's leg, onto her arm. Instinctively, Maggie squealed and shook it off, almost dropping her daughter. Then another appeared, its spindly legs dragging its fat body across her baby's face.

David gasped and swept it away. He turned on his phone light and froze. The room was covered in the creepy crawlies. The walls, ceiling, their bed. But most clung to the sides of the cot and to Kira's teddy bear; their sights firmly set on the little baby.

Maggie's blood ran cold. She couldn't deal with this. Still Kira squalled; an awful, rancid cocktail of pain and distress.

Together, the three bolted from the room, David slamming the door behind them.

"Keep them away from me, David. You know I can't cope with those things. Oh, Christ, her leg. Jesus, David, look at her leg." Kira's leg was bulbous, inflamed and angry. Around two tiny dots, the skin had turned an angry shade of purple. A spider had bitten her, that much was clear. "She needs a hospital. What if they're poisonous? Or she's allergic?"

"My dad's got the keys. I'll grab them and we'll get out of here. Sit tight, Mag. I'll be right back."

David burst into his father's room, surprised to see him up, hunched over his desk by candlelight. "Been bitten, has she? Don't worry, they're quite harmless. Though, I will admit it stings like a bitch," he said and held up a hand covered in purple welts. He didn't turn from his work. "The swelling will go down in no time; she's fussing over nothing."

"Christ, Dad. She's eight months old."

"Exactly. Why do you think they were attracted to her and not you?" He finally looked up, the candlelight casting dancing shadows across his craggy face, "The meat's far more tender."

"Are you mental? Seriously, you even listening to yourself? Next, you'll be telling us you only invited us up here as bait!"

His father didn't say a word.

David thought back to the sight of the spiders amassed around his daughter's cot and fought back the urge to swing for the man. Right now, he needed those keys. He scanned the desk, desperate to locate them. Beside his father's journal was a spider trapped in a jar. David couldn't believe how pronounced its fangs were. It shuffled, bristled its fat, furry body and launched itself at the glass. The glass shook, but it remained trapped. Beside it was a board with another spider pinned to it, vivisected. "Holy Hell, Dad. What have you been up to?" David spotted the keys and snatched them up.

His father grabbed his wrist, "You can't go out there. I was wrong. So wrong. If what I've found-"

"We're leaving, Dad. Stay here if you want, but your family are getting out of here." David pulled free and was about to make his way back to Maggie and Kira when he spotted his mother's luggage. "Wait, Mum's here?"

Puzzled, Henry followed his son's gaze to a suitcase poking from the wardrobe, "Oh, Christ. I hadn't even spotted... I hope to God she realised quicker than I did."

David didn't stop to listen. The bridges he'd hoped to mend with this holiday were well and truly burned now; his father's one-track mind had once again made his family an afterthought. He was done.

"David, please don't-"

David slammed the door behind him.

"Where's your dad?" asked a teary-eyed Maggie, nervously bouncing the hysterical Kira over her shoulder.

"Never mind him, it's my mum I want to know about. Her bag's in there. Dad thinks she's already left. The old bastard's gone off the deep end. I'll grab our bags, then we're gone."

"But what about him?"

"He can sort himself out."

Maggie looked on, eyes glazed and slack-jawed. She held Kira tight, her daughter's wails as thunderous as any storm. With that down her ear, she didn't hear the moans behind the cupboard door.

David pulled it open just as a flash of lightning hit to reveal the partially cocooned, sloughing body of his mother. Groaning, she lurched forward, having scrambled from the hole made by the luggage; a slimy slug-like trail oozed in her wake. Skin and flesh slid and dripped as the spider venom took hold, the skittering horrors having slowly feasted on her while the others slept. Spiders crawled from her hair, her body, even from the pustules that covered her face. Before David could react, she gasped and fell into him, her weight knocking them both down.

Maggie started toward him, but hesitated. She would tell herself she couldn't risk Kira, but knew the true reason was her crippling fear.

Lying on top, David's mother gurned and opened her mouth to speak, only for more spiders to emerge. They dripped out and dropped onto David's face. He tried to scream, barely recognising the woman who birthed him, but found himself being suffocated as they crawled into his open mouth, their little limbs clawing their way down his throat. More flooded his mouth, drowning his screams as more burst from his mother's body and from the rotted hole. Trapped beneath and at their non-existent mercy, David writhed as they engulfed him, skittering under his clothes, covering his entire body and entering every orifice.

He managed to turn to his wife, the terror in his eyes mirroring Maggie's, who could only watch on.

Desperate to get away and flee the horrific scene, she backed right into her father-in-law's room. On instinct, she kicked the door shut, her last glimpse of her husband being his screaming, misshapen face desperately pleading for help.

She turned to find Henry a gibbering mess on the floor, "We... We can't leave. This is their nest. We walked right into it. I was wrong, so wrong."

Through her daughter's cries, Maggie found herself bubbling with a rage she'd never experienced before, "You! You dragged us here!" With her free hand, she pummelled and dragged Henry across the room. "I wanted Butlins! Something relaxing! But, oh no! You had to drag us up the fucking back end of nowhere!"

Henry scurried back to the corner. Now huddled, he rocked back and forth, "Perygl. It's *danger.*"

"What?"

"Perygl. The warning signs you saw on the way here, it's Welsh for *danger*. Telling us to stay away. They came from the mines. They'd been closed for years, but no one knew why. Rumour was there was a huge accident; a lot of people went missing, but nothing was ever documented. Someone tried to reopen them last month. People died and they had to abandon it. A new species was down there, some said. We thought we could sneak in and take the credit. We didn't know..."

"Know what?"

A hulking figure shuffled past the window. Another lightning bolt illuminated its furry body, its fangs casting a drawn-out shadow on the floor around them. Something thudded on the roof and sent plaster cascading. The cabin groaned under its weight.

Under the door, smaller limbs scrambled and writhed, desperately trying to get in.

"They're spreading. And these ones inside, they're only the babies!" Henry was laughing maniacally by now, his mind having succumbed completely to the void, "This is their nest. They're just the babies!"

11. SOUNDS OF THE FOREST

by Brad Thomas

Kidderminster, England.

Dan had always thought of living off-grid. The thought of it excited him. He wasn't really a people person and loved his own company. He didn't have many friends and couldn't wait to get out in the wild. He woke up on this sunny Saturday morning, rubbed his eyes and sat up in his wooden framed double bed. *Well, it's time to get ready and go*, he thought while standing up and looking at himself in the mirror. He'd shaved his head the night before and had also shaved off a beard he'd been growing for months.

He had a shower, got dressed, and headed downstairs to grab his things; ready to go.

"Dad, I'm going now, okay?"

"Okay Daniel, make sure you stay safe. A little getaway will do you good."

"Dad, leave the small talk, okay? You wouldn't even have realised I was gone if I hadn't told you. At least I'll have my friends there with me," he lied to his dad as he closed the front door behind him. He knew himself that he was going alone. *Why did I even lie to my dad? He wouldn't even care if I went with friends or on my own anyway,* Dan thought to himself.

Dan had told his dad he was going camping for the weekend with his friends Andy and Kieran; his real plan was to check out what living in the wild would be like alone and if he liked it. Then, maybe, he could make it permanent to get away from reality. He wasn't completely lying to his old man because he actually *was* going camping.

He had grown up in Kidderminster in the West Midlands as an only child. His Dad, Stan, had raised him alone from the age of twelve. Dan's mother, Sharon, had passed away in a tragic hit-and-run six years ago. Dan and Stan weren't very close and always did their own things. Dan didn't mind, that's how he liked it.

Dan, now eighteen years old, walked down the long tarmacked drive at the front of their house. He was thinking to himself about how he would make it to the lake district for an adventure one day. He didn't drive but he had thought about hitchhiking there or even trying to get on a train without a ticket. He knew he had to lie to his dad, but there was no way Stan would allow him to go camping alone, especially as he still lived under his roof. Dad's house, Dad's rules.

Dan started walking down his childhood street, turning onto the main road. Wearing his brand new hiking boots, his blue rucksack on his back and a blue beanie hat covering his shaved head, he walked towards the signs for Wyre Forest. It wasn't far from his home and, if he decided to, he could maybe stay there the night.

It wouldn't take him long to reach Wyre Forest, he could set up a small camp and be settled before dark. *I should have eaten before I left*, Dan thought while taking a sip from his bottle of water. He wasn't a big eater, mainly living on Cup-a-Soups and bread, which he had packed in his rucksack for the journey.

As he walked along the country roads, it began to rain hard.

"Fucking hell, it wasn't meant to rain today," he said, fuming to himself. He turned to cross the main country road to the entrance of Wyre Forest. Without looking both ways, he stepped out and began to cross the road. As he was crossing, a white car came speeding around the corner. Dan had to jump out of the way of the car.

"You fucking arsehole, I'll get you," he shouted at whoever was driving the car.

The car didn't even slow down, never mind stop. Dan gave the driver of the car the middle finger. *That was close*, Dan thought, cold and shaking now. It had scared him, shocked him even. It always played on his mind how his mother had lost her life. He continued across the road and entered the forest.

I really need to find a place to set up camp soon, Dan thought while rubbing his hands together. Then he spotted an old tree that had fallen down, *This will do*. He began to take off his rucksack and place it next to the old fallen oak, as he got ready to set up his tent.

He knew he had to set his tent up quickly because it was getting dark, and he didn't fancy the idea of putting his tent up at night.

Right, let's do this...

He finished pitching the tent. Then, he lit a small fire, not too far away from the tent, but not too close either. *Now I can relax for a while*, he thought to himself smiling and looking at the campfire. He pulled a book from his rucksack, it was *Retown* by Boris Bacic.

Dan loved books by Boris Bacic, he was his favourite author. He had just grabbed his book light and had sat down when...

CRACK!

"Who the fuck is there?" Dan shouted, standing up from the campfire. He knew that sound was either a branch or a twig snapping. Something or someone was very close.

"Hello?" Dan called out, to no reply. *Maybe it was just an animal or something. There's no one out here*, he thought.

He sat down again and picked up the book. *Think I overreacted a little there*, he thought, giggling to himself.

CRACK! CRACK!

"RIGHT, WHO THE FUCK IS OUT THERE?" Dan shouted as loud as he could. He grabbed his torch from his rucksack and stood up. He was shaking now. The thought of the unknown scared him to death. *Maybe I should have invited my friends after all,* he thought. He took out his mobile phone from his rucksack. *Maybe I should call Dad?* He looked at his phone: *Oh crap, no signal.*

"Hello? Is anyone there?" he called out again into the forest. *Maybe it was someone camping too, maybe they were lost or, even worse, hurt.*

"Is anyone there? Does anyone need help? Dan called out to no reply.

CRACK!

"OH MY FUCKING GOD," Dan shouted, his voice echoing around the forest. *That crack was close.* To be honest, he loved camping, he loved horror, but the thought of them together, he was terrified. He began walking in the direction of where the cracking noise came from. The light from the campfire was becoming less visible the further he walked away.

What do I do? Shall I go back to my tent and just wait it out?

After walking for a while, the campfire was just a little speck of light in the distance behind him now, he shouted, "PLEASE, IF SOMEONE NEEDS HELP, MAKE A NOISE." No noise or response. *I best head back, I don't want to get lost in here*, he thought as he turned around to head towards his small camp.

"That's strange, the light from my campfire seemed smaller two minutes ago," he said to himself, looking towards his camp. He began walking back towards it. His walk turned into a jog, then into a sprint as he realised why his fire seemed brighter.

"NO! WHAT THE HELL? HOW?" His heart was racing now from the running, but also from fear as he kept his blue eyes fixed on his tent, which was now also on fire.

"OH MY GOD. OH MY GOD. WHO DID THIS? WHERE ARE YOU?" *Someone had to have done this, there's no way the tent caught ablaze from the campfire.*

Dan realised his rucksack was gone.

I need to get out of here, he thought. Maybe camping isn't for me after all. He picked up the only things that were left: his book and the flashlight that was already in his right hand.

He began walking in what he thought was the same direction that he arrived from earlier. *I'll be fine, it's someone just messing with me. Maybe it's Andy or Kieran, they knew I was coming out here*, he thought.

He continued walking.

After he had been walking for around half an hour, he thought, *I've definitely come the wrong way.* Then he saw something in the distance. As he got closer, he realised it was a small log cabin. It looked fairly new too. This was unusual because Wyre Forest was like a nature reserve and nobody stayed there; unless it was for the rangers who sometimes patrolled the forest. There were no lights on inside the cabin and it looked totally empty. Dan began walking around the front of the cabin. He was shivering from the coldness of the forest. As he turned to face the building, his heart sank, fear drained the colour from his face, and he began panicking. In front of it was a car, parked up behind a bush. Dan knew he had seen this car before.

"Oh God, that's the car from earlier," he whispered to himself. *Who was it? Why was it here? Are they messing with me?*

Dan knew he needed to find out who the driver was that had nearly run him over earlier, bringing memories of his mother's death flooding back into his mind. *I just need to get out of here, I don't think I want to find out who was driving this car.*

Dan turned to walk away. As he turned, he locked his eyes on a figure standing in front of him.

Whack!!

Dan was knocked out cold, whoever it was had hit him so hard that he just collapsed to the floor. Blood began dripping from his head as he just lay there.

Sometime later, Dan began to regain consciousness. His head was so sore, and he didn't know how long he'd been out cold. He looked around, *Where am I?* It was then he realised his hands and feet were tied together and he was lying in what seemed to be a deep hole in the ground.

"HEEEELLLP," he screamed.

"Well, well, well, look who's finally awake," said a very familiar voice that Dan recognised straight away.

Two figures wearing masks appeared at the top of the six-foot by six-foot hole.

"Hello Daniel, where was our invite for camping, bro?"

Dan knew who it was. The two figures then removed their masks.

"How are ya mate?" the other figure said.

"Andy? Kieran? What the fuck are you doing? I thought we were friends!"

"Are you serious Dan? You thought we were friends? Why the hell would we be friends with you?"

"I don't understand, why are you doing this?" Dan asked as he began crying.

"Why? WHY? You mean you don't know? Well let me fill you in then, MATE!" Andy said furiously.

Andy spat into the hole, it landed on Dan.

"Well, let's just say this is a little bit of payback. You see, your dad Stan, he ruined my life. Didn't you know about your dad and my mum's affair? My mum came clean and told my dad all about it, it drove him mad. He confronted your dad one day, and your dad attacked him. The affair broke my dad, he was never the same. So, he took things into his own hands. He knew your mum worked late Thursday nights and he wanted to ruin your dad's life, just like your dad had ruined his. My dad followed your mom in his car, then when he saw the opportunity, he floored the accelerator and began speeding towards her, sending her crashing over his bonnet and onto the floor. My dad even reversed back over her, just to make sure, mate."

Dan was absolutely sobbing now, fear flowing through his whole body.

"That's not true, it's not true."

"Yeah, yeah, it is, mate. It was my dad that ran your mum over, reversed over her and then drove off. It's why we tried to run you over earlier. Best thing is though, that isn't even the worst part. My dad killed himself the same night because of your dad sleeping with my mum. You know how I know all this? Me and Kieran here, found an old diary of my dad's, it's all in there."

"Stop this, please. I'm not my dad," Dan pleaded.

"You're right, mate. You aren't your dad. Your dad ruined mine and my family's lives. So, you know what? I'm going to ruin his. Come on Kie."

Dan's eyes opened wide and the fear in his face was like no other. Andy and Kieran began shovelling dirt into the hole where Dan laid.

"NOOOO, NOOOO, PLEASE, I BEG YOU."

"Sorry Dan, but it's our only way out of this now," replied Andy, laughing.

"Andy, you sure about this mate?" asked Kieran.

"Kie, are you with me or him?"

"I'm with you, mate."

"Well then Kie, keep fucking shovelling."

Dan's bone-chilling screams were so loud, but no one would hear them. He was being buried alive by two lads he saw as his best friends.

"Also, Dan, did you know my mum and your dad are still sleeping together? No? Thought not mate. Well, your dad, he's next!" Andy shouted as he finally covered Dan's body.

Andy and Kieran continued to fill the hole, flattening it as it got full, then covering it with leaves.

"Don't worry Kie, no one will ever find him."

The two of them walked away towards the car, got in and drove off.

"His dad is next. Let's go."

12. THE DARK HEART

by Jim Ody

Wiltshire, England.

His heart beat hard with expectation as his phone once again buzzed. He had known it would do, and yet he still felt the excitement.

Her thumbnail picture shot dopamine around his body the way it had done a million times before. The face he loved to see appearing, and the anticipation of words behind it for his eyes only, was sometimes too much.

This was the way it had been for a couple of weeks now. A chance interaction that had transported them to whatever it was they now found themselves in. A labelless relationship undefined by fear of others' perception. The world likes to judge, and label, and point fingers. Persecution was rife in history and in another time the situation could well have seen them in strife.

A gentle rap on his bedroom door had him panicked and dropping his phone onto his bed covers like some sex object he hoped would be hidden. His mother's smiling face looked at him like he was still a baby. In some ways he guessed he always would be to her.

"Hey Smoochums! You should be going to bed now," she said quite naturally, and walked over to him. She had been a stunning woman in her youth, and she was a beautiful woman now. She sat down on the bed and brushed the hair from his face in the same way she had always done. He usually had time for his mother, but at that moment he was distracted. His desires had him overwhelmingly torn between the two important women in his life.

"In a minute," he responded, his stomach doing summersaults as he thought about the unread message waiting for him; and her, clutching her device, waiting for his response. Perhaps biting her lip in wonder. And his mother, so full of unconditional love for her son.

"You need your beauty sleep for school," she said, kissing him on his forehead. The floral fragrance of her lotion breezed over him with a comforting familiarity. It was an invisible blanket that almost hugged him. It stirred up feelings of wanting to be held all night by her again.

"I know," he agreed, the words toppling out without conviction as he tried his best to smother the frustration he was beginning to feel. A new, unhealthy obsession gripped his throat.

She looked at him, sensing something was amiss. Her eyes stared into his, back and forth, searching for the lies she could smell permeating from his pores. "Is everything okay, Pumpkin?

Only… you seem a little on edge?" There was an edge to her voice. Her touch was a little more forceful.

He was on edge. In fact, he was wobbling and trying hard to control his feelings. He wanted to punch her in the face if she didn't leave him be. He knew that was bad, and he didn't mean it… but still. He saw her face, and then his phone. It was all he could do not to be drawn towards it. If he merely glanced in its vicinity, she would know. She would understand that a woman was to blame for his insubordination, and he knew his mother had a temper. She was a passionate woman. He had heard it through paper-thin walls, and he had seen the black eyes on retreating men running scared from the house still clutching their clothes.

"Just cramps," he winced, unleashing an Oscar-winning performance that would fool her.

She nodded, the answer satisfying her. "Then you definitely need to go night-nights."

For the first time in his life, her babyish talk embarrassed him slightly. A hot woman was waiting on his words, and his mother was talking to him like he was a toddler. But he loved his mother in a way others could never understand, and the whole situation filled him with deep sorrow. And this was why he was going to do what he knew was his only option left.

She bent in and kissed his forehead, her soft lips lingering. Then she slowly stood up, blew him another kiss, and sighed.

"Night, Mum," he said, as she waved with wiggling fingers and retreated out of his room.

The door was barely pulled shut before he had swiped up his phone and was using his finger to verify it was him.

He didn't have time to linger on her picture, instead tapping the bold message until the conversation filled the screen.

Let's meet up.

He looked at the words and felt the excitement build. The weight of the words couldn't be explained. That was exactly what he wanted. He swallowed, and tapped in the space ready to respond but his mind went blank. He didn't want to come across as too keen, but conversely, he didn't want to be dismissive. Eventually, he replied simply with:

Yes. Let's do it.

He added a heart, then deleted it. He pressed SEND.

She saw it straight away. He wondered whether he should've made an excuse about the delay, but in the time he took to forge a lie, the moment had passed.

The dancing dots told him she was responding, and a million things flashed through his mind. Then the response confirmed it all.

Give me your address. I'll come over at 12 pm.

She had switched up from her sweetness to demanding and he quite liked it. A taste of things to come. He tapped in to respond, starting then deleting each sentence as his mind bumbled over the words that would be deemed smooth and succinct. He had school so would have to get out of it. His mum wouldn't buy it but thankfully she was out all day, gallivanting with her friends and unaware of what he had planned.

I'll be waiting, he responded and added his address.

She was quick to come back with: **Get some rest. You'll need it,** and added a winky emoji. An inside joke.

He smiled to himself and was about to wrestle some witty line from his brain when he saw she had gone offline. He wanted to talk some more. Build it up. But she had cut him off. She was all business now and briefly he wondered whether he had gone too far.

With a sigh, and a mind full of dark thoughts, he turned off the light with the expectation of falling to sleep. His body was numb, but he laid there. The things from his mind sat in the corners of his room, whispering to him. Words goading him with a belittling passive-aggressive mantra: *You were never enough. You were never enough.*

Tomorrow everything would change. His life would never be the same again. He was resigned to the knowledge that it was better for everyone.

When morning eventually came, his body ached for more sleep. The night had been fitful, and far from restful.

A ray of light cut through the room as he opened his eyes. The covers were snaked around his legs and exposing his upper torso; he had wrestled monsters conjured from his mind throughout the night and as a result felt exhausted.

He showered thoroughly; not that he didn't normally, but today was different. She was different. Every time he thought he was spotlessly clean, he swore he saw the evil blemishes tattooed on his skin and had to scrub again until fully satisfied.

The comfort of a large towel around him couldn't be underestimated, and for a moment, the world almost felt normal. Almost.

The smell of bacon made his stomach growl as he followed the scent towards the kitchen where his mother stood over the frying pan, bothering the meat with the frequent pokes of a spatula. The fat popped and spat back in a familiar fashion.

"Hello, Sleepyhead!" She grinned at him, as he sauntered over, slipping an arm around her waist and kissing the cheek she had offered.

"Morning, Mum." He felt guilty he was deceiving her. His sneaky plans of heading back home to get up to acts of the taboo with the picture from his phone. The 2D version that would transform into an actual person. He knew he had to stop thinking about his mother's feelings and concentrate on his own.

She didn't get it. She would never get it, even if he tried to explain. His visions were too vivid, and his feelings too strong.

"I might have a surprise for you later," his mother suddenly said in a way he had not heard since the bike she had produced for him after Christmas one year. Guilt twisted his stomach into knots. A blanket of sadness worked its way up over him.

"Oh yeah?" He shoved the greasy food in his mouth as he responded. He was hungry but the anxiety of the day was making the food less palatable.

"You're such a good boy, aren't you?" she almost purred, standing over him and smoothing his hair. But it wasn't his mother's hands he was feeling doing that, but hers. Words less loving, but clipped and domineering.

"I-I am," he stammered, as her fingers tickled him. She pressed herself against him and chuckled.

*

It was a little after 10 am when he channelled his inner Di Caprio to feign a mystery illness. He had convinced those he needed to that home was the best place for him, and now he found himself fast-walking the familiar streets home in a whirlwind of excitement and expectation.

Once home, he cautiously checked out the house to make sure his mother hadn't decided to postpone her trip. It was overkill, but he even opened cupboards and closets just in case. She had form. She was a clever woman and ordinarily, he loved her for that.

When satisfied, he sat on the edge of his bed and looked at the single photograph he had of her. His mind filled it out into a full, 3D person, and he was gripping the sheets in a way he had fantasised about for days. He breathed in the room, taking in the seriousness of the situation he found himself in, and sighed with the decision he had finally got to.

He glanced at the clock, realising he was procrastinating, and stripped off his clothes to shower again. He wanted to smell his best, rid the world of anything foreign that might've attached itself to him when he went to school. No matter the situation, he wanted to look and smell his best.

He stood there in the stall, the hot water cascading down his face as he looked up into it. The steam surrounded him, engulfing him in a world of dark and dirty thoughts the water could never clean. He scrubbed himself diligently and roughly with shower gel and wondered what it would be like to feel the hands of something greater than life upon him.

Once dry, his fingers fumbled with buttons and he wondered whether a shirt was a mistake. Should he change it for a T-shirt that could be quickly removed? He was overthinking it again. In the grand scheme of his master plan, these details paled in irrelevance.

Obsessively, he looked at the clock once more and panicked slightly.

She would be here soon. There would be no turning back.

He once again looked at her picture, his mind conjuring up a montage of memories not yet created. All of the things in his life that could've been. His dreams would never become reality, and finally he accepted that.

Then the doorbell rang and snapped him back to reality. He swallowed, rubbed his hands nervously, and walked as casually as best he could to the front door. His heart and stomach portrayed the truth he was desperately trying to hide.

He took a final glance in the mirror, filled his lungs with a deep breath, and opened the door.

A middle-aged man stood smiling at him.

"Hello there!" The guy grinned cheerily.

The postman. A disappointing familiar face.

"Hi," he replied, taking the package dutifully with a sigh.

Undeterred, the man nodded and said, "Have a good day," and turned away, their interaction over.

"I hope so," he muttered, closing the door. *If only he knew*, he silently pondered.

She was late.

He wasn't overly bothered with her tardiness, but he was nervous and couldn't help but blame her for that. He paced the first floor of the house, his fingers fidgeting uncontrollably with anything, and everything.

Had he been stood up? He looked at his phone as he pulled up her messages. She wasn't online. A whole spectrum of emotions washed over him, and he struggled to wade through them and know which felt the strongest.

Then there was a knock on the door. She hadn't rung the bell.

He wondered why. His overthinking brain shouted questions he couldn't collate.

He tentatively pulled open the door.

"Hi," she smiled. It was definitely her, but she looked older than her picture.

"Grace?" he asked, looking her up and down.

"You're disappointed?" she said, looking to the floor then shifting her backpack. "My picture makes me look younger."

"It doesn't matter," he said. "We all tell fibs."

"I'm okay still?" She looked worried. She was maybe twenty and wearing a long, black coat that teased some skin around the neckline but fell to only black boots peeking out below. Her dark make-up couldn't hide sad eyes. She looked good and it would work.

"Come in, please," he said, stepping to the side and actively encouraging her over the threshold. This act being the same depicted in movies that one might do to a vampire, only to regret it later. He allowed himself to smile. The very morbid thought of it seemed apt.

When she walked, it was with confidence. "You didn't answer me." Her voice was now more direct and authoritarian. Like the house had stripped the introvert from her and now she was in control.

"You're fine," he said, but it wasn't quite what she wanted to hear. It had slipped out whilst his mind flashed images he was unable to stop.

"Okay, Mr Fine. Where are we going?"

He swallowed and felt himself heat up. This was really happening, wasn't it?

"Upstairs," he managed, controlling the quiver. His hands had a definite shake to them now. Nerves? Anticipation? Fear?

She stopped and looked at him for a second. He really did feel like a school boy. She was suddenly all domineering and he was weak and a complete nobody. "Then show me. I'm not a mind reader!" Her voice was strong and he was enjoying the way she was making him feel.

He nodded. "Of course." He led her up the stairs.

He walked into his bedroom and instantly felt embarrassed by the posters on his wall and the décor, however, she had little to no interest in the unrealistic models in the posters, pouting with false desire, pinned to his walls.

She expertly pulled out and unfolded a plastic sheet from her backpack, and laid it onto the floor. "I make a mess," she said matter-of-factly. "Take off your clothes."

He looked around, and then at her, like he was expecting eyes upon him or for her to humiliate him. "What? Now?"

"Yes," she demanded. There was no discussion. It was happening now.

He fiddled with his shirt buttons and wished he had gone with the T-shirt like he'd first thought. He slowly opened it up and turned to see she was letting her coat fall to the floor. She stood in just underwear in front of him. Nothing fancy - an off-white vest and panties. The irrelevance of the situation washed over him as he knew in another time and place he would be overwhelmed with desire.

Not that he wasn't now.

But now was too late.

"This is your last chance," she said, her face all Wednesday Adams and her hand deep-diving into her backpack.

His heart beat hard. He swallowed and nodded before saying with a slight breath, "I'm ready."

She held the knife like it was normal. He pretended it wasn't there.

She stepped closer and got down on her knees in front of him. She removed the last item of his clothing expertly. His underwear slipped down to his ankles and he nervously stepped out of them.

He looked at the large mirrored doors of the wardrobe in front of him. The sight of an almost teenage girl on her knees in front of a full-grown man unveiled the reality of the situation. A headmaster, no less. She wasn't much older than a student.

"You've been bad," she whispered in a tone that suggested otherwise. He couldn't look down at her. His mind was confused by what he was thinking. Now free from his underwear, he was growing in her hands. It wasn't meant to be this way.

"I'm sorry," he said, tears now rolling down his face. He was a middle-aged man who still lived with his mother and talked to teenage girls on the internet, a dark desire he was unable to quash.

"Which is why I'm here," she cooed, moving her gripped hand gently back and forth. That wasn't part of the agreement. This wasn't the punishment he deserved.

"I-I…" But he felt her mouth engulf him, and his words disappeared with a feeling he had not had in years. Instead, he steadied himself against the wall, the sound of his feet stumbling on the plastic. All he could hear was slurping. He was going dizzy.

He closed his eyes as her hand and mouth worked harder.

He felt so good as she continued rhythmically.

Until she stopped. And she screamed.

His eyes shot open as he saw the angry face of his mother. One hand of hers gripped the girl's hair, and the other held a knife that now dripped with blood.

"Who the fuck is this!" his mother shouted at him. The words spat past him, splattering saliva over a poster of a woman licking a guitar.

The sound of the girl's body crumpling to the side and her gasping for air through a gaping wound in her neck was too much.

"I just," he started, but had no words for his mother.

"I'm hurt," she said, shaking her head. "You wanted this?" she added, still holding the knife, the very knife the teenager had brought with her to kill him. Her eyes darted back and forth between the knife and the girl.

"I thought I did," he stammered, unable to convey his true feelings. The ones he had suppressed for too long. He was lost and wanted out of the world that could not give him what he wanted.

"Oh, son," she said, the words now melting as she stepped over the dying girl and embraced him. "I would've given you anything you wanted." She was unperturbed by his still rock-hard erection poking into her.

"You would?" He was confused. His mother had always promised to take care of him, but this was something else.

"You don't have to die," she said, dropping the knife and instead grabbing his manhood. "Mummy, knows best."

"But, I-I-"

"It's another body for the cellar. I understand now." Her hand moved with more expertise than the girl's had. Or maybe it was because it was what he truly desired.

She then took his hand and walked him over to the bed. He followed her without a word. He would do anything for her. Anything.

*

Through dying eyes, the teenage girl's last vision of life was an old lady, naked and having loud sex with her son. She was numb. And now she was dead.

Nobody truly knows how hard the dark hearts of suburbia beat.

Nobody knows.

13. MERRY BLOODY CHRISTMAS

by Alexandra Nisneru

Bath, England.

The streets were dark and eerily quiet, and it took him a moment to orient himself. He guessed that he was in London, but a cursory glance around this unfamiliar version of his past life told him a different story. He cautiously stretched, accounting for all limbs, and found his clothing intact as well. Physically, he felt different for the first time in more than a hundred years. The passage of time felt different in Hell, slower, and now it was as if no time had passed at all. Inexplicably, he felt incredibly strong, and surprisingly, not as confused as he should be, given that he had just landed Earthside for the first time in over a century.

The air took on a crisper, almost sweet note. It was quite the contrast to the stifling, sulfuric air in the fiery pit of Hell, from which he came. It was where he thought he would be spending his eternity, for the women he so viciously murdered in another life. But he was out, given a second chance, even if he had no idea who got him out, or more importantly, why. But he surmised that it was to continue his work.

He looked up at the massive building in front of him, with its surrounding lights giving off a warm sense of comfort in the coldness of December. He couldn't possibly know it was December, yet he did. Much like he couldn't possibly know the huge building front towering over him was the Bath Abbey, one of the most famous buildings in England, even from his previous life. He also knew that it was the year 2023, a hundred and ten years after his previous life. How he knew these things was as much a mystery to him as how he escaped Hell, but he figured their relevance was likely important to his success in a more modern era than he had previously lived.

In his previous life, he had died in London, in 1913, more than two decades after he shook the city with his killing spree, putting his imprint on history under the names of 'Jack the Ripper', 'The Whitechapel Murderer', and 'Leather Apron'. He was never identified, never discovered or apprehended, and even in 2023, authorities and historians still had no idea what happened to him. He chuckled at his infamy. Given the chance, he would murder on a much grander scale this time; somehow, knowing that spree killers these days had a much higher body count. But Jack couldn't be bothered with such inane competition - he believed in quality, not quantity . . . the 'tableau' of his work leaving an impression. And despite his penchant for toying with authorities, he wasn't unhinged enough to lead them to him. Thanks to whatever Hellish entity was responsible for his escape, he was free to traumatise yet another city. For what hidden reasons, he was yet to find out.

Even if it was almost Christmas time, nobody appeared to be milling around at this late hour of the night. The lights from the Abbey started flickering under the cover of a shadow, like a smoke was enveloping them and dulling their shine. Jack frowned at the sight and instantly knew that the shadow was coming for him. It started swirling and twisting until it caught the shape of a human being, but it was no human. Whatever *it* was, the swirling shadow was made of smoke, with eyes of pure fire. It hissed at Jack, in a whispery voice, that sounded like the wind: "Welcome back, killer!"

Jack froze. Even if he was one of the most dangerous killers the world knew, he was still afraid of the shadow. He understood that the smoky shape in front of him was what had pulled him out of Hell, and that he needed to please it if he didn't want to be dragged back into the pit of endless fire.

He stood, unmoving, in front of the human-shaped shadow. He waited without speaking, anxious to hear what it had to say. The hiss continued. "Do you remember who you are?"

Jack simply nodded.

"Good! I have plans for you. It's time to take your rightful place in history once more. Humanity has become worthless and pitiful, and they deserve to die screaming."

A glint in the dim lights coming from the Abbey attracted Jack's eye, and he saw the silvery, metallic, shine of a Liston knife taking shape. It was forming itself from nothingness, resting impossibly somehow, in the shadow's wisp of a smoky hand. The shadow raised its black hand, lifting the surgical knife that Jack had favoured in his previous life, and handed it to him.

"Get to work," the figure whispered, its words carried away on the wings of the wind.

Before Jack could even thank the figure, its shadowy form had already dispersed into the night air. The figure's absence was only noticeable by the lights from the Abbey shining brightly once more. Jack was left standing alone, holding the sharp instrument in his hand, staring fondly at it. A wicked grin crossed his face, and he began walking, going deeper into the shadows, looking for his first victim.

'The Whitechapel Murderer' was free to kill once again. And he craved blood with the immense thirst of a killer who hadn't tasted it in over a century.

***

He was walking around the central area of the town, where the little wooden houses were installed for the annual Bath Christmas Market, but they were closed at this time of night. The Liston knife was hidden comfortably in his pocket, and he wrapped his fingers around the silvery handle, ready to grab it and swipe at the first person he encountered. *If* he encountered anyone, he thought silently, letting out a small sigh.

He was disappointed about the lack of potential victims around, and he blamed the era into which he had landed. He got the sense that, in this century, the 'women of the night' he had previously preferred would be nearly impossible to find. Regardless, he was confident that he would come across a homeless person, drunkard, or some other easy target soon.

For stealth, he favoured side alleys, rather than the main, central aisle of the town centre. But he knew he had better chances of encountering an unsuspecting victim, likely sleeping it off, in front of a shop entry. And soon he did.

A hunched figure was lying on the ground, huddled in a sleeping bag, in front of a clothing store, squirming and trying to find a more comfortable position to sleep. Jack smiled intently and headed toward the hunched form.

The comically antiquated top hat that he was wearing did well to keep his face hidden, and combined with the raised collar of his jacket, he hoped that he was hiding his face well enough from the recording devices. He didn't quite understand them, but he inherently knew that they were something to be avoided in order to evade capture. The shadowy figure had neglected to tell Jack when he would be returning to the fiery depths of Hell and, assuredly, he was in no hurry to return.

He approached the figure on the ground and squatted next to the man, laying his hand gently on the material of the sleeping bag. A raspy grunting sound was soon followed by a sleepy face emerging from the tapestried origami that the man had folded himself into.

"Hey man, fuck off!" said a grumpy voice, accompanied by the face of a haggard-looking man who must have been older than sixty. Jack silently appraised this unfortunate member of society as the man was blinking away sleep and opening his eyes to look at him better. But the moment his cloudy, old eyes met the murderous, bloodthirsty, blue eyes of his soon-to-be killer, he was enveloped by a sense of comfort and peace like never before. The homeless man lost himself in Jack's eyes, mouth hanging slightly open in awe, unable to say anything else, and a smile crept across the old man's face. He saw Death in those blue eyes, and the old man felt no fear or remorse, just a silent acceptance of his fate.

Before he had a chance to speak, a short glint of light moved with such inhuman speed, that the homeless man didn't even have a chance to blink again. A strangled, gurgling sound followed, and the faded grey of the sleeping bag bloomed red, absorbing the initial spurts of blood coming out of the old man's throat. Despite the old man's tacit resignation to his fate, human nature took over once he felt the knife stab the tender flesh of his neck. He desperately grabbed at his throat to staunch the flow, which rapidly began decorating the shop windows and doors with an impressive spray of crimson before he finally slumped over the shop's front step, slowly exsanguinating into the empty street. He was dead in seconds, his eyes left open, staring vacantly into Jack's own eyes.

The Ripper grinned widely, thinking the shadow demon gave him a nice advantage if he could hypnotise his victims with just a simple look. Surely the old man hadn't given in so easily? Jack decided that whatever the case, he was happy to have finally spilt a bit of blood. The unblinking eyes of his first victim of the night, along with the electronic eyes from the corner of the shop's window, were a silent witness to what followed next.

Jack approached the slumped, bloody, form. He began slowly cutting through the fabric of the sleeping bag to reveal the body of the homeless man, his dirty and ripped clothes covering a body so thin, it looked like it had nothing more than skin and bones on it. He took his time to savour this first kill; he missed the rush of it, being deprived of the feeling of blood on his hands for so long. He breathed in the metallic scent of blood and death, and he shuddered with pleasure. He was truly back, and this was just the beginning of his new reign of terror. To celebrate, Jack decided to announce his return to the whole town: 'Ripper style'.

He returned his attention to the old man, tracing the knife slowly across the dead man's body, finally deciding where he should start cutting. He paused at the man's midsection, plunging the blade two inches above the man's belly button. He began dragging it upward, splitting away the papery, crinkly texture of the old man's skin. He stopped when he reached the diaphragm, expecting resistance as he met the tip of the sternum. But, to his amazement, the Liston knife proved itself once again: how thoughtful of the demon to provide him with an adequate tool for the job, rather than a simple scalpel, like most assumed that he used.

Jack stuck his hands into the old man's steaming corpse, loving the feeling of the slick, steaming blood on his skin. He enjoyed it so much that he couldn't stop himself from getting a taste of the salty liquid, smearing his lips and cheeks with the liquid of life. He shuddered again, a ripple of immense, nearly orgasmic pleasure crossing his entire body, and then he dug his hand back into the body.

He started pulling and ripping with his bare hands, a shredded pile of flesh at his feet, and then he reached for the ribs. With only the help of his trusty knife and his bare hands, he managed to split the remaining skin up to the collarbone. He spread the ribs, directing them outwards, leaving the man's chest cavity exposed. He stared in awe at the plump heart, full of blood that would never be pumped to the arteries, and at the lungs full of air that would never be exhaled. He spent a few minutes looking at the life-giving organs, analysing every curve and wrinkle of them, loving the miracle that was human life, and how quickly it was possible to end it.

He continued working, pulling the man's intestines out and spreading them as much as he could. Using their uncoiled length to his advantage, he roughly fashioned a harness out of them. He dragged the dead body toward one of the Christmas market wooden houses that was advertising Christmas ornaments. He thought it would be a good irony to offer the city of Bath the ultimate ornament for Christmas. Chuckling maniacally, he hanged the dead body on the edge of the wooden house's roof, using the harness made of the man's intestines to place him there.

He took a step back, admiring his work, and grinned. As he smiled upon his latest creation, he could feel the blood on his face drying and pulling a little bit at the side of his lips. His tableau was almost perfect, but he still felt that something was missing.

Jack contemplated his work for a moment, wondering if it was close enough to the killings from his past life. Even in his day, killers would leave a signature of sorts. That's how he earned his name, after all. But would the good folk of Bath, in 2023, recognise this display as his work? No, they had to. The world needed to know that Jack the Ripper was free to wreak havoc on the world once more.

He dipped his hands in the man's thoracic cavity once again, giving his fingers another taste. Then he started painting the ground, writing carefully, taking all the time in the world. He didn't have any worry that someone might come around and witness the gruesome scene. There was nothing that could stop him now.

When he finished, he took a few steps back and admired his work in a reverent silence. This decoration was complete, and now he could move on to find even more victims to add to his tally. The city was his for the taking, one by one, they would all scream and suffer as they met their fate.

He left the gruesome scene, walking slowly and started whistling a tune that could be very easily mistaken for a Christmas song.

***

The next morning, when the first workers of the shops around the town centre started showing up for their jobs, they had to witness the most brutal scene ever. A dead body was defiling one of the Christmas market wooden houses, hanged by a harness made by its intestines. As if that weren't gruesome enough, what was left of the man was on full display: his thoracic cavity split wide open, ribs sticking out like the wings of a bird, his heart and lungs fully exposed, and a pool of blood slowly congealing on the ground beneath the corpse.

And on the ground, the most horrific Christmas message was visible, written in blood:

"Merry Bloody Christmas! From Jack the Ripper."

A scream shattered the absolute silence of the cold December morning.

14. MURDER IN THE VIDEO STORE

by Bethany Russo

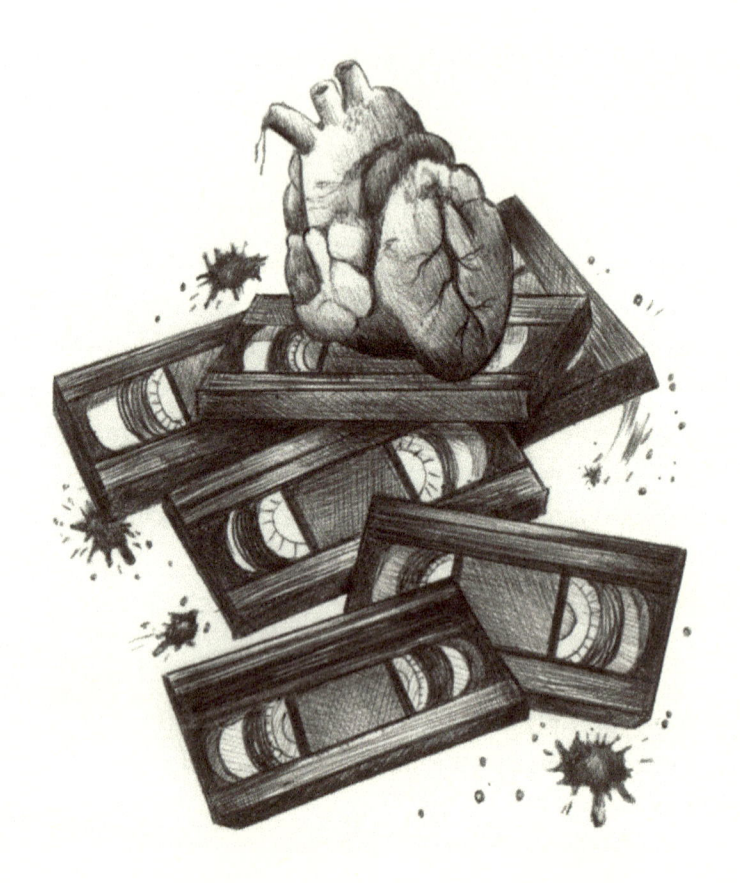

Weston Super Mare, England.

It's 1999 in Weston-Super-Mare. Katie is working the late shift at the video store, it would be boring, but she has Rory. Katie doesn't even hesitate when Rory locks the doors and pulls her into the staff room for some late-night fun! But things are about to go deathly wrong when Rory's vengeful girlfriend Tammy shows up.

*

Katie crossed her arms and sighed as she looked out at the dark sky. It was Saturday night and here she was, working the night shift at the video store. It was good money, better than the daytime shift, but my lord, it was boring. How many people in Weston-Super-Mare really needed a DVD at midnight? Surely not enough to make it worthwhile keeping the store open. But whatever, she thought, it was a job and as her mother said, "You're nineteen, it's time to pay rent, get a job."

It was fair, she told herself, to give her mum some money to contribute to the bills. She'd also have some for herself and she couldn't complain about that.

There was one perk of the job other than the money. Rory Michaels. Katie was sixteen when she met Rory at college, they were both studying Media. He only worked there while back home from university. She knew he had a girlfriend back in the dorms somewhere, a pretty blonde from London, a nice accent and a brain obviously smarter than her own, but when Rory was here… Well, it was her time. He was hers.

"Going to be a quiet one," Rory stated as he also looked out the window and into the empty car park. Katie glanced at him, knowing a blush was rising on her face. She felt so immature, but he was so handsome with his blonde hair, his muscles ripping their way through his work top. Every time he came home, he looked more and more like a movie star.

"It's always a quiet one," she replied, attempting to make her voice soft and appealing as she spun her brown locks around her finger, "But it's especially worse being January, it's so cold out there. Who would come out for a DVD?"

"That sounds like some good marketing for the store!" Rory turned and smirked at her. Katie's heart dropped, her stomach flipped. Oh god, that smirk, it would be the death of her.

"When do you go back to university?" she asked, hoping she'd have more time with him.

"Next weekend," he shrugged, "Tammy was upset I missed the New Year celebrations, apparently 1999 is a big year and she wanted a New Year kiss." He shrugged again as he scanned the "Hot New Releases" stand.

Fucking Tammy, she thought, *Tammy can fuck off.*

There was a moment of silence and all Katie could hear was her rapidly beating heart. She was so in love and she felt a moment of success when she realised that Rory had been content to not go back to Tammy. He didn't even look bothered by her, the way he shrugged as if she was becoming a nuisance to him. Maybe he was going to end things with her, maybe he was realising that he preferred it here, with her.

She was heartbroken when she realised university wasn't going to happen for her, she didn't have the marks, she didn't even have the willpower to study, but she wanted to be closer to Rory. Weston-Super-Mare to Brighton felt like such a long way for her and it felt like Brighton had so much more going for it. Even though Rory never initially showed more interest in her than just friendship, she loved every memory she had with him. Running down the pier holding hands. The late nights on the beach. Eating fish and chips on the bench looking out at the sea. He never asked her out, never made it clear he had any feelings for her. She felt destroyed when he came home that first time and told her about Tammy.

But then there was that Christmas kiss! Her mum was at work and so she invited Rory over, she wasn't sure how they went from standing in the kitchen to kissing in her bedroom. She wasn't sure how the kiss turned into her losing her virginity. She was heartbroken all over again when he went back to university with no intention of breaking up with Tammy. Would she have to wait until he came home for good? But she would wait for him. Always.

Two hours had ticked by and not one customer. No one buying, no one browsing. Rory had been dusting and Katie had been admiring him. She watched the way he strolled around as if he was something else and he was. He *was* something else. He was the most attractive man in the world. Yeah, she felt like a child thinking that but she couldn't help herself. Rory walked to the big glass doors and locked them.

Huh?

"What are you doing?" she asked, the store was never locked because the store was always open.

"This is fucking boring, let's go out back." It didn't even sound like a suggestion, more like a demand and Katie felt something in her stomach she couldn't explain. Did he want her to go out back for a drink, or… something else maybe? She listened to him like a little puppy and followed him back to the staff room.

It wasn't exactly romantic, the smell of coffee from the small and somewhat dirty kitchen area, the blue staff chairs that were mostly just itchy and uncomfortable.

Before Katie could think more, Rory pushed her up against the wall.

Her heart stopped.

Oh god, he was going to kill her.

He towered over her like a god.

She bit her lip as she looked up at him and considered spilling the news that she was madly and deeply in love with him, but she couldn't. Not only would it embarrass her but she couldn't open her mouth to speak anyway. She didn't need to worry though, Rory's mouth was on hers. He kissed her as if he was hungry. His tongue in her mouth. She put her hands on either side of his waist and gripped his t-shirt. She felt a fuzz down in her privates, but she was more experienced now and she wanted to show Rory that. She wanted to lead this as much as he was. She put her arms around his neck and jumped him. Her legs wrapped around his waist as if they were made for each other. As if their bodies were always meant to be together. She couldn't help the groan that escaped her mouth as she ran her hands down the back of his hair.

Rory chucked her down onto the blue sofa. Her breath caught as he threw himself on top of her, ripping off her jeans, ripping off her top.

Oh lord, she thought.

Her breathing was out of control and Rory seemed to love it. He was looking at her, scanning her body, like she was something special. It made Katie *feel* special. Powerful.

She didn't know if she wanted to have sex in the staff room of the video store, but it felt so good. It felt so naughty.

She was too weak with her lust to take his clothes off, so she watched him do it instead.

He wants me, she thought, *he* really *wants me!*

She felt the soft skin of his stomach as he got on top of her and put himself inside her. It didn't hurt like the first time; she got wet just by looking at him. She wrapped her arms around him as he pounded into her, thrusting with a fury she thought would rip her in half, but she didn't care.

This was good.

This was Rory.

She screamed out in delight as the tingle went from her privates, down to her toes. She had lost all control.

"I love you, Rory! I love you!" She didn't care, not anymore. Rory didn't reply but she could hear him grunting with every push. Did he get this from Tammy? Probably not, she bet that bitch was shit in bed.

He needs me, she thought again, and with that wonderful thought, she gripped the back of his neck tighter and screamed out. Rory hadn't even asked if she wanted sex, he just knew. They were one, this moment and every moment from here. She knew Rory was unable to control himself, he wanted to say goodbye to her in a way he couldn't understand, it was a panic deep inside him that made him want to claim her. Make her his, make her wait for his return. Rory didn't need to say it for Katie to know that's how he felt.

She wasn't sure how long they had been going at it, they were like dirty dogs, she was sweaty and she knew she'd be sore tomorrow but she was in love. *In love.*

Rory grunted, although this time it sounded different, it sounded like he had attempted to speak. Panic in his voice?

But she didn't worry, her eyes were closed, she was in heaven and she didn't want to rush Rory. He'd say those three magical words back to her soon.

But then something splattered on her face, her eyes opened instantly and she screamed.

She screamed as she tried sitting up but Rory's heavy body was still on top of her, inside of her.

There was a slit on his neck and blood was pouring out. She put her hands to her face, realising the splatter was *his* blood.

Katie looked up and saw a person holding Rory's head back with one hand and a knife in another. They didn't look tall, but they were all in black clothes and they had a white mask on their face. Like something from the theatre. If it wasn't for this situation, the mask would look comical.

Katie was in shock, but she couldn't stop screaming.

The person let Rory's head go and Katie felt like she'd been punched when he dropped down onto her breasts like a heavy ball.

She quickly pushed him off her and got up.

Her love was dead.

Murdered.

And now, even worse, she was alone with the murderer. How did they get in? Why were they doing this?

Was Rory really dead?

"Why? Why?" she screamed at the person, but they were too busy kicking Rory's dead naked body as if they hated him.

"You got the wrong people!" she shouted frantically, "Rory hasn't hurt anyone! How could you?" she sobbed, "How could you kill him?"

But the person didn't stop, they seemed furious and Katie wasn't sure if she was afraid or angry. How could the person she was just talking with, having sex with, just confessed her love to, be dead? How could life end so quickly, so suddenly? He was perfectly healthy and now…

"Stop kicking him! Stop it!" Her voice was weak. She wanted to rush over and fight the killer but that huge knife was a picture of a nightmare. She watched Rory's blood drop off it. All she could do was sob.

"Rory!" she whimpered finally, and with that, the person turned to look at her. It was chilling, the slow movement of their head turning in her direction. She couldn't see who they were, their black jacket was too big on them and the hood was covering the back of their head. Who were they? Why? Just why?

"It's your turn, bitch!" a female voice shouted, but before Katie could try to put the voice to a face, the person was charging at her.

Katie screamed and then she ran.

She couldn't believe she was running around the video store naked, blood covering her face and chest. She couldn't die like this. She didn't want to feel that knife going into her body. She didn't want her mum to find out that she had been having sex in the back room when a murderer walked in. How could she be in heaven one moment and hell the next? She ran for the doors, but they were locked.

"Help!" she screamed as she banged on the windows, the car park was empty and so were the streets. Weston-Super-Mare wasn't exactly a town of nightlife but she'd probably come across someone if she managed to escape.

Rory locked the doors. The keys were in his jeans. But could she get back to the room again?

"Let me kill you, bitch! I want to watch the blood pour from your body!" the voice said. Katie saw the person behind her, watching her frantically pound on the door for help that didn't seem to be coming. They were toying with her; she was like prey being played with. This person was the cat, and she was the pathetic mouse.

Cruel. So cruel!

They had the upper hand with that big knife. If they managed to kill Rory, then she'd be easy.

She ran again, this time god knows where.

The person followed; they were fast.

Katie pushed the DVDs off the shelf, the best-sellers, the not-so-best-sellers. All of them, on the floor, blocking the way. She ran towards the 18+ section and looked back. The person didn't seem fazed by the DVDs on the floor. Katie attempted to run but stopped herself, and the person copied. Their leg movement was creepy, they were ready for anything. They were not going to be fooled by her. It was like there was a football between them and Katie was trying to get the ball past her and into the goal, but this was no football match.

No.

This was a match to the death and this person in front of her had already scored one point.

"Was he good? When he was fucking you in there?" they spat. "Tell me Katie, how many times has he fucked you like that?"

How did they know her name?

Oh god, this *was* personal!

"I want to watch you bleed, let me stick this in your stomach just like he stuck his cock in you," their voice was so bitter. Katie felt the chills take her body, she sobbed again, she really didn't want to be stabbed. She'd rather be shot in the head.

Quick and painless.

Well, she assumed it would be so quick it would be painless.

She knew for sure that being stabbed would hurt, especially if the pain was prolonged by not being stabbed in a fatal place.

How did this person get in if the doors were shut, she thought? But she didn't have time to think.

"I watched the way he pushed himself in you, I heard you cry out that you loved him, you dirty little whore! Do you have no respect for yourself? In the back of a video store! Dirty," she shouted. "So fucking dirty!" She stomped her foot like a child throwing a tantrum. The person was psychotic, and Katie didn't think she would have a chance to reason with them. To beg for forgiveness.

To beg for understanding.

Had she been standing there watching them the whole time? Oh god.

Wait.

Katie had a sudden realisation, who could possibly be so angry about her and Rory having sex?

"Tammy?" she whispered.

"Oh, so you know I exist! You were just happily fucking my boyfriend?" she pulled her white mask off, which also pushed her hood off. Her blonde hair flicked around her face; her blue eyes shone.

God, she was beautiful! She was the perfect match for Rory in the looks department. But Katie didn't feel she needed to look this good for him, they had a connection on a deeper level.

They were soulmates, but now he was dead.

Katie took a deep breath, unsure what to do next, "I'm sorry, Tammy," she said. "We've known each other for so long and Rory started it." Her voice was weak, somewhat pathetic. But how could she be embarrassed by her fear? Tammy had a knife pointed at her, after all.

"That's not a good excuse, you little bitch and look at you, compared to me!" Tammy spat. Katie felt like she was being bullied at school again. She wanted to jump forward and smack Tammy right in her pretty mouth, but she was terrified by that knife.

"But why did you need to kill him?" Katie felt like the words were so far away, she couldn't risk losing focus, couldn't risk going light-headed or letting her shock and grief over Rory affect her. One wrong move meant certain death.

I don't want to die tonight, she thought. *No, I won't die tonight!*

"Because he deserved it, you know it's not just you, right? He's always cheating on me! But he broke up with me for you, told me he was in love with you!" Tammy screamed, stomping her foot again.

He broke up with her for me, Katie thought. *He was in love with me!*

She could have had it all, but this jealous cow who barely knew Rory had ruined it. She could have built a life with him.

No, I can't think this, she thought. She had to get away, she couldn't let her dreams for the future get in the way of this deathly battle. Especially as Rory had no future, and soon, neither would she.

"Please, I am so sorry he treated you like that, Tamm. He should have told you long before that he liked me," Katie tried to say it softly, she used the word liked instead of love in case it set Tammy off again. Although she wanted to scream it to the world.

He was in love with me!
Love!
He did want me. He did need me.
She wanted to tell her mum.

"You're not getting away from this," Tammy charged at her again and Katie ran. She felt a slice on her hip, it stung as the blood slipped out and leaked down her leg. It was just a slice though; it didn't matter, she tried to tell herself. She ran back into the staff room and looked around in a panic. She couldn't look at Rory's dead, naked and bloody body.

No.

Then she saw something, the coffee cafetiere, the hot water would probably be fairly chill now. Rory drank coffee way into the night, but still, she could use it.

She picked it up and turned quickly. Doing something she never thought she could possibly do to another human being, she slammed it into Tammy's face. Tammy fell back onto the floor, her hands on her face as coffee spilt over her. It wasn't the drink that was the problem though, it was the smashed glass. It was in her cheek and Katie thought she could see it in her eye too.

She jumped over her in almost a skip, but instantly hit the floor. Tammy had grabbed her ankle.

Fuck, rookie move, she instantly regretted it. She should have hunted the kitchen for anything else. Her own knife! How could she be so dumb?

Tammy climbed on top of her, her bloody face a mess. This felt so uncomfortable, not just in the *I'm about to be murdered* way but also the fact Katie was completely naked.

"Please!" she cried out, but Tammy slammed the knife into her stomach without hesitation. Blood shot out of Katie's mouth as she lifted herself up with a gasp. Tammy slammed the knife down again.

"Stop!" Katie croaked, she thought of her mum. She thought of her granny. She even thought of her cat. It was so unfair; she was being murdered simply for being in love. The spoilt brat Tammy couldn't accept someone didn't want her; she obviously had never been told 'no'.

Katie's back arched as she gasped out again, Tammy was slamming the knife into her non-stop.

Die already, she told herself, *I want to die, why am I not dying? Why am I being killed by the mean girl?*

Tears rolled down her face as she thought of Rory and the future they wouldn't have; the final tears fell into her bloody mouth when she thought of her mum. She didn't have future thoughts with her though, more so past thoughts, she wanted to crawl onto her lap like a toddler again and be safe.

Her vision started to fail her as Tammy forced the knife into her stomach again and pulled it all the way up to her chest, as if she wasn't a human, but just some science experiment. Katie was relieved as she finally fell into the darkness.

Tammy cackled like a witch as she watched the girl take her last breath.

Good! They both deserve it, she thought. How could Rory like Katie? Love her? Tammy knew she was a goddess, she was pure beauty. How could Rory not want her? She struggled as she dissected Katie, but finally, she cut her heart out. She had never seen so much blood. She didn't know why she wanted to make Katie suffer when she was happy for Rory's death to be so quick. Isn't it funny how he locked the front door but not the back? Dumbass.

She stomped her foot down on Katie's face, feeling satisfied as she heard the crack of her nose and the break of her teeth. Walking over to Rory, she kicked his head so it would be face up at her. His eyes still looked so full of terror.

"There you go! Have her heart!" She stuffed it in his mouth.

She looked down at him, a beautiful mess, she still loved him but he never loved her. He had cheated on her with just about everyone, but she thought he'd get over it, that he'd learn to love her. She wanted to talk to him when she found out he had sex with her childhood best friend Mary. How could he do that to her? How could Mary do that to her? She wanted to act like an adult and talk it out, but then he phoned her and said he was breaking it off. He didn't even have the audacity to do it in person! All because he was in love with Katie. That was it for her, the word *love*. Hell no.

She stormed into Mary's room, who initially smiled up at her like she hadn't betrayed her trust, and she punched her straight in the face. Mary fell out of her seat in shock. That was all Tammy was going to do, just a punch, but then she saw the knife that Mary had been using to cut herself some bread for a sandwich. It all happened so fast, she bent over Mary, put her hand on her mouth, watched the fear grow in her oldest friend's eyes, and then she stabbed her. She was strong enough to hold her down as she stabbed into her stomach multiple times, she didn't care as the blood flowed out. She didn't feel guilty as Mary wiggled underneath her in panic, fear and pain. She didn't even feel any sort of loss for her friend. Looking at Mary's crumpled dead body helped her establish what she needed to do next.

Tammy dragged her friend's body into the cupboard, Mary didn't have any of her own friends, like most girls, she was obsessed with her. But she wanted to give herself enough time to get to the little seaside town before someone finally noticed the body in the cupboard.

Tammy stood and looked at her creation, she wasn't sure what to do. Her parents would never give her money after this, would never accept her, she'd probably face life in prison. If she did get away with it, how could she go back to normal? She loved the kill; she felt so powerful when she plunged that knife into Mary's stomach. She felt herself getting off on the fear that took her eyes. She didn't even care when the vision of Mary's parents appeared in her mind. When she chased Katie, she felt like a beautiful monster, the way that pathetic girl ran and even begged her! It was such a moment. She wanted to strike again, but she had no more motives other than just the feeling of power. Would it be as fun killing someone who hadn't wronged her? Tammy picked up the knife that was beside Katie's dead body and stabbed herself in the stomach, she was too pretty for prison. She stabbed herself again and again until her hand grew too weak from the pain. Collapsing by the kitchen sink, a smile took Tammy's face, the video store morning shift workers were going to be in for a treat. The real horror movie was out back.

15. THE MOOR-FOLK AND THE POET

by Philip Alexander Baker

Devon, England.

Whiskey and gin and bottles of blue. Green glass surrounded by fifty thousand acres of green grass. Pretty labels. Local fables. Witty marketing language. I was taking it in, all that beautifully crafted penmanship that adorned the branded bottles.

I'm a bit of a wordsmith, you see, when I have the time. When the passion takes me. Like to write the odd poem on special occasions. Normally, I'm too busy, the pub's too noisy, and the abrasive kitchen staff are on at me because they're overworked. I understand though. I've been running this pub for a long time now. A very long time. But tonight was a special occasion. It was feast night at the pub. So, after getting some inspiration from the bottles on the back of the bar, I strung a few words together for you. Because, on feast night, that's what I do.

Perhaps you'll find it poetic. Just as the feast perhaps was. Depending on your perspective.

Shooting rabbits is cost-effective.

You know what else is poetic, in its own way? The view across Dartmoor from our beer garden. It is, quite possibly, the best pub view in the whole world. When the sun dips low in the sky, and the highland cattle roam by, it's the world's greatest view, let me tell you, and anyone who says otherwise tells lies. Yes, golden hour at the War Horse Inn beer garden is the greatest sight you'll ever see.

Now, I don't always have time for poetry, or much else on the busy summer days, but the view makes it all worth it. I can leave the poet in me buried deep in my heart, and bring him out through the cracks only when it breaks. Or let him yell when it beats fast in delight. It happens once in a while. Once in a very long time.

On feast night.

When my heart beats fast with delight, and the cooling sun slips into the golden magic light, just as the Dartmoor mist starts to form. It just makes me want to sing words. Once in a very long time.

I read a book once, a few years ago, that said to follow your passion. I never fell for that bullshit. But on a misty magic hour in the golden light, I'll grab a pen and a pint of beer, and write, and write, and write. And tonight, the moor-folk heard me recite. If just a line or two.

Anyway, I'm jabbering, especially for one who prides himself such on his choice use of words. I have a story to tell you. And it all started as I was looking at the bottles and jars on the back of the bar, enjoying the words that adorned them.

Early this evening when the wretched kitchen staff were swearing down the hallway, Neil, the new cook shouting some obscenity about the goose-fat spitting, I felt something stir. I had to apologise to the old posh couple who came into view as I turned, waiting patiently at the bar, a little shocked at Neil's profanity, they were. They looked positively shocked, angry, I tell you, and demanded a drink on the house. Behind them, through the window, something caught my eye. A little mist dropping. And my heart raised its pace just a little, and my breath fell as quiet as a mouse.

'Sure,' I said on a whispered breath, and the mist it thickened, and it whispered, *death*. 'On the house with apologies,' I said and I turned and released a grin the back of my head would not reveal.

The next customer up was an American man, bellowing his request for a beer and fries. *Chips, sir, we sell chips here. Fries are for fast food chains.*

'Coming right up,' I said, peering out through the window at the mist to see if death was coming in or passing by.

'Is it true?' the American asked. 'About the fire?'

My smile grew larger and then dropped the moment before I turned. Another clown asking about the fire.

'Oh yes. Never been out. In all the years I've been here, and all the landlords before me. As far as I know, never been out.'

'Bullshit.'

That word always sounds best in an American accent.

'I can only vouch for myself, and I've been here a long time.' A very long time.

The man slid his beer from the bar, paid in cash, and went and sat by the eternal fire. I couldn't help but notice the man's enormous feet as he walked back. Huge. It was like he was wearing clown shoes.

It's a good story, the fire. All the customers know it before they arrive. It's all over the internet. It's what brings the tourists in. It's down in local legend around here. They say the fire in the War Horse Inn has never been out since the pub first opened in 1854.

It's not true. It's been burning a lot longer than that. I believe the pub was built around it, not the other way around. Whether it's been out before or not, well that's just part of my story.

Another couple walked in, then another, and I saw thickening mist through the door. A group of four, then a bespectacled couple, all hastily shuffling in like a gaggle of confused geese, and I wondered, is this the night of the feast? I heard the cacophony of the cooks in the kitchen and hoped it would be.

'The mist is getting proper thick. Thought we'd come in and be safe, if it turns to thick fog we won't see a thing on those roads.' The sensible bespectacled man was quite right.

'Very sensible.' *As sensible as you look, boring man.* 'What can I get you?' I don't know if he really was sensible. I didn't know the chap. But he wore glasses and looked boring, so I'm up for the stereotype if you are. *Boring bespectacled man, I deem you sensible.*

The man ordered for him and his wife. Two sensible lemonades. *Knew it!* His wife called him Joe. A sensible boring name. The next wife ordered for her and her husband. They were all very welcome. Only one of them asked about the fire too, all preoccupied by the thickening fog that was trapping them in the pub. You might think I'd be tired of telling that story by now, but I'm not. It's a very special fire. And I like telling stories. If the light is right, and it's a beautiful night, I'll throw in a rhyme or two, or three, I'll throw in a rhyme or two.

To any clown who asks.

On feast night.

A man in plaster hobbled to the bar on crutches. He'd been here for a while, sitting at a table with dim-looking friends, one of which was particularly rotund. He ordered six pints.

'That's thirty pounds, please.'

'Woah,' he said with a look of surprise. Drinks in pubs like this aren't cheap. But then he spoke again as he happily paid. 'That's a good voice. You should do readings, or film trailers, or something.'

I smiled. I can hear my own voice bouncing off the old stone walls and wooden beams and rafters, and I love that it carries such weight. It helps put troublemakers in their place, and helps my poetry hit.

'I occasionally read poetry,' I said with a smile, 'just for me, and very occasionally, the moor-folk.'

'I'd like to hear some.'

'No, you wouldn't.' My face fell flat and serious.

The fire flickered, drawing my eye and I felt a sharp intake of breath. My heart flickered with it and the flames inside me lapped and burned. Confirmation: the feast was coming, and my smile immediately returned.

I've always had a nervous smile. Especially at feast time.

The man smiled back, then nodded to his fat friend who waddled over and picked up the tray. As they walked back, I heard the man in plaster.

'That guy's got a really good voice.'

And everyone was about to hear it. The moor-folk were coming, and the poet in me bubbled through my pounding heart.

But first, the food started arriving from the rushed cooks in the kitchen. Rabbits I'd shot my very self on the moor right outside the pub. Steak from the highland cattle that roam nearby. It's all grass-fed, all organic. Lamb from the local farmers. The local moor-folk.

I like shooting the rabbits. It's a pretty profit too. Doesn't cost much at all to fire off a shotgun, and the food sells for a good whack in a pub like this. As for the moor-folk, sometimes they come for a feast too. Once in a while. A very long while. When the fire starts to flicker and the mist comes in hard and fast. That's when the moor-folk come.

The American eventually ordered a beef pie, the beef also provided by the local moor-folk. He had to be talked out of driving away once the mist had fully come in, and instead reluctantly ordered a bigger dinner. Probably to sustain life in those massive feet in those massive clown shoes of his. Come to think of it, his nose was red and bulbous too.

Boring sensible Joe ordered boiled potatoes and rabbit stew. His wife had exactly the same. A young attractive couple ate moorland beef with chips and gravy (handsome he), and rabbit stew (pretty she). And the feast was about to begin.

When the fire flickered out, I felt my heart race. I knew it was time. The whole pub fell silent as their gaze fell on the smoking embers that floated around the fireplace and fizzled out and died. An audible gasp swished through the wooden beams and rafters. And I warmed up my tongue with a trill, and cleared my throat. The poet in me pounded at the inside of my chest, desperate to get out. It was time. And yet it's not the most polished stuff; I have to make it up as I go along, and fix a few bits as I recall it later and rush it down as pen on paper. But I love it and this occasion was looking to be a special one. It's my passion.

The fog outside thickened and the gold of the sun barely poked through. The deathly quiet in the pub was broken only by an American accent.

'Well if the fire didn't go out on us. I always knew it was bullsheeeet.'

Yes. Yes, it did. And the feast was about to begin.

The silence didn't last another few seconds before a raw and vicious scraping screeched through the door, which squeaked open and brought back my nervous smile. The whole pub was aghast at the sight they saw. There they stood: the folk of the moor.

There he was, Heilan, the second biggest highland bull of them all. His huge horns looked like they wouldn't fit through the archway and the couple at the table scampered away for safety, and I sat on the back of the bar and pulled my shotgun from its case. I knew I wouldn't need it. It just made me feel safe. And my tongue reached for a rhyme, and landed instead on a stutter and the sourness of a lime.

'Hi, Heilan. It's been a long, long time.'

The bull just looked back at me and nodded its massive head.

Heilan wasn't the only moor cow at my door. The next beast of golden brown to enter was Peadar. Peadar always was a handsome chap, and almost as big as Heilan. The two pushed their way into my pub and the rest of the customers backed away into all corners. And then another golden head poked through the door. Another face I hadn't seen for a while.

Flath.

Shit.

This was going to get messy.

Flath stomped in, and the other two huge cows faced me while Flath turned an ungainly one-eighty, hooked a giant horn through the door handle, and shoved it shut. And as the door banged hard, so did my heart.

No one was going to leave.

The moor-folk had arrived.

The feast was about to begin.

It's a fee we have to pay, you see, and these unfortunate tourists were just that. Unfortunate. Out of luck. Out of time. The final smoky wisps gently wafted through the pub, the fire well and truly out, the lingering smoke making the three massive cows look magical in the dim light of the chandeliers. Their huge horns look far more terrifying close up. And my lovely customers were about to see them closer still.

And I swallowed hard and cleared my throat, and readied my pen to scribble some notes.

And then it began.

Not the feast. As decades of cooks have told me, before the feast has to come the preparation. Neil and the current cooks slowly emerged from the kitchen with totally white faces and jaws that hung low. They were about to see a new kind of meal prep. A new kind of butchery.

And then...

It went a bit like this tonight, if I do recall it right:

Heilan went first as the humans dispersed, all but one fat man who fell frozen. The cow's horn immersed as the man's bubble-gut burst, and Heilan looked up sans emotion.

A man from the window-side table tried to run but he wasn't able. He froze in fear as Flath drew near, and I knew that this would be fatal. Flath walked on, slow, strong and firm, until he reached the man who sobbed once. When Flath got there, I froze too and stared as he wedged the man by his front. And yet Flath did not stop walking; the man looked ready to burst. Of all the feast prep deaths I'd seen, this wouldn't be the worst. The man's face crumbled against the wall, and Flath did not stop walking, a crushed body oozing out from the stone cracks around his mighty head. When Flath stepped back, the body collapsed, very, very, dead. With a flick of his tail, Flath turned around, his whole head and frontside now covered in blood. And I reached for a rhyme about cows, and found a crappy one chewing the cud.

It had started. They were just firing up. Better rhymes would come. As they warmed up, so would I. It takes a while to get going. The poet emerges but once every ten lifetimes. On feast night. I was rusty. But the rhymes would come. On feast night, trust me.

The man in plaster looked quite aghast as he rattled and smashed at a window. As Peadar eye's scanned, he was Schrodinger's man, now truly a life in limbo.

Peadar stepped, with barely a sound, as he approached the man from behind. With one swing of his head, the man was down dead, and now not just the window did rattle.

I've never seen a death rattle go on for quite so long, but I refused to be the slightest of flustered. He still twitched and spasmed while Peadar looked at me and said, simply, 'Ouch,' with such dry sarcasm that only a moor cow could muster. All my decor was covered in gore. And two metal crutches lay still on the floor.

The cows all looked in unison, and stared at a cowering couple. The pretty she and the handsome he fell to a ton of bovine muscle.

The cows stomped by and the handsome he cried and the smell was something rotten - as a horn slid in and his guts fell out as Flath split him top to bottom.

Peadar sniffed and grunted, and mooed a horn-like note. Then dropped his head and flicked it quick and his horn burst through her throat.

Flath then dashed, and quick as a flash, that bull did something quite reprehensible. Like a horse at the races, he charged several paces and skewered the man I had deemed sensible.

Not sensible enough to get out of the way, I thought, as I heard the tiniest of smashes. When I looked over to see, it quite amused me, that it was the skitter and crack of his glasses.

His wife, she sunk to her knees, and shouted, 'Please, no, God, please!'

She just knelt there frozen, while Flath wandered over, and you could see in Flath's eyes she'd been chosen.

Flath likes to play with his food, you see, and he lowered his nose to touch hers. He then licked her lips, his massive tongue dripped, and his eyes met hers as they widened.

Her mouth dropped low, and her whole body froze, and Flath's mouth did steadily open.

I was momentarily distracted, breaking the rhythm I was finally finding. The poet was awakening. But some frightful things will interrupt the most passionate of artist.

Movement in the mirror took my eye, and then, the whole beast, metres away, looking ten times the size he did in the reflection.

Yes, Heilan strolled by, his tail held high as he made his next dark and deathly selection. I averted my eyes, for to my surprise, the dirty fucker had half an erection.

When I looked back, there was Flath, and I wondered if I was still blushing, as Flath whipped his horn deep into her paunch and all her guts, they all came out gushing.

The old posh couple came crashing down next, and I shouted for my blood-soaked venue. And then I saw Heilan, standing ever so still, just staring at the menu.

Highland moor cow steak. £20.

Rabbit stew. £15.

Dartmoor lamb. £18.

All the moor-folk were listed, and my stomach began to churn. Heilan grinned a bloody grin and said, 'What's wrong? It's not often our turn.'

Now in this bloodbath, I noticed squashed under Flath, a man whose rump let out dirty water. A look of forlorn — and a swish of a horn — and his bowels came all slipping out after.

And the man in plaster stopped rattling.

And the whole pub lay dead on the floor.

And the front door did swing open.

And in walked all the folk of the moor!

The rabbits hopped in and the lambs danced in too, one gave me a look seeping sorrow. I didn't care much, this is a one-day event, and as such, they'll be back in the stew tomorrow.

Just once in ten lifetimes, the things get reversed, and the moor-folk they feast on the humans. But in the morning light, I'll put things right, and draw up a new menu and relight the fire that will burn again until the time is right for the reversal to happen again. Once in ten lifetimes. And more than ten lifetimes ended tonight.

That's just how it works. That's the law of the moor. It goes in cycles of blood. It's just nature, they say, and they're right anyway, and I've seen it for worse and for good. I must admit, in recent centuries, it's aided my passion a little.

Human beings. Oh so brittle.

The rabbits they feasted on sensible Joe, the lambs they gorged on his wife. The cows gobbled down the American clown with their teeth as sharp as a knife.

Neil was next. Oh, foul-mouthed Neil. The cook who became his own last meal.

'Cows!' I cried, 'Rabbits!' I bellowed and then scowled over at the little bunny beasts. 'I can and will not tell a lie. You'll soon all be in my fucking pie!'

A rhyme! My finest live rhyme in a very long time.

I'm a poet! And ALLLLLL the moor-folk will know it!

'Murder!' I screamed, 'Those people were innocent!' and then thought quickly for another rhyme. I stumbled and mumbled and Flath said, 'Magnificent,' and I knew I'd been out-rhymed by bovine.

He would be in the pot at the first opportunity. If it wasn't for the eternal impunity of this wholly holy cow. Fuck Flath.

And then the door opened with a bang once more, and I, with all the other animals turned to look.

Silence fell hard and fast.

There he was.

Angus.

The biggest of all the highland cattle stomped into my pub. I felt my heart race faster. Angus was the oldest. The wisest. The master.

The bunny faces lit up.

Angus squeezed himself between the tables, his huge horns shining. Monarch of the moor-folk, king of the cows. Angus had arrived. And the horns with the stars were aligning.

Angus was a good king, he looked after his folk. And the bunnies danced around him and the lambs they hopped and joked.

Angus, the protector, the good king of the moor. He'd rather save his animals. He wasn't one for war.

Here he was, ready for the feast. And look at the size of that beast!

He didn't live to kill.

He would bring the feast to a steady conclusion.

Though don't get me wrong, it wouldn't be long till that terrible bull would be full of a human.

As the moor-folk filled up and the flesh ran low, I looked around my pub, aghast. Now filled with blood from floor to ceiling, on the wooden beams and rafters, around the fireplace that still puffed the slightest of smoke. It would soon burn again forever after.

My poor pub.

My pub was flooded with blood.

Oh, right, fuck it.

A long night waited with a mop and bucket.

And then Heilan appeared from the kitchen, a dead cook between his horns, a rope around the corpse's bloody pink neck. With a flick of Heilan's head, the end of the rope flew up and lodged in the rafters, and the dead man swung, right in the centre of the pub. And all the moor-folk dived in and ate and ate, until there was no trace of the humans in the pub but a bloody head on a rope and layers of thick wet blood on every damn thing. Their parting gift to me, before I would once again hunt them in the morning. With the gun I still clutched as a warning.

This is the law of nature. And who am I to argue? It's as clear as day. And it only became clearer as the mists began to disperse, and darkness took over, and it was time for the moor-folk to leave my poor pub coated in blood, bones and gut-fall. I'll have to clean it up before morning. But first, I will get my pen and paper, and write this all down. Write some rhymes. Follow my passion. It only happens once every ten lifetimes.

They were to be gone soon. Angus snorted, and the last piece of person was slurped down a huge throat somewhere over by the fruit machine. Peadar gently nodded and turned. Heilan winked goodbye for now. Flath didn't look back as he laid a giant cow pat. Angus rested his giant nose on the human head on the rope, and gave it a gentle nudge, setting it gently swinging. All the animals watched it briefly, a dead dripping pendulum, and then Angus grunted again, and walked towards the door.

Goodbye till the morning, gentle folk of the moor.

The pub fell quiet and still. And I was inspired and felt a chill. The fire would need relighting. Just as soon as I finish my beautiful writing.

So, I'll pull me a pint of beer before I start my hard night's work, sitting in the half-light where brand new ghosts now lurk. I'll sit in stark shadow, a word aficionado, a pen in my hand; on my face, a sad and gentle smirk.

I'm a passionate poet with a pint and a pen. It would be ten lifetimes until it happens again.

It ended as the moor-folk vacated in satiated laughter. A lonely dripping head dangling low from the rafter.

So now there's a feast to write up.

An eternal fire to light up.

And the mop and bucket comes after.

16. SAND

by David Watkins

Cornwall, England.

Will opened his eyes and immediately regretted the last beer of the night before. Naturally, the other seven caused the damage, but the last one was a good one to blame. A quick glance at his watch told him it was way too early to be awake, but it was nigh on impossible to ignore Freddie.

Any second now, he would unzip the tent and physically drag Will out, laughing as he did so. Grunting, Will emerged from his sleeping bag. Grunts turned to curses as he hit the canvas and cold seeped down his back. Droplets of water ran down the inside of the tent. Will had a vague memory of a storm during the night, but the alcohol had done enough to let him sleep through most of it.

He pulled on swimming trunks, then a pair of shorts over the top. Yesterday's t-shirt finished the look, and he stepped into the gloom of pre-dawn. A combination of rain and dew soaked the grass underfoot, making his feet cold. Where were his flip-flops? Will scanned the area outside his tent.

They'd camped in the middle of nowhere to save some money. He could see Freddie's tent, and groans coming from it told him Freddie was awake but wouldn't be coming out for a while. Swearing to himself about lost sleep, Will went to the car. There were his flip-flops – underneath it but soaked. Why had he left them there? For Christ's sake, he really should stop drinking.

He and Freddie had long wanted to come to deepest, darkest Cornwall to surf, and the long summer break from uni gave them the chance. Freddie bought some book about hidden beaches in a charity shop, so here they were, miles from the nearest town, on a quest to find a quiet beach. It should have been the two of them, a couple of days filled with surfing, beers, and a little weed.

Why the hell had Freddie brought Savannah?

And what kind of name was Savannah for a home counties posh girl anyway?

Will retrieved his flip-flops and brushed off the worst of the mud. They were wet and cold, but they were all he had. He slipped them on, grunting with disgust, then opened the car and retrieved a packet of paracetamol from the glove box.

Will gulped down the tablets with the remnants of his bottle of water. He felt better immediately, which was surely psychosomatic as they hadn't had enough time to work yet.

He put the kettle on the cheap gas stove they'd brought, waiting impatiently for it to boil. The whistle of steam escaping the kettle did nothing for his headache, but at least he could make a hot drink. Clutching a cup of tea, he leaned on the bonnet of the car and took in his surroundings.

They had pitched off a tiny road, which was more of a dirt track. Trees dotted the hill behind them, trunks leaning at an angle of almost forty-five degrees. He could see the sparkling sea in the distance, nestled in the gap between two hills. The beach they'd come for was at the bottom of the nearby cliff path.

Giggling made him turn from the view. A topless Savannah emerged from the other tent, saw him and screamed, scurrying back into the tent.

"He's looking at me again," she said, loud enough for Will to hear. Canvas did nothing to dampen any noise.

"He's not like that," Freddie said. Did neither of them understand the principle of whispering? "Maybe put some clothes on."

"I didn't know he was out there."

"Who did you think put the kettle on? Now, come on, get dressed. Surf waits for no man."

Will sighed. It was going to be a long day.

***

The surfboards were getting heavy. Will adjusted his grip, nearly dropping the boards in the process as Freddie continued walking. They carried two boards between them, Freddie at the front holding the noses whilst Will had the tail of both. He had a backpack with their food and water. Will had a backpack of his own, filled with cans of beer and his wetsuit.

Savannah strolled ahead, wearing a bikini so skimpy she needn't have bothered. She giggled at everything Freddie said, stopping to kiss him every few metres. She made a show of rubbing the front of Freddie's shorts, kissing his neck, and making sure she made eye contact with Will as she did so.

Christ.

Will looked away, swallowing hard and trying to hide his discomfort. His shoulders ached, and the padded backpack straps rubbed despite his t-shirt. Sweat ran down his spine, plastering the t-shirt to him. It was hot already, even though it was barely past seven.

At least his headache had eased.

"How much further?"

"Can't be far," Freddie said, as Savannah ran ahead, giggling again. She disappeared around a bend in the path, covered by the trees lining it.

Will was pretty sure she could be more annoying, but only if she started banging a drum badly. "How do you put up with her?"

"Savannah? Ah, come on man, look at her. She's stunning, smart, and the things she does—"

"I don't need to know, man. Seriously, I heard enough this morning."

Freddie chuckled. "She is awesome."

Will bit his tongue. That she was beautiful was about the only thing he agreed with. He had introduced her to Freddie though, a couple of weeks ago at the Union Bar. Savannah and her friends had invited him along after lectures, and he'd dragged Freddie along as moral support. How *that* had backfired!

"I can see the sea!" she roared from somewhere ahead.

"About time," Will grumbled.

Freddie looked over his shoulder, his grin lighting up his face. "Think about the walk back up, carrying a *wet* suit."

"You are cruel, man."

Will's shoulders sagged at the thought. It had taken them at least an hour to walk down the narrow path from their pitch to this spot. They'd have to drink all the beer to lighten the load. Tough gig.

They rounded the corner, and the tree line petered out, revealing beautiful golden sand and a glistening blue sea. Two cliffs rose high above their heads, and the hill they'd come down stretched behind them. Will could see their well-worn path as a thin line scarring the hill.

This was an amazing spot. Beautiful didn't cover it. A postcard wouldn't even do it justice.

Savannah sat on a wooden fence, its rickety frame blocking the path. The sunlight caught her hair and her eyes, and Will looked away again. Why was she so irritating?

He examined the fence instead. It was the dictionary definition of old and worn and didn't look strong enough to hold Savannah's weight. Probably just as well she wasn't wearing much.

"There isn't a gate," he said.

"So what man? Wouldn't be the first time we jumped a fence."

"Yeah, but this beach is in your book, right? So why isn't there a gate?"

"Does he always worry so much?" Savannah said, somehow managing to scowl at Will and grin at Freddie at the same time. "It's beautiful here."

She jumped off the fence, landing with a flourish. "Come on boys, last one in the sea is a wuss."

Freddie dropped the boards and vaulted the fence by putting two hands on it and swinging his legs over. He shrugged off the backpack and set off after Savannah. Her screams of laughter disturbed the silence of the beach. Sand flicked up as he ran. It wouldn't take him long to catch her.

Will grunted and staggered in the sand. The boards weren't really that heavy, but the combination of Freddie's sudden movement and the long walk caught him by surprise. He bent to pick up one board. He brushed the sand off it and stood, putting it under his arm. Silence. Apart from Savannah's laughter and Freddie's shouts.

Where were the birds?

He clambered over the fence, swearing as the board banged against it.

"Guys, a little help wouldn't go amiss." His voice sounded odd in the silence of the woods. The giggles from the other two seemed quiet and a long way off. Will paused, gazing around the trees, shivering. He shook his head. What the hell was wrong with him?

It was a glorious day. He was on a beach – a beautiful one – with his best mate and his slightly annoying girlfriend. Alright, majorly annoying, but he could get in the water and surf until the beer started flowing. He'd never met anyone who remained irritating after a few beers. Grinning, he adjusted his grip on the board and jogged to catch up with the others.

Halfway down the beach, Freddie rugby-tackled Savannah to the sand, making her squeal with delight. They rolled so she was on top of him, and Will looked away again.

For Christ's sake.

About ten metres away, a deer stared at him with unseeing eyes. Will slowed, frowning. All four of its legs were bloody, pulpy ruins from below its knees. Its midriff had been torn open, revealing an empty cavity where organs should have been. He hoped the wind didn't change direction – his stomach was way too fragile to cope with what would surely be a putrid smell.

"Gross," he said and started walking. If they set up further down the beach, they wouldn't have to look at the carcass. Maybe it would help cool Freddie's enthusiasm for Savannah.

Not that Will blamed him.

Something else was bothering him. Other than the moans and groans coming from his friends further down the beach. Will looked at them. Savannah straddled Freddie, and his hands were roving over her body. She had her eyes closed; lips slightly parted as she moaned at Freddie's touch.

It was definitely too quiet here.

Will scanned the beach. Deer were herd animals – where there was one, there were usually more. Sand undulated across the beach, small ridges and troughs creating an effect like waves of sand across the bay. Holes dotted the sand, each about the size of a pound coin. Behind the deer, he saw another lump in the sand around five metres further away. Beyond that lay another and another. More deer. All dead.

What had happened to them?

Where were the birds?

The sand rippled beyond Freddie and Savannah, looking like a tiny wave moving across the beach. Will squinted, unsure as to exactly what he was looking at. The wave moved towards them, slowly but inexorably.

"Guys," Will said. Fear gripped his throat, and it came out as barely a whisper. He tried again, louder: "What the hell is *that*?"

He couldn't see the wave anymore, his view blocked by Savannah and Freddie's writhing bodies. She had her head back, hands in her hair, eyes closed. Freddie grinned up at her, hands roaming. Both oblivious to whatever was heading towards them. Both ignoring Will.

Savannah screamed. The high-pitched screech echoed around the cliffs. Freddie lay in the sand, but his hands were no longer on her body. They were twitching by his side, and his whole body convulsed like he was having a fit.

Will ran towards them, kicking his flip-flops off and dropping the surfboard so he could move more quickly. He was fifty metres away when Freddie spat blood over Savannah. She screamed again, recoiling from him. Disgust marred her perfect features.

Forty metres away.

"Freddie!" Savannah cried. She stood, legs trembling.

Thirty.

"Run," Freddie said as more blood bubbled out of his mouth. A lump grew on his shoulder, the skin stretching until it broke. Freddie watched in horror, his turn to scream. Something wriggled in the hole between skin and muscle. More lumps formed on his stomach, making the skin undulate like the sand had. Where the skin tore, blood and gristle splashed onto the sand and Savannah's feet.

Will skidded to a stop, fifteen metres away. He couldn't believe what he was seeing. A strong stench of sea and effluent hit him. Bile rose and splashed onto the sand. He couldn't help it. He watched, utterly impotent as Freddie's body disappeared beneath a crawling, wriggling mass. Freddie gasped, and choked on his own blood, even as his body was ravaged by whatever was under the sand. His screams stopped seconds later.

Silence enveloped the beach again.

Savannah stared at the pulpy mess, which was all that remained of her boyfriend, then she looked at Will, eyes pleading. Nothing moved. No sound. Freddie's body started to sink into the sand, shapes moving under his flesh. Savannah swallowed hard. She was trembling all over. Fat, translucent worms wriggled over Freddie's corpse. None of them were particularly big, but there were far too many to count.

Will's eyes filled with tears. Grief punched him hard in the stomach and he howled Freddie's name. He sank to his knees, huge sobs wracking his body. Even as he doubled over, he caught movement out of the corner of his eye.

The sand behind Savannah was rippling again.

Moving towards her.

"Run!" he said, but again his words died on his lips. She was oblivious to what was happening behind her. He swallowed hard, but his mouth was dry and it hurt. Somehow, he found his voice.

"RUN!"

His roar spurred her into action and without looking she sprinted towards him. Sand covered her feet and calves, sticking to the wet blood. She nearly reached him when she screamed, and her leg went from under her, sending her sprawling to the sand. She pushed herself to her feet, and immediately tumbled again as soon as she put weight on her foot.

Behind her, the sand rippled, a wave moving towards her.

Will grabbed her, dragging her to her feet and slipping her arm around his shoulder. She looked dazed, her face pale.

"It bit me," she said.

He ignored her, half dragging, half carrying her across the sand, heading for the discarded surfboard. The wave of sand stopped moving towards them, sinking lower. Will didn't look. He screamed with the effort of dragging Savannah forwards, trying not to think about the worms moving towards them underneath the sand.

Will dragged her onto the surfboard and laid her on it, taking care to make sure she wasn't touching the sand. His flip-flops lay a couple of metres away, out of reach. Were they thick enough to stop the worms biting through? He snorted at the thought. His flip-flops were so well worn, they barely prevented stones digging into his feet.

Savannah moaned and tried to sit up.

"Don't move," he said.

"Hurts."

He lifted one of her feet and brushed sand gingerly from her sole. A white shape lay there, burrowing into her foot. Swallowing fresh bile, he gripped it as hard as he could and pulled.

Savannah screamed.

Fresh blood splashed onto the board as Will withdrew his hand. He was holding a short, fat worm. It was a little longer than his thumb and about as fat. Instead of a head, it appeared to have a gaping maw filled with two rows of teeth. It didn't move as he held it and it felt fat, thick and slimy in his hands. It was also covered in Savannah's blood. He threw it away, hurling it as far as he could.

"You okay?" He winced. What a stupid question.

Her hair was plastered to the side of her head, and she was far too pale, but she managed to nod.

"I think you killed it when you ran."

"Great." She managed to sit up, and this time he didn't complain. She spotted Freddie's corpse and immediately looked away. Her eyes kept settling on the body and moving away, as if she were taking in the carnage in tiny bursts.

The visible bits of Freddie's corpse were covered in the white worms, although there was so much blood, they weren't white anymore.

"We need to run for it," Will said. "Now, whilst they're busy."

He swallowed. Yes, the worms were busy, but he didn't want to dwell on what they were doing. His friend was under that mess. His friend *was* that mess.

"What the hell are they?" Savannah said. Her voice was shrill, tinged with panic. "I've never seen anything like this."

"Look, for fuck's sake, it's irrelevant. Can you run?"

"I can bloody well run from here." Savannah jutted her chin out, but her eyes and trembling lips betrayed her attempted bravado.

Will stepped onto the sand, ready to run. A wave of sand rolled in front of him, and another came from the direction of the deer carcasses. He jumped onto the board, and the lumps of sand sank into the beach.

"Shit," he said.

"What are we going to do?"

Will couldn't meet her eyes. "I don't know," he said.

"Are we going to be okay on this board?"

"I don't know, Savannah," he snapped. "I don't know anything more than you."

She turned away from him and brushed her hair from her face. They stood near each other in the middle of the board. Will had brought his beginner board, so they had nearly ten feet of fibreglass to stand on. It was also wide, so they had plenty of room – if they remained standing.

"Someone will come along, right?" Savannah said, eventually. She had a bit more colour in her cheeks and was standing on both feet. She winced as she shifted her weight, but at least she was standing.

"We're the only ones here," Will said.

"So?"

"This isn't a particularly accessible beach, is it?"

She bit her lip. "Phones," she said.

"Mine's in the car and Freddie's is—" He looked at his feet, determined not to let Savannah see him cry. "Yours?"

Even as he asked, he knew it was a stupid question. She was barely wearing enough to cover herself, let alone a phone.

She shook her head.

"We're screwed," he said.

"What if these things crawl onto the board?"

"Let's hope they don't."

"That's not really comforting, Will."

"What do you want me to say?" He felt her jump as he shouted and felt guilty for a second. "My best friend is dead, okay? He's over there, covered in those shitty little things and—"

"He was my boyfriend," she said. The quietness of her tone increased the guilt but didn't quell the anger.

"He was just a shag."

"No. He was more than that, and you're a dick." She turned away from him.

Will stared at her for a moment, feeling more and more appalled with himself. He'd never been interested in her, beyond friendship. The day she'd invited him to the bar, he'd only wanted to chat, to get to know her better. It felt as though her relationship with Freddie had ruined any chance of a friendship.

The silence between them stretched, highlighting the utter silence on the beach beyond the crashing of the waves. Surf conditions were perfect for him: slight offshore breeze, excellent gap between the waves and not so big he'd get into trouble.

What the hell was he doing? His friend was dead, and he was looking at the waves.

"Sorry," he muttered as his gaze settled on Freddie's mutilated remains.

"It's okay," Savannah said. "We're both a little stressed."

He didn't bother to answer. They were going to have to run for it. He knew it was the only option. How quickly could the things under the sand move? Was he faster than them? He was in good shape, a winter spent in the gym helped offset the vast quantity of beer and shitty fast food he'd consumed.

It looked about a hundred yards to the fence. How long would it take? Twenty seconds? Less? He really had no idea.

"I don't think the worms are on the path," Savannah said.

"We don't know that."

"I didn't wear anything on my feet all the way here."

"So, we got to reach the fence then." He let out a long breath, even as his heart hammered in his chest. "How fast are you?"

"Fast enough. I was a sprinter in school."

Of course she was. He nodded, even though they were back-to-back. She was probably faster than him. Lighter too, so maybe the worms wouldn't respond to her as quickly as they would him. A distraction would help buy them a few more seconds. He scanned the beach again, taking in the deer and his friend's corpse. No birds. No people. Nothing to drag the worms away. The solution was obvious, but he didn't want to go there.

Not yet.

"How about your foot?"

"Hurts like hell, but it won't stop me."

Savannah pressed against him, surprising him with the warmth radiating from her body.

He took another deep breath. "Ready?"

"Yeah."

They turned to face each other. He scanned her face, again surprised at how her obvious beauty did nothing for him. All he could focus on was how irritating she'd been all trip. Who would miss her?

"Let's go on three."

Turning to face the gate, they both started rocking back and forth, stretching their legs. The beach looked so still and peaceful, even with the corpses.

"I'm not sure about this," he said, thinking, *It's not too late.*

"It'll be fine. We can't stay here much longer. You're right, no one is coming for us, not for days. Our food is over there. We have no drink. We go now, before we're too dehydrated to run."

He nodded and took a deep breath. He could work on his story later. *I'm really sorry, I don't know what happened, she was right next to me then she was gone.* Yeah, something like that.

Two hands pushed hard in the centre of his back, sending him sprawling onto the sand. He let out a grunt of surprise as he hit the sand with enough force to wind himself. How strong was she? He had time to see Savannah racing away before a wave of sand hurtled towards him.

What a bitch.

17. THE JOKE

by Tom Carter

Kent, England.

1

The palms of his hands are raw. They look as if he has held them under boiling water.

David once again places his hand on the bathroom tap and with all his strength, he tries to turn it clockwise. It doesn't move. He's turned it as far as it'll go but that doesn't stop him wanting to give it one last try – just to make sure.

Satisfied – kind of – he takes a couple of steps across the faded linoleum floor and wipes his hands.

Driiip.

The sound is barely audible but inside David's head it echoes as if his mind is nothing but a cavernous space. The *drip* stops him dead, his hands still enveloped in the cheap red hand towel he got from Dartford market. He swivels around and scowls in the direction of the sink. There's no water, no dripping – but he definitely heard it – didn't he? He grits his teeth and takes two purposeful steps back to the faucet, bends down and inspects with narrow eyes. After a second, he turns the tap back on so that the water is flowing freely – gushing like a waterfall – then immediately he shuts it back off. He repeats this action. Then again for a third time; *the magic number*. He clamps both hands to the tap and turns it as hard as he can, almost breaking the skin. Finally, he lets out a small gasp and inspects his palms. They're redder than before, if that's possible. He sighs and looks up at the mirror above the sink and studies his reflection. He looks older than his twenty-seven years. Mid-thirties, perhaps. Tired eyes, with purple rings that dust his lower eyelids. Evidence of last night's broken sleep. Two-day-old stubble prickles his clammy skin. There's not enough to grow a full beard, never has been, but there's enough to make him look scruffy and unkempt. Which in David's mind does nothing to help with his mental state and self-worth.

Finally, he turns to leave the bathroom, semi-satisfied that he's clamped the taps closed and no more dripping will occur. He reaches the bathroom door and flicks off the light. As he passes through the doorway he stops just outside, the darkness of the hallway engulfing him. He closes his eyes, attempting to control the anguish rising inside. He squeezes his hands into fists, his nails creating crescent shapes in his palms. Eventually, he turns and walks back through the open doorway and flicks the light back on – and then off again. A second passes and he repeats the action. Then a third time (*the magic number*).

Now he can finally get himself downstairs – mission accomplished.

David slowly descends the stairs, gripping the bannister as he goes. Halfway down he hears a high-pitched squeal followed by an incontrollable giggle. He pauses and his deflated features turn into an irrepressible smile. Taking a deep breath, he gives his head a little shake, as if by doing so he can dislodge some of the anxiety that is clinging relentlessly to the inside of his head. Like a gremlin, clawing at his thoughts trying to reach the forefront and create havoc. He starts to descend the stairs with more of a bounce in his step, more of a light-hearted smile on his face. Partly an act, for the ones he loves most. It's hard work, draining. But he doesn't want his OCD – his anxiety – to affect his family.

But it's hard.

David stands in the living room doorway, quietly admiring the scene that plays out before him. The screeches and giggles continue as Sarah – his wife-to-be, and Jimmy his five-year-old son – play on the floor. Sarah turns and sees David leaning against the door frame.

"Oh no, Jimmy. A monster's coming!" Sarah shouts theatrically, smiling at David as she does so.

Playing along, David raises his hands and curls his fingers into claws, a low rumbled growl rattles in his throat. Jimmy, half smiling, half terrified, hides behind his mum with a nervous smile on his face. After taking a few slow, creeping steps, David breaks into a run. He grabs Jimmy, lays him on the floor and tickle-attacks him. Jimmy's laughter echoes around the living room filling David's heart with pure happiness.

"What we playing then, mate?" David asks as he looks at the toys strewn across the floor. "Superheroes," David figures. "There's a shock."

They use the action figures to fight each other and for a moment, everything is perfect. Everything is as life intended.

Life though, has a way of kicking you firmly in the balls.

A loud knocking causes all of their heads to snap toward the living room window. No, not a knocking – a banging so aggressive you'd think someone was trying to bulldoze down the front door.

"Open the fucking door, Dave," booms a male voice.

Sarah looks at David, fear in her eyes. David slowly rises from the floor and makes his way to the living room window. He pulls back the net curtain and looks at the man on his doorstep. His tense shoulders visibly relax as he lets out a sigh.

"Who is it?" Sarah asks.

"I'll give you one guess," David answers as he marches past her and out into the hall. He yanks the front door open as Sarah half stands, half hides in the living room doorway, eyes angled down the small hall toward the front door. The man, David's age, stands with a Cheshire Cat style grin across his sunbed-kissed face.

"What the fuck do you think you're doing, Kev?" David asks.

Seeing who it is causes Sarah to march out of the shadows. "We've got neighbours ya know, and Jimmy is still awake you idiot."

"Oh, come on, as if he hasn't heard a swear word or two."

"Kev?" David prompts.

"You think I'm going to let my oldest friend get married without going out to have a few sherbets first? No way, Pedro."

"Not happening," David answers, waving his arms and shaking his head.

"A couple of drinks, Dave. That's it."

"It's never just a couple of drinks with you."

"Scout's honour," Kevin replies, holding up three fingers.

"You weren't in the scouts," David laughs, his frosty demeanour thawing out a little. "Kev, I told you I didn't want a stag do."

"What fucking stag do?! It's a few drinks with your best mate," Kevin exclaims.

David looks across to Sarah who's still standing next to him with a smile on her face. She gives him a little nod of approval. David lets out a huge sigh, a man defeated. Although if he was honest with himself, he'd love to go out with his mates. He could do with the distraction.

"Fine, but I ain't drinking," he says.

"Whatever. I'll get you a fizzy pop and ask the nice man to put a straw in it for you."

Shaking his head, David goes back to the living room to grab his jacket and say goodnight to Jimmy. Kevin stands outside with a big grin on his face, rubbing his hands together in glee. Once David's out of earshot, Sarah approaches Kevin. "Keep an eye on him," she says.

"You know I will, Ma'am," Kevin mocks.

"I'm fucking serious, Kev. Don't let him drink – you know as well as anyone what he gets like."

"Sarah, I promise," Kevin says, serious for a change.

As the exchange finishes, David walks back into the hall. Sarah pulls him close and kisses him passionately on the lips and wraps her arms around his neck. She has to go on tip toes to reach him. She drops her heels back down to the floor and they just stand there, looking at each other.

"He ain't going off to war you know," Kevin shouts.

David silently replies by lifting his hand up and shooting the middle finger Kev's way. He then gives her one small peck on the tip of her nose, an act he does often and one that Sarah loves.

After this she lovingly pushes him away toward the front door. "Now fuck off, I've got Love Island to watch before Sex and the City... and take a key. I'm not waiting up," she says with a sarcastic smile playing on her lips. David grabs his keys as he passes the sideboard and holds them up to show her. As he reaches the front door and is about to close it, Sarah calls him back. She holds something up and the frown he's sporting turns into a look of realisation. David holds out his wrist and Sarah slips a thick elastic band over it.

"Cheers," he smiles.

"My good God. Hurry up. I'm going to have to have another shave in a minute," Kevin hollers.

David turns and shuts the door, neither of them knowing they will never see each other again.

2

David opens his eyes, or half opens them at least. To open them fully would require a level of energy he just doesn't possess at the moment. Groaning, he sits up and swings his legs over the side of the strange bed he has found himself in. He tries to clear his throat. He's not sure if that's his tongue in his mouth or a sheet of sandpaper. Noticing a glass on the bedside table – half empty but still good enough – David reaches across and downs the stale, warm water.

Leaning forward he rubs his head, trying to clear away some of the fog that's clouding his memory. The last thing he can remember is Kevin talking him in to having one drink, (why did he say yes!?) and now here he is, in this strange room. He widens his eyes to clear away his blurred vision and hopes that by doing so, the marching band on full parade in his head might slip away. He studies the room in front of him. Definitely a hotel room. Putting the empty glass back he notices his phone. Tapping the screen to wake it up he sees he has a text message from Sarah.

'No problem. Everything okay? Have fun and we will see you tomorrow xxx'

Confused, David reads the message above.

'Gonna sleep on Kev's couch, babe. I'll see you in the morning xx'

Noticing his jeans and socks on the floor he bends down to pick them up. He slips them both on with the ease of a ninety-year-old man recovering from hip surgery. Screwed up on the chair opposite he can see his white T-Shirt. Unsteadily, he rises from the bed and zombie-walks his way across the old, patterned carpet you'd never find in someone's actual house, to his shirt. He picks it up and drags it over his head, flattening his tousled bed hair.

Then he sees it. Sees her.

Laying on the other side of the bed, unmoving, is a naked woman. David's heart stops as his stomach feels like a lift that's just descended thirty floors at breakneck speed.

He clamps his eyes shut and takes a deep breath before opening them again. "Fuck."

Her red thong is all that is covering her tanned skin. Her thick brown, wavy hair is – from this angle at least – obscuring her face. David slowly starts to move forward; each step like trying to shift a ton of weight. The closer he gets the more his heart starts to race, until he is finally around the front of her. He tries to avert his gaze, embarrassed as her small, but pert breasts are on full display. Moving to pull the sheet up from her ankles to cover her body, he stops, his breath catching in his throat as he chokes on a little of his own saliva. The woman is motionless, not breathing, a pool of vomit next to her mouth. David snatches his hand back as if scolded. His wide, bloodshot eyes slowly move from her to the bedside cabinet. On a small compact mirror – which he can only assume belongs to her – sits a small mound of white powder and a cut-in-half straw.

David ferociously rubs his hands across his face as if by doing so he can scrub away the image that's in front of him. He takes a step toward the body with his hand outstretched as if to touch her, to shake her awake. His eyes are fixed on the blank wall in front of him, he can't even bring himself to look at her. As his hand nears her, he snatches it away again. Turning rapidly, David flings the hotel room door open and disappears down the hallway. As the door closes behind him, a low vibrating begins.

His phone. Still on the bedside cabinet.

3

David falls through his front door. Stumbling into the hall, panting as if he's just run a marathon. He slams the front door shut behind him so hard he causes the windows to rattle.

"Sarah!" he shouts as he rushes into every room. He sprints upstairs, tripping as he goes. He knows she isn't there, she'd have answered by now, but it doesn't stop him trying. He needs to speak to her – she'll make it all better.

He knows it.

After finding nothing but emptiness, he goes into the bathroom and splashes cold water on his face. Rising up from the sink he catches his reflection. What he sees looking back disgusts him. He opens the cabinet door and slams it with all his strength. The mirror shatters and the cabinet comes loose from the wall. It dangles there, precariously held by one tiny screw. David grabs the cabinet and rips it from the wall and smashes it to the ground like a medicine ball. The contents of the cabinet cover the floor. An orange bottle catches his eye as it rocks back and forth. His anxiety medication. His nostrils flare as he stares at them, then he turns and through tears, stumbles his way back downstairs.

4

Slowly, the hotel room door opens. Kevin slyly pokes his head around. What greets him is an empty, but obviously slept-in bed. He enters the room and quietly closes the door. The sound of a toilet flushing in the eerie silence causes him to jump. He turns just as the bathroom door opens and out walks the woman, alive and seemingly in perfect health.

"Where's Dave?" he asks.

"He left here faster than shit off a sheet," she replies.

"What does that even mean?"

"He was panicked. I was just about to stop him and then I heard the door slam," she shrugs.

"He didn't even try to wake you?" Kevin laughs.

"No. Good job too, that vomit looked awful," she said.

"Well, I'm not exactly a props expert. I only thought I'd give him a quick scare – I thought he'd notice and realise it was just some banter."

"Yeah. Some friend you are."

"Friends play jokes on each other – especially me. It's how I roll."

"Well, you should know your audience. This is his phone by the way," she says as she throws it to him.

Catching it, Kevin slips it into his pocket as he pulls out a wad of notes and throws them to the floor. "Thank you for your...er...services," he says with a cocky grin. "You need to be out by midday."

5

Silence fills the whole house. The only sound David hears is that of his blood pumping in his ears.

Then – **SNAP!**

The noise echoes through the soundless house like someone is muting and then unmuting a television. Snap. Snap. It continues. A rhythmic beat.

David sits on the cold kitchen floor. Puffy, bloodshot eyes stare directly ahead. He's looking at a picture stuck to the fridge in front of him. Sarah, Jimmy and himself at the beach. Happier times. He's looking, but not *seeing*. His glazed over, unblinking eyes just stare, taking nothing in. He pings the elastic band on his wrist, hard. Each time he pings it, he pulls it back further and further. Snap. Snap. SNAP! The last one does it. It snaps completely and falls from David's wrist to the floor. It has some kind of waking effect. David blinks and the fog clears. He looks at the elastic band lying on the floor – his silent helper. Then he looks at his wrist. The red ring of despair stares directly back at him.

He slaps himself. Then again, harder. He runs his hands through his hair and then grips it, pulling it with all of his might. He roars. Then as quick as he started – he stops. Standing up, he grabs a pen and pad from next to the fridge. Usually used for adding items to their shopping list. He scribbles some words and drops it onto the dining table. He takes the family photograph from under the fridge magnet and slowly walks upstairs. After being up there for less than ten seconds, he walks back down and out through the front door. Slamming it shut behind him. Never once looking back.

6

Hours later, David sits on a bench as a beach stretches before him. He looks down at the family photo that he holds in his hand; it's the same beach. A place filled with happy thoughts. With memories of laughter. He raises an almost empty bottle of whisky to his lips and takes a mouthful. He grimaces as he swallows. Looking at what's left in the bottle he smiles; he's drunk enough to drop men twice his size, and yet, he continues. He drains what's left and throws the glass bottle into a bush opposite. It lands on another empty bottle. A plastic one. His tablets from home.

Empty.

Unsteadily, David rises from the bench and takes a second or two to balance his wobbly legs. He takes tentative steps forward and then staggers down a short ramp that leads to the alcove beach below.

7

"Just hang on. Once I've put the shopping away, I'll get you some Oreos," Sarah shouts at Jimmy. She struggles through the front door of their house carrying several bags. Kicking the front door closed with her heel she drops all of the bags and takes a deep breath. She feels exhausted. A day with her mother will do that to you.

After she left her mum's, she decided to go and do the weekly shopping. Something she now massively regrets. It's taken far longer than she anticipated, it's already dark out and Jimmy hasn't had any dinner. Picking up one of the bags she walks into the kitchen to begin the fun job of unpacking.

"Dave," she calls out on her way. "David!" she hollers more forcefully when she gets no answer.

Once in the kitchen she starts to unpack her shopping and notices something on the floor. Upon closer inspection, she can see it's David's elastic band. The tool was recommended to him by his therapist. Sarah thought it was a load of old twaddle – just man up and snap out of it – but the worse he got, the more it seemed to help. Seeing it here on the floor – broken – gives her a sinking, unsettling feeling. She picks it up and something else catches her eye. Making her way to the table she finds a piece of paper with David's untidy scrawl across it.

'Don't think bad of me. I love you...I'm sorry.'

Sarah doesn't have a chance to be confused by the note as a thudding at the front door takes her mind elsewhere. Through the frosted glass, she can see a figure standing there, illuminated by bright flashing lights. Trepidatiously, she makes her way to the door – as she passes the living room the only sound she hears is Jimmy's laughter.

8

Kevin pulls his car up on the street opposite David and Sarah's house. He looks down at his hands, he's still holding David's phone. He sits in his car, praying David has finally made his way home. He's spent all day trying to find him. Has already been here twice and had no success. He went back to the pub. The park. David's mum's, and even the lunatic office where Dave has his waste of time therapy sessions. The only thing he didn't dare do was call Sarah – that was more trouble than it was worth. He's sure David will be home now – in a state – but he'll forgive Kev eventually.

He was sure of it.

9

Sarah answers the door to the police officer. He has a solemn look on his face as he removes his hat. Another officer hangs up her mobile phone and enters the front garden. She trips on one of the scattered toys Jimmy had left out there.

"Sorry," Sarah says, her voice unsteady. "I was meant to clear those up but haven't had time."

The police officer holds up her hand in a 'no need to apologise' gesture and imitates the forced smile her partner had offered Sarah moments ago.

"Miss Smith?" asks the first officer.

"Yes."

"I'm afraid we have some bad news."

10

Kevin looks on from across the street as Sarah answers the door. He can't hear what's being said. All he can witness is distress on Sarah's face as her hand goes to her mouth and tears spill from her eyes. As if in slow motion, she drops to her knees at the exact time David's phone slips from Kevin's feeble grasp. Sarah's knees collide with the concrete steps in sync with David's phone shattering to pieces on the ground by Kevin's feet.

He continues to watch as a hysterical Sarah begins to scream. He can see a nervous and fearful Jimmy slowly walk to his mum. Kevin looks down at the shattered phone by his feet and then back to the shattered human on her knees. He runs across the road toward the house, pushes the gate open and steps into the front garden. The police look at him, wondering who this stranger is.

Sarah raises her head. Kevin looks directly at her. Her face, red and blotchy. Her eyes, bloodshot. The glow from the outdoor light shines against her tear-stained cheeks.

"You!" she screams. "You did this – I told you to look after him, but you can't can you? Everything is a joke to you, even Dave's mental health. And now he's gone! What did you do? You did something! You always do!"

"What? Wh…what d'ya mean – gone?" Kevin stutters.

The officers look at each other, and then both focus in on Kevin.

"Sir, we're going to need to ask you a few questions."

Kevin feels in a daze. His mind being able to do nothing but feel concern for himself. "No…" he mutters, "It was… it was just for a laugh."

He takes a couple of steps backwards as the officers start to approach him.

"Please, Sarah – it was a joke."

One more step and Kevin's foot catches something and slips. His legs go in the air as if he has just stepped on a sheet of ice. The thud of his back hitting the floor is nothing compared to the *crack* of his skull clipping the corner of the broken front wall.

Sarah lets out a little yelp. It escapes from her lips before she can stop it. Jimmy's scream pierces the night. Kevin's head is still leaning on the wall, the broken corner sticking into the base of his skull as warm blood trickles from his head, onto his neck and drips to the paving slabs beneath.

Kevin just manages to angle his eyes down to his feet and sees the small police car rolling away from him. The toy car flashes blue and red as it rolls into the glow from the real car parked just outside the garden.

All things considered; Kevin takes it well. A small smile tries to form on his twitching lips as he looks at the toy car.

Ironic, he thinks, before everything goes dark.

18. BROMPTON ROAD

by Elizabeth J Brown

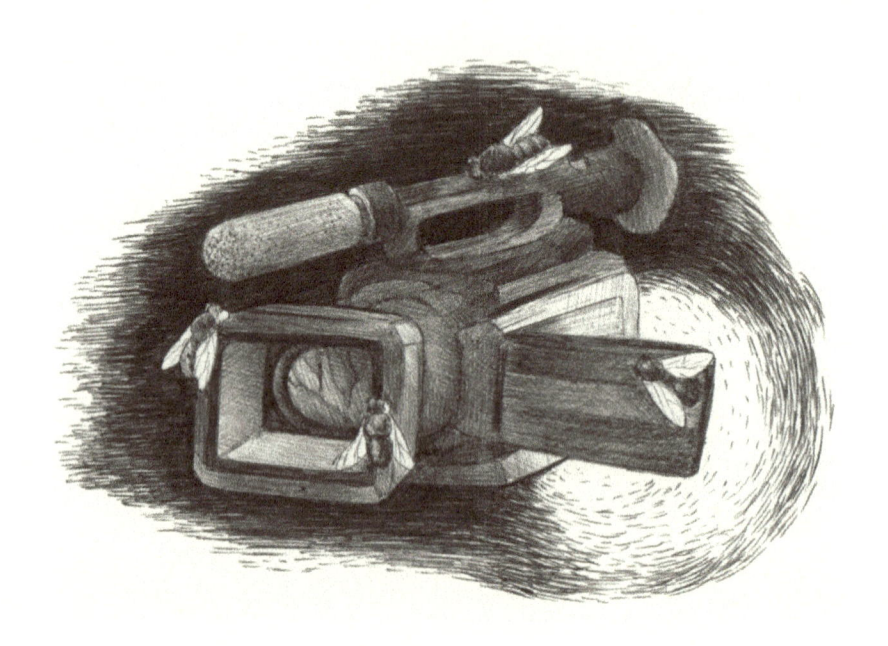

London, England.

Benjamin Oliver Aston rounded the corner into the little side street and tugged at the rucksack strap digging into his shoulder. Between the biting December chill and the fact that he'd had to lug the thing around for the best part of an hour, his arm was starting to go numb. He shook his head, cursing himself again for letting Liam talk him into this. He could think of better things to be doing at 1 am on a Friday, especially when he had uni at midday. But he'd made a promise, and he owed it to his childhood friend to try and keep at least one of his promises. He couldn't let him down. Not again.

Adjusting the rucksack with a nudge of his elbow, he stuffed his hands into his pockets and slowed to a stop, gazing up at the building in front of him. Brompton Road Station. Disused. Abandoned. A ghost station.

Ox-blood red terracotta tiles—rendered almost black by the creeping shadow — swept up the walls curving in two wide arches at the first floor. Beneath them, empty windows stared back at him. A chill fingered its way down his spine as he imagined movement there, someone watching him. He chewed on his lower lip, a vague memory nagging at the back of his mind. Something had happened here. Something bad. He just couldn't recall what. His gaze darted between the blackened panes, sudden and unwanted thoughts screaming inside his head. A flash of white caught his eye. He gasped, taking a backwards step, until he realised it was just a crumpled piece of paper resting on the other side of the glass. With a nervous chuckle, he blew out a breath and checked his watch.

'Jesus, Liam, where are you?'

'Ben, I'm right here.'

'Shit!' Ben shrieked. His cheeks flushed with warmth. He lowered his voice an octave, 'Where the hell did you just come from?'

Liam made an amused sound, his lips curling into a half-smile. 'I've been here the whole time.'

Ben opened his mouth to speak, but snapped it shut when he took in his friend's face properly. Liam looked ill, his grey eyes sunken in dark, bruise-like circles, his skin ashen. Even his dark-blond, usually immaculate hair was dishevelled. 'A—are you okay?'

Liam's smile dropped.

'You look…' Ben paused, not wanting to cause offence. Aside from the out-of-the-blue call he'd received yesterday, it'd been months since they'd spoken, let alone seen each other in the flesh. He rubbed at the back of his neck, breaking eye contact. 'Tired.'

'Dead on my feet. Come on, let's get inside before someone sees us. I think our subscribers are really gonna love this. Hopefully, this'll make up for the fact we haven't uploaded anything in ages.' He hobbled towards the pair of black, heavy-duty-looking doors.

Ben nodded. His momentary relief quickly gave way to concern as he noticed Liam's limp. 'What happened to your leg?'

'I fell.'

'Fell? When? Are you sure we should be doing this if you're hurt?'

Looking back over his shoulder, Liam shrugged. 'I'm fine. It was a couple of days ago. It's all good.' He rolled his eyes at Ben's unconvinced expression. 'Come on, if we don't start posting some new content soon our channel's going down the crapper.'

'And Hannah's okay with this?' Ben winced, knowing immediately that mentioning Hannah was a mistake.

Liam stiffened. His hand hovered above the doorknob. 'She's fine with it.' The words were clipped.

'Look,' Ben said, closing the distance between them. 'I'm sorry. I didn't mean—'

'It's fine.'

A frigid breeze whipped around them, sending an empty crisp packet skittering across the pavement.

'No, really. I'm sorry.' Ben reached out a hand instinctively to squeeze his friend's shoulder, but Liam shrugged away before he could make contact. His fingers swept through the air.

As Liam regarded him through narrowed eyes, the temperature seemed to drop.

Ben suppressed a shudder, the hairs on the back of his neck standing on end.

'Let's just get inside.'

Ben let his arm drop. 'Sure.'

Stepping to the side, Liam gestured to the door. 'After you.'

With a frown, Ben closed his hand around the silver doorknob and twisted. To his surprise the door opened without any resistance. He strained to see within the darkened room, then glanced at Liam.

And then the memory hit him. 'Didn't someone die here?'

'Plenty of people have died here.' Liam waved a hand dismissively. 'Accidents, suicides, murders.'

'I've changed my mind. This is creeping me out.'

'Don't tell me you're *still* afraid of ghosts?'

Ben cleared his throat, trying to ignore the knot forming in his gut. It was easy to forget just how much Liam knew about him. 'No, I mean, shouldn't this place be locked? Isn't it supposed to be owned by the MOD or something?'

'I don't know. I think it got sold to some property developer. Does it matter? Just go in already.' When he didn't move, Liam let out an exasperated sigh. 'If this place is owned by the MOD, or whatever, do you really want to find out what happens if we get caught trespassing? Plus, you've come all this way, might as well get the footage now that you're here.'

'I'm not sure about this.'

'Ben, please, our channel needs this.' His body sagged. He stared down at his feet, his voice losing some of its strength. '*I* need this. Since Hannah and I broke up I haven't known what to do with myself.'

Tugging at his collar, Ben averted his gaze and gave a single nod. 'Okay, man. Let's do it.' With a final backwards glance, he stepped inside the building.

The door clattered shut immediately behind him. Swallowing him in shadow. Cutting him off from the world outside.

'Jesus!' He leapt forward with a start, heart hammering inside his chest, and fumbled in his pocket for his mobile. His numb fingers swiped at the screen, his desperation to switch on the torch making his movements clumsy. The phone slipped from his grip, hitting the floor with a sharp crack.

'Liam?'

An icy chill ghosted across his ear. He shrieked, spinning back towards the door, grasping blindly for a way out.

'Liam? Liam, this isn't funny. Let me out! Let me out, Liam, now! I mean it! Liam, where are you?'

'Dude, relax. I'm right here.'

A circle of white light bloomed beside him. Liam stood watching him with a curious expression, pointing his own phone towards the ground so as not to blind either of them.

'Holy shit.' Clutching at his chest, Ben gulped a breath before releasing it in a choking cough. 'How did you... I—I thought you...' Wheezing, he fished his inhaler out of his coat.

'You thought I locked you in? Christ, what kind of arsehole do you take me for?'

Ben shook his head, sucking on the mouthpiece. After a few seconds, he exhaled and returned the inhaler to his pocket, feeling the weight of Liam's glare.

'The door closed right behind me. I thought you were still outside.'

Raising an eyebrow, Liam tsked. '*Why* would I want to lock you in?'

The knot in his insides was back. Ben flicked his gaze to the floor. 'Sorry. You know I'm not a fan of places like this.'

'We're urban explorers. Places like this is what we do.'

'No, you and Han—' He stopped himself just as his friend's face became rigid. 'You're the urban explorer. I'm just the camera man. Anyway, we used to do this sort of thing during the day. Why did we have to meet at this time of the morning?'

'You know why. We're not supposed to be here. This place is strictly off limits.' Liam turned to face the inside of the room, waiting for Ben to do the same, before sweeping his hand through the air theatrically. 'It's why our subscribers are gonna love it. Subterranean tunnels. Gun operation rooms from World War 2. Most of these ghost stations were just converted into air raid shelters during the war, but not Brompton Road. It's a piece of history. This is the shit that goes viral. I'm telling you, the views are gonna be off the charts! We might even *finally* get that silver play button.'

Now that his heart rate had returned to normal, Ben attempted to take in his surroundings. Shadows stretched around the edges of the phone light, clawing and grabbing, desperate to drag him back into their soulless embrace. He could see little of the room they were in, besides the edges of the walls where the moonlight leaked through the windows. It smelt wrong. Musty with a tinge of decay. Liam couldn't be right about it being sold off; there was no way a developer would just leave a property to collect dust. Unless there was something wrong with it…

The door rattled behind him.

He jumped, spitting out a curse.

'Seriously, Ben, chill. It's just the wind.'

Part of him wanted to all but beg Liam to call this off, but he already felt like a coward and they hadn't even started yet. Plus, he owed him. Shaking off his unease, he bent to retrieve his phone.

'Shit.' Scowling down at the spiderweb of cracks across the screen, he tried the power button. Nothing happened. 'Fuck. It's dead.' He held it up so that Liam could see.

'Unlucky. Good job you've got that student loan.'

'What I've got is two years' worth of student debt and counting. I can't afford another phone.'

'I'm sure your parents would front you the money. Bank of mum and dad and all that.'

Ben heaved out a sigh and stuffed the useless device back in his pocket. Sometimes he wondered if all the stress, all the debt, was worth it. Liam could never understand what he was going through, he'd dropped out of uni after the first term and landed right on his feet. As usual.

'Right. Is this where you want me to start filming?'

'Nah, I thought we'd start with the good stuff. You brought the lighting, right?'

Ben patted his rucksack in response.

'Awesome, let's get a move on then. Follow me.'

Hurrying to catch up, Ben stumbled after the dim glow of Liam's phone. With every step it seemed to get colder, the mouldering smell of rot stronger.

After several minutes, and more stairs than he cared to count, Liam stopped. Ben swiped at his brow with the back of his hand, the muscles in his thighs throbbing with a dull burn. At least he'd warmed up.

'Here?' Ben asked hopefully, adjusting the strap biting into his shoulder.

'*Here?*' Liam scoffed. 'This is the basement.' He shone the torch around them to illustrate his point. 'We've still gotta get to the platform.'

'Oh.' Ben filled his lungs and looked around, exhaling through his teeth.

Thick silver tubes snaked up the cracked, flaking white brickwork of the walls, filtering into a network of countless smaller pipes above their heads. He couldn't get over how quiet it was. Without the distant hum of traffic and the general activity of London at night, he felt completely cut off from the world. Thoughts of Freddy Krueger's boiler room edged their way into his mind. He shuddered.

The light on the mobile flickered off, plunging them into darkness. Ben froze.

'*Liam?*'

'I'm right here. Hang on,' Liam sighed.

After a few seconds, the light came back on.

Ben blinked. Cold, dead eyes stared back at him.

He yelled, staggering backwards as he flung his arms up to shield his face.

'What the fuck, Ben?'

'I… I thought I saw…' he lowered his arms. The eyes were nothing more than two spots of light reflecting off the silver piping in front of him. He groaned, relief warring with embarrassment.

'Saw what? A ghost?'

'No. It was nothing.'

'It's a good angle.'

'What?'

'The whole ghost thing. Might help to get more subscribers.' Liam stroked his chin and broke into a wide grin. 'Brompton Road. A haunted ghost station. Steeped in history, and plagued by the vengeful spirits unable to seek retribution on those who wronged them in life.'

Ben shifted uncomfortably. 'Why do they have to be vengeful?'

'They're always vengeful. It makes sense. Pain, loneliness, anger. The manifestation of all that negative energy with no outlet? That makes for one pissed off ghost. Nope, Casper's day is well and truly done. You gotta give the viewers what they want, and what they want is risk-free thrills and jump scares.'

The light flickered again.

'What's wrong with your phone?' Ben asked, eager to change the subject.

'I dunno. I dropped it when I fell. It's been acting up ever since.'

'It did sound kind of weird when you called. Like there was some sort of static interference.'

'Yeah?' He gave a casual shrug. 'Probably on its way out then. Ready to keep going?'

Taking another glance around the basement, Ben nodded. 'Sure, let's get this over with.'

It wasn't long before they were descending a spiral staircase. Once or twice, Liam stopped him to point out something that he thought their followers might enjoy. Like the strips of original green and brown tiling that ran in parallel with the dust-smothered wrought-iron handrail, to which Ben now clung. Sure it was interesting, but he just couldn't bring himself to be excited about tiles. Especially not when the rust bleeding down the walls made him think about every horror film he'd ever seen involving abandoned buildings or tunnels.

When they eventually made it to the platform area, Ben's legs were on fire. The air was stifling, carrying a dusty weight that clung to his every panting breath. His hands were covered in grime, his clothes too. He'd already had to use his inhaler again. Liam, on the other hand, didn't seem in the least bit affected. Even his limp hadn't slowed him down. Maybe if he'd had to lug the rucksack full of camera equipment around... He hadn't offered to help once. In fact, he hadn't so much as opened a door.

'This is it,' Liam announced. 'Brompton Road Station. Just through that cross passage is the Westbound tunnel that links to Knightsbridge, I thought we could start with the Eastbound tunnel.'

As Liam moved his mobile around, illuminating their surroundings, Ben took a moment to recover. On one side of the tunnel, the station's name had been fired in large letters across the dingy, soot-stained white tiles. Above and below it were more of the brown and green strips he'd become familiar with during the descent. Every surface was smeared with a fine, gritty film of grey.

He wrinkled his nose. 'Jesus, it smells like something died down here.'

'Lots of things die down here. Do you know how many hundreds of thousands of rats and mice there are living in the underground?'

'I don't want to think about that.' He could almost hear the skittering of tiny claws. 'Where's the track?'

'It was excavated so this part of the tunnel could be used as a communications room during the war. That's why the floor's so low.'

'You want me to start setting up?' Ben frowned at the grubby surface beneath his feet, yanking the rucksack off his shoulder and placing it down. Thankfully the material was predominantly black; even so, he hoped he'd be able to get all the soot and filth off it later.

'Yeah, go for it.'

Keeping the phone light in place, Liam waited while Ben set about removing the tripod from the bag's side panel and began adjusting the legs.

'I thought I'd hear from you more.'

Ben paused. His stomach clenched. 'I uh… I'm sorry, man. What with Uni and my part time job…'

'No, I get it. You're busy. It's cool.'

Offering a tight smile, Ben unzipped the rucksack, focussing on the lenses inside instead of Liam. He could feel his friend's gaze on him.

'It's just it's been six months since Hannah and I broke up, and other than you taking my call yesterday, I haven't really heard from you.'

He knew this might come up. Knew the conversation would inevitably become about Hannah. But he'd hoped that six months would've been long enough for Liam to have moved on. It suddenly felt even hotter inside the tunnel.

He swallowed, not meeting his friend's eyes. 'I'm sorry. Like I said, I've been busy with studying.'

The silence stretched. Ben looked up.

A dark expression flickered across Liam's face, gone in an instant. Had Ben imagined it? He'd been jumping at shadows ever since he got here. Letting his nerves get the better of him.

'How much longer?' Liam asked.

'Not long.' A bead of sweat trickled down his back. Focusing on the bag, he plucked the adaptor from one of the partitions, slotted it into the camera's hot shoe, and attached the LED lighting panel. 'There. Let me just put the camera on the tripod and we're good to go.'

'Nice.' Liam shuffled back a few yards.

Once the camera was secure, Ben switched on the light. Compared to the phone, it was so bright that, for a fraction of a second, it bounced off the dust coating Liam's clothes giving the illusion of an ethereal glow.

'Let me get into position.' Liam pocketed his mobile and, after a quick backwards glance, took a few steps to the right. With a satisfied nod, he gave Ben the thumbs up.

A couple of adjustments later, Ben held up his hand gesturing for Liam to start.

'I'm standing in the Eastbound tunnel of Brompton Road. A ghost—'

'Hang on a sec, something's off with the focus.' Squinting at the display, Ben scrolled through the menu options. His forehead creased. Muttering, he removed the camera from the tripod. 'The settings are okay. I'm not sure what the problem is.' He pressed the shutter button, listening to the stuttering click as the camera attempted to autofocus. Liam's outline became sharper. 'There. I think…' he trailed off, his attention drawn to a shape on the floor a few metres behind his friend. From this distance, he couldn't make it out, but there was something familiar about it. Something disquieting that made his flesh prick with goosebumps.

Liam cleared his throat, arching an eyebrow in question.

'Behind you, it kind of looks like a—'

'You never asked why we broke up.'

The statement hit him like a fist to the gut. All else forgotten, Ben's jaw dropped.

His friend continued, his voice taking on a hard edge. 'She was cheating on me.'

'W—what?' he stammered, his insides roiling.

'Yeah. She was taking a shower, left her mobile on the side. She got a message. Now, normally I wouldn't think anything of it. But then she got another one. And another one. I thought maybe something was wrong. Someone was obviously desperate to get hold of her, so I check it, y'know, just in case.'

Ben swallowed, his mouth dry.

'I read the first message. I couldn't believe it. It made me feel physically sick, but I couldn't stop scrolling. Turns out it had been going on for months.'

'Did you… do you…'

'Do I know who it was?' Liam's jaw ticked.

Ben couldn't bring himself to say another word, instead he nodded weakly.

'Some guy called Olly.' Liam shook his head, his teeth grinding together. 'I must've looked at hundreds of their messages. I was numb. My whole world was crumbling. He even sent her a fucking dick pic. So there I am, sitting on my girlfriend's bed staring at some other dude's cock, at full mast. I lost it. I fucking lost it.' He took a breath, his eyes wild. The light on the camera flickered. 'I ran down the hall to the bathroom and burst through the door. I shouted. She cried. I asked her if she loved him. She wouldn't answer me. Her flatmates eventually told me to leave, so I got my shit and I went.'

Ben exhaled, unable to think of an immediate response.

'I'm sorry, Liam. That... that really sucks.'

'Oh, that's not even the best part.' Liam hobbled towards him, dragging his injured leg behind. 'You see, the image of that cock was seared into my mind. I couldn't get it out of my head. And then I remembered something.' He stopped walking. With only the tripod between them, and the light from the LED panel illuminating his face from below, there was no mistaking the loathing in his cold, grey eyes. 'There was a birthmark on his right thigh. Now, you and I, we've known each other since we were five. Went to school together. Had swimming lessons together. And I happen to know that you've got that exact same birthmark on *your* right thigh. Haven't you Benjamin *Oliver* Aston? Or should I just call you Olly now?'

Time seemed to stop.

Ben couldn't breathe. Couldn't think over the sound of his pulse racing in his ears. His entire body tensed. Liam knew. Liam knew *everything*. And now he was stuck 70 feet underground with him in an abandoned tunnel.

'I... I didn't... we didn't... it just—'

'Shut up!' Liam bellowed, his voice a deafening echo that resounded in the space around them. 'You were my friend Ben.

You were my fucking friend and you betrayed me. You both betrayed me.' He took a breath, his mask of rage smoothing into something more composed. A cruel smile twisted at the corners of his lips. 'I've waited for this moment for so long.'

Ben stumbled back. Every fibre of his being screamed at him to run, but his legs were dead weight. The camera quivered in his white-knuckled grip. A high-pitched keen was the only warning before the LED panel flared blinding white. It exploded with a crack, scattering shards of plastic in all directions.

Darkness swallowed him whole.

A shriek ripped from Ben's throat. He turned on his heel and sprinted, lurching blindly through the pitch-black tunnel. There was no telling which way he was fleeing. He stumbled, righted himself and stumbled again.

Laughter resonated around him, coming from nowhere and everywhere all at once. Ominous. Menacing. Hateful.

Ben's eyes bulged, tears streamed down his cheeks. He was blind. Helpless. His chest was burning, every rasping breath fire in his lungs.

His foot caught on something firm. His ankle twisted. Unable to keep his footing, he pitched forward with a yelp. The camera jammed painfully into his chest as he landed on top of it. Scrabbling to his knees, he lunged out wildly — sure that Liam was right behind him. His fists met nothing but air.

The laughter stopped.

Ben waited for the blow, muscles trembling. Dust coated his skin, filled his mouth, so that every wheeze was more painful than the last. He rummaged in his coat for his inhaler.

Gone.

He must have lost it when he fell. Blind panic set in. He clawed at the floor around him, stone and grit tearing at his hands. His fingers brushed something hard. He grabbed at it. The camera!

Jabbing at the display, he choked out a sob as the glow of the screen burst into life — frozen on a still of the empty tunnel. If Liam was looking for him it would give him away for sure, but he had no choice. In the dim light, he saw the inhaler. Lunging forward he snatched it up and rammed it into his mouth, sucking the medicine into his lungs. Releasing the breath, he shoved the inhaler back in his pocket and, hands shaking, cast his makeshift torch around. There was barely enough light to see more than a few inches. If he could just make it to the passage that linked through to the Westbound tunnel, maybe he could follow the track back to Knightsbridge.

Pausing, he strained to listen. There were no footsteps. No sounds of movement. Nothing to indicate where Liam was. Just the buzz of flies and the putrid stench of decay.

He shuffled on his knees, trying to orientate himself. Throbbing agony lanced through his ankle with every movement. It wasn't broken, but there wasn't a chance in hell he'd be able to walk on it. There was nothing for it, he'd just have to crawl on his hands and knees back the way he came until he found the tunnel's edge.

Ben lowered the light, there was something in the dirt just in front of him. A trainer? His chest tightened. Slowly, deliberately, he moved the camera upward, trying and failing to keep it steady. The trainer was immediately followed by a leg, its jeans slashed open where a warped piece of gore-coated metal protruded from the bloody fabric beneath. Fat, greedy blue bottles flitted around the wound. He barely noticed them, his attention fixated on the mass of maggots writhing inside the open gash.

He gagged, bending to the side just in time to vomit the entire contents of his stomach across the floor.

After several dry heaves, he straightened and swiped his sleeve across his mouth. His hand moved almost of its own accord, forcing the light further up the body. He didn't want to look, but some part of him needed to know. Needed to dispel the intrusive thoughts invading his brain.

Slowly, reluctantly, he peered at the pallid face of the corpse. Sunken grey eyes stared vacantly up at nothing. Its jaw had dropped, exposing a reddish froth oozing from its mouth.

'*Liam?*'

It didn't make any sense. It couldn't be Liam, they'd been together just moments ago. He knew very little about dead bodies, but he knew enough to understand that this one had been dead for at least a couple of days. But it looked just like him…

What the fuck was happening?

He had to get out of here. Had to get away.

Forcing his limbs to move, he shuffled back. His palm struck something smooth and solid. He glimpsed down. A phone! He could call for help! He snatched it up, stabbing at the power button with his thumb. Bringing it closer to the light he cursed. The screen was smashed. But then how had its torch worked earlier?

Liam's words rang in his ears: *I dropped it when I fell.* Ben's gaze locked onto the piece of metal skewering the corpse's leg, remembering Liam's limp.

The pieces clicked into place.

An invisible force wrenched the camera from his grip, pitching it through the air. It landed with a crack, plunging him once more into darkness.

Absolute darkness. Suffocating, all-consuming, darkness.

Paralysed by terror, Ben made a strangled noise. He was alone. Injured. Trapped beneath the ground with no way to call for help. No one knew where to find him. And he'd gone willingly; like a lamb to the slaughter.

He could hear nothing above the sound of his own breathing and the rabbiting thump of his heart. Warmth spread down his inner thigh.

'*Liam?*'

'I keep telling you. I'm right here.'

19. SKATE *BORED*

by Tim Stephens

London, England.

She saw him for the first time in the record shop, having seen movement on the opposite side of the vinyls display. This part of the story though, isn't about 'an instant attraction' or anything like that. No, this is actually towards the end of the story. Maybe even *after* the end.

Sian had been focusing on the titles in the display in front of her, as she flicked through the vinyl covers. She was after quite a rare artist to add to her collection, to be used for her next set maybe. No, she knew this person, she had been in anticipation of him appearing at some point; she just didn't know when he was going to show up. It was like a final promise he had spelt out to her.

Sian had been in the shop alone; she had nodded to the owner, whom she knew a little. He had come out of the back with a coffee, having heard Sian enter a few minutes before. She had noticed the figure in her line of vision, **nodding at her,** jumping when she focused in on him. There he was.

Adam had always turned up unexpectedly; he was kind of the stalking type, if there is such a type. He seemed to get a kick from covertly watching people – not joining in, just observing. In return, she had observed that his tattoos seemed to have faded almost, up and down both arms and around his neck. That was what attracted her to him in the first place, **way back, what, four years ago?** She had thought he was 'cool'. He knew how to dress down well. How to arrange himself for 'the look'. The chains, the piercings, the skateboard, the swagger - he had it all, and she loved it. Adam's massive tattoo of an eagle, wings outstretched across his torso, with a human skull in place of the bird's head was something else. Sian had covered her mouth with her hand the first time she had seen it, it was that impressive. He had travelled quite a way to get that one done. But, aside from all the accessories, it was just the rest of him that was the problem and what had been going on in that head of his.

Let's go back to the beginning, to what started as a story of young love. Sian met Adam through a friend – they all hung out in the local park. They would go to the skatepark, drink alcohol and smoke down there and generally waste time. It was great in the summer, with a huge crowd gathering regularly. Adam was one of them – he was so good on his board, doing loads of tricks, almost effortlessly. Sure, he had a lot of gear and no, he didn't have a job. But Sian wasn't really at an age where you start questioning things like that. She was just so caught up in it all. It really was fun – back then.

She had heard Adam showing off at the park about what he had been 'lifting' from shops, and when she first started going out with him, she quite liked the fact that he kept getting things for her. The smoking wasn't a problem, nor the drinking, as he didn't actually drink that much in the early days, since being only slight in build, it didn't take much.

As things got more serious, Sian noticed more behaviour traits she didn't like. She found it quite thrilling if she was honest, in the early days. He definitely had a dangerous side, did Adam. He seemed to be attracted to risk, it was literally like he played with fire and thrived on the buzz. Yeah, he definitely got a thrill from it, but it was okay when he was in control of it. As time went on though, the balance changed, and it didn't go unnoticed by Sian. As the years passed, what she was originally content with became less appealing. She knew he used to like to smoke a lot of weed, but so did most of the kids down the skatepark. It was when Adam started messing about with the 'crystal meth' that things took a dramatic change for the worst.

Sian started pulling back, as it really wasn't her thing. While Adam was changing, so too was Sian. She was wanting more out of life. She was aspiring now to greater things. Her DJ-ing was starting to take off and she had quite a good following on social media. Her part-time fashion studies course was also taking her mind elsewhere. She wanted more than this; hanging out locally was not doing it for her anymore. She wanted to 'go places'.

Adam's character changed when he started on the crystals. Some of his worst traits came to the fore. Along with the weight loss, Adam was becoming more impulsive; he had zero patience and his rationality was non-existent. They had had a few bad arguments over the years – and while Adam had never laid a finger on her, when he lost it, he became dangerously violent. He was destructive, to the point that he would smash things up and kick people's cars for example. Anything that he saw as being in his way, he would bash, smash, scratch or lob. It had scared Sian when he was like this on quite a few occasions. Sian continued easing back, doing other things, coming to the park less often, choosing to head up town instead. But this didn't sit well with Adam. They had had quite a few run-ins, and, while Adam never turned on her, he would make threats instead.

He started messing around with knives – she knew he always carried one with him. But, he started to threaten to cut himself if Sian chose to do other things. He did it a few times – it was pretty gross as he opened up his arm in front of her. Probably because he was on that stuff, it was like he wasn't feeling the pain. Staring at Sian, grinning at her, as his skin parted and the blood trickled down his arm. He would stop when the flow got too bad. Somehow, he knew when to stop. Then, he would get patched up and turn up the next day at the skatepark, with a bandage around his arm. When kids asked him about his injury, he would make something up about having a bad fall on the way home while doing some stunt or trick. The younger kids would always be impressed, not knowing the truth about the source of his troubles. A couple of times his dad had to take him to A&E to get stitched up. It was a shame his dad didn't take more notice of his son, given the change in his appearance, the mood issues and the general downward trend. Sian thought that, maybe, if Adam's mum was still around, she would have noticed.

It all came to a head last summer, as Sian increasingly withdrew from Adam's company. They had had a couple more 'incidents', in which Adam had threatened to cut himself, if she didn't spend more time with him. Sian didn't want to and she didn't like some of the new 'friends' Adam was hanging out with; they were older than him and clearly into some serious stuff. They must have been supplying Adam with 'the gear'. She had heard on the grapevine that one of the new acquaintances had been in trouble with the police a few times – generally, there was a bad air about them all.

Sian was going to go to a friend's big party in the West End. Adam, however, wasn't invited as he was in the other crowd. This was a 'clean party': a modest amount of alcohol, lots of soft drinks, definitely no drugs, smart casual – i.e. clean clothes. Adam asked Sian not to go, but to come to the park instead and hang out with them. They were going to start late at the park, as a friend was coming down from another area who was bringing some strong gear with him. However, Sian refused to change plans, but Adam had been texting her repeatedly over the last few days, asking her to come and meet his new friend at the park. Sian didn't want to as it just wasn't her thing anymore. She liked the look – the emo style, the fashion, but all of the stuff with Adam was getting way out of hand. The original sentiment wasn't there anymore – what she thought it all stood for had shifted. Or had she just been blind? Had she misinterpreted it all, as she fell head over heels in love? She didn't feel safe with Adam anymore as he was like dynamite, with erratic behaviour. His humour was really dark, his interests were becoming more unsavoury. It scared Sian – he had gone over the line of where Sian wanted to be, with the 'alternative lifestyle' stuff. She didn't want to be associated with that.

So, she told him quite firmly she wouldn't be coming. He repeatedly texted her in response, to the point where she told him she didn't want to see him for a while. He took this really badly, telling her he would come down to her flat and talk her round. She lied and told him her parents were there and not to come. The messages kept coming and they were getting more demanding. It all culminated in Adam saying in his final message that 'she wouldn't see him again'. She replied, asking what he meant. She had been through this a few times with him before, when she wanted things to cool off a bit. It was all or nothing with Adam. He had threatened to do himself in, but hadn't followed through, thankfully. Sian had last texted Adam to say they should both do their own things on the Saturday night. She tried to soften the blow by lying that they could meet on the Sunday. Adam had replied simply with a 'bye'. At that point, Sian just hadn't realised the significance of that term in his message.

Back in the record shop, Adam could not be seen by the owner, Sian was in full view, not that she was light-fingered – she was happy to pay her way. Adam grabbed a handful of the street-style jewellery that was on the display, which was popular with the skater crowd, and dropped them into the inside pocket of his gilet. He gave Sian a knowing grin and winked. She didn't respond, as she knew the shop owner would think she was the one who was up to something. Sian also didn't want to connect with Adam anymore. She didn't want to encourage him, as he was still unpredictable in her mind, even in this state. He held up his arms to reveal his wrists to her. She turned away – she couldn't look. It was still too raw in every sense.

Sian turned and headed towards the exit – she stopped for a second and caught the attention of the guy on the counter, asking him if he could keep an eye out for anything by this particular artist. He said he would check his suppliers for the next time she came in. As she was about to leave, he asked her who she had been looking at just before, he said it creeped him out. He must have noticed her staring across to Adam, which must have come across as strange. She denied any knowledge of what he was talking about and left. She crossed the pavement to head across the great expanse of the main road. It was unusually quiet for an A-road, heading into the capital. She stopped on the central reservation to let a couple of cars pass, glanced down and jumped. She could see a trail of fresh blood, leading across the road. Looking across to the other side, she could see Adam had beaten her in getting across the road. He was standing there grinning, leaning against a parked car, with his skateboard propped up against his leg. He would have looked quite cool if it hadn't been for the fact that he was bleeding excessively from his wrist and arm. It looked like Adam had had another go at opening up his arm further. He had a vest on, but the flesh on his left arm – with the tattoo sleeve - was hanging off, literally like a loose sleeve of a patterned shirt. The 'material' had a sickly, deep-red lining. It matched his raw forearm underneath and the deep-red blood trail that had dripped down the car, which was particularly dramatic, as he had chosen to lean against a white car.

Sian stopped on the pavement – shouting across to Adam to leave her alone. She said she just wanted to get on with her own life, and that she was sorry for what had happened. A woman came out of a shop and saw Sian shouting, pulled a disapproving face and steered a wide course away from her. Sian looked back across the road and saw the record shop owner standing in the doorway, watching her, a puzzled look on his face. Sian looked back to Adam, who had turned and sped off down the road on his board. He was doing his usual flips and spins, despite the state of his wrists. Adam had obviously listened to Sian, as she never saw him again after that. It was like he had come back in the form of an apparition one more time to hear what she had to say. Maybe "sorry" had done it for him.

Last summer - the night of the parties - was when it finally all unravelled and the extent of Adam's problems became catastrophically clear. Adam's text messages had stopped after Sian suggested not seeing each other on the Saturday, preferring to meet on the Sunday. Maybe Adam knew she was fobbing him off and had no intention of meeting him the next day. **She didn't get a reply all day Friday, or during Saturday after the sudden 'bye' message.** She had gone to the park to see if Adam was there – which she was reluctant to do, as she feared it might be sending out the wrong message. His friends said they hadn't seen him since the previous day.

Sian carried on as usual, and returned to her flat, having been shopping in town with a couple of friends after leaving the park. She had bought a new outfit for the party, and, with not much time left, she got herself ready to go out for the night. She made an extra effort as she anticipated making some contacts at the party to help with her fashion ambitions, since her friend had said a few of her acquaintances were in the business.

Catching a taxi, en route to the party and a couple of blocks away from her flat, Sian, by chance glanced down an adjacent road and thought for a moment she had seen Adam heading in her direction. It was strange to see him in this neighbourhood - if it *was* actually him - as he rarely came this way. He had always said it was 'too posh' an area and made him feel uncomfortable. She dismissed it as a mistaken identity and focused on the evening ahead.

Sian had a great time; the new restaurant in Covent Garden was a really pleasant surprise, with the rest of the evening at the party making a lovely change from her usual activities. In fact, it was the best night she had had in a long time. She was able to clear her mind of some of the traumatic things that had been going on in her life recently, what with Adam and his erratic behaviour. Her close friends had been growing increasingly concerned for her and had been making more direct suggestions that things were not right. Maybe Sian should have listened to them in the early days, but she had unfortunately chosen to ignore them.

As Sian got back to her flat, she could tell something was amiss, as the lock on the external door to the building didn't feel right, as if it had been tampered with in some way. She headed up to the top floor, where, on turning the corner to her flat, she could see her door was slightly ajar. She chose to go in, probably as she had had quite a few drinks – ordinarily, she would have called the police. As she walked in, she could tell Adam had been in her flat; it looked like he had forced the lock. She could smell he had been smoking joints in there. His skateboard was in the hall. But where was he? She glanced into the bedroom and could just make out someone lying in her bed. She pushed the door open further and could now see it *was* Adam. She called out to him, but he didn't respond. He looked restful, so she thought he was either in a deep sleep or had passed out, having smoked too much. The covers were right up to his neck. She tapped him, then rocked his body. Something didn't seem quite right. She slowly pulled back the covers and immediately shrieked; he was literally soaked in blood, including the underside of the duvet, as well as the sheets, which were all completely covered. She ran back across the bedroom, holding a piece of paper that she had pulled out from between Adam's fingers. In turning on the light, she could see Adam was completely white. She touched him and felt he was cold. She ran through to the kitchen where she was violently sick in the sink. She looked at the piece of crumpled paper – it was titled **'He was a sk8er boi - she said see you l8er boi…'**

Adam had cut his wrists hours before. He had quickly lost consciousness soon after writing the note for Sian, so had been dead for quite a few hours when she discovered his body. It was as if all his blood had drained from him into Sian's bed. A strong, pungent smell of blood was in the air. After calling the police, Sian sat on the floor of the hall sobbing, reading the note over and over again. Adam had said he was sorry, that he couldn't face slowly losing her and that he felt this was his only way out. He apologised again, signing off with a final 'p.s.', saying that he would come back. This was why Sian was not completely surprised to see Adam, which, in the circumstances, is quite something to say.

He had caused a lot of inconvenience for her, what with being evicted from her flat, her landlord having pointed out that he would have trouble re-letting the flat now with it linked to a suicide. She lost her deposit and had to move on. She had to move back to her parents for a while, until she got over the shock. She felt traumatised for a patch of time, understandably. Things moved on though and Sian worked her way through her studies. She kept her part-time job as well as doing the DJ-ing at weekends around London. She took on another flat on the riverside overlooking the Thames, and started developing another network of friends. Some were linked to her music interests, some were into fashion and worked in the industry, while others were associates she had met through her everyday job.

It was during the first week in her new flat, that the final 'surprise' came. She had had the flat warming party in her new place - quite a modest, civilised affair really. Maybe it was a gift from him – the skateboard that appeared in the hallway as she returned home from work one day. It was a top-of-the-range model; it had some great wheels on it. It was almost a waste really as she wouldn't be using it – having 'moved on'. She still whistled as she picked it up – as she flipped it over, she saw the unique design on its underside – the eagle emblem, wings outstretched with a human skull in place of its head. The board had a kind of super gloss finish; it would have cost a lot of money. She felt bad for wondering if Adam had stolen it, even in death, but thinking about it more, she realised this was a proper custom job. Adam had somehow had this made for her. He had also left her some of the skater jewellery he had lifted from the record shop when she had last seen him.

With time, as Sian had sorted out her flat, the board had pride of place on the wall of her new lounge, in the corner over her DJ decks. It had the skater jewellery draped off it. She saw the board as a memento of an earlier phase in her life. She had no hard feelings now; she had come out the other side and wanted to put it in a prominent place, while she got on with her new life. When Adam had 'come back' that time in the record shop, he looked kind of happier than he had ever been before. More content in death, off the stuff and free, maybe, even if his tattoos had taken a turn for the worse. He left Sian a gift, and that was the end of it. Nothing after that, so he must have departed finally, perhaps even heading to a skatepark in the sky. Who knows? It just left Sian with one more thing to do. She hurried across the lounge as her emotions took her and flung open the French doors that led to her balcony, overlooking the Thames. She inhaled a huge gulp of air and shouted at the top of her voice – "THANK YOU ADAM." That was thanks for two things. It was of course a thank you for the farewell gift, but also a thank you for letting her get on with her new life.

20. BONE ZIPPER

by William Long

Hertfordshire, England.

Emily Ruskin woke up hungry. It was probably two or three in the morning, which was the time her stomach's growls normally woke her up. She'd never had this problem at home but since moving to St. Joseph's Boarding School in Hertfordshire, which felt a world away from home, she had found her appetite would peak at the most inconvenient times.

She opened the drawer beside her bed, pulled out her phone, and saw that it had just turned 2:45. She listened to see if anyone else in the dorm room was still awake but couldn't hear anything but gentle breathing and light snoring. There were thirteen other girls in her dorm room, and as far as she could tell, they were all fast asleep.

Excellent, Emily thought as she slipped out of bed, pulled on her school blazer, and quietly tied up her black leather shoes. She pulled an extra pair of socks *over* the shoes, so that she wouldn't make as much noise as she disappeared out of the bedroom and into the hallway.

The hallway contained a dozen other doors that led to a mixture of fourteen-bed dorm rooms, four-bed dorm rooms, and single rooms with en-suites, which were primarily occupied by the wealthiest students. One of the doors led to the communal bathroom and the final door led outside into the cold.

She unlocked the door as quietly as she could and flipped the latch to lock it open, so that she could come back in without having to use the number pad, which beeped loudly as she entered the passcode.

Emily walked outside into the chilly playground. A few spotlights illuminated the concrete as a breeze blew the rustling leaves across the concrete. Emily buttoned her blazer and immediately regretted not putting on her hoodie instead. There was no time to change. Returning to her room meant risking waking up one of the girls.

She could make her way from the dorm room to the cafeteria by almost staying in the shadows the whole way, so long as she kept close to the bushes that lined the classrooms. The only time she had to pass through the light was when she moved from the front door of the music block to the back door of the cafeteria. Emily stood in shadow and looked around her to make sure the security guard wasn't on one of his night-time patrols. He wasn't. He would have either been in his office, watching the security cameras, or, Emily hoped, on a toilet break.

Emily dashed across the lit playground in five long strides until she landed in the safe darkness by the rear entrance to the school cafeteria. After hours, the student buildings such as the dorm rooms and the sixth-form block only required a six-digit passcode to enter but the other rooms, such as the classrooms, offices and, in Emily's case, the cafeteria, also required a key.

Being as resourceful as she was, Emily had taped over the door latch with a piece of duct tape earlier that day. She had eaten her dinner slowly to ensure that she was one of the last students to leave the cafeteria. She had palmed a small piece of tape and, as she left, she had stuck it to the latch in one swift movement.

She hoped that it was still there.

She tapped in the passcode - 091856, which was the month and year the school was founded: September 1856 - and winced as each number beeped. If she was going to be caught, it would be now. She braced herself, anticipating that the security guard would shine his flashlight upon her and catch her in the act.

Nothing happened. She was safe.

She opened the door to find the tape was still there and the door hadn't locked. She ducked in before she could be found.

The cafeteria was warm and quiet. Even though she wore her socks on the outside of her shoes, the echoes of her soft footsteps ricocheted around the whole cafeteria. She heard a light scuttle in the far corner. A mouse. Lizzy MacDonald had sworn she'd seen one the previous week.

The kitchen was easy to get into. All Emily had to do was jam her ID card into the door crack, which pushed the latch away from the lock and allowed her to simply pull down the door handle, remove her ID card and open the door without a problem.

Now, what have we here? Emily wondered as she headed straight for the walk-in fridge. It felt icy inside. She peered around at the fresh fruit, vegetables, meat, and fish, that would be served over the following weeks for breakfast, lunch, dinner and, in Emily's case, a 3 am snack.

'Bingo,' Emily whispered as she eyed a tray of left-over iced buns. She knew that they were just hotdog buns dipped in icing and topped with sprinkles, but my gosh they were delicious, especially when they were stolen from the kitchen in the middle of the night. Emily always thought that stolen food was the tastiest food, ever since she had snuck into the school kitchen during her third night at St. Joseph's.

She scoffed one iced bun on the spot, barely allowing herself to taste it. It was cold, sweet, and ever-so-slightly stale, but it hit all the spots. She felt her hunger start to subside and snatched up another one to eat on the walk back.

She left the kitchen, removed the tape from the cafeteria door, and retraced her shadowy steps back to her dorm room.

All in all, it was another successful night-time excursion, and as Emily finished the last bite of the second bun and licked the icing from her fingers, using the gap in her front teeth to scrape the icing trapped beneath her fingernails, she was grateful that she hadn't been caught.

As she entered her dorm room, she heard a sound that sliced through the silence. It was a slow zipping sound, as though someone was quietly opening their gym bag so as to not wake up the other students.

Zzziiiiiiiiiiipp…

Crap, Emily thought, fearing that she was going to be found out. She hadn't told any of her friends about her night-time adventures, not even Claire Savoy, who was her default best friend because their fathers were both partners at the same law firm and they had grown up two roads apart before coming to the same boarding school the year they turned eleven.

She heard another long, slow *zip*. She glanced around the dorm room that was only dimly illuminated by the cracks in the curtains but then realised that the room was brighter than it was when she had left. One of the curtains was wide open and she saw the dark shape of someone move away from Lizzy MacDonald's bed.

Emily let out a silent sigh of relief. Lizzy and Jacob Brindleford must have gotten back together. By the end of the last school year, they were always sneaking into each other's beds in the middle of the night to make out.

The window opened, sending a quick burst of cool air through the dorm, and then closed again as Jacob left.

As Emily pulled the covers back over her, with her hunger now satisfied, she heard several sleeping students shuffle beneath their duvets.

They must have felt the chill from the open window, Emily thought as she fell asleep.

'Help!' A girl shrieked, jolting Emily awake well before her alarm was supposed to go off. 'Someone get the nurse!'

The screams were coming from an athletic girl called Hannah Oak, who was in Lizzy's close-knit circle of friends and played on the school's lacrosse team.

A crowd had already formed around Lizzy's bed by the time Emily had reached it. She looked past the other students and saw Lizzy, blue as ice, gasping for air. Her face contorted in hideous ways as she struggled to breathe. Her eyes were wide open, staring at the ceiling, unable to see the other students.

'Give her my inhaler!' Karen Millstream shouted over the noise, reaching towards Hannah with her asthma inhaler. Hannah snatched it out of Karen's hands and held it to Lizzy's blue lips. She pressed down on the canister so Lizzy could inhale the medicine.

The school nurse burst into the room and sent the gawking students outside so that she could address the situation without thirteen teenage girls getting in the way.

Within fifteen minutes Lizzy was on the way to hospital, and within two hours she was dead.

Much to everyone's surprise, it turned out that Lizzy MacDonald only had a single lung. Her parents hadn't known, and Lizzy had never had any chest x-rays, so her doctors hadn't known. The day she had died was the only time that Lizzy had ever complained about her breathing – except for that time she had tried to get out of cross-country because it was her birthday, and she couldn't wait to see what Jacob Brindleford had bought for her as a present.

That night, none of the students could sleep and everyone was still chatting well past midnight when Emily was ready to eat. The headmistress had cancelled classes for the following day and had announced that any student who wanted could return home for a week or could temporarily relocate to another dormitory. Five girls had chosen to return home, including Hannah Oak, who was a complete wreck the last time Emily had seen her, and another three girls had asked to move dorms and were temporarily sleeping in a four-bed room in the boy's dormitory.

At three in the morning, the conversations had died down and the seven remaining girls finally decided to go to sleep. The other six girls had decided to pair up and squeeze into three of the skinny beds for the night. Emily insisted that she would be fine sleeping on her own but moved into one of the beds that was closer to the other six girls, which had belonged to Chloé Hamilton who was now sleeping beside Susie Lambeth. As she fell asleep, she couldn't help but remember the strange noise that she had heard the night before:

Zzziiiiiiiiiiiipp...

Emily Ruskin woke up feeling cold.

This is a new one, she thought, expecting to either need to pee or for her stomach to be rumbling in anticipation of whatever dessert the lunch ladies had prepared the day before.

She pulled her duvet up to her neck and shivered beneath her covers. She then heard the window slide shut and she snapped open her eyes, suddenly realising that it probably hadn't been Jacob Brindleford sneaking in the night before.

Emily immediately felt wide awake. She looked around at the three other occupied beds: Julia and Isabelle were in one, fast asleep with Julia's arm cuddling Isabelle over the duvet. Priya and Fiona were in a second bed, also fast asleep, and in the third bed were--

A dark shape moved in front of the third bed. The curtain by the window hadn't been closed all the way and the dorm was much lighter than it was supposed to be this late at night.

Emily realised that it must have been the chill from the window opening that had woken her up.

Susie and Chloé were sleeping in the third bed. Emily could just about make out Chloé's face. She was sleeping with her mouth open as the dark shape moved in front of Susie and blocked her from Emily's sight.

Emily felt her body tense. She didn't know if she should shout for help or shut her eyes. Maybe it was fine. Maybe it was the nurse, or a teacher, or the security guard checking up on them, making sure that they were all fine and sleeping sweetly and--

Emily struggled to quieten her breathing as she heard the same sound as the night before: that horrid zipping sound that made her bones rattle.

She tried to see what was happening, but the dark shape had its back to her. Instead, she heard a wet slopping sound, like a raw steak being laid on a chopping board. Emily's eyes were cracked open just enough for her to see out of, in the hopes that whoever - or whatever - was in the room would think that she was fast asleep. Emily then saw them pick something up from the bed and place it with a soft rustle into a large leather bag.

What are they doing?

Ziiiiipp...

The second zip was shorter and faster than the first. As the dark shape moved from one side of the bed to the other, Emily could see that it was a man because of the broadness of his shoulders.

No, she thought as she saw the curves of their hips, *it's a woman...*

As they stopped moving and the dim moonlight emanating from the window lit up the figure, Emily realised that she may have been wrong a second time. It neither looked masculine nor feminine. It had long thin arms, and wide bowing legs that moved with such horrid grace that its head stayed level as it walked.

Emily caught sight of its face but there didn't seem to be any distinguishing features. There was the shape of a nose, and the divots of eyes, and the curves of lips but they all seemed to be lacking any recognisable definition.

It climbed up onto the bed, its wide legs straddled Chloé's body as she slept. Emily opened her eyes further.

It's wearing a mask! Emily thought, realising that whatever was crouched over Chloé Hamilton had smooth porcelain features that reflected what little moonlight reached into the room.

It held something in its hands that Emily couldn't quite make out. Her vision buzzed with grainy noise as her eyes strained against the darkness. The intruder held something in their hands that looked like an ivory-white zipper, with two rows of jagged teeth, clasped together, and a large, ornate pull tab that connected to the slider that zipped and unzipped the teeth—

The zip! Emily realised as she looked at the zipper, which she would have sworn was made of bone. She had seen zippers like it in textiles class when they were learning how to make pillows. The students had fought over the different coloured unattached zippers - Emily had landed the only silver one - and then sewed it into their pillows. The zipper in the intruder's hands was like that: unattached.

It laid the bone zipper over Chloé's chest and gently pressed it in place. The intruder slowly unzipped it with a long, slow *zziiiiiiiiiiipp*...

It pulled the zipper apart, which almost looked like they were opening Chloé's body, and plunged their hands into the zipper and into Chloé's chest. After a few seconds they pulled out a large chunk of meat... an organ...

Her liver! Emily realised, recognising the organ from their biology class last year.

It then dropped the liver into a large black bag, zipped up the bone zipper, and lifted it from Chloé's chest. After a few moments, her breathing died down, almost completely.

It's stealing our organs!

Emily instinctively gripped the top of her duvet even tighter, causing it to rustle.

The creature jerked its head to look at Emily, despite not having any eyes that Emily could see. It cocked its head like a curious dog and then reached into its leather bag, the one that contained Chloé's liver and whatever organ it had lifted from Susie. It pulled out a thin, bone-white mask. It took the featureless mask that it was already wearing off its face with a terrible rip, as though the mask was fused to the skin beneath. Its head was pure black and round as though it was crudely moulded out of wet clay, yet Emily *knew* that it was looking right at her. It was staring *into* her.

The nightmarish creature then placed the new bone-mask to its face, finally giving it features that Emily recognised as almost human: large black eyes, a long, thin nose, and a grin so wide that it looked like a crescent moon.

The creature lurched forward, never taking its fake eyes off Emily, and Emily felt comforted by it. Its large eyes started to feel less like unending pits, and more like the eyes of a sweet puppy, and its wide, thin smile made Emily feel safe, and happy. It reminded her, in some ways, of her own mum's reassuring smile. The mask helped to soothe her fear, as the creature slid over the bed and silently scuttled across the dorm room floor towards her.

Emily took a deep breath and closed her eyes, knowing that there was nothing to worry about. She felt a comforting weight lower itself on top of her, as the creature found her bed. It felt like a purring kitten asleep on her chest. As the duvet was pulled back from her, she no longer felt the coldness of the room, instead she felt a sweet, comforting warmth. Emily smiled as she allowed herself to drift off to sleep, listening to the restful sound of a long, slow, *zzzzzip*…

21. PLOUGH MONDAY

by Benjamin Langley

Cambridgeshire, England.

As the last peal of the church bell signals the arrival of Plough Monday, Mary tightens her grip on Albert's hand. Four decades of harsh farm labour have made it coarse and strong, but Albert returns the grip with the tenderness that has been present through the thirty-five years of their marriage. Together, they've faced adversity in the past, but never before have they been so tense on this night. But never before has the harvest failed so badly, and never before have they left such a small offering. Albert mutters a curse for the water that flooded his land for the first time since the failed attempt to drain the Fens around Whittlesey, back when he was still a boy and his father was responsible for the offering. At least there were sufficient potatoes and a pile of onions not rendered worthless by the maggots of the onion fly, but was it enough? It hadn't been for his father all those years ago. Albert looks around his kitchen, wishing to commit it to memory in case he will see it no more after this night.

Sensing his worry, Mary rubs the back of Albert's hand with her thumb. They hold their breaths for an eternity, all effort concentrated on listening, hoping. Mary eventually draws in a breath, but it's a relief that comes too early as bells tinkle from outside. That chime conjures an image quite contrary to what Albert suspects is out there as he recalls those monsters that stole his father away leaving only a pile of ash.

Albert swallows. His throat is so dry it feels like he has a coarse stone lodged in his throat. He struggles to moisten his lips. "Go light the bedroom candle," he says, withdrawing his hand.

He remembers his mother being sent to do likewise. Then, the townsfolk stayed away, claiming, when they turned up days later with condolences and guilty offerings, that they never saw the light.

If they don't come, if they ignore the call, Albert thinks, then the day's frivolity was merely a show. They gathered to perform the dance as they made their way through the town, knocking on doors and taking what their neighbours could afford to give, a contribution to the great feast which now sat heavy in Albert's gut. The performance heralds the beginning of the new farming season — a show of strength to ward away the forces of evil and protect those households who didn't leave enough for them. He wonders if Tom Parsons will come. He'd worn the straw bear, that woven head and torso of straw, and stood eight foot tall in the town square, beating his straw chest — a performance to strike fear into the Devil himself. Or so Albert had thought.

Perhaps the denizens of Hell were not so easily put off, for it was they who gathered outside.

From outside, a shrill whistle joins the bells. Albert places his hands on his knees and pushes himself up. Notes continue to play a haunting melody, a sound he remembers from before. He can hear his father's woeful cry, and the way he cursed that bog oak pipe. That was the last time the harvest was so poor: the last time the offering was so meagre.

The sound of footsteps coincides with the jingling of bells as the midnight visitors grow closer and another sound becomes apparent, the trundling of the painful plough, said to be constructed from human bones.

Albert knows he needs to go upstairs to prepare for the confrontation if he is to survive until dawn, but he can't help but approach the window and twitch the curtain to gaze out upon them. Immediately, so suddenly that he feels like his blood has frozen in his veins in that very instant, Albert knows he has made a mistake. Repressed memories from bygone years rush to smash him in the face — his father trudging out to face them alone. They'd fallen upon him, those red-skinned devils, and driven him to the ground.

Had he not seen them, had that memory not taken a chunk of his courage, he may have found the strength to face them, as his father had done. Now, with the image of their red-skinned faces, their bulging eyes, their hungry salivating mouths, he doesn't even know how he can take another step.

"The candle's lit." Mary's voice saves him, as she has done with her every action in their years together. Mary makes him a better person, gives him a reason to get up those stairs and to prepare. He pauses on the bottom step to look around the heart of his home one more time. A thousand memories flush out the image of what waits outside.

Mary has spread out his clothes at the foot of the bed. She stands by the wardrobe as he undresses. From outside, the intensity of the bells grows, joined by the pipe, and a new musician, a drummer, who drives the pace of the song to greater intensity before it breaks, only for a new song to emerge, slower. Albert immediately recognises it, and while the broken voices of the demonic choir distort the lyrics, he knows them well:

> *Come you worthless ploughmen, who farm the failing field,*
> *Your labours have been wasted on such a meagre yield.*
> *You promised us a mighty feast, and we demand it now,*
> *Make yourself the offering, beneath our painful plough.*

As they continue their song, Albert buttons up his white shirt. He pulls on his stockings. He ties the bells around his calves. When he removed them this evening, he was hoping it would be the harvest festival before he had to wear them again. Alas, no. As he ties the second set of bells on his other leg, another jingle draws his attention. For an instant, he fears one of the demons has entered his home. But it's worse: the bells are in his wife's hand. She too wears the attire that matches his, the uniform of the dancer, they that guard that thin veil between the world of darkness and our own.

Albert shakes his head. "Mary, you can't."

She ties the bells around her leg. "Am I to stand at the window and watch you fall alone?"

Albert gulps. "I won't fall alone. They'll come." He glances out of the window. While his candle flickers, he can see none reciprocating from the nearby farms. Have his fellow dancers really forsaken him? Have they forgotten the sacred and ancient pact which they celebrated only hours earlier? Will another generation come to pay their respects in days to come with excuses of a light unseen? Albert knows his neighbours would have stayed up late. They too would have listened for the bells. They too would have waited in fear that the forces of evil would fall upon them if their offering was deemed insufficient. But they had not lost their crop as he had.

Albert glances at Mary, dressed as he is. "And whether they come or leave us to our fate, I can think of no one I'd rather have by my side."

Mary rushes to her husband and they embrace, bells jingling with every movement. Outside the drums rise once more to a crescendo, and the first hands fall upon the door, scratching at the wood.

Albert reaches into his wardrobe and takes out the sticks, each a yard long. He hands one to Mary, and they take the stairs together. At the bottom, they stand before the door. From outside they hear the creatures screech through the song again, At least, for a moment, their assault on the door is paused. With their focus on the song, Albert knows there will be no better time to head outside if they are to avoid falling on their own doorstep. He battles with self-preservation, the instinct that insists he stay barricaded inside and hope help will come or the sun will rise before they make it inside. He cannot help another look around a room so full of warmth and memories. But legend says they always make it inside. He doesn't want this place tainted by their presence, even if he is to see it no more. Mary is poised by the door. Albert knows they have to do this. Holding his breath, he pushes the door open, grabs Mary's hand and dashes out, immediately hit by the intense heat that radiates from the creatures who pause for but a second before continuing their song. Albert and Mary stand back-to-back, surveying the scene around them. The painful plough, its bone glowing in the light on the moon, stands on the path, still held by two of the creatures. The door is flanked by four more. A dozen have taken up positions all around them, meaning there are no gaps to dart through. The piper continues piping and the drummer keeps drumming, and the circle of red-skinned hell-spawn closes in.

"We must dance," whispers Mary. Albert knows it's true, but the moment had fazed him, knocked him out of rhythm. He starts to pick up the beat, and, in tandem with his wife, he kicks out his left leg, sending the bells jingling against one another. A shrill shriek comes for the creatures in unison, and they too kick out in mimicry, their own bells repeating the sound. Albert, now, understands the nature of the bargain. With his produce too meagre, he must provide something more. The Devil and his minions love nothing more than the dance. If they can keep it up until sunrise, it may be enough. The creatures kick out again with their other leg. Albert and Mary this time are the ones to imitate which draws more delighted wailing from the beasts. Albert and Mary continue alternating kicks, but each iteration draws less amusement, and once more the creatures draw closer.

"Face me," Albert calls to Mary as they synchronise another kick.

Mary turns.

"On the fourth beat, kick to my side." Albert nods to his left and starts to count drum beats. When the time comes, he kicks out as Mary does likewise.

The creatures cackle, and he knows it's bought them a little more time. They continue the pattern, alternating kicks to each side, before Mary glances at the stick she holds in both hands and makes prolonged eye contact with her husband. He nods to signal his understanding, and when the time comes, when the beasts expect a kick, instead they smack those sticks together. They clash with a crack too loud for the size of the piece of the wood, too mighty for the force used. Even though the majority of his focus is on the continuing dance, over Mary's shoulder he notes some of the creatures recoil. Albert and Mary twist the sticks 90 degrees and clash them together again and Albert wonders if the sound is reminiscent for those beasts of Hell of the crack of the Devil's whip for, again, they step back and their cackling distorts into a panicked growl. Mary and Albert's sticks collide once more, but the demonic drummer, forever in control of the rhythm, stops.

Mary kicks out, but without the rhythm of the drum, it has no effect.

The creatures close in once more so they're near enough to smell, their sulphuric stink stinging Albert's and Mary's nostrils.

Albert watches, trying to hold off a shudder of revulsion. He shakes his leg, but without a beat, the creatures don't react.

"We set the rhythm," Mary calls. "Together, heel, together, heel."

Albert nods. "On three, two, one."

Their sticks collide. Still the creatures move. Together they lift their right legs, turn into a figure of four and hit the heel with the bottom of the stick, causing the bells to ring in a manner more manic than before. They twist the sticks, knock them together again before raising their left legs and hitting that heel. Without the drummer, without the piper, they play their own tune. Instead of closing in, the creatures start to circle, skipping around in time to the repeated clashing of sticks and the jingling of bells.

"It's working," Mary says. But Albert can feel the burn in his legs. With each hit, he can feel his arms weaken. Each breath is a struggle, and the position of the moon tells him there's still so much night left.

"Keep going," Mary says, sensing his weakness. But he detects something else in her voice, too, a glimmer of hope that has no place in her tone at all, considering what they're up against, unless…

From a distance comes the sound of a pipe, and it sounds natural, manmade, unlike that monstrous demon pipe. There comes the beat of an additional drum. The demon drummer responds with a rapid beat. The monster piper plays the same shrill note over and again, and the creatures stop, stand bolt upright, then turn as one to face Albert and Mary. Step by step, they close in, no longer affected by the jingling of bells or the clashing of sticks. They move now to the drummer's rapid beat, stirred on by the chaos of the pipes and the gnashing of their hungry teeth. The devils have decided it's time for the debt to be paid, and they demand flesh. The dance will no longer suffice.

Albert and Mary turn to look at the closing creatures. The approaching townsfolk grow nearer, too, illuminated by torches and marching to the beat of their own drum.

But they're too far away to arrive before the creatures take their feast.

"What do we do?" asks Mary, knowing the dance has lost its power.

Albert knows he would have fallen long ago without Mary beside him. The blood runs thick through his veins. Every motion sends a judder of pain into his chest and his limbs feel so heavy as if they're clad in iron. And yet he makes a defiant suggestion: "We make the music of sticks on skulls."

Despite their exhaustion, Albert and Mary begin a new dance, their choreography still entirely in step. Back-to-back, they circle slowly. They both clench the stick in two hands, and simultaneously swing. The sticks connect with the heads of the creatures with a crack that's followed by a thump as the minions of Hell fall to the earth with a final jingle of bells. They repeat the move and two more fall.

The townsfolk are close enough now that the white of their costume is visible, the bells around their calves audible, and the squeak of the wheelbarrow their leader pushes growing ever louder. Some of the creatures dart away, drawn to the visitors. Albert and Mary swing again, knocking two more down, and at this point, panic sets in among the devils. No more are they in the thrall of the piper. No more are they moving to the drummer's beat. Chaos rules, and they hunger no longer for flesh, but for survival. Some make for the plough. Others dash across the field on all fours, hoping to find safety in the lights, unaware that those very same lights have drawn many to their doom.

With the creatures retreating, Albert and Mary bring their dance to a close. Albert massages his chest as he draws in a breath. With his other hand, he still holds the stick aloft. He can't drop his arm. It's tingling, how he imagines it would feel if a bolt of lightning struck the stick and ran through his limb. He knows if the arm drops, he'll never lift it again. Mary gives him a nudge, concern painted on her face. There's something else in her eyes too, an orange glow that makes Albert forget about his pain and turn to look at what she sees. Yes, the rest of the community are near, two holding flaming torches to illuminate what's in the wheelbarrow: the straw bear.

The flaming torches illuminate the people of the town as they dance around the wheelbarrow, around the straw bear, carrying their own sticks, reaching out to clobber any creatures who close on them in time to their piper's song, a song of hope, not of the flesh-rendering frivolity that the demon piper played.

"Quick!" cries Mary. She grabs Albert's hand and leads him into the throng of human dancers. Now, among friends, Albert moves more freely, eagerly cracking another demon skull. The piper keeps piping, the dancers keep dancing and the creatures continue to fall, and as the song reaches it's crescendo, with the wheelbarrow pulling level with the bone plough, Albert realises only that lone demon piper remains. The drummer's drum lies beside the painful plough, its skin torn. The demon piper sits, cross-legged, a few yards beyond the plough, unaffected by his status as the lone representative of Hell. The human piper, Gerald Oakley of Birchover Farm, brings his song to a close, and the people of the village stop their dance. Tom Parsons, who has pushed the wheelbarrow all the way from his farm, takes a step back and urges those holding torches to light his cargo. Flame spreads across the straw bear, rising high, threatening to lick the moon. The heat it provides is comforting, not that searing, painful heat that radiates from the creatures. Fire spreads to cover the entirety of the straw costume, which somehow holds its shape. It can only be the enchantment of the night that maintains it for this finale.

Albert doesn't need Tom to direct him, for he knows the writing in the old book, the records of the old ways. He never thought it would come to this.

"Gerald," calls Tom, a croak breaking it after the first syllable. "Hand Albert the pipe."

Albert rubs his arm which continues to throb. He coaxes it down and releases the stick, letting it fall to the floor. It will crack no more skulls, not this night, not by his hand. He takes the pipe.

It is an effort even to bring it to his lips. His heart beats at a rhythm way beyond that of even the most joyous tune, but he knows his duty.

"It is your household that failed to provide adequate tribute. It is you who must play the song, drive him into the bosom of the straw bear."

Albert glances first at the flames dancing on that straw costume, then at the creature calmly awaiting their duel. Surely, the fiend can hear the tattoo of Albert's heart and knows this is no contest.

The creature stands. The time away from Hell's fire has diminished its glow. Patches of its skin are charred and blackened, other parts are an angry red, tender and juicy. It brings its pipe to its mouth and blows a single morbid note, signalling that it is ready to commence the duel.

Albert takes a heavy breath. It feels stuck, like he cannot breathe in again until a gasp rasps its way into him. He brings the pipe to his mouth, but it's so dry, the wood sticks to his lip. He has no breath to give, no song to play, save the beating of his heart which is surely audible to all around him. It's all he can hear, the pulse matched in the throbbing in his head, closing up his ears until Mary's voice breaks through.

"It is our household which failed to provide. I am a member of that household. I shall play the pipe."

Albert hears muffled protests, but none come from him. He relinquishes the pipe to his wife. Their fingers linger in a moment's touch. Albert wants so many more fleeting touches.

The creature grins, but only until Mary plays her first note, the one that signals the beginning of the final part of the night's encounter, then its fingers become a blur as it plays note after note at a frantic speed.

Mary fails to reciprocate. Knowing she cannot possibly imitate the devil's song, she plays a tune of her own, slow, mournful, each note lingering.

The creature again tries to stir Mary into a fevered response with its own blasts, still carrying some semblance of rhythm, but a tune of the damned.

Mary doesn't break. She continues with her low tone, until she springs a quick chirp of a pair of higher notes, mimicking birdsong, the break of day.

Albert eyes the horizon. The sun can't hide long in the Fens, for there are no mountains, no hills, barely a perceptible change in the gradient for it to hide behind. Even in the depths of winter, nights are shorter than in those lands with a greater variety of landforms. But it's still the domain of the moon.

The chirrups have unsettled the demon. He casts a glance over his shoulder, as Mary draws another chirp from her pipe.

Fearing the break of day, he renews his assault on the pipe. Each time he threatens to achieve some semblance of a tune, Mary blows into the pipe mimicking the starlings that refuse to leave for the winter.

The devil's song breaks down, becomes a series of discordant blasts, a raucous and incoherent cacophony of failure.

Mary plays a couple more chirps.

Defeated and confused, the demon piper throws down his instrument. He cannot be caught on the surface when day breaks. He seeks the salvation of Hell, the fires from which he arose. He sees the flames flicker in front of him, and he leaps for them.

As soon as his body enters the flaming mass of the straw bear, Tom overturns the wheelbarrow. The townsfolk hurry forward, their bells ringing as they stomp the fire, taking the life from it, and the demon, too, driving it down, into the land.

This is their offering. They hope it is sufficient.

Albert stumbles over to Mary and places his arm on her shoulder. Tom nods before leading the townsfolk away. They've righted a wrong from a generation ago, many of them the sons and daughters of those that betrayed his father, but they won't linger to celebrate; they've a day of farm labour to start in but a few hours when the sun truly rises, when the starlings start to sing.

But first, they'll remove the bells and the attire reserved for this day. They'll put away their sticks until next time they're required.

Albert bends down and picks up the demon's pipe. How is it so cold to the touch when everything about the creature was flame? He'll donate it to the museum. He'll write an account of the events of the night so should the crop fail and the offering be insufficient for those that follow, they'll know what to do. Albert massages his chest once more. He knows he won't be around much longer to pass on the story himself. No, he doesn't have long, but it could have ended on this night, and he'll treasure every last moment he has with Mary, who danced with him to confuse the creatures of Hell, who cracked demon skulls alongside him, who took the pipe and refused to play along to the Devil's tune.

He takes Mary's hand, and the feel of her flesh calms him. Together, they return home. There's still time to make more memories.

22. MEMENTO MORI

by Marie Sinadjan

Lincoln, England.

Death and I first met on a crisp spring day.

I was busking at the High Bridge that morning, setting up camp early to seize that prime spot across from Stokes. It was my first time back out after winter; three years in the country and I still couldn't stomach the cold.

There wasn't much of a crowd, but there wasn't any competition either, so I took my sweet time and remained far longer than I normally would. I didn't notice her until I took a water break in between sets and turned to gaze towards the river. She just sat there, on one of the rainbow-coloured benches, looking nothing like Death and more like a university student in her bright yellow cropped padded jacket, joggers, and white trainers. She had a sketch pad on her lap and was busy drawing — I assumed — me.

I kept looking back at her for the next quarter hour, stealing glances as I sang. Back then, I thought it was because she reminded me of my ex, Lillian, with her long, dark hair and equally dark eyes. I also wanted to give her a good angle, particularly of my jawline. My wife always said it was one of my best features.

I grabbed a coffee when I finished and sat next to her on the bench. She didn't look up or give any indication that she noticed me or my fantastic singing, still engrossed with her drawing. I cleared my throat, then made some comment about the weather in my YouTube tutorial British accent, but she only hummed noncommittally. Either she was deaf, or she didn't understand me.

Overpowered by my curiosity, I shuffled closer to peer at her work.

Don't get me wrong, it was fantastic. She was clearly talented, rendering people with an uncannily lifelike quality. But while she drew the white-and-black timber framed shop in front of us with incredible detail, as well as several of the passersby — I recognised the stingy old woman in a funny red hat from earlier, who'd dropped only coins into my guitar case — she left *me* out of the sketch. I was disappointed, to say the least.

"Don't you want to draw me?" I offered. I've always had confidence in spades.

She gazed up at me then, frowning. "Why?"

So she wasn't deaf. She even sounded like my ex with that smooth American accent. I used to be jealous of how well Lillian spoke, charming crowds left and right during our performances. She told me she did it to land us more gigs, but I knew better. She was a diva and an attention-seeker, and to her, I was competition.

"I make a great model," I proclaimed to the woman who I didn't know then was Death, flashing her my winning smile. The same grin that garnered me thousands of followers on TikTok.

"Huh," was all she said. Then she turned away and resumed sketching.

* * *

After that encounter, I saw her whenever I went out. She seemed to prefer loitering around the rainbow benches of the High Street, but she also had other haunts, most notably along Brayford Pool. She constantly hunched over a pad, sketching people, regardless of the weather or whatever was happening around her.

Yet she refused to sketch me every single time.

I didn't know why I was so drawn to her. She was hot, sure, but she was also *weird*, like Lillian had been.

"Draw me," I tried again that afternoon when I came across her in the Arboretum. She was sitting cross-legged on the grass by the pond, sketching a trio of tourists and the ducks they were feeding.

She didn't even spare me a glance. "No."

"I'll make it worth your while. Are you doing anything tonight? I cook a mean *adobo*." Well, it was technically my wife who'd cooked the dish and I only had the leftovers from our lunch, but she didn't have to know that. Neither did my wife; she was going to be on a night shift at the County Hospital later and, as always, would be none the wiser about my occasional overnight excursions.

That, finally, seemed to catch the artist's attention. She paused in the middle of outlining a fourth duck and gazed up at me. Her eyes were deep pools of shadows. It felt like staring into two black holes and just... falling.

"What about your wife?"

"How—"

She pointed at my wedding band with pursed lips, just like Lillian had been in the habit of doing.

"Ah, it's fine." I waved my hand with the ring dismissively. "She won't be home until eight."

"It's already four."

"*A.M.*," I emphasised, smirking.

She stared at me for a long moment. If I had known any better, I would have realised she'd been peering into the depths of my tainted soul and searching for (and failing to find) my name in St. Peter's book or whatever it was you believed about the afterlife. Dumb fool I had been, I thought she was finally reciprocating my interest — and how beautiful she would look pinned against a wall covered in her sketches, moaning breathlessly against me.

Let her draw *that*.

"Okay," she agreed, to my delight.

* * *

The night passed in a blur, mostly because of the bottles of prosecco we had over dinner. I told her about my life in the Philippines, and my frustrations as a musician who couldn't even make it to Britain's Got Talent. She was a good listener. She never once interrupted, and when she did, it was only to ask more questions that I was all too happy to answer, or to refill my glass.

She insisted on sketching me before we proceeded to the bedroom, though she'd only managed a rough outline, unable to ignore my wandering hands. She pretended to protest when I pulled her into my lap, but boy did she sigh when I kissed her neck. Hah. And I thought Western women were well beyond prudish pretensions.

She was long gone by the time my wife arrived, but I dreamed of her every night thereafter.

* * *

"You never let me finish," she complained as I grabbed the sketch pad and pencil from her hands and threw them on the coffee table. Today, it was a sketch of me busking in front of the mural wall near Starbucks. She had rendered the wall first, and she had taken so long that by the time she started outlining my figure, my impatience had become a fever on my skin.

I could not recall any other woman who had that effect on me — except Lillian, but that was first loves for you. This artist of whom I was the muse of stirred a fire in me that was growing out of control. It was infuriating. Yet it was also just so… addicting.

What was happening to me? She was haunting my waking moments now, too. She consumed my thoughts so much that my wife had been wondering about my unusual enthusiasm in our relationship that had long become perfunctory.

The artist picked her tools back up with that indifference I found so endearing. Maybe because she'd been playing hard to get when this all started, pretending to not be interested when, in fact, she'd been into me all along. Women could never truly resist me. They would eventually give in and bend to my will. It was a game I enjoyed playing.

And I was far from done with her.

She still had not given up her name.

* * *

When she finally surrendered, a whole sketch pad later, she leaned over me and whispered, "I am Death."

I cried out in delight. God, it was so *hot* when women waxed poetry while they pleasured me.

* * *

My wife was on annual leave for a week. It drove me mad not being able to see my artist, with my wife's itinerary of housecleaning, grocery shopping, and Netflix and chill. I became irritable and moody, choosing to spend most of my time in bed instead. Thinking of my artist made my hunger worse, however, and sleeping it off only ended in fever dreams that left me weak.

I decided to go out and busk on the High Bridge, certain that she would be there, sketching. Talking to her, or even just catching a glimpse of her, should help.

But I collapsed and had to be taken to A&E. *Dehydration,* the doctor said.

It was a string of sicknesses after that. Hay fever, pneumonia, gastroenteritis, cold sores. I grew weaker by the day. I couldn't work up an appetite. I couldn't get a good night's sleep. Nobody could explain why, not even the doctors. Weakened immune system was as close as they got, which meant quarantine and masking up and being bored to death in our tiny flat.

My wife called a priest for an anointing. I almost begged for an exorcism. Whatever had to be afflicting me was no disease, was it? I just wanted it to stop.

But when he asked if I had something to confess, I said, "No, Father."

* * *

"Maybe it's witchcraft."

My wife, who was as religious as she was superstitious, crossed herself when her friend from work suggested the possibility of dark magic at play. "What, like *barang*? They have that here?" *Barang* was a form of black magic that inflicted pain or disease upon a victim via insects or poppets. I didn't know anyone who actually got cursed that way, but we had plenty of stories and enough instalments of the horror film franchise *Shake, Rattle, and Roll* back home.

"Maybe they chipped away his soul," her workmate mused, shrugging.

Why was her voice familiar?

Was it her? My artist?

I forced myself through the veil of exhaustion that enveloped me, latching on to the voice I'd just heard. But my hold was slipping, and I only caught fragments of their conversation after that. My wife wondering who would want to hurt me. Her friend asking her if she knew me at all.

Their voices grew hushed. A weight settled upon me, heavy and stifling. Though it felt like I was half-asleep, I could sense dread settling into the pit of my stomach. Something was wrong.

My wife left the room in tears.

Her coworker was nowhere to be found. Instead, Death stood in her wake, wearing that ridiculous yellow padded jacket I first saw her in. I should have felt relieved, but there was none to be had. There was too much pain, too much discomfort.

I just wanted to know what she was doing here now. What she'd told my wife.

"I finished your sketches," she answered with a smile, before moving to perch on the side of my bed. But there was no warmth in her voice — or in her touch, as she tucked away the stray strands of hair that had stuck to my sweaty forehead.

She reached into her tote bag and pulled out a sketch pad.

The sketches were breathtaking. I never cared much about drawings and paintings—I beheld the Mona Lisa in person when my wife took me on a trip to Paris for our anniversary, yet I couldn't see what the big deal was — but these were just exquisite. It was a collection worthy of an art gallery or a museum, and it featured *me* in all my glory. Damn it, I looked great. She'd captured my essence with incredible detail: my smile, my hair, my jawline, my youth, my abs.

Tears welled in my eyes. I would be lucky to get back into that shape after all the trips to the hospital and the bouts of illnesses. With these, however, I was beyond death.

I was immortal.

"So you understand," she said, watching me with that indifferent, clinical expression.

I tried to ask *what,* because I *didn't* understand, but all that left my throat was a weak croak.

"You asked me who I was. But you never believed, did you, Tommy?" She sighed, like an exhausted parent whose child had messed up once again. "You know, you're not supposed to die. Not for a while yet. But you saw something you couldn't have, and, as you have always done before, you stopped at nothing to take it."

"I... I didn't—"

"You traded away everything. Your dignity, your marriage, even your soul... and for what? For the ego boost of being an artist's muse?" She snorted, then shook her head. "I normally don't interfere and let your lives run their course, but you were just *begging* for it."

She turned the full force of her glare at me then, and in her eyes, I found a darkness that had no end. A void that was meant for *me*. I whimpered in fear, entirely against my volition, and I shrunk back into the pillows as if they could protect me from my fate.

However, she had not finished pronouncing her judgement. She held up the sketch pad again, flipping past the innocent drawings of me busking on the High Street or posing by the Cathedral. I wanted to squeeze my eyes shut as she showed me page after page of my indiscretions, but I couldn't, so I lay there, helpless against the detailed account of my misdeeds.

Pride.

Greed.

Wrath.

"That's not me," I vehemently denied, somehow finding the strength to raise my voice. "I didn't do it. I didn't do any of it! How *dare* you—" Anger coursed through my veins, scorching my fear. This wasn't fair. Why must my life and my value be determined only by my mistakes? Typical of people to only see the failure in others!

Envy.

Lust.

I swatted away the sketch pad, and her arm along with it. "You're not real. Do you, what, draw people in your little pad of paper until they wither and die? Is that what you did to that old lady? To those ducks?" My thoughts drifted to those superstitions about mirrors and cameras capturing pieces of people's souls. *The Grim Reaper came for me, armed with a sketch pad and a pencil.* I laughed at the incredulity of it all.

Gluttony.

Sloth.

But what if she *was* Death, truly? What if this was my last chance at redemption? My hysterics turned into pleading cries. I begged for forgiveness, for her to pardon my imperfections. I was only human, after all. If anything, *God* had made me imperfect! Why must I be punished for the mistakes of others?

Death would not be moved, however. She simply watched.

Realising that, I started to cry. But even that did not move her. There was no bargaining with Death now. All that was left was for me to accept my doom.

She stood up and closed the sketch pad. "I'll leave this with your wife."

23. THE MILL OF SHATTERED BONE

by Mark M.J. Green

South Lincolnshire, England.

Keys rattled, followed by the click of a lock opening. The door hastily pulled open, allowing an inch of light to escape before the security chain halted its progress with a jolt. A frustrated cry, almost a sob, loosened in frustration as the door pushed shut once more, and the clatter of the chain being slid free could faintly be heard from behind the heavy paint-chipped wood. With all impediments removed, the door flung open, fully this time. The rectangle of light that spilt forth was not overly bright. Compared to the darkness that clung to seemingly every surface outside like a black coating of tar, it may have appeared as a beacon, announcing to anyone foolish enough to be stumbling through the gloom that here is a sanctuary from the horrors of the night. Except that would be untrue. There was no safety within this particular house. The murky bloom issuing from within was more of the bioluminescent glow from the ghostly lure of an angler fish than one of shelter and warmth. Step inside, it said, and you would feel safe until the jaws slammed shut and the thin, needle-like teeth punctured your flesh.

Only pain and torment awaited within.

The girl knew that all too well.

With the door open, she lunged forth, putting the light behind her as she ran into the impenetrable stygian gloom outside. She was small for her age. Not especially in height but in build; her arms and legs seemingly nothing more than flesh-covered sticks wasted by malnourishment. Her ribs, if not hidden beneath a tattered and filthy nightdress, would have stood out visibly, each pressing against thin flesh. Despite her weakened, sickly appearance, she ran faster than one would expect, faster than she had ever moved before. Her bare feet darted over stones, fallen leaves and fragments of broken twigs. Each step brought pain digging into her soles from the rough terrain, but she barely noticed. She was used to pain. Only this was different. This discomfort was born of freedom and carried a sensation more of euphoria than of despair.

A smile, something she hadn't experienced for a long time (unless ordered to smile or suffer a beating), pulled at her lips, and she couldn't stop the cry, filled with an exultant wave of liberation, from bubbling out. All she had to do was run. Run and run and run. If she kept moving, she would be free.

Her eyes adjusted to the gloom, and tears, a mixture of terror and joy, couldn't stop her from seeing that she was approaching the tree line.

"Hannah! You fucking get back here, you little bitch! Do you hear me?"

The voice of the man she called her father punched through the night, striking Hannah like a physical blow. The exultant cry that had been forming warped into a wail of fear. Her stomach knotted about itself, twisting and writhing as if it were full of eels that churned over one another as they fought to find a way out. He wasn't her biological father, but that is what he demanded she and the others call him. Hannah had never heard him filled with so much anger. So much hate. Her guts clenched as she fought against the burning sensation of vomit trying to crawl up her throat that forced her to double over. That sudden hunching from the stomach cramp saved her.

She wasn't sure what happened first - logic dictated it must have been the noise - as a thunderous boom roared behind her. The nearest tree trunk exploded, spewing shards of wood and bark. The air caught the scents of fresh wood and heady sap before the wind bore it away. Splintered fragments of wooden shrapnel sprayed outward, piercing her left arm, fragments burying into her shoulder and back. More wounds. More pain. More layers of misery overlapping until they merged into one another. Scars upon scars, heartbreak upon heartbreak.

Not that it mattered at that moment. She was alive. If she could keep running, she would remain that way.

The eels swimming in her guts ceased their wriggling. Fear became replaced by determination. She would survive this.

Having reached the trees, Hannah had shelter of a sort. Using the darkness and the sturdy trunks as cover, she continued her flight into the wood.

Once more, the shotgun boomed, its roar of death and destruction echoing through the night. The nearest trees remained intact, but Hannah heard the pellets whoosh through the air and the papery shredding of leaves as ferns were torn apart. She did not stop running. Not the gun, the one who wielded it, or the myriad of fresh wounds upon her bare feet and back would stop her.

A bright talon of torchlight lanced out behind Hannah, illuminating the trees and foliage. It hadn't pinpointed her with its luminous gaze, but it would if she didn't keep moving.

Large fronds slapped against her shins; moisture from an earlier rainfall clung to the leaves, giving them a cold, clammy feel. Other plants, unseen in the dark, seemed to reach out at her legs as if conspiring against her, trying to make her stumble and fall as they snatched at her bare feet and legs.

Torchlight, weak from the distance between Hannah and its source, caught her in its cycloptic eye.

"I see you!" The man's voice had strength, but an underlying rasp from years of smoking gave it a bestial gruffness.

Resisting the urge to stop and look back, Hannah ran on, her body involuntarily clenching as the fear of another blast from the shotgun coursed through her. She tried to stop her imagination from conjuring images but couldn't halt the visualisation of the lead shot peppering her back and transforming her nightdress into one decorated with red flowers that bloomed and spread until the petals met.

There was no further bellowing cry from the twin barrels, but it didn't stop fear from grasping her bones in icy fingers, numbing her limbs as terror and fatigue began taking their toll. Her emaciated form couldn't keep up the pace for much longer.

The torchlight danced wildly. One moment, shining upward through the trees, sending a shaft of light piercing the branches and disturbing sleeping pigeons into annoyed flight. The next, swishing through the air in a strobing effect, creating a chiaroscuro of nightmarish zoetrope images.

Light. Dark. Light. Dark.

Shadows cast from tree trunks elongated and then shrank with the shifting of the light, creating the illusion that they had chosen to uproot themselves from the damp earth and join the chase. The rainfall had saturated the ground in places, and the wet odour of dirt, loam and foliage only enhanced the sensation. Were there more hazards littering the floor? Did the entire woodland conspire against her? The trees were closer together now, weren't they?

Hannah's chest felt as if it were being squeezed. Pain, sharp, needle-like, jabbed at her as she struggled to breathe.

And then, through flickering glimpses caught in the beam of the wavering light, she realised the flora was not conspiring against her as she saw the trees coming to an end. Despite her tiredness, despite the pain and fear, she felt a joyous wave at leaving the wood. The trees she had initially thought would shield her from prying eyes and aid in her retreat had failed to do so. All she wanted was to be out of the claustrophobia and away from their snatching limbs.

The torchlight, still bouncing from the heavens before falling back down to earth, had veered away from Hannah as her pursuer drifted off course.

The trees came to an end. An ocean of blackness awaited her. Another flicker of fear dragged a cold, decaying finger down her spine as her next step took her into the dark sea.

Grass. That's all it was. A clearing covered in cold, wet grass. It caressed her toes and bathed the bottom of her feet as she entered. What she had mistaken for waves upon a slick and oily expanse of water was simply rain-dappled blades gently swaying in the breeze.

Pain lanced into her ankle. A dozen points bit through Hannah's skin, puncturing flesh and drawing forth scarlet droplets. She stumbled, trying to free her leg from whatever had her in its grasp, but the points penetrated deeper. There was no stopping the muffled cry that rose from her throat: not one of pain, for she was used to that, but a sob born of frustration. The torch beam swung its roving eye across the grass, seeking her out. Raindrops sparkled like miniature gems as the light moved this way, then the other. It halted in its search when it fell upon an object in the centre of the clearing.

A tower of brick, perhaps four or five storeys in height, loomed like a lone sentinel.

The light crawled over the building, clearly abandoned, judging by the empty oblongs that must have once held glass but were now nothing more than egress points for birds and other animals.

The sight was enough to make even her self-proclaimed father cease his pursuit and examine the structure.

The remains of windmills were a common sight around the Southern part of Lincolnshire, including sections of Cambridgeshire and Norfolk. A few were holdovers from the Middle Ages, but this one looked newer, something from the 1800s, perhaps. Once used for grinding corn into flour, the flat landscape proved an ideal, obstruction-free area for the wind to do its work powering the sails. Why anyone would choose to build one in the middle of a forest seemed an absurd notion. The mill had clearly been long abandoned. Nature had reclaimed the surrounding land, and a shadowy expanse of vines almost covered one side of the tower. As with most of its empty cousins, it appeared to be nothing more than a hollow tower of stone. The wooden cap, the sails and whatever mechanisms powered them likely stolen away by time's steady decay.

He continued shining the light over the mill, curiosity driving him until the torch beam glinted from two discs of yellow light - the eyeshine of some unseen creature lurking in the upper window. His insides twitched from involuntary fright. A moment of weakness that annoyed him. How dare he flinch. He, of all people. He was the one to be feared. Not the other way around. Resolved, he passed light over the ancient stonework once more. Nothing was revealed this time. Whatever had reflected had either fled or been nothing more than a flicker of imagination.

Turning away from the edifice, he pointed the torchlight back at the frail form of the girl.

Words were not necessary when he saw her tangled form sitting amongst the foliage, the tears in her eyes sparkling like the moisture on the blades of grass. A grunt of smug satisfaction rumbled in his throat. No longer in a rush, he approached at a leisurely pace; allowing the light to dance over Hannah. She struggled again, not willing to give up. Hands fought to untangle the clasping limb from her leg, the thorns digging into her fingers and the palms of her hands. Whatever plant held her was wrapped too tightly, the thorns too numerous.

She was still struggling in tear-filled frustration when her father reached her. He stood motionless, staring at her as she battled against the thorns. Drops of blood looked black in the haze at the edge of the torch beam, transformed from rubies into puddles of liquid onyx.

"You shoulda' known you wouldn't get away, my little Hannah. Nobody gets away." The shotgun was in his right hand, resting on his shoulder, the twin barrels pointing skyward. A finger tapped tunelessly against it until he sighed as he reached a decision. "Can't take you back. Not alive. You know that. The others need to learn there are consequences." He looked around, shining the light toward the windmill. Pieces of wood, like the ribs of some forgotten creature, were visible against one side of the structure. It looked as if they were what remained of the sails, gathered together and stacked in a heap. The doorway was open, the doors long gone, either rotted away or removed. Overhead, a ghostly shadow flew on silent wings, a lone owl passing into the trees, presumably looking for a perch or a meal. He realised it was most likely responsible for the eyeshine he had seen earlier.

Moving to the trees, he rested the shotgun against it, giving himself a free hand, and returned to Hannah, crouching beside her. She had ceased her struggling.

"Please, Father. I'm sorry."

"I know," he replied. "They always are when caught. Such a shame." He ran a calloused palm down her face, dry flesh scraping roughly, coarse and unpleasant. "You were one of my favourites."

Sighing, he put an arm around her. "Still, no reason we can't have one last playtime first, eh?"

Before Hannah could respond, he stood and began carrying her toward the ruin. The thorny tendril around her foot punctured deeper into her flesh as it tightened enough to impede his progress. Rotating at the hip, he twisted his body, simultaneously striding forward. The thorns scratched against her flesh, miniature razors carving through her skin, ploughing small furrows. Some of the thorns broke from the plant, remaining embedded in her ankle, and she screamed out against the pain as traces of fire filled her foot and lower leg.

The vine snapped.

Satisfied, the man she called Father carried Hannah's screaming, crying form into the dark entryway of the mill.

The interior of the building was surprisingly dry, considering the open doorway and the holes where windows once sat. Somehow, the recent rainfall seemed not to have gotten inside.

The ground was a mixture of brick and weeds; a carpet of dried rodent faeces, mounds of crusted pigeon excrement and the occasional broken piece of wood was the only decoration. The air inside felt dry. Stale. A mixture of ancient animal deposits and something earthier. A twinning of dirt and animal not too dissimilar from that of a wet dog.

Hannah was dropped to the floor, her back and shoulders slamming onto the solid ground. The pain in her leg from the thorns felt worse than the sudden thump, but what she feared most was the inevitability of what would happen next. Hannah had endured his vile intrusions before. The thing he called love was a spear of cold, barbed metal that twisted mind, body and soul, seeking to pull away her humanity and leave her compliant to his whims. Hannah had seen the other children back at the house, whose existence was nothing more than vacant stares. All emotion, all life, stripped away by this monster and his evil, malicious wife.

Keeping her eyes on him, Hannah scuttled backwards. She struck the brickwork behind her and glanced around the circular chamber. The only exit lay behind Father. There would be no escape other than the one that awaits all of us at the end of life.

Hannah would have prayed if she thought it would help. She had tried before, but her prayers, and those of the other children, had gone unanswered. Either God didn't care, or he didn't exist. Not in that house.

Father shone his torch around the tower, curiosity delaying him. He was surprised to see a stone floor at the third or fourth storey. There was a section cut out of it where a hatchway allowed access, but the torch wasn't powerful enough to illuminate what lay beyond it. Probably roosting pigeons, or even the owl he had spied earlier.

He turned back to face Hannah, who was cowering against the far wall, and placed the torch on the ground so the beam would keep her under its watchful glare.

"Now, where were we?" he asked rhetorically, reaching toward his waist and undoing his belt.

Hannah's body had turned to ice. She couldn't move, could barely breathe. She wanted to squeeze her eyes shut, to look away and wish herself someplace else, anywhere other than here, but her body remained unresponsive.

Considering what happened next, she was glad her eyes had refused her demands to shut out the sight before her. If they had, she would have missed the glorious moment of salvation.

The man she was forced to call her father had loosened his belt, fumbling with the button on his trousers when the shadows came alive. At first, Hannah thought she was seeing things, madness making the world warp and deform as a patch of darkness dropped from the murk above. She only knew it wasn't the fabrication of a broken mind when it landed upon her father's shoulders. He screamed. A sound she had never heard from an adult, much less from him. Fright and pain sent him into a confused panic, spinning around and around, trying to dislodge whatever had him in its grip.

He screamed. Roared. Movements frantic as he pawed ineffectually, trying to reach whatever had hold of him. Clawed toes dug into his back, puncturing flesh and scraping against his ribcage. He could feel them sliding against bone and causing a shuddering cold vibration to emanate through his body, raising his skin in goose-flesh. He struggled against it, flailing and shouting, but it held him tight. Clawed hands dug into his shoulders. Blood flowed freely from each laceration. He tried to grasp at the arms of the creature, a feel of revulsion loosening his bladder when his hands met coarse hair. His movement brought him into the torchlight; the resultant shadows hurtled across the brick. In a last-ditch effort to dislodge the thing, he ran backwards at the wall, crushing the beast between himself and the brickwork. The effect didn't go to plan: all he seemed to achieve was driving the thing's claws deeper into the meat of his body. The animal hissed at him. Hot breath carrying the cloying odour of rancid meat washed over him. Despite his own wounds, he took the hiss as one of pain and prepared to bash the thing against the wall again.

An unexpected blow to his stomach knocked the wind from him, doubling him over as bile clawed up his throat.

As he curled into himself, the creature relinquished its grip and leapt free. Before Father, a length of wood clasped in her small hands, was Hannah.

She had surprised herself when she struck him in the stomach, launched into bravery by the strange being that had rescued her.

Whatever it was, its arms and legs were long, much longer than anything human. The body was covered in short brown hair, giving it a simian appearance. The face, however, was curiously feline. Large eyes, yellow and slitted, looked quizzically at Hannah. The being trilled, tilting its head to one side as it studied the girl.

At the top of its skull, two large ears pointed upward, adding to the cat-like aspect of its face.

Muffled swearing began to cut into the air from the groaning figure on the ground. The creature looked at Father, trilled once more and returned its gaze to Hannah. Extending a finger, it pointed at her, then at the floor, rotating its hand in a circle.

"What? I don't understand."

Point at Hannah. Point at floor. Circle.

"Turn around?" Hannah asked. "You want me to turn around?"

Her saviour's face split into a wide smile - pointed teeth showing between black lips. Hannah almost refused. She wanted to see what fate had in store for the monster - not the creature before her, but the real monster bleeding and cursing amongst the rat turds and pigeon shit. But then Hannah realised that perhaps she had witnessed enough horror in her short life, so she obeyed and turned her back on the pair of them.

Walking to the open doorway, she breathed in the fresh air and smiled.

Behind her, the man she once called Father but now no longer would, screamed. His agonised wails pierced the night in a screech that wound on and on until terminating in a liquid gurgle. The sounds funnelled up the hollow insides of the old mill until only the dying echoes remained, drifting away with the breeze.

In the silence that followed, Hannah's new-found friend emerged from the gloom of the tower. Together, they walked back toward the house. There were others to save this night.

24. WORST HALLOWEEN EVER!

by M.L. Rayner

Peak District, England.

Ever since the move, life had lost its familiar charm for the Beasley family. The decision to uproot and relocate hours away had not been an easy one. It weighed heavily on each of them, especially for Seth and young Addie, who had to bid farewell to everything they once held dear — their school, their teachers, their entire lives.

Their new house, nestled in the heart of the countryside, appeared desolate to their young eyes. So desolate, in fact, they thought they were the only people left on Earth. The house was a small three-bedroom bungalow, surrounded by vast open fields that dropped away into the horizon. It goes without saying there were no other children to play with, no neighbours to talk to—just an eerie stillness that enveloped the lonely home which sat upon the hill.

The decision to move had primarily been driven by their father, Dean, who had secured a job detailing cars at a reputable auto dealer in the nearest town, some several miles away. Their father saw it as a gracious opportunity, one that would shield his family from financial hardships. But for Seth and Addie, such matters held little significance. After all, what was money to them? Merely a collection of shiny coins and fancy paper they occasionally stumbled upon as their mother rummaged through their father's pockets during wine time (or so she often called it). Why should their lives be turned upside down because of it?

Adding to the whirlwind of abrupt changes, the young siblings couldn't understand why their grandfather, Papa Dennis, had to accompany them on this journey. Dennis was an elderly, cantankerous man who Seth guessed must have surpassed the remarkable age of 100 by now. The old man had always been curt and impatient toward his grandchildren, often forgetting their names midway through conversations or signalling them with a stern, sudden flick of his fingers. Despite their father's persistent attempts to explain it, Seth and Addie struggled to grasp the true nature of the elder's illness.

"Your grandad…" their father tried to explain, casting a gaze upon his children who stood blank-faced in the doorway. "He can't remember things very well."

"Why?" asked little Addie, swinging from the door frame in a way that bored children often do.

"He…" Their father considered his words. "He has a poorly noggin," he said, tapping a finger to his temple.

"A wah?" scowled Addie.

"His brain doesn't work properly, stupid!" voiced Seth as he tightened the straps on his rollerblades.

"That's right," agreed their father, although disapproving of his young boy's manner. "He'll be staying with us for a little while," he added. "Not long."

"Why?" piped up Addie again, watching as her father slowly knelt to his knee.

"Well," he whispered discreetly, his best attempt so as not to be overheard, "you know how Grandad lived in that big house with lots of other old people?"

"The hotel?" asked Addie, nodding her head in agreement.

"Sure. Kind of like a hotel," replied her father as he playfully pinched Addie's cheek. "Well, with us moving all the way out here, it wouldn't have been very fair to leave Grandad all alone with no one to visit him, don't you think?"

The young girl considered the question for a moment before swiftly nodding her head again.

"That's why we've brought Grandad with us," continued her father. "We'll find him a new hotel nearer to the house. A nicer one, too. One with lots of things to do. He'll be closer, and we'll get to see him as much as we want. Won't that be nice?"

"Will the new home smell like the last one, Dad?" butted in Seth as he stepped onto the driveway. "Mushy peas and pee?"

With a heavy sigh, their father climbed up to his feet and collected his keys from the hook.

"All that matters right now is that we are nice to him," he said. "Papa… He's an old man and can't remember where he is right now, or even how he came to be here, I bet. Be respectful. Remember manners. Yes, manners are important. And before you know it, we'll have Papa in a new place before you can say, 'Mum's passed out again.'"

***

Months had slipped away since that unforgettable conversation — a precise count of eighty-two days, to be exact. As the summer months passed to the growing dreariness of late October, the countryside leaves, once vibrant green, now smothered the landscape in the warmest hues of orange. And with this transformation, the children's hearts quickened with anticipation, for Halloween loomed just around the corner, reviving their excitement like a long-lost friend.

In the Beasley household, Halloween had always been a cherished affair, a momentous occasion that transported the children beyond the confines of screens and their collection of gadgets. It was a time when their young minds roamed free. Clad in whimsical costumes of their own creation, they ventured into the city's streets to partake in the mirthful festivities as their parents had done many years before them. It was a time of door-knocking escapades and spirited games, a night woven with laughter and delight. Oh, the children cherished those moments, their capes billowing in the wind as they embraced the wonders of the night.

Yet, this year brought a new change of scenery. No longer in the bustling city where they once lived, the children found themselves amidst the dullness of the countryside. No lights, no trick-or-treating, no decorations of ghosts, vampires, and werewolves displayed along the country lanes. And as much as they yearned for the same fervour and excitement they once had, the youngsters soon discovered that Halloween, like most of their precious memories, remained far, far away from their secluded house and had been abandoned with the life they left behind.

On that night, a silence fell upon the family as a ferocious storm unleashed upon the countryside. The gusts grew fiercer by the minute, tearing through the land with relentless fury. By some cruel twist of fate, it left the family to rely solely on the feeble glow of several candles salvaged from an old box within a dusty pantry.

"Come on kids!" encouraged their father, leaping from his favourite chair and waggling his fingers in a ghostly sort of way.

"Let's not cry over spilt milk now. There's still plenty of things we could do."

"Oh, yeah? Like what?" mumbled Seth, his brow just visible through the haze.

"Well... trick-or-treating is off the cards, there's no doubt about that," replied their father, scratching at the nape of his neck. "But we could still have some good old family fun! How about a game?"

"We haven't got any games..." sighed their mother drearily as she nestled farther back into her chair, glugging on a glass of red and holding her book to the candlelight. "They got lost during the move, remember?"

Their father thought for a second, determined not to be beaten. "Then we shall make a game!"

"Make one?" questioned Addie, who up until this time had sat contently on the living room rug. A pumpkin mask half concealed her face.

"Yes, make one?" echoed their mother. Her attention momentarily strayed away from her book. "And how do you suppose to do that?"

"Have you all forgotten what night this is?" shrugged their father dismissively. "It's Halloween! There are plenty of games we can play."

"Go on then?" pressed Seth.

"How about apple bobbin'?" suggested their father, spouting out the first game that came to mind. He always loved it as a child. The bite of the cold water as he submerged his face. The thrill of the competition. The skill in catching the stem with his teeth.

"We don't have a bucket," remarked their mother between pages.

"We could use the sink?"

"Or any apples..."

Seth was impatient as he raised his hand through the darkness. "What about pin the tail on the donkey?"

"No good," replied their father, shaking his head at the notion. "I'm afraid the only picture of a donkey we have around here is a poster of that author your mother keeps framed behind her bedroom door. Jim what's his face?" He clicked his finger in deep thought, hoping for the name to come to mind.

"Odie?" voiced Seth. "Like the dog from Garfield."

"It's Ody. With a 'Y'!" snarled their mother, who snapped her book shut and, with one large swig, threw back the dregs of her glass.

"Yeah... close enough," muttered their father, rolling his eyes as he watched her.

This would have been her second bottle this evening, a habit she had grown quite accustomed to these past few months. She had already cleared the several bottles of gin they were storing away for Christmas, not to mention the miniature bottles of Malibu that came free with the house. What was next? The stash of Toilet Duck from under the bathroom sink?

"Don't you think you've guzzled enough tonight, my sweet pig?" asked their father, whispering beneath his breath.

"What did you say?" she snapped. Her eyes stared daggers through the dimness.

"I said, don't you think you've had enough for one night?"

His wife said nothing at first but instead did what most people in this situation often do. She took back a long, deep breath.

"I'm simply saying you should think of the kids, dear," explained their father, hoping she would see sense. "They may be children, but they aren't stupid." He quickly glanced at his children, whose heads panned left to right. "The last thing they need to see is their mother getting sauced every night."

"Oh, like you're Father of the Year!" remarked their mother through gritted teeth. Her miserable attempt to stand ended quickly as she slumped drunkenly back in her seat.

"I never said that, did I?" insisted their father, holding up his hands in surrender. "I just—"

"Just play your pissin' game, Dean," she snarled and, without further argument, swivelled herself around to block him.

A hush fell upon the room, lasting a few moments. And for a time, no one dared break it. The only sounds that filled the air were the gusts of wind, howling mournfully as it swept past the lonesome house, and the rhythmic clatter of raindrops, drumming persistently against the windowpanes, causing the children to shudder.

Their father sighed heavily, his frustration straying away from his wife. "Come on now, kids," he assured them. "It's only the weather. A spot of rain, that's all."

The sound of thunder suddenly clashed in the distance, followed by the brightest spark that illuminated the room with a flash.

"…And a little thunder," continued their father, slightly taken aback by the uproar. "Don't you worry though, we're as safe as houses in here. Nothing to fret about." He smiled uneasily whilst rubbing his hands together. "About that game?"

"I don't like these games," moaned Seth. "They're for kids."

"OK…" replied their father, witnessing his son draped in the finest vampire costume Amazon had to offer. "Then what do you want to do?"

Seth thought for a moment. His decision was watched with great interest under the eyes of his sibling. "I like ghost stories."

"Yeah!" clapped Addie happily as her mask slipped down on her face. "I like ghost stories, too."

Their father paused for a moment, considering the aftermath of such a story when he would attempt to settle his children to bed. It was always the same, one always too frightened to sleep alone, the house lit up like Blackpool Illuminations. That or he would end up on the sofa for the night, again.

"A ghost story?" he echoed. "I… don't know, son."

"Why not?" barked Seth.

"You very well know why."

"We won't get scared this time, Dad. Honest," urged Seth.

"Yeah. Honest," mimicked Addie, her fingers woven together in prayer.

"I know a story," said a voice. Its tired, gravelly tone came from the darkest corner of the living room.

The old man sat in his same old spot. A couple of blankets were thrown over his knees, and an old, wooden walking stick rested idly by his side. He never used it, mind you, but found it was the perfect appliance for pointing out tasks he wished to be done around the house, like removing empty dishes once he was finished or turning on the television in time for his favourite show (not that he knew what he was watching). If it was a bad day, which was often more than not, he would simply use it to make himself heard, striking it upon the carpet in order to gain attention. However, today was a good day. And a good thing, too. The last thing their father needed was to deal with the old man's tantrums right now.

"A story, Papa?" asked their father with an expression of hesitance on his face. "I don't know, Dad. Why don't you just sit back over there and enjoy your peppermint tea?"

The old man's brow deepened. His lip trembled slightly as he attempted with great effort to push himself forward on his seat. "I said, I want to tell the story." His hand drifted to his side. His bent and ridged fingers curled around the handle of his stick.

"Oh, just let him tell his bloody thing, Dean!" said their mother as she pinched the bridge of her nose. She continued quietly. "He'll likely forget what he's talking about halfway through anyway."

"Uh?" the old man grunted. "What did that hag just say?"

Dean shifted a look to his wife, who by no surprise to him had already matched his gaze.

"Nothing, Papa," exhaled their father. "She was just saying how much she's looking forward to it."

Due to this response, the old man released his grip on the stick, falling back into his chair, exhausted. "Very well then," he groaned breathlessly. "You!" He curled his finger. "Boy. Girl. Come here."

Seth and Addie looked to their mother for approval. It was a process they often followed before accepting a request from their elder. And for good reason.

"What are you looking at her for?" remarked the old man, uttering his words discreetly. "Drunken whore."

"Dad!" remarked Dean, his voice raised whilst slapping his palm to his forehead. "That's enough! Kids," he looked down to the floor, "go sit over by your grandfather. Let the man tell his story."

Without further delay, the children made themselves comfortable on a rug near the old man's feet, sharing the candy their father had purchased that morning from the nearest store. How else were they supposed to obtain it? The spoils of trick-or-treating were not available this year.

Lightning lit up the room once again, sending an array of sinister shadows across the old man's wrinkled face. He shuffled himself back for comfort, drumming his fingers on the chair's worn leather. For a moment, he seemed distant. His gaze vacantly wandered to the ceiling as he moistened the roof of his mouth. And just when the children were about to look back at their father with questioning eyes, confused about what they should do, the old man cleared his throat with dramatic effect. The noise he made broke through the awkwardness as he calmly began to speak.

"Well now, let's see…" He thought back. "It must have been around sixty years ago, or was it sixty-five? I suppose the exact year doesn't hold much importance. Back in those days, I was living in a rural area, a place known as Hulton House Farm. A rather old house located on the outskirts of Staffordshire. It was a desolate place from what I recall, lacking any nearby homes or neighbours. Very much like this one, wouldn't you agree?"

The children nodded in reply.

"Even the closest house, about three miles away, didn't harbour any children. None of my age, at least.

"As a child, I was frail and undersized, living with my mother and aunt. My father had passed away some weeks prior to my birth, according to my aunt's account. She told me he died in the army, his leg severed by a landmine. However, it held little meaning for me back then. After all, I had never met the man, so I suppose I never really felt a true sense of loss. He was merely a photograph that hung in the hallway, a name my aunt occasionally mentioned in brief conversation. Strangely, my mother never spoke of him. In fact, I cannot recall a single instance where she uttered his name.

"As a small boy growing up in such a place, I spent most of my years alone, just like any boy in such a setting. Though, despite my lack of friendships, I never found myself lacking in tasks to keep me occupied. Like most farms, there was always work to do, and even as a child, a measly boy, I took on my fair share. Being the only one with muscles, as my aunt often reminded me, I was considered the man of the house. And regardless of my stature, this made me feel proud and capable.

"My mornings were typically dedicated to the usual chores: cleaning the pigsty, caring for the livestock, and collecting eggs from the chicken coop. I always did enjoy that part. And if there were more eggs than usual in the basket, my mother would always allow me a couple for breakfast. Two eggs of my choosing. It was a real treat back then, you know? Unlike the sugary rubbish you take for granted today. We didn't have the means for such things back then. If we were lucky, my Aunt Clare would occasionally bake a pie using apples from a tree that stood outside my bedroom window. However, she always failed to pick them at the right time. The taste was often either salty or undesirably sharp on the tongue. It would linger for days, too. An unpleasant reminder.

"Speaking of pies, my wife had a knack for making them, particularly cherry pies. Delicious, so they were. She had the perfect recipe. One that would make any man's taste buds dance with joy. God bless her for that. She would–"

"Dad..." their father interrupted, coaxing the old man back on track. "The ghost story..."

"Hold your horses, Dan!"

"It's Dean, Dad."

"Uh? What was that? Speak up!"

"It's Dean. Your son... Your only son..."

"Yes, yes," waved the old man dismissively. "Hold your horses, Dan. I'm just about getting to that part." He looked down to the two children, his eyes somewhat lost in his innocent glare. "Are these your children, Dave?" he pointed at them, confused.

"Yes, Dad," replied their father, struggling to hide his frustration. "They're my children. Your grandchildren."

The elderly man panned back down to the youngsters, struggling to distinguish their features in the gloom. "Both quite ugly, aren't they?"

"Please, Papa." He cringed at the statement and reached for his glass on the coffee table. "The story..."

"Hmm?" hummed the old man, who now had taken to picking at the skin around his nails. "Ah, yes," he remembered. "Right you are."

"It was on a cold winter's evening during late November when it happened. I had just about finished milking Shirley, a fine cow with large black spots that covered the length of her hide. A rather unusual animal in some respects. I suppose this was mainly due to her only ever having one udder."

From out of the darkness, Dean spat out his drink, choking on the dregs that lodged in his throat and grabbing the children's attention.

"That's right!" continued the old man whilst cocking his eye peculiarly. "One udder. Damaged stock from birth, you see. The cow still supplied milk, plus the old girl was affordable. That said, I never used to understand the looks I received from people as they passed the house. Not until I was much older. Strange sight to witness, a cow with one udder being milked, don't you know?" He gazed about the room, waiting for someone to answer. "Anyway," he continued, "I was just about finished with Shirley when the strangest of noises caught my attention from outside the barn. It sounded like a whine at first, or so I thought, but after just a few seconds, I heard the noise again. A moan of some sort, low and mournful. At first, I considered it to be nothing other than the wind, blowing over the barn. I had often experienced similar noises when lying in my bed at night. All it took was a steady breeze.

"Curious, I collected the pail of milk and made my way out of the barn, following the short path back to the house. It was when I reached the porch that the same thing occurred again. A moaning, or should I say weeping sound, much louder than before, spilled out into the night, travelling with the leaves across the air. I spun on my heels to look behind me, sloshing the milk as I did so. Yet, there was no one to be found. No one. Not a soul. The land was just as barren, just as soulless as it always was. I paused there, gazing up to the house, and noticed a small window on the landing that had been left open but a crack. This was of course nothing out of the usual. My mother often had a habit of leaving a window open. 'Fresh air will do us good,' she used to say, 'whether come rain or shine.' But as I continued to listen, standing alone on the porch steps, my mind became frozen. It was evident the haunting sound was not of the bellowing wind but a voice coming from the house itself.

"I was scared, as you could imagine. Utterly petrified. And as I stood there motionless, a cold sweat pouring from my brow, I had come to realise that it was none other than Sunday night. My mother, just as she always had, would have been at her usual church service by now. And my aunt Clare would be visiting the Miller's house a mile or so down the road. Neither would be back home at such an hour. Not until the clock struck nine.

"I couldn't help myself, and as I stared up at the window, remembering all the haunting fables I'd come to learn as a lad, a bitter chill spiralled up my spine. It went without saying that the farmhouse had stood the test of time. It was old and tired. Its roof bowed slightly to the right, with windows and doors that rattled in response to the winter's breeze. Many houses have their stories, and this house was no exception. I had overheard a group of boys talk about it in the village. Many years before, a girl, no older than I, was found buried just on the outskirts of the house. Her younger brother was found buried behind the barn. Killed in cold blood by their own relation. It was said that the bodies were not discovered until this relative had reached their timely end. Still, I thought little of such things. Stories can often be exaggerated. After all, I never had reason to believe that the house was haunted. Not in the slightest. And like my mother always said, if ghosts were real, why would they want to stay in a place that had caused them so much pain? I remember always taking note of that.

"The wind swept furiously across the ground, whisking up the cuffs of my trousers and cooling the sweat on my neck. I didn't know what to do. Should I run or hide? And as I listened intently, my ears pricked, bound to the haunting moan which seeped through the cracks of the house, I instead did something that to this day I never thought I would."

"What?" asked Seth.

"Well, I began to ascend to the door."

A hushed stillness plagued the room. Every breath, from the children to their mother and father, seemed to pause in anticipation as rain poured down beyond the windows, mimicking the sound of a thousand heartbeats.

"I stepped into the house," the old man continued." The hall was lit only by a dim lamp that cast shadows of the staircase railing on the walls. Gradually, the sound grew louder — a muffled groan drifting down the stairs, drowning my ears with its sorrow. I lingered on the bottom step, my feet reluctant to go further. And it was at that time I noticed the large photograph of my father that hung on the wall was missing. I must have blanked out for a moment... Maybe a little longer. Before I knew it, I was standing on the landing, my eyes fixed on the place the sound seemed to be coming from: a closed door at the end of the hall — the very same room that once belonged to my father.

"I crept along the landing with fearful caution, the floorboards creaking under my feet as the moans grew louder and louder. A faint light glimmered beneath the crack of the door, its glow flickering like that of a waning candle. Without any further delay, my trembling hand grasped the doorknob, slowly twisting it until the latch clicked. Letting go, the door sluggishly began to open on its own accord, revealing the sight through the gap. The pail of milk, which I somehow had forgotten I was carrying, was released from my grip with a tremendous clatter, its bone-white fluid covering my shoes and spreading wide across the surface of the floor.

"Inside the room, a candle stood on top of an old forgotten counter, dancing with the draft of the open door. On the bedcovers, the framed photograph of my father had been placed near the centre. His eyes peered out at me through the shadows. At the foot of the bed stood my Aunt Clare. A hand clasped tight around her mouth, if only to conceal her voice. At first, I believed her to be weeping, mourning the loss of such a courageous man, a true soldier. But as I peeked farther around the door, I noticed my aunt suddenly hunched forward. The hand that had once smothered her lips now leant trembling, upon the bedpost as she let out a series of splutters. It also appeared that she had lost some of her clothing, as her skirt lay ruffled around her ankles on the floor. With her one free hand, she dug deep into the front of her knickers, gasping as she–"

"Christ, Dad! Jesus!" barked Dean, springing from his chair as his wife rushed over to the children, pressing their heads against her bosom, desperate to clamp their ears.

"What?" remarked the old man, raising his brow in defence. He gazed up at the tall figure standing before him, a man for a brief moment he almost swore he knew.

"You were supposed to be telling the kids a ghost story!"
"A what?"

25. THE HARLEQUIN

by Elijah Frost

Sheffield, England.

The Harlequin public house was a very popular venue, not just with the older clientele during the week, but also with the younger crowd and the hundreds of students that made Sheffield their temporary home whilst they went about their educational lives, safe in the knowledge of what the weekend would bring.

This was one such weekend and the raucous laughter and clinking of glasses could be heard despite the amount of traffic that was merely three streets away. It was coming up to midnight and the fun was still well and truly in full swing, with people coming and going all the time. For some it was the place to end the night and for others it was the start.

Even the cloud cover that obscured the full moon wasn't enough to put off the partygoers. When the moon made its appearance from behind the enshrouding clouds, The Harlequin pub was like the proverbial younger brother living in the shadows of its elder brother. The brother in this case was a huge derelict building that was close enough to be connected to it without actually being a part of it.

The building in question was a part of the old steel works which had dominated a major part of the city of Sheffield for years, not just in terms of the square foot of each of the various buildings that made up the far reaching industrial complex, but also the financial aspects as well. However, that was quite some time ago and in recent years the Sheffield steel industry had decisively downsized its operations and abandoned select buildings.

This particular building had long since been left to rack and ruin but it had weathered time and the elements well with hardly any damage to the structure, whilst the pub was fairly recently refurbished. Lights from the thriving, bustling pub brightened the surrounding area but were unable to penetrate into the derelict building's interior.

Skulking through the darkened alleyways in between the pub and its gargantuan brother was a creature that created its own kind of fun. At this moment though it wasn't in the mood for fun, it wasn't smiling or giggling to itself. In fact the anger and rage that flowed through its malformed body almost permeated the very ground that it stomped along. So engrossed was it with its own fury that it took no notice of its surroundings.

It furiously mumbled to itself, making wild hand gestures as it absentmindedly marched through the dingy alley. The sound of bells tinkling away, barely noticeable over the noise from the pub, was lost to the surrounding darkness. They emanated from the wooden stick that it clutched furiously in its uninjured hand. As it got closer to the end of the alley its voice and tempo rose in angered volume all the while keeping its synchronicity.

"Who was that child? How was he able to see me? Hear me?" it violently cackled, almost to the point of screaming at itself, then it quietened as it looked down at its hand, if it could indeed be called a hand, "Hurt me? How? How did he hurt me? That pathetic mewling child," it squealed at the thought of what it had endured at the hands of a mere child. Like its hand, the pain from the momentary touch was burned into its memory. Its burned appendage would take a few seconds to heal whereas the memory of the blasphemous pain would never heal.

Hidden underneath the dirty, aged and dishevelled clown costume, the creature's body had fallen into such disrepair that a qualified coroner would declare the body a walking corpse. After so many years of tortured existence, the monstrous creation's body had taken on the dull grey hue of overripe fruit. Boils and blisters, long since burst to quickly become infected, adorned its rotten body, only its face had any semblance of colour to it.

Its entire head was almost shockingly pure white in colour. Its yellow eyes appeared sunken deep into its skull thanks to a darkened black rim around them rising up to a point and ending just below what would've been its hairline, had it had one. Unknown symbols, slightly reminiscent of ancient Egyptian hieroglyphics, were permanently etched into its forehead. The finishing touch was a bright red mouth that cut a swath through half of its face when it smiled.

Although its skin was relatively in one piece, it had taken on a papery texture, splitting where it covered the joints. The tears in the dried out skin looked to have pulled themselves apart as the fluids in the creature's body evaporated over the years, exposing the muscle and tissue beneath. As old as its body was, the injury that it had sustained from the brief encounter with the child was clearly agonisingly and painfully fresh.

The creature's costume was of duo colours, red and black, but the red half was of a deeper shade, almost the colour of blood and it was dirty, grimy from years of unwashed usage and stained randomly with splashes of what appeared to be blood. It was nearly unnoticeable, would've been, but for the fact the dried blood was flaking off the costume. It was still gawping at the offending clawed hand, cursing it under its breath for its obvious betrayal to a child, when the costumed beast stopped mid-stride.

Its yellow lizard-like eyes opened wider than they were ever supposed to, the remaining muscles in its decaying jaw relaxed just enough to reveal row upon row of razor sharp teeth as a realisation dawned on it. A mix of unknowable fear and confused shock flashed over its contorted features as the undeniable truth flooded its chaotic, vengeful thoughts – whatever, or whoever, this child was, he or it could hurt him – and cut short its bloody thirst for vengeance. That was something it could not allow.

As understanding cleared its thoughts so did it clear the fog that had dulled its senses. Dazedly it looked around at its surroundings, its gaze instinctively drawn to the sounds of laughter and joy exuding from the building it stood next to. Looking further up, it spotted colourful writing above the windows but the awkward angle at which it saw it made it difficult to see, so it casually strolled around to get a better view.

As it became clearer a smile blossomed on its ruined lips, a smile of recognition, of mischievous delight. The creature was from a time when they believed in signs, had faith they were from the multitude of gods worshipped then. Its smile was because it believed this to be a sign from those gods.

"So they name this building The Harlequin, a name derived from fool or buffoon. A court jester to be ridiculed or mocked," its face contorted and twisted. The smile faded and melded into a cruel sneer as its gaze dropped from the sign to the brightly lit windows with its thinly veiled silhouettes moving this way and that, "Do they think me a fool too? Is that what they find so funny? Sheut-Ren-Ka is a buffoon, to be mocked because it lets a mere speck of a child cause it pain. Was it even pain? It has been so long since I have felt it, it is a near forgotten sensation."

Its eyes slipped back down to its wounded hand, the fury and the rage and the thirst for vengeance building slowly, but with each passing second those volatile emotions were rising quicker, preparing to boil over. Like bile in its throat, its emotions began to grow in substance as it stared at the blistered, burned mess of its hand. Its palm was pockmarked with tears of varying sizes as its skin had split under intense heat. It wrapped its undamaged hand around the wrist of the offending hand.

It raised it slightly to its face just as a long, black snake-like tongue wound its way out of the deep gash that was its mouth. Thick gelatinous mucus dripped onto the concrete beneath it. As it hit the ground it spider-webbed out from the impact site, almost as if it had a desire of its own to infect the earth. Like dried paper, the tears had curled over themselves to expose raw muscle.

The creature's tongue flicked over the trauma of its hand in a near sensual manner. It took its time as it enjoyed the taste of its own flesh. The sneer that had dominated its lips soon gave way to a murderous grimace as its desire for revenge turned into an insatiable need to cause pain to someone, anyone, if only for a momentary release of pleasure.

"How dare they mock me! Ridicule me!! I am Sheut-Ren-Ka, the Jester-God of the damned and the one true devourer of souls. I have lived for a thousand years and fed on twice that number of souls," it squealed to no one in particular as it angrily paced back and forth, stomping its padded feet on the cracked slabs of the pavement. "I have caused untold chaos, shaped the destiny of many of my mortal playthings, moulding them to my will, my desire and I have sown the seeds of fear like a cancerous tumour that cannot be cured. They should fear me for I am true fear."
The grimace, foreboding and devilishly hostile, mellowed and the mischievous grin, sadistic in its very nature slowly returned and blossomed into an impossibly wide smile, parting ever so slightly

to give the merest hint of broken, bloodstained razor sharp teeth, "I'll make them fear me."

With its back to the pub, Sheut-Ren-Ka turned its head to glance behind it, not stopping until it had fully completed its turn and was staring mercilessly at the building before it. Mere seconds later the rest of its body spun slowly on the spot until Sheut-Ren-Ka faced the pub that now was the focus of its sadistically violent attention. Without another word, the Jester-God closed its eyes, and without reopening them, walked with a scary deliberation to the main entrance.

The music that flowed from inside rose considerably in volume as Sheut-Ren-Ka gently pulled open the double doors. The frosted glass with the image of a harlequin in the centre of it prevented the demon jester from seeing inside clearly. That soon changed as the doors parted though.

A near overwhelming concussive onslaught of sights and sounds assaulted the jester's senses and it took a split second for it to adjust itself to take it all in. A momentary pause in its stride was all it took before Sheut-Ren-Ka continued its merry jaunt on its path to vengeance.

He stopped a few feet just shy of the bar, its feet quietened by the heavy burgundy carpeting underfoot, and scanned the sizable room in which he'd entered. Silently twisting its ghostly white head to the left, it took in a multitude of sights and sounds. Slowly it turned to look to its right before returning to face the bar again.

As it stood there in silence it couldn't help but smile to itself. All of these playthings in one place meant only one thing to it, it was going to have so much fun. Closing its eyes it went through a mental list of all the different ways it could and would inflict pain on them all.

Busy contemplating all the fun it would have, it didn't hear when the barman called out to it. Not at first anyway. Eventually, it opened its eyes and stared directly at the puny mortal that dared to interrupt its cruel contemplations. Never blinking, it just stood there and smiled at him.

"Cool Halloween costume dude. You do know that it was last month though, right? I mean you can take it off now 'cause you do look kind of silly wearing it this close to Christmas," he said, the beginnings of a smirk appearing. As brief as it was, Sheut-Ren-Ka noticed it before it vanished.

"Ah, so I was right. You do mock me. I shall play this game with you if you will play a game with me. Do you accept?" the demon jester asked, its own smile lingering at the prospect of all the fun to be had. Its outstretched finger never wavered as it indicated the man before it.

"Ok sir, well I have absolutely no idea what that's supposed to mean but go on then, I like a good game. I accept," replied the barman willingly. If only he knew what he'd accepted, he might not have been so eager, but only Sheut-Ren-Ka knew what game it wanted to play.

"Yes, I do know when All Hallows Eve is, as I have for hundreds of years. What I wear is not to amuse or scare small children but to amuse myself as I devour the souls of you, my pitifully mortal playthings," its hoarse, raspy voice sounded like nails on a chalkboard, "Now it's time to play my game."

"Talk about getting into character. I love it. Go on then what do I have to do?" the barman asked the costumed patron.

"Much like yourself, it's simple," the twisted jester answered in return, its smile widened when he saw the look of primitive confusion awash his childlike face, "All you have to do is die," it giggled as much to itself as to the delicate thing in front of it.

In the next moment, Sheut-Ren-Ka started writhing and the barman was reminded of a candle, the way the flame flickers when a gentle breeze passes through it. As the jester flowed and gyrated one after another of the pub's customers began to take notice of it. The pub quietened down till there were only hushed whispers to be heard amongst the spectators.

Everyone was on the edge of their seats as to what the finale of this strange and mesmerising dance was going to be. Unfortunately for them, they didn't have to wait long. One minute into the performance Sheut-Ren-Ka sped up its gyrations until it appeared as though after every movement it froze, only to resume a second later.

At the peak of its gyrations, Sheut-Ren-Ka's body stiffened and the movements appeared more forced. Faster and faster it moved until something entirely unexpected happened. Its flesh began to split, starting at the top of its pure white skull and sliding all the way down, never stopping even at its groin. The blurring movements caused the split to widen.

Shocked cries resonated around the pub, replacing the confused silence. The crashing of plates joined the melee, with freshly cooked meals splashing all over the surrounding carpet. Chairs scraped along the deep carpet, tumbled over as people began to hastily rush for the exit in their attempt to escape whatever the terrifying finale of this bizarre show was going to be. Getting to the double doors they soon realised to their dismay that the doors, for some unknown reason, wouldn't open. Closer inspection showed they weren't locked, they just couldn't be opened.

Cries of pain and anguish could be heard rising from the deepest pits of the jester's soul as the split grew. Beneath the torn flesh was not the expected muscle and tendons covered in blood. No, underneath was another jester. This one was different to the one that had stood before the bar. Under the thin layer of blood, the jester's face was half black and half white.

Once the outer flesh had cleared the jester's head underneath, horns sprouted out at irregular angles, crowning its head. As the skin moved further apart, the left side of the jester began to change until it was significantly different to the right. After the whole process had finished, roughly ten seconds later, three jesters stood side by side opposite the barman who had remained frozen to the spot through fear. Wide-eyed, glassy, with a couple of tears streaming down his face, he couldn't remove his focus from what he was watching, no matter how hard he forced himself to.

Unable to cry out in fear, all he could manage was a strangled gasp which was cut short when he saw the three jesters in front of him were themselves splitting again. This time, however, it was a lot faster and, like the previous time, as the skin parted the left side changed and morphed into a different jester. In the space of a few moments, there were now six jesters, each one's appearance differing radically from the others.

The third time that it happened was the final one and, by the end of it, there was a line as long as the bar of jesters standing motionless but grinning maniacally with their arms at their sides. Quiet ensued when the patrons realised that for some inexplicable reason, all the doors and windows refused to open. Instead, they all turned and watched the jesters, each of them, waiting anxiously, fearfully, to see what was going to happen.

And then it happened, the jesters moved off, splitting off in different directions but each making straight for one of the trapped humans. No longer working in synchronicity, as soon as a jester reached its intended prey, tendrils snaked out of its abdomen and ensnared the human, pulling them closer together.

As soon as all the jesters had trapped someone in their tentacles they began to fade away. The humans captured in their grip each began to convulse, their bodies twisting and contorting until, eventually, their captors had fully disappeared. Standing stockstill the now freed customers began to smile, one after the other. The much too big smiles on their faces almost tore the skin at the seams.

Then, as with the jesters before them, the possessed humans reached for anything that could be used as a weapon. From cutlery to wine bottles and glasses, they all picked something up. A couple of them even smashed the legs off toppled chairs and clutched the splintered wood in their vice-like grips. Now armed, they turned on the people that hadn't yet been in the tender embrace of the jesters.

In a flurry of speed and motion, the battle-ready patrons began attacking their fellow man and woman, furiously beating and stabbing them with whatever had been their choice of weapon. Thankfully there hadn't been any children in attendance this night. A few fought back but, for the most part, the number that cowered away hoping to be spared was just that little bit higher.

Maniacal giggling mixed with tortured screams, and begging pleas of mercy reverberated around the walls of the pub. High-pitched squeals of delight followed as one by one they were gradually cut down. Blood coated the walls and lush carpeting, soaking in and staining everything it touched.

In the struggle to survive the brutal onslaught by their family members, friends and work colleagues, most of the tables had been overturned in desperation to defend against the barrage. By the end of it, the floors of the pub were littered with the dead. Bodies were contorted in agony and pain. Wooden chair legs, blood-soaked cutlery and broken glass bottles jutted out from many of the fallen.

Pieces of bone and brain matter were crushed into the carpeting. Broken crockery, glasses and all manner of silverware were left strewn around the unusual battlefield. Silence had once again descended as soon as the last person had fallen.

The only people left alive were the twelve whom the jesters had taken up residence inside of and the barman, who, while all the violence and bloodshed had taken place, had remained stoically glued to the spot. Eyes permanently looking straight ahead, he never broke eye contact with the wall in front of him, even when the jesters came together in a circle directly in his line of sight.

Facing outward, the jesters each brought their right hand up. Seeing as they were ahead of him and he hadn't blinked once during the entire bloodbath, the barman noticed that every jester had a steak knife gripped firmly against the throats of the jester next to them.

Sheut-Ren-Ka stared back at the barman, splashes of blood decorated its face, adding to its gruesome facade. Its sinister smile widened until it looked as though its face would split under the strain and in a slow, deliberate motion it brought the index finger of its left hand to its lips. In a barely audible tone, it shushed him. The pursing of its lips to make the sound was even more terrifying than the smile, if that had even been possible.

The demon jester still had its finger pressed against its lips when in one singular and fluid motion, each of the jesters dragged the serrated edges of the steak knives against their own throats. Just as the last throat was slit, Sheut-Ren-Ka relinquished control over its victims. Clutching their wounds they dropped to the floor coming to rest in their own individual pool of blood.

With Sheut-Ren-Ka no longer present in the pub, the doors were also released. Police burst in through the doors, only to be stopped by the sight before them. Out of the twenty officers who had responded to the calls of horrifying screams, nearly all were unable to withstand the sight of the carnage and rushed out to vomit away from the crime scene.

When it was decided that whatever had happened had ended, paramedics were hurriedly allowed inside to see what they could do for the survivors. Their job and their presence were cut short though when it was determined that there was only one survivor. If he could even be called a survivor. He may not have been butchered in the melee or had his throat sliced open by the deranged jester but the barman that had inadvertently mocked Sheut-Ren-Ka was forever trapped inside his own mind.

Taken to the best psychiatric hospital in the country the doctors determined that whatever horrors had occurred that night were simply too much for his fragile mind to comprehend and so, in defence of that, he had retreated into his own psyche as a form of self-protection and to shield himself from it all.

However what was really happening was that he was replaying all that he'd witnessed over and over again, being tortured by it all by the very thing that should have protected him. The police visited him on numerous occasions following the shocking events that took place at The Harlequin pub on that disastrously eventful night, and each time the doctors advised them against it, they were never able to get a statement from him.

Every time they went and every time they asked him the same questions, he mumbled the same two words. Two words that the police were never able to make use of in their efforts to investigate what really happened that night, how so many people were killed and how little evidence there was as to who the perpetrators were.

Two simple little words that, if had been said to the right person, would've solved everything and ended so much pain. And those words he kept repeating to himself day and night?

The Jester.

26. DOWN T'PIT

by Sarah Jules

Barnsley, England.

"Have you ever seen a ghost?" a little girl asks. She clings to her mum's leg and peers up at the ruddy-cheeked miner.

"A good question, is that," the miner, Stan, our tour guide, says. He kneels down on creaking knees so that he is at eye level with the little girl. "Personally, I've never seen a ghost, but some of t' men I worked with 'ave."

"Here?" she asks, eyes wide with what I interpret as fear.

"No, not 'ere," he says. His Barnsley accent is thick on his tongue. It sounds like home to me. It's the same accent as my dad. "I've worked at t' museum for nigh on twenty years and, as far as I know, no ghosts 'ave been spotted 'ere."

"Then where?" the girl asks. She bravely steps towards Stan.

"Back at Woolley Colliery, a fitter I worked with, Pete, claims t' this day he saw a ghost. Ya see, down t' pit, yer determined by yer cap lamp. That's what yer holding in yer hand.' Stan gestures to the small lamp in the girl's hand. She's pointing it at the floor. 'If you were an actual miner, that'd be fixed to yer cap. Now, we used t' charge the batteries on them overnight and hope they'd last a full shift t' next day, either eight or twelve hours. Sometimes they didn't. What do yer think'd happen if battery died on yer lamp?"

"You wouldn't be able to see."

I watch as the girl's bottom lip begins to quiver.

"Well, luckily for Pete, his light lasted 'til almost very end of his shift. And, also, Pete knew the coal face like the back of his hand. He knew how to get back to t' cage, but he had t' do it in dark."

Stan looks around the rest of the group. I'm the only loner on the tour. I'm accompanied by the little girl and her mother, a couple who look to be in their early thirties, and an elderly gentleman with his sullen teenage grandson.

"You must 'ave read mi mind," Stan said to the little girl. He groaned as he stood. "Because next part of t' tour is the best bit. Follow me."

Stan led the way, his neon orange clothes glowing as the lamps we're holding ricochet off them. We follow behind him, and I find myself at the back of the small group. Stan opens a swollen wooden door and we file through. He looks pointedly at me as I fulfil my duty as the last one through. We'd been taught about the importance of closing these doors when we first stepped out of the cage about 140 metres below the ground. It kept us all safe and kept the gases where they should be, or something like that.

Stan gives a shallow nod and a wink as I close the door tightly behind me. The underground tour promised a *charismatic Yorkshire miner*, and that's exactly what we got. Promise fulfilled, National Museum of Mining. Gold star for you.

I bend my head low so as not to hit the top of my *cap*, as Stan calls it, on the wooden beams above. We've already had a history lesson about why miners preferred wooden beams over steel beams... because wooden beams *speak to you*. They creak and groan, much like Stan's knees, when the earth above them becomes too heavy. It gave the miners warning... RUN. Steel doesn't do that. Steel is silent.

"And here we are. This is my little mate James," Stan says. He gestures his thick fingers toward the tiny mannequin of a little boy. "How old d' yer think James might be?" Stan looks at the little girl again and smiles.

"Go on Isla," the girl's mum says.

She shakes her head and ducks, once again, behind her mum's leg.

"Isla's Mam? How old d' yer think my little mate James is?"

"He looks very young," she says. Her accent isn't thick like Stan's. It's sharper at the edges; modern Yorkshire.

"Yer not wrong. James could be anywhere from five years old. Although, he looks younger because he dunt get much sunlight. He's down here ten to twelve hours a day in t' dark."

"Didn't he have a light?" The teenager says. Stan does well to keep the shock off his face that the boy asked a question. The teenager's grandfather chances a small smile.

"Lamps were expensive, and children, like James here, didn't need one. He's a trapper. His job is to open and close that door next to him. He doesn't need a lamp to do that. But his mam or dad or older brother, who are working on the coal face itself or moving the coal through the mines, they'd need a lamp. *Hewers*, the people who get the coal, or *hurriers*, the people who move it. But he couldn't do that until he was bigger and stronger."

"So he'd be down here in the dark on his own all day every day?" the teenager asks.

"Yes. Have you noticed that James is tied t' door?" Stan says. He waits a beat before he continues. "Why d' yer think that is?"

'So that he doesn't run away?" Isla answers, her voice confident.

"Nope," Stan says, smiling and biting his lip. The man is a born performer. He clearly loves his job. "Any other guesses?"

The group shake their heads in unison.

"I'll show you why," Stan says. "On the count of three, we're all gonna turn our lamps off."

I glance at Isla, expecting her to protest. Instead, she looks almost gleeful at the idea.

"Three, two, one."

Our lights flicker out one by one, as we flick our switches, and we're plunged into darkness.

"Bloody hell," the teenager says. I hold back a laugh.

"This is what James saw all day, every day," Stan says. The dismembered voice is strangely unnerving. "Any ideas now why he was tied t' door?"

I lift my hand in front of my face and see nothing. This is like no dark I've ever experienced before.

"So that he can find the door," I say. My voice is hoarse. I cough and catch myself. "So that he can open and close it."

"Exactly," Stan says. I can hear the smile on his face.

"Right, lamps back on," he says.

It takes me a moment to find my switch. I direct my lamp at James. He's a creepy little dummy but my mind aches for the Jameses of the past. To sit in the dark, alone, for twelve hours a day opening and closing a door. It must have been terrifying.

"Isla?"

Without meaning to, I point my lamp towards Isla's mum. She looks around her frantically.

"Isla? Where are you?" Her eyes are wild. She shines her lamp sporadically around.

"Don't panic," Stan says. He reaches out a hand but Isla's mum slaps it away.

"Are you being serious?" She smiles, it is a smile of disbelief, of amazement.

"She can't have gone far. It is perfectly safe down here."

"We're in a mine!"

"An old mine. It's a closed circuit. We've blocked off all the old shafts and tunnels."

"Then where is she?"

"She'll have just wandered off, as young 'ens do. We'll find her. Shout her name, but wait a few seconds before you shout each time. I'll radio and let t' lads upstairs know what's happening. They might want t' send down Steve."

"Who the hell is Steve?" Isla's mum says, mascara has already started to dribble down her face. I can't imagine how she's feeling. I'm childless, although more by circumstances than choice, but when my friends have lost their children in a supermarket or a play centre, they always say it's the worst feeling ever. I didn't know Isla until half an hour ago, and my heart feels like it's in my throat.

"Health and Safety," Stan says. He pulls the radio off his belt and speaks into it. "Steve, one of our guests has gone walkabout."

The radio beeps. "Copy that. Let me know if you need a hand."

"Will do, bud." Stan attaches the radio to his belt. "Right, can y' shout yer daughter, please? And we'll all tek a look around. Better you shouting her name than a bunch of strangers."

Isla's mum does as she is asked and shouts her daughter's name. The word echoes down the shaft, bouncing off the tight black walls and roof. She waits a beat, and continues. "Isla, you need to come back. Now! You're not in trouble. Just," she breaks into sobs, "come back."

I turn and shine my lamp back down the shaft in the direction we came. Nothing. There is nowhere to hide in that direction, just one straight *corridor*. Corridor doesn't seem like the right word but… The corridor ends with the door I shut. The one that groaned loudly when opened and closed, we'd have heard if she'd slipped through. I'm certain.

The group begins to move onward. Isla's mum shouts her name, and the woman belonging to the couple in their thirties has her arm shoved under her armpits, keeping her aloft. Up ahead, there may be branches from the main shaft, hiding places and recesses, areas that would be easy for a little girl to get lost in.

James. The mannequin of the trapper has a wooden door tied to his wrist with rope.

"What about in there?" I say, gesturing to the open pathway through the door. I don't wait for an answer. I squat down and shine my lamp into the doorway. My heart slams into my chest as a pale face, blackened with dirt, stares back at me.

"Fuck," I say. I try to steady my breath as I stare down the dummy.

'That's James's mam,' Stan says, letting out a nervous laugh. "She's a hurrier. If you look further back, you'll see his dad. His dad's a hewer."

I shake my head at my own stupidity. "Isla?" I say. "Are you in there? Do you need help?"

"There's nowhere to go in there," Stan says. "It's a dead-end, for illustrative purposes, the gaffer said."

I ignore his comment and get down on my hands and knees so that I can stick my head through the door. It would be the perfect hiding spot.

The air feels colder inside the faux-shaft. Isla's mum's frantic shouts feel distant, like they're happening beyond a veil.

"Isla?" I say again. I crawl further, the rough floor biting at my knees through my jeans. Holding the lamp awkwardly in one hand, I inch forward until I'm fully inside.

"Isla?"

Sitting back on my knees, I hold up the lamp. The spotlight illuminates a single circle that I slowly move around the space. I try to ignore James's mother, who is bent forward so that she's almost on all fours, a belt around her waist attached to an overflowing tub of coal behind her. I can feel her presence. It eats into the close space. Every cell in my body tells me to move away from her. To retreat.

Get a hold of yourself. It's a well-known fact that our brains don't do well in the dark. They like to trick us. To make us think of what *could be* rather than *what is.*

"Isla?" I say again. I'm determined to check the whole space before I let my brain get the better of me. If, on some off chance, the little girl decided to hide behind James's door... It was better safe than sorry.

I shine the lamp ahead. Stan was right. It looks like a dead end behind James's dad, who lies on his stomach holding a pick-axe at an awkward angle with his right arm. Poor bastard. I put the cable from the lamp in my mouth, trying to forget about the number of people who've had their grubby hands on it, and crawl forward. Why the museum didn't think to include a slot on the helmets for the headlamps is beyond me. It would make looking for lost children in tiny pretend mine shafts a hell of a lot easier. Ignoring the sharp pains in the palms of my hands, and my knees, I crawl forward.

When I get to James's dad I stop. It's quiet.

I hold still and listen for Isla's mum's voice; for the others shouting her name too. There's nothing. Nothing at all.

"Stan?" I shout. "Everything okay?" I laugh a little to hide the anxiety I'm feeling. "Hello?"

Nothing.

I take a moment and try to think rationally. Maybe the group continued on without me. Maybe they heard Isla from up ahead and didn't wait for me.

The mannequin of James's dad lies adjacent to me. He's holding a pickaxe up to the coal face from his awkward position. I have to crawl over his legs to pass him, to reach the end of the tunnel. I have to make a decision. To continue forward or turn back.

My pulse thrums painfully in my neck. I don't know how much further the shaft goes. I hold up the light and say a silent prayer that it dead-ends soon. But, I can't tell. The lamp doesn't focus on anything, the large circle of light dissipates before it reaches a hard surface, which is strange, because Stan said it was a false shaft, for *illustrative* purposes. How far would the museum dig a false tunnel, just for illustrative purposes?

"Isla?" I shout again, reminding myself of why I'm there. If the little girl did go through James's little trapper door, and if she did get lost, or get scared, it makes sense for me to search the rest of it.

"Just in case," I say aloud to myself. "Isla? If you're in here, I'm coming to find you, okay? Can you let me know where you are?"

There's a significant chance that I'm talking to myself but speaking the words aloud makes me feel less alone, it fills the empty tunnel with something other than my unjustified anxiety.

I take a deep breath and climb over James's dad's legs. Whatever he's made from feels slick, greasy under my hands.

"Isla? Your mum says you're not in trouble. If you're in here, you need to come out." I attempt to keep my voice light and breezy, despite feeling anything but.

A noise startles me and I drop back onto my haunches. It sounded like a cough, or a laugh. Maybe a cry. *She's here,* I think.

"Isla? It's okay. Where are you? My name's Alice."

I freeze and listen, straining against the silence.

I hear something but I can't quite make out what it is.

Scurrying.

The sound of tiny feet.

My skin prickles in goosebumps. A crawling sensation fills my body.

Rats.

I don't move. I *can't* move.

I hold my breath and listen.

Stan said that there were no rats down the mine anymore because there were no miners leaving food behind, but I know what I heard.

My breath hitches. Above me, there's the scuttle of tiny feet.

I close my eyes. I won't look up.

"Isla, please? Are you here?"

I want to go back. I need to go back. But if she's there, she's scared. Maybe she's hurt. I can't leave her alone because of a rat.

I keep the lamp pointed forward and talk myself into moving again. *It's just a rat. A rat can't hurt me.* I just have to check to the end of the tunnel and then I can leave.

"Isla?" I say, edging forward.

"Help me." The voice is weak, faint, but definitely Isla.

"I'm coming," I say, scrambling further into the tunnel. It is tight with no hiding places and so I push on. I move quickly. "Isla, are you okay?"

"NO, SHE'S NOT." A deep low growl, barely words. *My imagination.*

I attempt to hold the lamp steady as I move as quickly as I can. My whole body aches with exertion. I can't see the end of the tunnel.

"Where the fuck is it?" I snarl through gritted teeth. At least she's here. I know she's here because I heard her.

"Isla?" I say again. I need to hear her voice again. I need to.

Instead of words, I hear laughter. A childish giggle.

"What the-" I say. I hold the torch before me, in the direction of the laughter, but there's nothing there. I half expected Isla to have been playing a practical joke on us, but there's nothing but empty tunnel. The sound came from right in front of me. I'm sure of it.

Then I hear movement again. Not the scuttling sound from earlier, but running footsteps, heavy footsteps, a drumbeat against the floor, coming from behind me. I turn around, and aim the light back towards James and his family.

Nothing.

I have to get out of the tunnel.

"Isla, I'm going back now. If you're in here, you need to tell me now, or I'm leaving."

I try to steady my heart rate, to tell myself that I'm being dramatic. My mind is playing tricks on me. That's all. It's a normal reaction to crawling through a pitch-black tunnel with only a handheld light to guide me.

"Alice!" My name smacks me in the face and knocks me sprawling onto my back. I land on the battery pack attached to the miner's lamp in my hand and a shock of pain radiates through my hip. The lamp falls from my hand and blinks out.

Blackness surrounds me. My shaking fingers find the battery pack and trace the cable to the lamp. There's a small metal switch on the side of it. I flick it up. And then back down.

"Please please please please please," I mutter under my breath.

I flick the switch again and wait for a second.

"Fuck," I breathe. Desperation weights me to the spot. If the light doesn't work, I'll have to find my way out in the dark, that's all. It's one tunnel, all I have to do is turn around and go back the way I came. Carefully, I move onto my hands and knees and begin to crawl back towards James and his parents. I move as quickly as I can but the pain in my hip feels like crunching shards of glass.

"Come on come on come on." My hands are ripped to shreds but I can't afford to stop. I have to keep moving.

"Is anybody there?" I shout, my voice filled with hysteria. It feels like I'm approaching the little wooden door. I can't be far away from it.

My breathing is loud, it reverberates off the walls of the tunnel. "Hello?!"

I'm way past the point of caring what people think of me. I'm happy to be the girl who panicked on the underground tour experience. I don't care. I just want to see again. I want to laugh it off, to pretend that it wasn't a big deal.

"Please! Stan, anyone?!"

I'm not aware that I'm crying until I feel the wetness on the back of my hand. I don't stop to wipe away the tears. It makes no difference. I can't see anyway.

Something hard slams into the divot of my kneecap.

"Fuck," I snarl.

James's dad's legs. The hard plastic of his body. I'm almost there.

I force myself to keep moving despite the pain. *You've dislocated your knee,* a voice in my head says. I ignore it. Ignore the agony each time I touch it to the floor. I'm near the door, I know I am. When I get there, I'll feel the wooden slat signifying the door and-

THUD.

My head hits something hard and lights float across my non-existent vision. I blink the floating lights away but my head swims and sways. Dizziness and nausea wash over me. Slowly, I pick up my hand and press it tentatively to the closed door.

I push my hand against the moist wood. The door doesn't give. It doesn't move an inch.

"HELP ME!" I break into heaving sobs. "Hello? Please, anybody?"

I bang my hand repeatedly against the door.

"You're ours now," a voice whispers in my ear. A young boy.

I reach out in the direction of the voice but my hand grasps only at the air.

"Do we get to keep her forever, James?" a different voice says.

"Yes, Isla, we do," James says.

MISSING PERSONS APPEAL – SOUTH YORKSHIRE POLICE – FACEBOOK

14.02.24

Have you seen ISLA CLARKE or ALICE DUDLEY?

Missing from the Mining Museum. Last seen on an underground tour of the pit on February 14th, 2024. ISLA CLARKE is 7 years old, with long blonde hair, and was wearing a yellow coat and blue jeans at the time she went missing. ALICE DUDLEY is 31 years of age. 5ft 5. Has short red hair, and was wearing black jeans and a black coat. If you see either of these persons please contact either South Yorkshire or West Yorkshire Police in the first instance.

MISSING PERSONS APPEAL – SOUTH YORKSHIRE POLICE – FACEBOOK
14.08.24

Today marks the six-month anniversary of when ISLA CLARKE (7) and ALICE DUDLEY (31) went missing from the Mining Museum during an underground tour. If you know anything about their disappearance, we urge you to contact either South Yorkshire or West Yorkshire Police. At this time, police are investigating all leads and are actively encouraging anybody with further information to come forward.

Bonus Irish Story:

27. THEY STALK THE ROWS

by Leigh Kenny

Wicklow, Ireland.

The minibus rumbled down the rutted lane, the rough terrain jostling its occupants in their seats. It screeched to a stop and with a final shudder, the engine died.

"Welcome to Ballybeg Farm, folks! The finest guesthouse in authentic Irish hospitality."

The aged driver turned in his seat, grinning at the handful of tourists behind him who were too busy oohing and ahhing at the verdant landscape before them to hear the old man's welcome.

"Oh Hank, isn't it magnificent?" crowed the tall, thin woman in a Texan drawl, as she leaned across a small Norwegian woman cradling a sleeping infant. The woman flushed, embarrassed by the sudden invasion of her personal space, and moved away from the American. The sudden movement disturbed the child who began to fuss. The tall woman cast her eyes down upon the seat's occupants and clicked her tongue in annoyance.

"Imagine Hilary, this is the kind of view my great-great-grandfather got to witness every morning," her husband responded, pushing past an Asian family to reach his suitcase. "I can practically feel my blood turning green just by looking at it!"

The driver, Patrick, rolled his eyes.

For the most part, he loved the tourists that frequented his guesthouse, and always had a great time mingling among them, and in turn helping them to become immersed in the Irish culture. After all, that was the point of Ballybeg Farm.

His family had owned the land for generations, employing most of the nearby village on the farmland upon which the quaint guesthouse sat. Things had taken a bad turn a long time ago, and the family had come close to losing what had been theirs for so long, but Patrick's father had been a clever man. He had found that paying tribute to the land, and all it held, was the solution to their problems. The old farmhouse had been renovated and marketed to tourists who wished to experience the "real" Ireland. It was a massive success, and now Patrick and his younger brothers Joseph and Shay, worked the business between them. Joseph ran the guesthouse, ensuring the most authentic experience for each guest who stayed. Shay was responsible for the farm. It was no small feat, their farm being one of the largest vegetable suppliers in the province. The Hennessey brothers' logo was known across the island, emblazoning bags of potatoes in most Irish kitchens.

Despite the years that had passed, Patrick still remembered those dark days as a boy, watching his father and uncles come home from the fields day after day, mud and defeat marring their weather worn faces. They had come so close to losing the crop entirely. It always warmed him to see their produce on shelves. The crop was bountiful now.

Patrick was an all-rounder, helping both of his brothers across all areas of the family business.

He didn't roll his eyes at the tourists out of cynicism. So many years spent mixing with people of all nationalities, and there wasn't any single country whose people he was at odds with, but he had developed a knack for knowing the ones who were loud or obnoxious or inclined to turn their noses up at the very experience they themselves had requested. Patrick was quite happy for everyone to hold their own opinions, but he hated to see it interfere with the enjoyment of the other guests. And it usually did.

With a wry smile, he remembered the group of German college students from a few years back. They had been rowdy and disruptive, and Ballybeg Farm wasn't the place for that behaviour. Patrick chuckled at the memory of the dressing down he had given them. They had been indignant, but he knew they weren't a problem he'd ever need to deal with again.

As he watched Joseph hand out information leaflets with a beaming smile, Patrick had a feeling that the noisy American duo were about to be the latest problem that needed to be solved. Lifting a hand to shield his eyes from the dying glare of the late summer sun, he watched as the couple spoke over the other guests, as though theirs were the only questions worth answering. Over the thin woman's shoulder, his eyes met those of his brother. Joseph knew it too.

Patrick followed his brother and the gaggle of awestruck tourists as they hauled their luggage across the dusty yard, their heads on a swivel as they drank in the beautiful scenery that surrounded them. The evening light had bathed the outlying crop fields in a soft golden glow. Patrick loved this time of day. The gentle cast of the waning sun lent an air of magic to the countryside. Sucking in a lungful of the crisp air, he saw Shay across the yard, pulling the gate across the opening that led to the fields. Lifting a hand to his brother in greeting, Patrick waited until Shay had returned the gesture then turned and followed the group inside.

**

The flames danced inside the grate. Tossing another log to the greedy fire, Patrick poked at the embers and watched as a shower of sparks erupted from the pile. He settled back in his armchair, closing his eyes as he listened to Shay's rendition of 'She Moved Through the Fair' on the tin whistle. He had heard it countless times but never grew tired of the haunting melody. The tourists loved it too.

It had long been a tradition at Ballybeg Farm to gather the guests in the parlour after dinner for music, songs and stories. Most of the guests loved the tradition and were enthralled by the brothers' varied entertainment.

Patrick's eyes snapped open as the American lady, Hillary, broke out in song. She was attempting to shoehorn the lyrics of some pop song onto Shay's melodious efforts. Whispers and disapproving glances were cast around the room, but Hillary either didn't notice or didn't care. Patrick could see the pained expression in Shay's eyes as the music faltered. Enough was enough.

"How about a story?" he called from his chair. "Ireland is famous for its storytellers. The Land of Saints and Scholars, as they say."

A rush of excited chatter and enthusiastic nods greeted his suggestion, and he chuckled to himself.

"A story it is, then! I'll allow ye all to do the choosing. Are there any mythical creatures that come to mind when ye all think about our fair land?" he asked slyly, knowing he was sure to get the answer he sought.

"Fairies!"

"The Banshee!"

"Leprechauns!"

Patrick whirled at the last suggestion, pointing at the young Asian girl who'd spoken it.

"And tell me, girl, what do ye know of leprechauns?" he asked.

The girl blushed, smiling shyly at the sudden attention that was thrust upon her.

"They are small men in green suits, and they hide gold at the end of the rainbow."

Her words faltered as she spoke, aware that all eyes were upon her, but Patrick gave her an encouraging wink.

"Very good, lass. That is exactly how the world knows a leprechaun to be," he said, smiling.

Behind the gathering of guests, Joseph gently lowered the lights in the room. So gradual was it, that nobody noticed the room plunge further into darkness. Soon, all that was left was the orange flames of the fire in the grate, its light casting eerie shadows upon the walls that elongated and danced in the gloom.

"That's not what Leprechauns are *really* like though," Patrick said, lowering his voice until it was almost a whisper.

Everyone in the room leaned forward to better hear his hushed tone, their faces eager with anticipation for whatever secrets he was about to impart upon them. Patrick looked out at their faces for a moment. The undulating shadows cast by the flames thrust them into a half-darkness and turned their faces into grotesque masks that rippled and shimmered in the low light. The frightening effect sent a cold shiver darting along Patrick's spine like a bolt of electricity, and he quickly lowered his eyes and coughed to dislodge a sudden tightness in his chest. When he lifted his eyes again, all was as it should be.

"No, not at all," he continued. "Leprechauns are nasty creatures. They're only small little things, maybe a couple of feet tall. The gold they guard is real, but it's not what everyone thinks. No, the gold they guard is more precious than any metal, for it has fed the people of this land for many generations. The gold they guard is what you and I know as the simple potato."

The small crowd gasped, their eyes wide with rapt attention.

"Potato fields, just like the ones out there, are where you will find leprechauns," he said, nodding towards the darkened windows. "But believe me when I tell you this. You don't want to find a leprechaun, and you don't want them to find you! They're vicious creatures with a mouth full of sharp teeth and a black tongue full of the taste for human flesh. And t'isn't their suits that are green, no. It's their very skin."

Patrick paused, watching with satisfaction as the young Asian girl huddled closer to her mother, her eyes fearful. Scaring a child didn't satisfy Patrick at all, but saving her life did. And people don't go looking for things they're frightened of.

At least, not most people.

"But they aren't real!" tittered Hillary, her tone uncertain.

Levelling his gaze upon her, Patrick responded, "Oh, they're real alright, Miss. This very place is named in their honour. In our native language, Ballybeg becomes Baille na Beag. That means 'Land of the Small'. This countryside is rife with the critters! They say if you can manage to steal a potato from the ground during the nights leading up to harvest time without alerting the leprechauns, it will become real gold. My brothers and I have spent our whole lives surrounded by the potato fields, but not once have we chanced our arm at it."

"Why not?" she whispered.

"Because we aren't damn fools, that's why! As boys, we once caught a glimpse of the aftermath. It was enough to keep us out of the potato fields at night ever since."

"When is the harvest?" her husband asked.

"A week or two from now."

More gasps rang out, and the American couple's eyes widened.

Glancing towards the young girl, Patrick could see tears glistening in her eyes and his heart softened.

"That's enough about leprechauns for one night," he said. "Who's for a drop of whiskey? Maybe a little red lemonade for this young lady. You've never tasted red lemonade? My girl, you are in for a treat!"

As one of his brothers discreetly raised the lights once more and chatter resumed among the guests, Patrick shuffled to the dark wood cabinet that stretched along the back of the room. Shay appeared beside him, stuffing a bundle of keys attached to a worn leather strap into one of the drawers. Together they fished out the good whiskey and a bottle of TK red lemonade for the youngsters.

"Do you think they'll chance it?" whispered Shay, as he pulled the foil back from a tray of sandwiches.

Casting a furtive glance towards the American couple who were whispering conspiratorially with each other, Patrick nodded.

"Course they will," he replied. "Imagine what an adventure it'd be for them to tell their friends back home. Imagine they got the gold? They won't be able to resist trying."

**

The guesthouse was silent but for the gentle ticking of the old grandfather clock. It stood sentry in the darkened hallway, its motionless face the only witness to the shadows that passed it by, their dual silhouettes reflected in the dull glass. The shadows coalesced before separating from each other, and as the front door clicked softly closed behind them, all that remained was the quiet echo of their hushed laughter.

"The field gate is unlocked!" whispered Hank.

Hillary followed her husband across the dusty expanse that lay between the guesthouse and the potato fields.

"Yes!" she hissed in hushed tones. "This is a sign that we're supposed to get that gold!"

Hank looked sceptically at his wife. The harsh lines of her normally stern face looked almost soft in her excitement.

"You don't really believe that bullshit, Hill, do ya?"

"You saw his face, honey. The man was downright scared of his own words!" Hillary tested the gate, swinging it open gently and preparing for any squeaking hinges. "Besides, if it is bullshit, it'll be some story to tell the gang back home!"

Hank grinned, already picturing himself holding court at one of their backyard parties, the guys enraptured by his Irish escapades.

The pair stepped silently onto the rough dirt track that ran parallel to the fields, each one parcelled neatly into a large rectangle and bordered by thick, thorny ditches. Hank stepped towards the first field gate as Hillary gently closed the gate they had just come through. She crossed the lane to join her husband, the bright cone of light from the torch on his phone casting eerie shadows on the uneven terrain that surrounded them.

"This gate is labelled," whispered Hank, motioning towards the sign.

Printed in large, scrawling letters was the word **CARROT**, a cartoonish, hand-drawn carrot pictured beneath it.

"Well, that sure is helpful," giggled Hillary.

She grabbed Hank's hand and smiled up at him, her eyes shining with an exuberance not normally present, and together they headed further down the lane, the darkness swallowing them whole.

As they approached the fourth gate along the lane, Hank aimed the light at the sign.

POTATO.

"This is it," he hissed, squeezing his wife's hand. He didn't know what had gotten into Hillary tonight, but it was infectious. Hank would be happier to call this crazy hunt off and return to the guesthouse to ravish his wife. It had been too long.

Together, they climbed over the metal gate, and Hank clicked the light back on.

The field before them was huge, bigger than any they had passed so far. The earth was divided into deep furrows, all set uniformly apart from each other. And there, in tidy rows, sat the potato plants. They were taller than Hank had expected, but then what did he know about potatoes aside from grabbing them at the grocery store, clean and ready to cook?

Hand in hand, the couple wandered along the edge of the field, the light scanning the dark rows as far as it could penetrate. The darkness did not wish to be disturbed though.

"We're gonna have to pick a row and go that way," said Hillary, her hand pulling from Hank's larger, warm one. She marched off into the rows, disappearing instantly in the black of night.

"Hold up, Hill!" Hank hissed. With an exasperated sigh, he took off after her.

Hank jogged through the darkness, hissing his wife's name.

He had followed her in a straight line, so she must have branched off into the next row, he thought to himself, silently cursing her adventurous spirit while simultaneously rubbing at his crotch, gleeful thoughts of where the night could take them filling his mind in a smoky, red haze.

Hank pushed through the plants to his left and peered into the next row, but his wife was not there.

Doubling back on himself, he crossed to the right of his starting point. As he pulled the first plants aside, there was a sudden crashing sound. Something was moving close by and at great speed. Hank stepped backwards, away from the softly swaying plants and listened for sounds of movement. Pulling the phone out, he shone it along the edge of the plants and stalks, crying out as a dark shape moved back into the foliage out of sight. Hank swung the light towards the area again, fear like a cold fist in his stomach as he watched the stalks and leaves quiver in the wake of whatever had stood there just a moment ago.

Watching him.

The light suddenly fell on an item, and the fear was instantly replaced with a burning desire. It was Hillary's shoe.

The fresh, country air appeared to be rolling back the clock on his normally straight-laced wife. Hank remembered when they first met, how wild Hillary had been. No matter where he took her on dates, at some point of the evening, she had usually begun to shed her clothes, urging him to follow her behind a tree, into a lake, through the cornstalks back home.

Hank grinned.

He moved the light further along, and there, hanging from one of the huge potato plants, was Hillary's jacket. With a grin on his face, Hank lifted a foot to follow the trail of discarded clothing when a scream rang out, slicing through the still air like a knife.

The grin froze on Hank's face, the fire in his groin replaced quickly with ice in his veins.

A second scream rang out, this one jagged and shrill, like an animal in pain.

But Hank knew it was no animal.

"Hillary!" he cried, instinct kicking in and forcing him into action.

Without a second thought, Hank flung himself through the rows of plants, the large leaves and thick vegetation pulling at his limbs as though they were alive and trying to slow his progress. On and on Hank ran, from one row to the next, slowly becoming attuned to the noises that surrounded him. Something was moving near him. A lot of somethings. He could hear them as they crashed through the rows in his wake, a multitude of whispers that surrounded him like a heavy fog.

As he pushed through the plants of yet another row, Hank skidded to a stop. Hillary lay in the dirt, her pale skin glowing in the silvery moonlight. Her half-naked body was sprawled across the mud, her head turned at an unnatural angle, her dark eyes staring at him and yet seeing nothing.

Hank raced to his wife, dropping to his knees in the dirt beside her. Her skin was covered in scratches and bites, small chunks of flesh removed from her soft body. Where the soft skin of her neck had once been, now there was only a dark, jagged crater. Cradling her face, he gasped as the eyes that had been shaded in darkness now showed only empty sockets, blood that looked black in the moonlight still wet on her porcelain cheeks.

Hank roared, his anger and loss pouring out in one mighty bellow that tapered away to a hushed moan.

When he finally lifted his head, every space between the stalks that surrounded him was filled with creatures. Small creatures with oozing, green skin, whose sharp teeth flashed in the darkness as they moved quietly towards him as one. As the leprechauns began to feast upon him, Hank screamed. His voice floated off into the night sky and was swallowed by the stars.

**

The smell of rich butter, toasted bread and fresh fruits still lingered in the dining room. Muted tones of a variety of conversations in colourful languages drifted in and mingled with the shafts of morning light that pierced the windows.

Patrick stuck his head through the doorway and grinned at Joseph.

"All taken care of, Pa?" Joseph asked as he hoisted the clattering tub of soiled cutlery onto his hip.

Patrick nodded. "Our American guests left early. Bags, passports, everything gone."

"Anything left in the fields?"

"Hardly a scrap. Sure, it's been a while since *they* fed. Shay is out there now doing a final walk-through."

Joseph nodded, his shoulders visibly relaxing.

"I'll take over here. You go see to our remaining guests," smiled Patrick.

"Cheers," Joseph said, placing the cutlery tub on the table. As he passed his brother in the doorway, he stopped, a thoughtful look in his eye. "The crop is sure to be great for the next year or two now. The German tribute of four saw us good for a few years."

"Aye, indeed," grinned Patrick. "It's sure to be bountiful."

Patrick moved around the dining room as light as a feather. As he wiped crumbs from tables and straightened up chairs, he hummed a haunting melody, a smile playing around his lined mouth. From a different part of the house, his brother's voice drifted in, filled with good cheer as he spoke to the assembled tourists.

"Some guests decided to leave during the night without paying their bill. The experience wasn't for them, but they're about to miss out! Who wants to learn how to make some Irish soda bread from scratch??"

Acknowledgements

First of all, I have to thank the authors who took a leap of faith and agreed to be part of this anthology. I was absolutely blown away by your talent, your passion, and your support. Thank you all for lending me your stories, and allowing me to be the one to share them with the world.

Second, a huge thank you to Rachael Rose who, when I floated the idea of her illustrating the anthology, snatched my hand off. You have taken this anthology to the next level. As always, I cannot wrap my head around your ability to take words and turn them into the most beautiful illustrations.

To William Long whose story *Bone Zipper* is included in this anthology, for putting together the most amazing trailer.

To Mary Hoyle for your proofreading. Once again, I'm embarrassed by how many things you caught. Thank you for helping me to polish this book and get it ready for public consumption.

To the indie horror community. I'm going to go out on a limb and say that horror authors (and horror readers) are the most supportive, kind, and talented people on the planet. I feel incredibly blessed to be part of this community.

To YOU, the reader...

As I said in the dedication, without YOU there would be no US. Thank you for allowing us to tell our stories. Readers who pick up self-published, independent press, and traditionally published books without discriminating between the method of publication are THE BEST! You're a special breed of people. Thank you for what you do to keep our dreams alive.

Sarah Jules

About the Authors

Dr. Stuart Knott

Dr. Stuart Knott is a PhD graduate and a writer of horror fiction. Primarily influenced by the writing of Stephen King and H.P. Lovecraft and the films of David Cronenberg and John Carpenter, Dr. Stuart Knott has published several short stories, novellas, and novels that infuse mundane everyday life with dark comedy and the macabre.

Threads: @drskspawner

David K. Slater

David K. Slater is a novelist and screenwriter, specialising in horror and literary fiction. His home is in Teesside where he lives with his fiancée and their three children. He is putting the finishing touches on his first novel, *Air Conditioned Nightmare*, and has a planned release for it in 2024. Much like *American Werewolf in London*, David loves stories that are too scary to be comedy and too funny to be horror.

Facebook: David K. Slater - SlaterTheWriter

Jessica Huntley

Jessica Huntley is an ex-British soldier and Personal Trainer turned author of addictive psychological thriller books. She has spent almost three years writing and is now the author of eleven books, including two trilogies, two standalone thrillers, an anthology, a co-written horror project and a novella. She writes books for thriller readers who like their stories dark and twisty with complex, yet memorable characters, who often suffer from relatable mental health disorders. When she isn't writing dark books, Jessica is either keeping fit, copywriting, walking her dog or looking after her young son.

Instagram: @jessica_reading_writing

MJ Mars

MJ Mars is the author of *The Suffering*, which was published by Wicked House in 2023. MJ has featured in a number of anthologies including Dark Peninsula's *Negative Space*, *Colors* in Darkness' *Deadly Bargains*, and Silver Empire's *Secret Stairs*. You can also find MJ's work on The NoSleep Podcast and The Dread Machine.

Website: www.mjmarsauthor.com

J C Michael

J C Michael is the author of the novel, *Pandemonium*, as well as two short story collections, *Everything's Annoying*, and *Old Tales Reborn*. Citing Stephen King, James Herbert, and Clive Barker, as major influences, his work firmly sits within the horror and dark fiction genres.

Facebook: James C Michael

Ashley Lister

Ashley Lister is a UK author. He holds a PhD in creative writing and teaches in the North of England.

Website: www.ashleylister.com

Stephen Barnard

Stephen Barnard is a suspense/horror writer from the North West of England. He's been indie publishing titles for a number of years, and has a range of novels and short story collections in the genre. He's taught high school English for nearly 30 years and has two sons studying at university. When he's not writing, he's binge-watching horror movies. His wife is very understanding.

Facebook: Stephen Barnard – Suspense/Horror Writer

EC Samuels

EC Samuels was born and raised in North West England. She still lives there with her family.

Instagram: @ecsamuels_writer

Lee Allen

Dark fiction author Lee Allen was born in South Wales, UK. An avid reader and lover of books from a young age, he began developing his fascination with mystery, intrigue, crime, horror, and the supernatural early in life, writing stories of his own long before he can even remember. He completed the manuscript for his first full-length novel while still in secondary school, which was later published as his debut crime thriller *Those Crimes of Passion* in 2012. Seven books later, he continues to reside in Wales with his feline writing companion, immersing himself in imagination and research.

Instagram: @LeeAllenAuthor

C S Jones

C S Jones has been a keen horror enthusiast for many years and finally decided to pick up a pen and contribute to an already brimming horror scene. From Wrexham, Wales, he grew up a timid child, who was drawn to (and scarred by) anything scary — much to his parents' frustrations. A family man at heart, he looks forward to dragging you along on his journey of more grim discoveries.

Facebook: C S Jones

Brad Thomas

Brad Thomas is an English author of horror, thriller books, and short stories. He is also writing his grandmother's life story. From a young age, all he wanted to do was become an author. Growing up in Tipton, West Midlands, England, he never thought it would be possible, but he never stopped chasing his dream.

Facebook: Brad Thomas Author

Jim Ody

Jim is a Wiltshire based author with a dark sense of humour who is considered a bit odd. He loves horror, coffee and chocolate. All the rumours are probably true.

Facebook: Jim Ody Author

Alexandra Nisneru

Alexandra was born in Romania but lives in the United Kingdom with her husband, two kids,
and their cats. She has always dreamt of becoming a writer and is finally fulfilling this dream. She has always loved the horror genre, even as a child, but she knew she wanted to write horror when, as a young woman, she came across John Saul and Stephen King's books. When she is not working (as a sales assistant in a bookstore) or spending time with her family, she enjoys reading and writing what she loves the most: horror and dark fantasy.

Facebook: Alexandra Nisneru - Author

Bethany Russo

Bethany Russo is an indie author from the Southwest of England. Her favourite genres to read and write are fantasy and horror. Her debut novel *The Devil Inside* is out now.

Instagram: @bethanyrussowrites

Philip Alexander Baker

Philip Alexander Baker is the author of the *Hanging Hill Lane* trilogy.

Facebook: Philip Alexander Baker

David Watkins

David Watkins lives in Devon in the UK with his wife, two sons, ridiculous dog and psychotic cat. His most recent release is *St Neith*, from Demain Publishing.

Instagram: @david.watkins.writer

Tom Carter

Tom Carter lives in Kent with his wife, two boys and cat, Bauer – named after TV's greatest character, Jack Bauer. His published work includes the horror novel *The Doctor Will See You Now* and the YA novel, *Swish*. His favourite authors are Stephen King, C.J. Tudor and Harlan Coben and he worships at the altar of Steven Spielberg.

Twitter/X: TommyCarter14

Elizabeth J Brown

Elizabeth was born in Kent, England. This probably explains her obsession with tea and cake. She currently writes the *Brimstone Chorus* series - supernatural horror featuring demons, witches and a whole host of things that go bump in the night.

Website: www.elizabethjbrown.com

Tim Stephens

Tim Stephens writes fictional, chilling short stories in his leisure time. He self-published his first short collection of short stories - *Fast Lane and other short chillers* in 2019 (available on Amazon Kindle) and is looking to publish his second longer collection - *Message You Back and Other Short Chillers* later in the year. This is Tim's first contribution to a horror anthology. Tim lives in Kent with his family.

Facebook: Tim's Chillers

William Long

William Long works full time as a film editor and has edited four feature films and several horror short films, which have been shown at film festivals around the world. His debut novel, *Unholy Gods* was published in 2022 by Severed Press. He currently lives in Hertfordshire with his wife Agnes, and two Khaki Campbell ducks called Chester and Marjory.

Instagram: @williamlongauthor

Benjamin Langley

Benjamin Langley is the author of quiet horror stories with a creeping dread, and noisy, blood-soaked, demon-infested alternative histories. He has released six novels and one novella. Much of his work is set in the Cambridgeshire Fens where he lives.

X (Twitter): B_J_Langley

Marie Sinadjan

Marie Sinadjan is a UK-based Filipino speculative fiction author, singer-songwriter, and musical theatre actress. She writes mythology/folklore and fairytale retellings, horror, and sci-fi. She is the co-author of *The Prophecies of Ragnarok* series, and her short stories have been published in anthologies, magazines, and literary journals.

Website: www.mariesinadjan.com

Mark M.J. Green

Bald, bearded and bumbling, Mark likes the spooky side of life and things that go bump in the night. Although that's usually him wandering into something as he didn't bother to turn a light on.

Facebook: Mark MJ Green

M.L. Rayner

Born and bred in the county of Staffordshire. Matt is a keen reader of classical, horror and fantasy literature and enjoys writing in the style of traditional ghost stories.

Facebook: M L Rayner Author

Elijah Frost

Elijah Frost is a 46 year old bus driver with a desire to bring a whole new face of fear to the world. He wants to write something so terrifying it scares even himself.

Facebook: Elijah Frost

Leigh Kenny

Leigh was born and raised in the garden county of Wicklow, Ireland. She lives by the Irish Sea with the love of her life, two wonderful boys, a black Labrador, and a three-legged cat that hates people. You can find out more about Leigh's work and any upcoming releases on her social media pages.

Facebook: Leigh Kenny Writes

About the Editor

Sarah Jules is an indie horror author from South Yorkshire. She is a self-professed accidental hipster (who refuses to apologise for this). She is also the owner of Sarah Jules Writing Services, a job that allows her to work in her pyjamas, which she is immensely grateful for. She is the author of FOUND YOU, DON'T LIE, and YOU INVITED IT IN. This is the first anthology she has edited.

If Sarah isn't working (or writing), you can find her with her nose stuck in a book, travelling the UK with her partner and her rescue pup, or sweating it out in the gym. She is a mental health advocate, coffee-addict, and loves all things spooky and/or creepy. Sarah blogs (super-hipster, she knows) about all things books, writing and publishing on both her Instagram (@sarahjuleswriting) and on her website www.sarahjuleswriting.com.

Facebook: Sarah Jules Writing

About the Illustrator

Rachael Rose is an artist and illustrator originally from South Yorkshire. She has a background in fine art, animation and illustration and has been a professional artist for over 12 years. She specialises in fine detailed pieces drawn in biro and ink. When she isn't drawing you can probably find her with her chihuahua, Obi, lost in the woods or up a mountain with a coffee and muddy boots.

Instagram: @the_rosemoth

If you enjoyed this book, please consider leaving a review on Goodreads, Amazon, and social media. It helps to get more eyes on the anthology, and therefore on these amazing authors.

Milton Keynes UK
Ingram Content Group UK Ltd.
UKHW030718030824
446082UK00011B/33

9 781738 487226